The
Demon Girl's
Song

Susan Jane Bigelow

Dreaming Robot Press
quality middle grade and young adult science fiction and fantasy
• Las Vegas, New Mexico •

DREAMING ROBOT PRESS
Las Vegas, New Mexico

1 3 5 7 9 10 8 6 4 2

First published in the United States by Dreaming Robot Press. 2016

Publisher's Cataloging-in-Publication data

Names: Bigelow, Susan Jane, author.
Title: The Demon Girl's Song / Susan Jane Bigelow.
Description: Las Vegas, New Mexico: Dreaming Robot Press, 2016.

Summary: In a world on the verge of an industrial revolution, Andín dal Rovi wants to escape to
university; instead, she gets a thousand-year-old demon stuck in her head, and in a race against
time to uncover the secrets of her world – and save it from utter annihilation.

Identifiers: ISBN 978-1-940924-15-1 (pbk.) | ISBN 978-1-940924-16-8 (ebook) | LCCN
2016939892.
Subjects: LCSH Fantasy fiction. | Adventure fiction. | Paranormal fiction. | Love stories. | Lesbian
teenagers--Juvenile fiction. | Minorities--Fiction. | Identity--Fiction. | BISAC YOUNG ADULT
FICTION / Fantasy / Epic.
Classification: LCC PZ7 .B4825 De 2016 | DDC [Fic]--dc23.

Cover Illustration by ilza
Cover design by Pixel Dizajn
Map creation by Beee

For Tasha

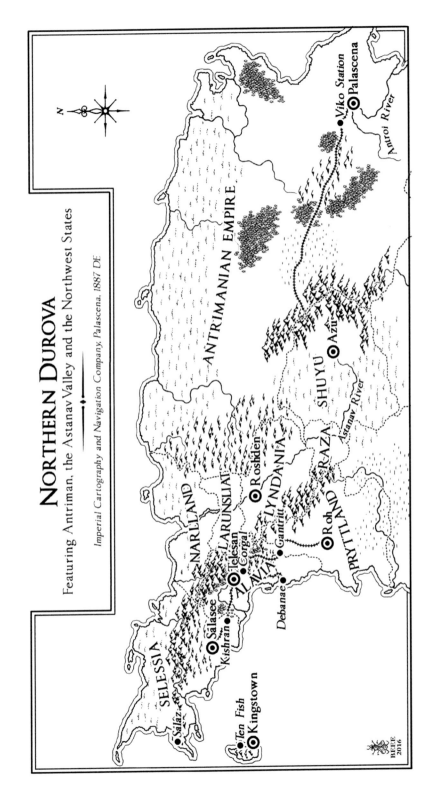

NORTHERN DUROVA

Featuring Antriman, the Astanav Valley and the Northwest States

Imperial Cartography and Navigation Company, Palascena. 1887 DE

ANTRIMANIAN EMPIRE

Palascena
Viko Station
Antroi River

Azu-
SHUYU
Astanav River

NARELAND
LARUNSLIAT
Roshden
Telesan
Corgal
LYNDANIA
RAZA
ALAVIA
Gantrit
Rohd
PRYTTLAND

Debanac

Salasec
Kishran

SELESSIA

Salaz

Ten Fish
Kingstown

BEEB
2016

PART ONE

Chapter 1

Peasant Girl

"When the sky shatters, everything is possible."
—old Shuyan saying

Andín hummed a nameless little tune to herself as she bustled around her father's shop, stacking tins of dried pork, refilling jars of spices, and neatly arranging cigars in their wooden boxes. The store smelled of cigar smoke, spiced tea, and sweat, and every inch of wall space was covered with shelves heavy with every imaginable kind of good. The only clear spot was reserved for a small framed photo of the emperor right above the doorway, which Andín had to dust twice a week.

Outside, the streetcar rattled past, and Andín could just hear the bells of the tower clock chiming.

Papa was playing the jovial shopkeeper with two men, laughing and joking while trying to draw their eyes to some trinket or another.

She caught a snatch of conversation and froze, her spine suddenly ramrod straight.

"—and next year my boy Palyar will be off to the university in Palascena! We just received his acceptance. He'll study business and—"

Cigars tumbled across the floor as their box hit the ground. "You promised!" Andín shouted at her father and the two stunned customers. "You promised!" she repeated, and fled from the shop.

◆ ◆ ◆

"It isn't fair," Andín seethed at her father, who sat cross-armed and dour in the parlor. "Why send Palyar instead of me? He just wants to play his fiddle all day. He's not even old enough—he's still in school!"

Papa's gaze floated heavenward. "He'll graduate in the spring, and then he'll go. And you have to know why, Deeny. Do I have to make it plain? I can only afford to send one of you right now, and there's boundless opportunity there for a man looking to go into trade!" He put stress on the word 'man,' but Andín chose to ignore it.

"And what if *I* want to go into trade?" Andín pressed. Not that she did, but it was the principle of the thing.

"You may think you have an idea of what it's like at the university," Papa continued after huffing and running a hand over his thin, slicked-back hair, "but you'll find it very different. Palascena is no place for a naïve young lady on her own."

"Is that what this is about?" Andín said, fighting back tears. "I am *not*—I'm not naïve!"

"But you don't know what you want," Papa retorted. "You said you wanted to go and study history, then it was economics, then science!"

"So?" demanded Andín at the top of her lungs. "That's what the university is there for! I could find out what I want!"

"Your temper, Andín," her father reminded her.

She almost tore into him again, but she caught herself. Barely. "You *did* promise," she said sulkily.

Her father's bushy walrus mustache actually seemed to droop. "I did."

"And?" she demanded.

"And it's not possible. You know it's not as simple as all this. Women at the university… it's not done often, Deeny."

"It has happened," she snapped.

"It's not just that, but it's the money… the store," he continued, his voice taking on that wheedling tone he used when he was trying to placate a customer. "You know how things have been this past year. I'm sorry, kitten, I am. Maybe... maybe in a few years, when we have a little more money to spend on luxuries."

"Luxuries?" she shouted, filling the house with her voice. "Luxuries," she repeated, disgusted.

He heaved a disapproving final *harrumph* and gave her that utterly implacable look over his glasses.

"Fine," she said, voice tight. "Have it your way. If you won't send me, I'll find another way. I'll get out of this town. I'll go to the university. I'll have a brilliant life. And it'll all be no thanks to you!"

"Oh, now, Deeny!" he said, rising from his chair. But she was already gone.

◆◆◆

Her mother would be out back gathering in the washing from the line; Andín bolted in the other direction, towards the street. She couldn't face Mama today.

She ran into Palyar coming in from school. "Deeny!" he said brightly. "Did you—?"

He never got to finish his question. "Go away!" she screamed at her little brother, her control shattering. "I hate you!"

"Whoa!" he said, backing away. "What did I do?"

She threw up her hands in disgust and marched determinedly away, eyes full of tears.

◆◆◆

An angry wind blew from the east, driving her out into the countryside.

The abandoned hill of the Vintoi property made a fine place to sit and brood. She glowered back at the little town of Viko Station below. The line of brick factories by the railroad tracks still belched smoke from their stacks; it was not yet dinnertime. The town's lone streetcar rumbled down the cobbled main street, carrying people towards the station. Beyond the town, the wild forest stretched towards the horizon.

An old Lofkand song she'd sung in school floated into her mind.

Little girl, oh little girl, where do you run,
Beyond the road, toward the setting sun?
Beware the wolves, oh beware the sight
Of the Forest King, stealing through the night.

She sighed dejectedly, her fury melting away as quickly as it had come.

A rusty iron pot with "VIKO IRON WORKS" etched on it was embedded in the dirt next to her; she rested an arm on it, tracing the familiar edges with her finger. Long ago, she and Palyar had played a game called Wash Pot Land here, where she was the queen and he her knight. The pot was the throne, and the lumps of stones on the hill were villages. It had been such fun, creating a whole world from their dreams.

This whole sorry mess wasn't Palyar's fault. He hadn't made or broken any promises; he couldn't control what Papa wanted to do. She'd have to find him and apologize later.

Still, it was hardly fair at all! It had already been a year since she graduated from the girls' academy in town, while Palyar wouldn't be done with his own schooling until next spring. Her teachers had always said they expected great things from her, but all she'd done since was stand behind a counter in her father's shop each day, smiling half-heartedly at the leering factory men who came to buy filthy cigars and tins of snuff.

At night she raced to her room to escape into dusty histories and exciting tales from distant lands. She read about the marvels of the cities, the rugged beauty of the mountains, the wonder and magic of the ancient lands of the western coast. There was so much more to learn and see. The world was vast, and it called to her. The university was a stepping stone to those endless horizons.

Papa didn't understand that. Nobody in this tiny little factory town possibly could.

She had to get away from here. Valsin, her only real friend, always said that if they stayed much longer in Viko Station they'd both start to rust away like this old pot. Valsin didn't care about the university; she had a long list of eligible noblemen she wanted to track down and try to marry, but both she and Andín longed to be away from the dull sameness of home.

The sun had begun to set in the faraway hills off to the west. The already brisk wind picked up, blowing her hair around her face as clouds loomed overhead. Was there a storm coming in?

When she was established as a great scholar and world traveler, everyone would finally see. A cruel little fantasy unwound in her mind. Papa's business would fall on even harder times than now, and he'd have to come, hat in hand, to wherever she was living in academic luxury. Her shelves would be stocked with trophies from her travels and all the volumes she'd written, and she'd deign to offer Papa a few pitiful moments from her busy schedule. She was leaning back, thinking of all the choice things she'd say to him when fingers gently touched her arm.

Andín yelped and almost fell over. A young woman sat next to her on the hillside. She wore a simple brown robe with complex patterns sewn into the tattered fringes. Her skin was darker than Andín's and her hair much shorter. She looked like she might be Alavesh; the empire had many poor Alavesh living in it, traveling from place to place.

Her tired eyes regarded Andín steadily.

"I didn't see you there! Are—are you lost?" Andín asked.

The young woman smiled warmly. "You're Andín dal Rovi, right?" she asked. Andín nodded. "Then I'm not lost."

Andín's eyes grew wide, and she started gibbering in panic. "Why are you looking for me? I don't know you! What do you want? I don't—I don't have any money."

The Alavesh woman laughed. "Antrimanians. No, I don't want your money. Hey, I just wanted to be sure about you." She sniffed the air. "You seem about right. You smell right to me."

A strange buzzing sound began to vibrate the air all around her.

"I—what?" Andín asked, looking wildly around. "What's that? What are you doing?"

"It's time to wake up," said the girl. "It's been so long. I'll be seeing you again soon. And for what it's worth, I'm sorry."

The buzzing continued, getting stronger and stronger. She held her hands over her ears—and yet it continued unabated.

"Stop!" Andín screamed. "Stop!"

But the young woman had vanished.

The buzzing amplified now into the overwhelming blasting of a thousand little horns that rattled and shook her skull. She clutched her head, moaning with sudden pain.

All at once she felt as if she wasn't quite alone in her own mind any longer.

«*Oh, no, no, it's gone wrong,*» something very distinctly said. A dark, hot energy seemed to swirl around her. «*This is some peasant girl!*»

She passed out.

♦♦♦

It was a dream, and something more than a dream. The colors were too vivid, the sounds too sharp.

Two men who looked like they'd stepped out of a centuries-old painting sat nearby, pointing at an irregular-looking map spread on the table. The men wore unkempt beards, and there was a stale smell she couldn't place. "There," said one, pointing. "The rebels have come as far as Lodt. They've picked up men and supplies."

"They're within two days' march of here," said the other. "What do we do?"

"We must firm up our defenses," she said without meaning to, her voice deep and gravelly like a man's. "Dig trenches on the hillsides. And then we must hope that General dav Peoro is swift."

"Your Imperial Majesty," the second said, his tone soft and wheedling. Why had he called her that? "May I suggest we retreat to Palascena? We can regroup, and it's far more defensible."

"Retreat again?" she snarled, standing. She vibrated with dark power. They stepped back a pace. "I will not hear of it, Ulan! I will not!" She banged her fist on the table. Her hands were large and hairy. She noticed for the first time that she was wearing a bright red outfit with stockings and a long coat, garments that a nobleman would have worn hundreds of years ago. "We stand here at Viko Castle, as planned! Prepare your men. This discussion is over."

They bowed, fear in their eyes. She sat back down as they hastily left.

"Cowards," she said to no one in particular. "The world is shaped by will and dreams alone."

◆◆◆

Her eyes snapped open.

Clouds passed over the moon, shining high overhead, and the gas lamps were lit in the town below. The stacks of the factories were silent. Hours had passed.

Rebels, Lodt, General dav Peoro… those were all pieces from a history of the empire she'd been reading. Her books were starting to intrude into her dreams.

She scrambled to her feet, the world swaying before her. The wind blew ever stronger, and she could smell rain on the way. Her head throbbed and she almost threw up, but she got control of herself. She dimly remembered a young Alavesh-looking woman, the sound of buzzing, voices…

Andín wanted nothing more than to lie back down and let the pain pass, but she knew she had to get home before the storm hit. She hiked up her long skirts and trudged wearily back down the hill toward the town, her head throbbing.

◆◆◆

She didn't quite make it. The rain started as she crossed the streetcar tracks by the station, and she was dripping wet by the time she opened her own front door.

Her father was waiting for her. "Where were you?" he demanded, worry on his face.

"I'm sorry," Andín said, holding her pounding head in her hands. She felt even worse. "I was out on the hill, and I fell asleep. I won't do it again."

"This is just the problem," Papa fumed. "How can I trust you in a place like Palascena when you're irresponsible enough to go out to the field by yourself, without telling anyone where you were, and sleep there? In the rain!"

"I said I was sorry!" Andín snapped, her temper flaring again.

"You asked why I'd send Palyar," her father said as she tried to push past. "Because he wouldn't *ever* do this! He's responsible!"

"Good for him," Andín said as sharp pain lanced through her head and body. She felt too strange and weary to fight any longer.

"Are you all right?" her father asked, concern chasing the anger from his face.

"I'm fine," she said faintly. "I didn't mean to worry you. I'll... I'll see you tomorrow."

She left her father to worry in her wake as she climbed the stairs to her room.

◆◆◆

Andín tossed and turned in her bed that night, unable to find rest or relief. Vivid dreams tormented her.

Worse, she couldn't shake the feeling of something foreign lodged firmly in her mind, like a piece of meat stuck in her throat. It drew her through places she'd never seen or even imagined, through strange horrors and incomprehensible sights. Waking was a relief.

Someone was pounding on the door. "Deeny?" her mother's voice came through the door.

She tried to tell her mother to go away, but all that came out was a sad little whine.

Her mother cracked the door and peered in. "Deeny! It's morning! You need to be down in the shop; your father's been asking after you!" Andín groaned and sat up. Her mother's eyes widened in shock. "By the Holy Pair's grace, you look awful. What were you *doing* last night?"

"Nothing," said Andín said. The world swam in front of her. She swallowed hard.

"Nothing indeed! Your father says you were out until all hours!" Her mother bustled into the room and threw open the curtains. Early morning sun streamed in. Andín winced. Mama whirled to face her, hands on her ample hips. "And what were you doing out on the hill in the middle of the night, anyway?"

"I fell asleep! I was just out there to be alone. Papa—" Andín swallowed what she was going to say. She didn't want to involve Mama in any of this. "It's where Palyar and I used to go to play," she finished limply.

"Not with some boy, I hope! That Mansar dav Palyen has been giving you such looks lately, I had better not catch you with the likes of *him*."

"Ugh, never!" Andín protested.

"You can do much better," said Mama with a sly grin. "If you have to spend time with any boys, the dal Gari boy is a nice one, or Kavín dav Iusco's son."

"Mama," Andín groaned. She could never muster much interest in boys.

"You'll have to think about it sooner or later," Mama said with a sad little smile. "Now get dressed. Papa's waiting in the shop."

◆◆◆

Andín listened to her mother's footsteps receding down the creaky stairs, then sighed and dragged herself out of bed. Her head still ached.

What had happened out on the hill last night?

There had been that horrible buzzing, and then the bizarre, vivid dream. What had that been about?

Viko. The Battle of Viko? She knew the story well enough. The emperor at the time had faced down a rebellion led by one of the western barons who had designs on the crown, but Andín's head was so fogged that she couldn't remember which one.

«*Ropan.*»

"Who said that?" she exclaimed, shocked. The voice was deep and alien.

«*Ropan. He was the baron. You should learn your history better, peasant girl.*»

"How dare you!" she said, stinging from the insult. She looked wildly around to see if she could see where the voice was coming from. "I know my history very well, thank you! And where are you? Show yourself!"

She waited. No answer.

"Hello?" She checked around the bed and picked up the little pen she kept on her nightstand. If some strange man were to come at her, she could stab him in the eye with it.

And yet, no one came.

I refuse to be insane, she thought, putting the pen down with trembling fingers. I refuse!

♦♦♦

She stumbled down into the shop attached to the west side of the house, hoping for some strong tea. She knew she looked awful despite her feeble efforts to tame her hair and scrub her face, and she hoped that maybe her father would take pity on her and send her back to bed.

To her despair, the store was already packed with men clutching newspapers and speaking in animated tones. Her father would barely notice her now.

"You're late," her father said distractedly as she settled herself gingerly onto the stool he kept behind the counter.

"I'm sorry. I didn't sleep well," she said, yawning for emphasis. She took the cup of delicious-smelling tea he handed her. Papa had the best teas. "I think I may be getting sick."

"You must really be sick if you're apologizing to me," he said, smiling a little under the mustache.

"What's going on?" she asked, changing the subject. "Busy this morning." *For a change*, she thought but didn't say.

"The paper says the emperor is near death," he said, perking up considerably. "And someone saw a detachment from the Army in town this morning. They may make the proclamation."

"Oh," she said. Her head started throbbing again. "I see." Whenever an old emperor died, the army went to every town that had more than a handful of people to proclaim his death and the ascension of his heir. She'd never seen it done; the current emperor had been in power since her father was a little boy.

"It's a moment of great significance and solemnity," he said, glancing around with an avaricious gleam in his eye. "Everyone's buying plenty of newspapers and mourning caps."

"That's only right and proper," she said, her voice coming out deeper than she expected. She suddenly remembered dozens of facts about mourning caps that she couldn't ever recall learning. "You're aware that they were originally made of sheepskin, painted blood red, and were meant to signify a son who had fallen in battle?"

"You're always full of facts, Deeny," he said absently as he waded back into the crowd to hear the latest rumors. The shop was one of the centers of social life for the men of the town, and they often gathered here to gossip, smoke, and clap each other on the back.

She sat on her stool, reading a book of old poetry through her pounding headache, enduring the customers and the stale air for a good hour before an excited little boy burst in.

"They're setting up in the Station Square!" he said. "They say to get everyone together!"

The men all streamed for the door *en masse*, like excited boys going into a show.

"Lock up and follow!" her father ordered, his eyes bright.

◆◆◆

When she arrived in the open square in front of the railway station, she had to stand behind what seemed like the entire town. An honor guard stood off to the side holding flags and ceremonial pikes. Imperial flags with their stylized stocky northern horses and crossed swords, the emblem of the ruling Molasca family, fluttered in the breeze next to the green, white, and blue Antrimanian state flag. At the center of the square stood three Imperial Army officers, resplendent in their green coats, peaked hats, and shining buckles.

The crowd hushed, eager to hear. One of the officers stepped forward and unrolled an official-looking proclamation.

"People of the town of Viko Station, Lofkandi province, hear the will of Heaven!" he said, his clear voice ringing through the square. "Be it known that His Imperial Majesty by the Will and Call of the Glorious Pair, the God and Goddess Eternal, our sovereign Askar Molasca of Antriman has departed this mortal realm."

A sigh went through the crowd. At last, what they'd come to see.

Behind the honor guard, a good two dozen soldiers raised their rifles to the sky and fired. Andín jumped. They shot into the air again and again until Andín's eardrums rang.

This didn't help her headache. Spikes of pain lanced her, and she clutched her father's arm to steady herself. He glanced down at her, concern in his eyes.

She couldn't respond; her mouth felt full of cotton. Worse, a strange energy seemed to pulse and grow within her. It felt like her body was being consumed by some dark fire. She felt woozy, like she might be sick. Something was very wrong.

The smoke cleared, and the lead officer read the next part of the proclamation.

"Viko Station, Lofkandi! Hear the will of Heaven!" cried the army officer again, in the same lilting, rising and falling tones. "Be it known that His Imperial Majesty Hular Molasca, late Grand Prince of the Realm, has ascended to the Imperial Throne of Antriman in his capital at Palascena. Long life to the Emperor Hular Molasca!"

The crowd, loyal subjects all, applauded enthusiastically.

The dark energy had built inside Andín to the point where she couldn't control it any longer. Something felt like it was bursting out from within her.

"No!" she screamed. Everyone turned to look at her. "No!"

She tried to stop herself, but she couldn't. Some other voice from deep inside her had clawed its way to the surface.

"That ungrateful brat!" she cried. "How dare he! He is not the emperor! *I am emperor! I am emperor!*"

Her knees buckled, and she sank to the ground, wild with terror as the soldiers ran toward her. Her father's eyes were wide with horror.

"I am the emperor!" she shrieked in a voice that wasn't her own.

She repeated herself over and over, unable to stop, until she passed out.

Chapter 2

Viko Castle

Her mother hovered anxiously by Andín's bedside, her expression drawn down into a worried frown. She kept changing a wet towel on her daughter's forehead, even though she wasn't warm, and bringing her more cups of tea.

"Mama," said Andín, feebly batting her mother's arm away. "Stop. Stop! I'm fine."

"No, Deeny, you are most certainly *not* fine." Her mother's voice quavered. "Do you know we had to persuade those army men not to cart you off as a traitor?"

"What? No, no, I'm not a traitor," she insisted. "I—I'm sorry, Mama. I don't know what happened. I wish I could explain it—"

"It doesn't need explaining," her mother said briskly, cutting her off. She had the tone that said she had a theory and was going to run with it. "All of this… all of this is wrapped up in this university nonsense. You've been obsessing over it! You spend all your time locked away with books and stories up here when you aren't working, having fantasies about running off to Palascena. It's too much for a young lady. It isn't any surprise that you've had, well, a 'falling down.' This runs in your father's family, this kind of thing. I'd hoped you'd be spared. I had the priestess at Temple say a special Lady's Blessing for you this morning."

"Mama…"

"It will be a temporary trouble, nothing more," Mama said firmly. She wrung out the towel and dipped it in the water again.

"You must move beyond it, and we'll see that you do. Your father and I have talked about him hiring one of the local boys to help at the store. It's time you thought more seriously about your future."

"My future is at the university," Andín said weakly.

Her mother sighed. The anger drained from her face, only to be replaced by anxious worry. "Oh, my dear Deeny. You're seventeen already; you need to think seriously for once. The university? What would you do in Palascena? What would you study? Did you have a plan for that, or for how you might live after? You're not an average girl by any means, but you've never had the first idea what you wanted to do with all those brains you have."

Andín bristled. The whole point of university was to find something she loved doing, wasn't it? Why did she have to choose before she even went? "That's not fair."

Her mother just shook her head. "And how will you meet the kind of man you could marry there, in such a strange place?" She put a small emphasis on 'you'—the implication was clear. Plain country-girl Andín would be out of her league in Palascena.

"I don't care," Andín shot back. "I don't want to be married!"

"You've said that for years," her mother said. "But, sweet, dear girl, you don't want to be twenty-five and alone. You don't know what a hard life that can be." She put the wet towel on Andín's forehead again. "Well. For now, just rest. We'll discuss it all when you're feeling better."

"Mama..." Andín tried to protest.

"Sleep, if you can. I'm going to go downstairs and try and explain this to people." She stood and drew a holy sign in the air. "What a dreadful start to a new era."

◆◆◆

Andín fidgeted in bed, unable to sleep.

They were talking about her out there. Everyone thought she was crazy, or worse.

A new era, her mother had said. A new emperor.

"You," she said softly, addressing whatever it was inside her head. "I know you're there."

Something inside her mind stirred but said nothing. It wasn't a comfortable feeling, like someone had put a snake in her bed.

"You must be real," she said, summoning her courage. "I'm not crazy."

As she spoke, lurid visions danced through her imagination. Andín the madwoman, just like Old Mama Yava from children's stories who lived in a haystack, only coming out at night to blither and rage and steal...

She'd be crazy Old Mama Andín, who lived with her nose in a moldy book, who wanted to go to university just like a man, who said strange things at the wrong time and embarrassed her poor family. She pictured herself as an old woman, bent and dressed in filthy rags, hobbling through the square mumbling to herself. She'd never get to go anywhere or do anything but stay in Viko Station and rant.

She sniffled, tears welling up in her eyes. She wouldn't. It was impossible. She didn't want to stay here. She didn't want to be crazy!

«*Stop crying,*» a deep voice said in the back of her mind. «*You are not crazy.*»

"You!" she whispered, sitting up. If this thing was talking, she was going to talk back. "I knew it! You made me say those things, didn't you?"

«*I made you say nothing. I said it.*»

"Who *are* you?" she demanded.

But it said nothing more, retreating back to sulky silence.

"Curse it all!" she swore.

Her brother poked a concerned head in.

"Are you all right?" he asked hesitantly. "I thought I heard you..."

"Go away, Palyar!" she snapped, her temper flaring again.

He shrugged and withdrew without another word.

She lay back on her pillows, letting the impact knock a sigh out of her, guilt chasing the anger away. This wasn't Palyar's fault. He wasn't responsible for her father's decisions. He hadn't chased her out of the house.

He hadn't put voices in her head.

"Whatever you are," she said to the air. "I despise you."

As she finally drifted off to fitful sleep, she thought she heard a deep, quiet laughter.

◆ ◆ ◆

She rode through a deep, lush green forest in sweltering humidity, at the head of a long column of men and pack animals. She felt an immense satisfaction; something had gone very, very right. Beside her rode a beautiful young woman with long, perfectly straight black hair and a complexion far more fair than Andín's own deep brown.

Andín felt an overwhelming desire for her, not just to be near her, but to possess her, to *do* things to her. A few of them made her stomach lurch. A few of them made her flush and squirm. The woman glanced back at Andín and smiled secretly.

She awoke to find a familiar face staring down at her. For a heart-stopping moment, she thought it was the woman from her dream; then she opened her mouth, shattering the illusion.

"Andín! You're awake!" her best friend Valsin shrieked.

Andín started, heart pounding. "Val! What do you—what are you trying to do? Scare me to death?"

Valsin smirked. "I could probably get permission from the mayor to do that." The mayor was her father.

Andín glared at her.

"Fine, poor taste." She spun around and sat on the bed with a *whump*. "Everyone's very, very wroth with you. Papa says they had to convince the soldiers not to drag you off in chains! You made the town look horrible!" She grabbed her friend's hands, eyes bright. "It was wonderful! I only wish you'd told me you were going to do that ahead of time!"

Andín shook her hands free. "I'd never! I didn't plan it, Val, you have to believe me."

Valsin's face fell. "Oh. You didn't? I thought it was some sort of glorious prank gone wrong."

"It wasn't," said Andín sulkily.

Valsin lowered her voice. "So does that mean you *are* …affected? In the head?"

"No! I don't think so... I don't know," protested Andín, struggling to find words. "I can't exactly explain it."

"Oh, please! Try me."

"Well..." Andín began hesitantly. "The other night I was up on the hill above the Vintoi land—"

"What were you doing there?" Valsin interrupted immediately. "At night? Were you with a boy? Oh, Andín, finally!"

"No, there was no boy! Why does everyone keep thinking that?"

"Well, we all figure you're overdue," Valsin said matter-of-factly.

"Look," said Andín, "I was up there because I was mad at Papa over the university issue. Palyar and I used to play up there, so that's where I went! That's all."

"Oh," said Valsin. "That. Did your father say you couldn't go?"

"Yes," grumbled Andín. "Palyar's going instead."

Valsin gave her a pitying look. "There are other ways out of Viko, you know. You told me yourself you didn't even know what you'd study there!"

Andín scowled at her.

"Well," said Valsin with false cheer, "it could be worse, right? You'll get to stay here with me!"

Andín rolled her eyes. "Right." Valsin wanted to get away from Viko Station, too. They'd concocted plans for leaving since they were both little. Valsin seemed to have given up on it lately. "Um, so I was angry and I went up to the hill so I could be alone. There was some other girl up there, Alavesh maybe. And then I heard this buzzing... and I blacked out. When I woke there was something in my head. It talked to me. And yesterday it... it talked. Through me."

Valsin's gave her a look.

"It's true," said Andín weakly.

"The voices in your mind told you to say it?" Valsin said at last. "Oh... Deeny. You do know that doesn't sound quite sane, right?"

"I know," muttered Andín.

"Oh, you poor thing!" Valsin grabbed Andín and gave her a huge hug. Andín made a little strangled sound. "You poor mad thing! Well, I'll do whatever I can to make you well, yes?"

"Thanks," said Andín. "Really."

♦ ♦ ♦

As the sun slipped down in the sky, Andín decided she'd had enough of sitting in bed worrying. Valsin had left long ago, and no one else had been up to see her.

She looked west towards the setting sun, trying to figure out what to do next.

Palyar practiced his fiddle in the next room. She had to admit, he was getting pretty good. When had that happened? Soon he'd be old enough to leave school here and go to the university. What would happen to her then?

She read to distract herself. She tried and failed again at sewing, and she sorted out her room twice before giving up and going to sleep.

The next morning, she ventured downstairs. No one spoke to her, but her father gave her a tight little smile before he headed over to the store.

Was she that toxic now?

Andín sat alone at the kitchen table, anger warring with the dreadful suspicion that things had changed for good.

♦ ♦ ♦

The next few days passed in a whirl of tension and worry.

The voice in her mind refused to return. She knew it was still there—she still felt that strange, dark spot in the back of her brain—but she couldn't do anything to prod it back to life, no matter what she tried or said.

Maybe, she concluded, she was crazy after all, but she was getting better. Maybe she could ride this out. A return to normality dangled in front of her, tantalizing in its nearness.

Andín made some noise about returning to work at the shop, but her mother strictly forbade it, and her father reluctantly agreed. He even hired a local boy to work the counter as her mother had suggested.

This left Andín with nothing at all to do with her days. She woke up and thought she should be at the shop, perched on her familiar stool, until she remembered that someone had taken her place. She found, unexpectedly, that she actually missed working with her father.

Her mother dragged her to the local temple every day so she could be blessed and re-blessed by the priestesses. They sat on the women's side of the elegant building, and while her mother chanted and prayed, Andín found herself looking up at the statue of the Goddess—in this aspect a matronly woman with a baby on her hip—and sent up a little prayer of her own. She'd never been much of a believer, but it couldn't hurt.

Apart from that she mostly helped her mother with the cooking, the washing, and the cleaning, but otherwise she stayed up in her room reading. She re-read familiar history, folk tales and adventure books, willing the world to make sense again. She read so much that she began to daydream of the university again—a different place where she could be on her own and read and study as she wished. History! Music! Literature!

Still the feeling of wrongness nagged at her. It was like having an itch she couldn't scratch. She simply couldn't shake the feeling that the voice was still inside her, watching and waiting. Every night she dreamed of awful, unsettling things in places she'd never seen. Bodies in the streets. Gallows, full of swinging corpses. Armies churning fields to mud. Swords clashing, axes falling, men dying...

Early one morning she awoke from yet another night of terrors, shivering and shaking, and made a decision. This had gone far enough, and it wasn't going away. It was time to act.

She pulled on her heavy boots and traveling cloak, fixed a snack to carry with her, and set out for the ruins of Viko Castle.

♦♦♦

Andín hiked out of Viko Station down the dusty road that led to the cramped, run-down hamlet of Old Viko. Before she actually reached the ancient village she turned down a barely visible trail that led to the ruins. In her dream, the vivid one she'd had on the hill that first terrible night, she had heard herself say, "We stand here at Viko Castle."

That had to mean something. If she went to the castle, maybe she had a hope of jarring this thing, whatever it was, loose.

She cut through a wide, empty field on her way to the hilltop ruins. There, as she tromped through the mud and broken wheat stalks, she was suddenly surrounded by the ranks of a great army.

She stopped dead, her heart pounding. The army was ethereal; it came and went like a fading memory, both here and not here.

Strange languages fell on her ears in snippets, mixing with the calls of birds and the sound of her own labored breathing. Were they speaking a form of Antrimanian? Or something else? The answer seemed just out of reach.

She shook her head and marched determinedly forward, leaving the ghostly army behind. This was a sign that she was on the right track, she was sure. Whatever was in her mind was waking up again.

Finally, as the sun loomed high in the sky, she pulled herself up onto a deserted embankment. Viko Castle wasn't much to look at; hardly one stone stood atop another. The Antrimanian Empire was covered in old ruins and tumbledown castles like this.

She picked her way through the ruin, trying to figure out what was what, and where the room she had seen in her dream might be. When she blinked, she saw whole walls, tapestries, guards and grizzled, worried-looking generals in the firelit corridors. When she blinked again, they were gone, and only the ruins remained.

Past and present seemed to be mingling in her mind, as they had in the field. She forced herself onward, her legs shaking.

At last she came to a breathtaking view of the western approach to the hill. She wearily plunked down on one of the stones and looked out over the fields and rolling hills. She fixed on a particular rise many miles off, now crowned with waving wheat, and she saw very clearly six long columns of men marching over it. There were men with tall pikes and sturdy helmets, archers, mages with their distinctive scarlet cloaks and tri-cornered, plumed hats, men on horseback, and more. They carried green banners with a snake and a tree on them, very unlike the imperial flags she knew so well. At the head of the host rode a tall man dressed entirely in green; his helmet was made to look like the branches of a tree.

She knew what she was seeing from the history she'd read. This was something that had taken place hundreds of years ago—the Battle of Viko, one of several battles between the emperor and a rebellious baron.

«*They called him the Forest King,*» whispered the voice in her mind. It had grown somehow less distinct and softer, though still perfectly clear. «*Pyoral Novark, Baron Ropan, the Forest King. He always dressed like that. Ridiculous. His people worshiped him. They thought he was an incarnation of the God Himself. It was only a matter of time before he marched against me.*»

"There you are," she said. She was too weary to say much more. "I knew you'd come."

«*I stood here and watched him march toward us. You saw it, too, just now. We're beginning to blend, you and I. Those are my memories you're seeing.*»

"That was hundreds of years ago." The breeze played with her long, straight, black hair. "I am going mad," she said matter-of-factly. It was the only logical conclusion.

«*You aren't.*»

"What are you, if not madness?" she asked.

«*I'll show you.*»

The world vanished again as she was abruptly plunged into foreign memories.

♦♦♦

She lay in bed, her chest struggling to rise and fall. Every little movement was agony. She was so, so old, and this body was so frail... She had only a little time left.

Dark, choking energies swirled around her, waiting.

"My son," she croaked, and again her voice was that of an old man. "Bring him... bring him here."

"Yes, your Imperial Majesty," said a tall, gaunt man dressed in elegant robes. His name popped into her mind; Syr fan Porlab, the court wizard. He had an unreliable smirk on his face as he bowed his way out of the room.

She glanced to the right. A grizzled, withered face below a shock of unkempt white hair stared back. The mirror, she realized. This was her body and her face.

She had seen that face in photographs and on coins. The emperor, the one who had just died.

She was propped up in a bed piled high with gaudy, expensive covers. The room was stifling hot, and yet she shivered.

Then the shivering stopped, and everything seemed strangely calm.

The feeling was leaving her body; she knew death when it approached. She'd died so many times before. Memories within memories surfaced... here, death came as she lay in unspeakable agony on the battlefield. There, she tripped and fell down the stairs, her last thought one of acute embarrassment. And there again, like now, she died in her bed, but this time covered in furs in a rude wooden room. Strange, for a warrior prince to die in bed so often. But maybe that was the ultimate success. She struggled to clench a fist in triumph.

I have made this country safe enough for its emperor to die in bed, thought Andín-who-was-not-Andín. It would have to be enough.

She wheezed and coughed. Her chest rattled and seized with pain. Soon.

There. Her son entered, trailed by the wizard, Syr fan Porlab.

"Father," he said, his eyes bright. He looked like he had won something.

He thinks he'll be emperor soon, but he'll have a surprise, she thought. A terrible, wonderful surprise. She wondered how it would be this time. They all fought it at first, but in time... there was almost always acceptance, merging, and the strength of a new bond.

Visions swam in her mind. Hallucinations, perhaps. A young Alavesh woman bent over her, frowning, and placed her hand on the dying emperor's forehead.

And then, the shock of death hit her. She felt herself ripped away from her body. The dark energies in the air swelled to a crescendo.

She closed her eyes—

—Only to open them and not see, as she had expected, her own corpse lying in the bed before her, but the stars above a small village in the remote provinces. Her body was gut-wrenchingly wrong, not the Grand Prince's, not even a man's! She felt a terrible, sickening disorientation. "Oh no no," she shouted. "No, it's gone wrong! This is some peasant girl!"

♦♦♦

Andín gasped for breath as she returned to the present.

"You—you—" She couldn't find words for what she had seen. "I don't understand!"

«*No. How could you? You're just a peasant girl,*» he said, and his voice was cruel and bitter.

"I am *not* a peasant girl!" she retorted, stung. "You don't know the first thing about me!"

«*Nor do I care to. Clearly something has gone wrong with the transfer. I'm supposed to be inhabiting Hular's body, a man's body, not... this.*»

She tasted the sense of his voice, the feeling and meaning below the surface, and found the sharp tang of distance, dissonance, disappointment, and revulsion. *Where is my penis?* she wondered idly before flinching from the thought in revulsion.

"There is nothing wrong with being a girl, whatever you are," she snapped. "I don't care what you think! And if you don't like it so much, why don't you just go away?"

«*I would if I could, but it's not that simple. My spirit leaves at body's death, and only then,*» he said. «*It follows the crown. And the crown always goes to a man.*»

"Ridiculous," she snorted. It had always been that way, she knew. But now the thought of the emperor always being a man seemed utterly absurd. "Why is it that way? Other countries have queens."

«*Tradition, girl. Something you don't understand.*»

"I understand that you're in my head without my permission!" she said. "I should be able to be rid of you."

«*We are stuck together, sadly. This is the way the sorceress constructed the magic at the beginning. I can't just* leave *you.*»

"Well—we have to do something!" She sputtered. "My family and friends think I've gone mad. I'll never be able to earn enough money to go to the university at this rate."

«*The Imperial University in Palascena? You?*» He laughed. «*You're only a provincial girl!*»

"What are you, my father?" she said, fighting back tears. "What do you know about women?"

A series of very descriptive and lurid images flashed before her.

"Stop! No, stop!" She tried to shove the images out of her mind. "I don't want to know about that!"

And yet his residual lust and pleasure lingered as an aftertaste of the memories. She squirmed uncomfortably. These were not memories she wanted to be having right now. A few stray thoughts of her own filtered through; she banished them quickly. "I don't want to know about your man's life."

«*And you wanted to come to Palascena? To my city? That's how it is there. That's life. Men and women. How ignorant you are. Ask your father and brother, they'll tell you.*»

"No! No, I won't hear that," she said firmly, trying to regain control of the conversation.

Conversation! She was talking to a voice in her head. She laughed at the absurdity of it all.

«*It seems absurd now,*» he said, responding to her unspoken thought. «*But soon you'll get used to it. We'll merge more fully, and it won't be a conversation at all. It will seem like we're the same person, depressing as that is for us both.*»

"That won't happen," Andín said. "I can't think of anything I want less than to be yoked together with some foul spirit!"

«*You know who I was. I'm not just a foul spirit.*»

She had tried not to think about that, but she couldn't avoid it now. "You really are the ghost of... of the emperor?" she asked, barely daring to say it aloud. "The emperor who died?"

«*Yes,*» he snapped, impatient, «*and all the emperors before him, going back a thousand years. And I'm no ghost.*»

"So what are you?" she asked. "You're telling me that the emperor is—was—some kind of... immortal spirit?"

«*Yes,*» he informed her grandly. «*I'm a demon.*»

◆◆◆

As midday turned to afternoon Andín walked back to town, furiously working it over in her mind. She could feel him perched in there, observing her thoughts like a spectator at a game.

If what he said was true, every emperor for a thousand years, all the way back to Antriman's beginnings as a loose band of tribes living along the Antroi River, had been possessed by a demon spirit. When each emperor died, his heir inherited both the throne and the demon. When dynasties changed, the demon followed the crown.

If all that was real, she didn't just have one man in her mind, but more than eighty. It was a chilling, world-bending thought.

She stopped dead as she reached the dusty road leading to Old Viko, looking right and then left. No one was around.

She began to talk through her options out loud.

"So," she said, trying to keep her voice from shaking. "This is intolerable. You agree?"

«*I agree.*»

"I don't want to believe in you," said Andín. "I hate the idea of you. But you are here. If I'm mad… then I'm mad."

«*You're as sane as I am.*»

"How reassuring," Andín said dryly. "So I see it like this. If I'm hallucinating voices in my head, fine. I can't do much more damage to myself than I've already done. I hope. But if you are real… then I need to deal with you somehow."

«*Indeed.*» The demon seemed amused.

"Well," she said, trying to hold on to her steadfast practicality. "If you can't simply leave me under your own power, what do you propose we do?"

«*I'd wondered how long it would take you to ask. You have a high opinion of your own intellect, but I see little evidence of it. Let me ask you then, girl who wants to insult my great university with her presence: what should we do?*»

"It seems," she said slowly, pushing her anger aside, "that we need help. Was there anyone in the—your court who knew about magic, demons and whatever it is you do to go from body to body?" Her heart leapt; she could kill two birds with one stone.

"What about at the university?"

He considered this. «*Yes, the position of court wizard is an ancient one; Syr fan Porlab would know. And I have instructed the university library to collect many, many books on demonology.*»

There was something else, too, that she'd only just been able to fish out of the overwhelming mass of information she was processing. "That Alavesh woman you saw at the end, right before you… died." She gulped. "Do you know her?"

«*A mere hallucination, a sign of death,*» he said dismissively. «*It is common.*»

"No," insisted Andín. "She was here. I remember her. Right before you came to me, I saw her. She talked to me, she said she was sorry. She must be real. She must know something about this."

That actually seemed to make him pause. «*I don't know her.*»

"No one else does, either," said Andín. "And no one has seen her here, but we both saw her."

«*Interesting,*» allowed the demon after a moment.

"If she was in the city," mused Andín, "maybe she's still there. She certainly isn't here."

«*So what must we do, then, peasant girl?*»

"My name isn't 'peasant girl,' it's Andín dal Rovi," she said haughtily, "and we should go to Palascena."

«*At last. Yes. We should.*»

Chapter 3

Dreams

That night Andín lay restless in bed, trying and failing to sleep. If they were going to Palascena tomorrow, she needed her rest.

Excitement kept her awake. At last, at long last, she would leave Viko Station. She would get to see all the places she'd only read about in books!

But even as she thought of how it would be in Palascena, strange memories kept seeping into her consciousness like moisture through the walls on a humid day. Faces, smells, sights, sounds, all from a life—lives—she'd never known. It was unpleasant and disorienting. She wasn't sure which memories were hers and which were someone else's.

The feeling of an invader lurking in her mind made her want to scream with frustration. Try as she might, she couldn't grow used to his jagged, foreign presence, especially now that she knew what he was. A demon. *A demon.*

The hope that soon she'd be rid of him forever was her only consolation.

At last, exhausted both mentally and physically, she drifted off into a fitful sleep.

♦♦♦

She walked down a shadowy corridor, her footsteps silent. The dark-skinned, serious Alavesh woman Andín had seen on the hillside waited for her there, somewhere deep inside her own mind.

"You again!" Andín exclaimed.

"Hello, Andín," said the Alavesh woman.

"You did this to me—to us!"

The woman held up her hand. "We are alone together, Andín. The demon, such as he is, can't see or hear you right now."

"W-what? He's gone?"

"Not gone, just… not quite here," she said. "He may sense your memories later as the two of you grow closer, but for now, we can talk without interruption."

It was true, Andín could sense it. That awful foreign feeling was gone. Gone! She almost cried with relief.

The Alavesh woman watched her. "This isn't permanent. When we're done, you'll be connected again. I can only pause the link between you for a few moments."

"Why did you do this?" Andín demanded. "Please take it away!"

"I can't," said the other woman. She actually looked sad about it. "But it will get better, I promise. Soon, it'll be like the two of you have always been one."

Andín shivered. "I—I can't imagine that. You have no idea what it's like, having your mind be not completely your own."

In response, the other woman took Andín's hand. "There's something I want you to see, all right? Are you ready?"

"No," whispered Andín.

"Good," said the other woman.

There was a flash, and then Andín was looking out through the eyes of someone else.

♦♦♦

There was a crate, or maybe a chest, inside a darkened room. It was made of wood that looked like it was about to start rotting away.

Something inside was singing to her.

Andín knew that she inhabited the body of someone else. The way she moved wasn't quite right, the way her hands felt, the way the world seemed a little smaller.

Whoever this was looked down at the crate and slowly, softly opened it.

A rusty piece of metal lay deep within. She glanced around, as if afraid she'd be caught at any moment, then rummaged it out. The song grew louder.

"Oh, good," sighed the someone else's voice. "A magic sword. Just what I hoped he'd bring home from the sea. Couldn't have been something worth money, oh, no."

But she picked up the sword anyway, grasping the rusty, thin hilt with both hands.

At once she was struck speechless by strange, ethereal visions. A glowing form spoke to her, choosing her, loving her, granting her a mission.

A quest. A *holy* quest.

"Oh, no, no, no," she whispered. "I can't. Not me! Please, pick someone else. You're not even mine!"

But it was done. The sword hummed happily in her hand, and she began to sob uncontrollably.

◆◆◆

The scene shifted abruptly as Andín's heart went out to whomever it was she'd just left behind. She now stood in line with a dozen others, dressed in ragged uniforms that might, at one time, have matched. They had assembled on the front lawn of a ramshackle country house; a red and white flag whipped nearby in the stiff breeze.

Someone dressed in uniform, who bore a striking resemblance to the Alavesh woman but older and with burning eyes that twitched every which way, swaggered down the line.

The uniformed woman looked up at the sky, and her face drew taut.

"Something's happened," she murmured. "I can feel it in my blood."

◆◆◆

The scene shifted. Now she sat at a table, her hands huge and calloused, the hands of a man who had worked his whole life. Blueprints were scattered everywhere on his table, designs for massive, arching sections of… something.

"They may come to you, Rikan," murmured someone in his ear.

"One with a sword, one with the future in her mind. Two girls, one Alavesh, one Antrimanian. Be ready for them. Help them go north. Help them heal the world."

"I understand," she said, and her deep voice seemed to resonate in her shoes.

◆ ◆ ◆

The scene shifted again to a warm little house in the middle of a valley ringed by steep hills. The briny scent of the sea was on the air.

She walked out of a little cabin, leaning on her cane, and looked up.

"So soon," she whispered. "Too soon. Oh, I'm not ready. Not ready at all."

She closed her eyes and said a few words. There was a flash of power, and then she saw an old, gaunt woman with steel in her eyes standing in front of her. She dimly understood this to be her own shape.

"God and Goddess above, I hope it's not too late," she said. "Go, now, to Alavia."

◆ ◆ ◆

The scene shifted yet again, and she flew high in the sky. Her thoughts were those of a bird, a predator, winging higher and higher, looking for food.

She wheeled around and shrieked. A crack had appeared in the sky itself.

Andín hurtled back into herself as the crack swallowed the bird whole.

◆ ◆ ◆

She opened her eyes, her head swimming. It took her a few panicky, disorienting moments to realize where, and who, she was.

The Alavesh woman was nowhere to be seen. Somewhere in the back of her mind, the demon was nestled, waiting, watching.

"What was that?" Andín whispered.

« *A dream*,» grumbled the demon. «*The world is made of dreams. Go back to sleep. Tomorrow, Palascena awaits.*»

Chapter 4

Palascena

Andín got dressed, packed a light bag, and gathered together all of her meager savings from various hiding places all over her room. She assembled the assorted crinkled bank notes and worn coins on her dresser.

It wasn't enough. She'd known it wasn't enough before she started. She'd stared up at the fare to Palascena at the railway station far too often not to know what it cost, and she didn't have it.

«*Well? Let's be off,*» the demon prodded.

"What's the rush? Afraid you'll be here when my time of month comes?" she muttered. It was an unfathomably rude thing to say. But she was in a hideous mood, and it was worth it to feel his panic. She smirked.

«*This isn't enough money,*» he observed.

"What intellect," she spat, embarrassment making her cruel. "You can even count. So, Your Imperial Genius, what should we do now?"

He bristled at being talked to that way. Tough, she thought. You're in my head.

«*It's my head now, too,*» he reminded her.

Chills ran down her spine. She didn't like that thought at all.

«*Sell a few things,*» he ordered. «*Look, some of these trinkets you have here must be worth something. Like that round thing.*»

"This?" She picked up a tiny locket and watched it turn in the morning sunlight for a long moment. "My grandmother gave this to me. She died years ago."

«*A cheap memento of the forgotten dead, how droll. Sell it. You'll never miss it.*»

"No! And... it's not like it's worth much anyway. It wouldn't be nearly enough."

«*You could sell yourself,*» he remarked dryly.

She flinched. "You're hideous," she said.

He seemed to chuckle. She caught a whiff of wretched old man thoughts and wanted to throw up. She was about to tell him off when three heavy knocks hit her door.

"Deeny? Are you all right?"

"I'm fine, Mama! Go away!" Andín called back.

"There's breakfast," her mother said. Andín listened to the stairs creak as her mother trudged back down them.

"If you have any *useful* ideas, I'd love to hear them," she whispered after she was certain her mother had gone.

He said nothing more, withdrawing to lurk in the back of her mind. She rummaged through her jewelry, pronounced it all either cheap and worthless or too dear to part with and searched the rest of the room.

"Maybe this," she said, pulling an old green dress from the closet. "No. No, it's threadbare. Yet the lacework is fine..."

Her door creaked a little, and Palyar stuck his face in. "Deeny?"

She sighed as loudly as she could, trying to get him to leave. "What?"

"Breakfast."

"Mama told me," said Andín. "Go away."

"Are you okay?" he asked. "I heard you talking to yourself."

She glared at him.

"Is... is there anything I can do?" he asked hesitantly.

«*Ask for a railway ticket to Palascena,*» the demon prodded.

"Not unless you have enough money to buy me a railway ticket to Palascena!" she snapped without thinking, and immediately covered her mouth. She hadn't meant to say that out loud.

"Truly?" he asked quietly. "You're going?"

Andín's mouth was suddenly dry. "I didn't say that," she

stammered. But he had seen the coins and bank notes on her dresser; he'd seen the bag she'd packed. She looked away. "Please don't tell Mama and Papa."

"I won't. I'll be right back," Palyar said.

"Palyar!" she hissed, but he was gone.

She heard him withdraw, floorboards creaking in rhythm to his footfalls. Andín, wondering how she could possibly salvage this, sifted through the bottom layer of her closet. These shoes that no longer fit might have been expensive once. Surely someone would pay a few coins for them? Had these old wooden dolls been hers? So long ago. Her mother had carved them and put the hair on; she always had a way with crafting. Andín sighed regretfully and put them back in their box.

Her gaze fell on her bookshelf. The volumes there were old, the bindings falling apart from constant re-reading. They were the world to her, but worthless to anyone else.

She sat on the floor of her room, willing back the tears. Her whole life, everything she was and everything she loved, wasn't enough to buy her way out of this horrible mess.

Her door creaked again. She glanced back, annoyed to find Palyar's face there again. He had a little leather bag in his hand.

"Um," he said. "I heard the fight you and Papa had, before. And now... I... I don't think it's really fair. That you can't go to Palascena and the university."

She blinked, surprised. "Well, no. It's not."

"And maybe it'll make you well if you get to leave and go there. Do you think it will?"

"Yes," she said truthfully. Once the demon was gone, then she would return to herself. She could live her life again. "I'm sure of it. I'll come home well. And I *will* come home, I promise."

"I don't want to go to Palascena at all," he said, unable to meet her surprised eyes. "I'd rather stay here. I like Viko. I don't think I'd like the city, and I know I wouldn't like finance and business. You were right: I just want to play my fiddle." He smiled and flushed, embarrassed to have said that. "Maybe you can have my place in Palascena. They'll understand, someday." He put a collection of coins and crisply folded bank notes on her dresser. "Here. I hope it's enough."

Open-mouthed, she glanced over the money, counting it rapidly. It was more than enough. "Palyar…"

"Okay. I'm glad. I'll go."

"Wait!" she said, and he paused. "Thank you. This means more to me than you know. I'll make it up to you someday."

He nodded at her in such a quiet, determined way that for a moment she could glimpse the man he was becoming. Then he turned and was gone.

«*That worked out nicely,*» drawled the demon.

"Shut up," she whispered through her tears.

◆◆◆

Andín ate breakfast and drank her tea as if nothing was wrong, avoiding Palyar's eyes the entire time, then dashed back upstairs to gather her things. When Papa was in the shop and Mama was busy out back, she stole out of the house. The door closed behind her with a click.

I'll be back, she promised. As soon as I can.

She dragged the only travel bag she had, crammed full of clothes, books, and other items she figured she might need, to the railway station in the center of town. The train to the capital would be here around midday; like every other person in town, she had the schedule memorized.

The board posted the fees. Viko Station lay on the Cross Empire Line, which stretched from Palascena in the east all the way across forests, mountains, and deserts to the remote western border with Shuyu. The mind-boggling price of a ticket to the distant western terminus, over a thousand miles away, was a stark illustration of the vastness of their empire.

Some of the men who had returned home from the war with Yarun had spoken with reverence of the astonishing sights and wide-open spaces of the lesser-known, western parts of the empire. There existed people in those places who rarely heard from imperial authority, and didn't even know the name of the emperor. She longed to see those places someday.

On cue, images flickered through her mind as she looked over the names on the destination board. The demon, of course, had seen them all at one point or another. The empire was an open book to him.

She found she envied him that. But she would do it on her own, without his help.

Andín unsteadily approached the ticket counter. Jova, one of the men who frequented her father's shop, smiled broadly at her when she approached.

"Well, Andín dal Rovi! Glad to see you up and about. What brings you to the station?"

She pushed the money at him with what she hoped was brisk efficiency. "One ticket for Palascena, please."

He frowned, and her heart stopped.

"Does your father know about this?" he asked. She kicked herself for not buying the ticket ahead of time, when someone less nosy was on duty.

"Please," she demanded politely, "a ticket for Palascena."

"I don't know," he said, shaking his head. "If Goen finds out I sold a ticket to his daughter, he'll never let me back in the store. Why don't you go home and talk it over with him?"

"Jova, please," said Andín, trying to keep the desperation from her voice. "Just sell me the ticket. That's your *job*."

A high-pitched whistle sounded as the train pulled into the station. She had no time!

"Well…" he said, making a show of considering, "after all that happened with you lately, I don't think it would be right. You aren't well."

«*Who is this arrogant fool?*» the demon's voice snarled in her mind.

Hush, she willed him. Thank the twin gods, he listened.

She turned back to Jova, improvising quickly. "Believe it or not, I've been called to Palascena to account for what I did. And if I don't get on that train, I could be in a lot of trouble!"

«*What? That's the silliest thing I've ever heard. We don't—*»

Jova scratched his head. "I don't see any police or army with you. And where are your documents?"

"Andín!" a familiar voice rang out behind her.

Andín flinched as Valsin ran into view, dress and hair far too elegant for the station plaza. "Deeny, what are you doing here?" she asked.

Jova beat her to it. "She's trying to go to Palascena! I didn't think it would be right in her state."

"Val," Andín said, grabbing her arm and holding it in a vise grip. "Tell Jova here that I'm not making it up that I've been called to Palascena to explain myself for the other day! By the army."

"Ow!" Valsin complained.

Andín gave her friend a pleading look. "Val!" she hissed.

"Oh?" Valsin's eyes lit up with mischievous glee. "Oh! Yes, of course, Jova! You should take her at her word, that's exactly what happened. I saw my father get the notice himself this morning. She's had to pack in an awful rush! I can vouch for her myself. She must go."

Jova's frown deepened as he thought. "So this is... imperial business?"

"Yes!" Andín and Valsin chorused.

"I don't know..."

The whistle sounded again. The train was pulling in. She had to be on board quickly. "There's no time!" she insisted.

"Listen to her," Valsin advised. "Unless you want my father to be very wroth with you, indeed."

His brow furrowed so deeply that Andín could have planted grain between the folds. "Do you swear that this is imperial business?" he asked, gazing solemnly at her.

"Yes," Andín said without hesitation. "I swear it on the name of the great Goddess herself."

It was technically true.

He sighed and took her money, passing a ticket back to her. "Well. Good luck then. I hope they're not too hard on you."

She swiped the ticket from his hands. "Thanks!" she called, sprinting through the doors toward the waiting train. Valsin gave him a little wave and smile and dashed after Andín.

"What was that about?" she said, eyes wide. "Are you really leaving?"

"I am," said Andín, pausing in front of the hissing, groaning train. People started getting off and on. "And thank you! I swear, I wouldn't have been able to do it without you. Thank you for trusting me. I can't thank you enough!"

"You were just going to leave without telling me?" Valsin looked hurt. Andín gathered her in her arms, squeezing her tight.

"I'm sorry, Val. I am. I have to. It was last minute!"

"Are you going to try to go to the university?"

"Something like that, yes. It's terribly important! I'll tell you all about it later, promise."

The conductor was shouting; she had to be on board right now.

"I'll be back soon! I promise!" she said, running for the train.

"You'd better!" Valsin called.

Andín bolted through the crowd toward the gleaming metal monster. Her hand grasped the metal pole on the side of the door; she pulled herself up and inside the coach.

Travel, at last. At last! *Palascena.* She was going. She was finally going.

She'd promised Val she'd come back, but right now all she could think of was how wonderful the train was and how exciting the city would be.

She settled into a vacant seat in a compartment full of women, all of whom were better dressed than she. They made a point of ignoring her. She glanced out at the little town of Viko Station as the train jerked forward.

Wheels squealed as they pulled out of the station, and her whole life rolled right out of view.

♦♦♦

The train chugged through the low hills of Lofkandi province, then descended into a broad flat plain full of vast fields of wheat and rye. Station stops, rare during the first hours of the trip, became more frequent as fields turned to towns. Soon they passed from Lofkandi into Antroi province and the empire's heartland.

Andín tried to glance around the woman sitting by the window to see the scenery, but she kept giving her icy stares. She contented herself with staring off into space instead and catching sidelong glimpses of Antriman as it passed.

They were about 65 miles from Palascena, which meant that on this slow, local train, the trip would take the rest of the day. They wouldn't be there until nightfall.

She wondered in a sudden moment of panic what she'd do once they arrived at Highgate Station. Where would she go? She knew no one in the city. She'd been so excited about actually leaving that she'd forgotten to figure that part out.

«*You only thought of this now?*» said the demon with barely concealed contempt. «*Patience, country girl. We'll be fine, I know where to go. And now, so will you.*»

She yelped in pain and clutched her head as she felt information about Palascena well up and then somehow unpack itself into her consciousness. It felt like someone had shoved an umbrella into her brain and opened it.

"Are you… quite all right?" one of the well-dressed women asked, giving Andín a look.

"I'm fine," said Andín. The pain was receding. "Thank you for asking."

Hesitantly, she began to explore this new knowledge. Now she knew many things she hadn't before: the layout of the city, the major avenues and neighborhoods, the immediate area adjacent to the station. The quiet River Park Palace was close to the station; they could go there first.

«*This is my home. They'll let us in.*» Visions of a beautiful, well-appointed palace with abundant gardens, brightly lit corridors and room after room filled with graceful furniture and sumptuous works of art filled her head.

Home?

«*One of many. You'll see.*»

"I can't wait," she murmured. The woman gave her another look, and she fell silent. The train chugged on towards the city.

◆◆◆

She first saw it as a low, angular darkness crouched on the horizon, but soon the teeming imperial capital of Palascena was all around them. The buildings here were made of the same brick and plaster as back home, but they were so much larger, and there were so many more of them! Buildings stretched as far as she could see. She thought surely they must come to the heart of it soon, but they passed through the rambling outskirts for what seemed like hours. Grand buildings rose here and there like beacons, towering above the rickety tenements and crisscrossing elevated rail lines.

The women in her compartment started talking excitedly about the places they loved to frequent in the city—the theaters, the shops, the wonderful parties! They were from Casima, the Lofkand provincial capital, and there were simply so many things they couldn't get there!

She'd gone with her father to Casima once; it was ten times the size of Viko Station. Andín felt, for the first time in her life, like a base, provincial nobody.

The voice in her head stayed mercifully silent, though she could feel him looking hungrily out through her eyes. She thought she could feel longing, though—for the women, the city, or both, she couldn't quite tell.

◆◆◆

At last the train groaned into the huge terminal in the center of the sprawling, dirty, teeming, painfully beautiful mess that was Palascena. Andín and hundreds of others were spat out of the train into a roiling mass of people. She had never seen so many human beings in her life! She had to fight just to get by.

Go, she thought. Forward! She couldn't afford to just stand and gawk; she'd be run over.

She spied an exit at last and joined the stream of travelers bound in that direction. Suddenly she was outside in the cool evening air on the far side of a huge square surrounded by lofty gray stone and painted brick buildings. The names of stores and products were painted on every surface. Boys held up newspapers and called out headlines; vendors pushed carts of food or goods and sang out their wares. Everywhere, people rushed by. Carriages, trolleys, horses, and even a few puffing, clanking motorcars competed for space with thousands of brightly dressed men and women. Amazing foreign sounds and smells filled the air.

It was overwhelming. Andín stood stock-still at the station's entrance, goggling like the country girl she was.

"Get out of the way, girl!" someone hollered at her in a clipped Palascena accent. She started and stumbled forward, trying not to drop her luggage. "Bloody hayseed!" he spat.

Andín's anger caught. "I am *not* a hayseed! Ignorant lout!" But he'd already disappeared into the crowd.

No one seemed surprised by this in the least. She squared her shoulders and set off, irritated, across the cobblestones.

She was here—here at last. The great capital of the Antrimanian Empire, the richest and largest city on the entire continent. Her heartbeat quickened. This, at long last, was an adventure worth being on.

Except that the sun had already set and the lights were flickering on. All by themselves?

"Electric lights!" she cried in joy. "We have only gas lamps at home!"

«*A new innovation, and one well worth the expense to the treasury,*» the demon said, very much the emperor now. «*Much cleaner, and easier to maintain. Ah, look up. One of our finest innovations floats above you.*»

She looked above and gasped as she saw the long shadow of an airship whirring by overhead.

"Incredible!" she exclaimed.

«*We developed them during the war. There are still only a handful of them in the world, all but one of them in this country. The other belongs to the Selessians, I believe.*»

"So. Where do we go now?" she asked, exhilarated. Her feeling of being overwhelmed was fading fast, and now she drank in the sights and sounds of somewhere new. She'd been dreaming of this for so long, and now she was here.

«*Ahead, towards the avenue by that red-roofed building. I'll guide you. Fear not, it isn't a long walk.*»

"I can walk just fine!" she snapped, then looked around guiltily. No one seemed to care that she was clearly talking to herself. One advantage of the big city, perhaps?

She walked on, listening to the demon laughing at her in her head.

◆◆◆

Andín pushed her way through the square and onto one of the wide avenues radiating out from it. Here horse and motor traffic moved slowly in both directions, while policemen in bright green outfits and marvelously plumed hats signaled with their whistles and white gloves. Andín lugged her bags down the street, trying not to stare too openly at the huge stone buildings.

A man standing on a box harangued a crowd. "The expense of this coronation could feed the hungry, clothe the poor! And why do we need an emperor in the first place? Are we not a modern nation? Can we not look to the west? Can we not see the waves of freedom and self-determination coming from those ancient lands?" he crowed, gesturing wildly with every other word.

«*Anti-monarchist scum,*» the demon said sourly. «*He should be lucky the police don't throw him into prison and forget about him. In the old days, they would have.*»

"Oh," said Andín, shocked. She had no idea people would ever dare speak out about the monarchy like that. In Viko Station, it simply didn't happen. Her outburst was perhaps the closest anyone in memory had ever come. She walked by, avoiding eye contact.

Two young boys stopped her. "Need a guide to the city, ma'am? Need to know good places to stay? Best shops and restaurants?" One edged around behind her.

«*Ignore them, and watch your things! They're Alavesh children. Dangerous, crafty.*»

"Shoo!" she said, swatting at them. "Go away!"

They ran off to bother someone else. "Why are they like that?" she asked.

«*The Alavesh migrated here a century ago when their country was conquered. I should never have let so many in. Vermin!*»

Andín remembered the Alavesh woman from her dreams, from

the hillside… she didn't like thinking of people as vermin. But she said nothing as she clutched her bags close; her few remaining coins were still in their places, thank goodness.

The sense of being in a completely new and dangerous place threatened to overwhelm her again as the night air became colder. The coins she had wouldn't buy a ticket back home. She had no idea what she'd do if the demon's plan to get him out of her and into Emperor Hular didn't work out.

«*Of course it will work,*» the demon said, projecting a clear sense of what a ninny she was being. «*The palace is my home. The people there know me. My steward is well aware of my nature, he will be expecting me.*»

"Right," she said, "but what if he decides I'm just some mad girl from the country and throws me back out?"

«*He won't,*» the demon said firmly.

I guess we'll see, she thought.

◆◆◆

She rounded a sharp corner in the avenue and was immediately confronted by the red stone edifice of River Park Palace looming in front of her. She caught her breath. It was so, so huge. Electric light poured out from every window, and a massive imperial Molasca flag at half-mast fluttered atop it.

«*Do you like that?*» The demon asked. «*The architect was very interested in the principle of 'surprise.' He nattered on about it endlessly.*»

"It's only a building," she said, trying to cover for herself. She strode toward the palace with what she hoped was confidence.

«*To the gate. Speak with the guard. Tell him you wish to speak with Pero, the steward.*»

"All right." She mustered her courage and marched right up to a tall guard clad in green, gold, and black ceremonial finery. He stood below an ornate lamppost and wore a black armband on one arm. She realized that he was in mourning for the being perched in her mind, and she almost turned right around.

«*Stand your ground,*» the demon snapped, and she stood firm as he looked her over. «*Get on with it.*»

"Ah, hello? Yes. Uh…" She fiddled with the ring on her finger. "I need to speak with the steward."

"And you are?" he drawled, bored.

"Oh! My name is Andín dal Rovi. I-I'm from Viko Station. In Lofkandi province? I… I really do need to speak with him. Pero? The steward?" She straightened herself up and tried to sound commanding. "It's a matter of imperial importance!"

Somewhere in the back of her mind she could hear the demon groan in exasperation.

The guard rolled his eyes. "So they all say. You have an appointment?"

"Er, no. But he'll want to speak with us. Me. Please."

His eyes narrowed. "No appointment? Get lost."

She found herself shoved aside as the demon roughly took control of her.

"Do you know who you're talking to?" she—or more precisely, the demon—hollered at the top of her lungs. "I am your emperor! I am Askar Molasca, and I insist on being allowed entry to my home!"

He snorted a laugh. "A dead emperor in the form of a country girl!" he said mockingly. "That's a new one. Piss off, wench!"

Andín struggled for control again, shrieking with horror. She couldn't move her arms, her legs! No sound came from her lips. She fought and thrashed, but the demon held her firm.

"I'll see you hang for this!" he was saying with her voice. "What's your name? Who's your commander? Is it Pol Davna?"

"Pol Davna's retired, little Miss Emperor," he retorted, an amused sneer on his face. "Years ago! But nice try. Now step away before I have you thrown into an asylum!" He looked over her head and out at the street, pointedly ignoring her. The conversation was at an end.

Andín suddenly had the use of her legs back. She took control of her feet and sprinted away.

"Don't ever do that!" she panted, shivering with fear.

«*The impudent fool! The moron! I'll have his hide!*» fumed the demon, ignoring her.

"Well, what do we do now?" she demanded. "We have nowhere to go!"

The demon was still lost in his rage and frustration; she could feel him railing and ranting back there. He was going to be useless.

She glared back at the guard, irritated and embarrassed by his arrogant dismissal. There was nothing else to be done. Unless...

Decided, she marched back up to him. "I would like you to tell the steward, Pero, that a woman claiming to be the old emperor was here," she said quietly, trying to project calm sanity. "I know it's an odd request, but humor me. Tell him—tell him something went wrong in the transferral. He likely knows this already. I will return tomorrow, and he will permit me entry then. Here." She gave him one of the last coins from her precious stack. "Will you do this for me?"

"Well..." he said, "it isn't a lot of money."

She braced herself, then stood up on her toes and gave him a quick kiss on his cheek. "Please? Just tell him."

The demon flinched, shocked. She felt a fierce satisfaction at having caught him off-guard, even as she recoiled from what she'd just done. It felt much worse than the bribe.

The guard chuckled softly and shook his head. "I'll tell him. I promise, my word as a member of the Guard. But he won't care, I guarantee you! Don't blame me if he doesn't."

"That's fine," she said. "It's fine. Just tell him."

"All right, crazy miss," he said. He gave her another appraising look, all up and down her body this time, and she wanted to sink into her boots. "You should go now. I'll be here tomorrow in the early morning."

"I'll see you then," she said, just barely keeping the tremor out of her voice, and walked away as fast as she could go.

Chapter 5

The City and the Palace

Her dreams that night were filled with the demon's memories of the palace and the city. She marched through the muddy streets alongside guards in half-armor, the acrid tang of human filth and wood smoke in the air. The buildings were all of wood, the weapons and helmets of iron. Then she was sailing in a long, narrow riverboat toward the Horn Palace and her new empress from distant Larunsliat, the brick and wood buildings of the city crowding the banks on either side. Then she was in an open carriage, the buildings of stone, brick and marble all around, on her way to the Obsidian Temple in the heart of the city for a ritual. People waved, she lazily waved back.

She dreamed of street battles, fires and riots; she dreamed of celebrations, cheering crowds, wonderful shows and games. She saw the city as a filthy collection of huts behind a stone wall and again as a modern metropolis.

The demon had actually lived through all these things. She drifted through his memories—so many of them were of Palascena. He had clearly spent most of his days here.

She stood before a window, gazing out over the modern city. She felt old and infirm; she might not see it with these eyes again.

Soon, she'd see it anew. She grunted in satisfaction. Rebirth would feel wonderful.

The world is a dream, she, or maybe someone else, said. *And now we wake. Now we wake.*

◆ ◆ ◆

Andín jolted back to her senses as someone beat a pot and yelled "Go on! Awake, lazy! Now!" in broken Antrimanian. She sat up, her back groaning in protest. She'd been sleeping on a bed that was little more than a wood shelf covered by a threadbare sheet. She kicked off the sheet and heard ominous scuttling noises as it fell to the floor. In the rest of the cramped, narrow room a dozen other women were getting up.

An old woman with a pot stood, arms folded, at the door. "Up, up, up!" she hollered. "All leave now! Go, go!"

One of the other women fired something back in a language Andín didn't know. They both had darker skin and curlier hair than Andín.

«*Alavesh,*» the demon said with a little sigh, and Andín felt that strange, uncomfortable sense of unpacking again. She winced in pain and held on to her head until it passed. No one seemed to notice.

Then, all at once, she knew the words they were saying and understood the grammar and structure of their rapid-fire sentences.

"And you! This place is filthy! You could sweep the floors every now and then!" the other woman said to the landlady. The landlady made a rude gesture.

"Don't like it?" the landlady sneered in Alavesh. "Then don't stay!"

You know Alavesh? she thought at the demon.

«*I know the languages of the people who live in the empire. Many Alavesh came to Antriman when their country was conquered by the Prytt a century ago. Precious few have returned now that it's independent again; in fact, more come here now than ever before. I can't blame them. Alavia is a backward place, as is much of the west. I've made it my business to know as little as possible about them. They are an unpleasant, loud, and criminal-minded people. Still, I thought it best to learn their language, and so I did.*»

And now I know it as well, Andín thought. A new language! She felt the foreign words and grammar settling into her mind. She'd tried to learn Yarou, but that had not gone well. Everyone had told her not to bother in any case. Antrimanian was the *lingua franca* of the empire, and when would she ever leave that?

Andín found the communal chamber pot and grimaced. It smelled horrible, but she used it anyway. At home they'd stopped using these things when running water and blessed toilets had been installed. Some parts of the capital city were less well-off than even her provincial backwater, apparently.

The Alavesh women stared at her through heavy, worried eyes. She thought of the young Alavesh woman she'd seen on the hill and in her dreams. She—and these—didn't seem particularly loud or criminal-minded, just… weighed down.

There was a lot the demon didn't know. She was sure of it.

Once she'd finished, she grabbed her things and spent a few moments at a cracked mirror combing her hair and smoothing out her rumpled dress. There were other clothes in her bag, but she didn't dare change in front of all these tough-looking Alavesh women.

When she left, the early morning streets were still misty from the fog that had settled over the city at night. The world seemed ethereal and dreamlike.

She walked through the crowded, crooked lanes of the poor immigrant neighborhood where she'd finally found a hotel willing to put her up for so little money, trying hard to ignore the stares and the smells. She couldn't help that she looked like a native-born Antrimanian; her straight black hair, light-brown skin, and round face made her stand out in a street full of people who were darker, taller and more delicate-featured than she was. The crowds parted for her, she noticed. It made her feel both uneasy and embarrassed, though she wasn't quite sure why.

A confusing mish-mash of languages babbled all around her. She caught one word in ten.

She trudged down the hill, feeling lost and overwhelmed. Any sense of exhilaration at finally being able to travel had long since vanished into the mists.

♦♦♦

When they reached one of the wide squares that seemed to be a border between neighborhoods, Andín found herself crushed in a mob of people just as dense as the one outside the railway station. Streetcars clattered through, horses clopped by, and everywhere were men and women, Alavesh and Antrimanian, hurrying along to whatever their days had in store.

Somewhere she smelled fresh bread baking, and her stomach rumbled. She had no money and only the few crusts that she'd thought to bring with her.

Inside her head, the demon was giving her an obnoxious guided tour.

«*Over there is the place where the original Visno Gate was; it was named after an old baron of mine who lost his head during a riot. Literally. And down that hill there used to be a neighborhood of craftsmen. It seems to be gone now. Pity. You can see the river from here when it's clearer… it's foul these days, but it used to be gorgeous. Clear and lovely, no terrible smell. But that was many centuries ago.*»

"That's great," she said wearily.

She paused for a moment to catch her breath. She was more tired than she thought; sleep on a hard, unfamiliar bed had done her little good.

A woman's voice rang out, clear as a bell, from the side of the square.

"And who does the labor? Who is made to stay in the home all day, looking after children, cooking and cleaning, and never setting foot out in the wide world? Whose labor, whose *backbreaking* labor, do the men of the world rely upon?

"The labor of women!"

Andín caught her breath.

"And what payment is there for this labor? None! What voice does a woman have in society? None! We may neither vote for our city council, nor stand for office, nor be hired to any position in government. Under imperial law we have no rights of property; we may own nothing save that which our fathers and husbands give us! We may be crushed at the whim of a man, simply for being ourselves, and all the while we are told this is our due. This is how the God and Goddess planned the world, that men should rule while women toil and suffer! But it is not so. Woman is equal to man, as the Lady Goddess is equal in every way and power to the Lord God!"

A few well-dressed women nearby clapped enthusiastically. Others glared sullenly.

«*We must be off,*» said the demon in her mind. «*This is prattle! Useless nonsense.*»

"No," said Andín, suddenly very interested. "I want to hear this."

«*Just the ravings of an extremist. Worse than the anti-monarchists. Should have them rounded up for disturbing the peace.*»

Andín ignored him. The woman continued to speak, gesturing with her closed fists to emphasize her points.

"But still men rule in the temples, and in the halls of government, and in the home. Man has endeavored, in every way that he could, to destroy the confidence of woman in her own powers, to lessen her self-respect, and to make her willing to lead a dependent and abject life!"

Across the way several men began jeering. One even threw a rotten piece of fruit at the woman, who stood on a little crate. It hit the sign next to her which read, "ALL-PALASCENA WOMEN'S UNION – We Demand a Voice," and slid down.

"My name is Fevín dan Halda, and I demand to be heard!" she cried.

High-pitched whistles blew nearby, and men in bright green coats and tall hats, waving batons, swaggered into the scene.

«*Police. Go now.*»

"But—"

«*Go now! Do you want to be arrested?*»

Andín took off as fast as she could in the opposite direction. Behind her, the police were arresting Fevín dan Halda and leading her away to the jeers of the men who had thrown the rotten fruit.

Andín burned with helpless fury as she stormed out of the square, her former hunger quite forgotten.

◆◆◆

«*There's always some group or another trying to get everyone to listen to them,*» said the demon as they walked. «*Fanatics. They disturb the peace. Bad for order. This is the trouble with letting people vote for their local officials; it leads to nothing but this chaos. As I told them it would.*»

"Can you be quiet for a bit?" Fevín dan Halda's words still marched through Andín's mind. "We're almost there."

«*You won't kiss him again, will you?*»

She grimaced. "No." The thought was revolting to her. She'd taken a terrible risk yesterday. She didn't think of herself as the type who kissed boys.

«*Ah, wait a moment. This may interest you. Stop and look to your right.*» She did; she saw more city in that direction.

"What am I looking at?"

«*Over there, do you see that spire? That's the Master's Temple on the campus of the university.*»

A spire rose through the morning mist, hazy but visible. She stared at it and felt an ache somewhere deep inside. "That's it? There?"

«*Yes. Beyond are the College of History and the College of Music. Next to it is the Emperor Askar Library. I gave a generous gift to the university to build it.*» She could feel his smugness oozing through into her mind.

So close. She wanted to reach out to it, run to it. Her dreams were all right there. The university. Books. Scholars. Knowledge.

«*They almost never admit women. You do know that?*»

She felt that same helpless fury she'd felt when Fevín dan Halda had been hauled away. "I know. I... I thought I could convince them. I'm very good at music, writing and history. I've read many books... but that doesn't matter, does it?"

«*No. That's the way it's always been. Your dream of going to the university was nothing more than that. It could never have been a reality.*»

She straightened again, her anger catching fire. "I'm looking forward to getting you out of my head once and for all! Damned *parasite*."

He fell silent as she marched up to the palace, still angry.

♦♦♦

The same guard was waiting for her. His expression was far different from before; today he focused on her with brisk professional interest.

"Yes, Miss dal Rovi," he said smartly, with none of the boredom, irritation, or flirtatiousness of the previous day. "You're late. Come in at once. Steward's orders." He opened the gate for her and pointed her inside. "They're expecting you."

"Th-thank you," she stammered, inclining her head in gratitude and to hide her surprise. Her heart was pounding. He nodded back, an appraising look in his eye. She wondered what the steward had said to him.

The guard closed the gate behind her with a soft *clunk*. She looked around and decided to go for the front entrance. Another guard waited there; he sniffed disapprovingly at her wrinkled country clothes.

"Your name?" She gave it. "Ah." The disapproving look vanished. "This way Miss dal Rovi." He turned smartly on his heel and led her into the palace.

She couldn't help but look around. The entrance was plushly carpeted, with ornate paintings and ornaments hung on every wall. She could feel the demon inside relax.

«*Home,*» he sighed contentedly.

Not home for me, she thought testily. How anyone could call such an opulent place a home was beyond her. This was as far from her own experience as that cramped Alavesh hotel. She missed her own tidy room back in Viko Station. She wouldn't know what to do with herself in a huge place like this.

Andín followed the guard into a plush waiting room. He guided her to a chair and said, "The steward will be with you soon." He then bowed and left her alone.

A clock ticked. Somewhere, footsteps creaked on floorboards upstairs. Everything seemed very still, bound by stuffy protocol and perfection.

«*This is the room where I met my lovely Lansi,*» the demon said, «*and where I once received the diplomats from Yarun, long before all the wars. I didn't use it much otherwise. This is a young palace, only two hundred years old.*»

"I don't need a history lesson now," Andín muttered. She felt like she was balanced on a knife's edge in here. Like someone was going to come and chase her out.

«*You're in the heart of imperial power, girl! Surely it must awe and fascinate you.*»

It didn't. Maybe before everything had happened it would have, but now she looked around and saw not the power of an entire empire, but ostentatious furnishings, sterility, and the hand of the vicious creature that lived in her head. She thought about what Fevín dan Halda had said, and she saw the trappings of power to which she would never have access. If not for the demon, she would never have been allowed in here.

She didn't particularly want any of it. She just wanted the demon gone.

«*What will you do when I'm gone?*» he asked, picking up on her thoughts.

"I don't know," she said truthfully. She hadn't thought that far ahead. "I'd like to travel more. I'd like to see the world. But... I—I don't have enough money to get home. Or to stay."

«*I will take care of that,*» he said, not unkindly. He was apparently feeling generous now that he was back in his opulent 'home.' «*You were drafted into this through no fault of your own. Your service to the empire will be rewarded.*»

"I'd like to try the university," she said impulsively. "I would. I don't care if they won't see me because I'm a woman. I'll wait outside their doors until they do. I was a good study at home. I can learn well. I'd make them proud."

«*Perhaps,*» he said. She had the feeling he was only humoring her. «*The term has yet to begin, I think. But you can try.*»

Let him think what he liked. He might be inside her head, but he didn't know her.

A man in colorful livery appeared at the door. "The steward," he announced as a portly man with a shiny bald head bustled in.

The demon took complete control of her, and this time she

forced herself to step aside for him. He would fix this. She stood at his command and spoke with the emperor's voice.

"Pero," she said. "I'm home."

The man put his hand to his heart. He looked like he might either faint or start laughing. "Great God and Goddess," he said. "Is it true? I don't believe it."

"Yes," the emperor said through Andín. She found it utterly bizarre to watch as her body moved and spoke without her. His movements and speech were so different from hers—it felt like her muscles were moving all wrong. "Something went amiss. I awoke in this peasant girl, not in Hular at all."

She bristled but held herself silent.

"I don't understand what occurred," the demon continued in Andín's voice. "I must speak with Syr."

"The wizard is often with His Imperial Majest—His *current* Imperial Majesty, your son. I suspect that is where you would find him. But this is unexpected. Your Majesty informed me some time ago that the, ah, spirit always followed the crown."

"And so it has been, until now," the emperor said.

"Begging your forgiveness, but I must know—" the steward said hesitantly.

"I told you these things under cover of night, atop the roof of this very building, in the private garden of my sister, the Princess Isva," said the demon, waving Andín's hand impatiently. "You were much thinner then, and you had more hair. The watchword we used was *holdings*."

Pero the steward seemed to shiver then bowed deeply. "I am honored to have been entrusted with such important information, Your Imperial Majesty."

He waved Andín's slender hand again, this time dismissively. "I have many servants who know. You are but one of them."

The steward stared at the ground, flustered and embarrassed.

"I would speak with the wizard. Can you bring him here in secret? My son is not to know."

The steward looked nervously around the room. "I... I would be breaking my oath to do so, ma'am—sir. *Sir*. He is emperor now, by the law."

"And I was emperor for a thousand years before him! He has had, what, a few days? Has he even been crowned? Bring the wizard here as I command," the demon said.

The steward trembled as he bowed yet again. Was it necessary to torment the man so, Andín wondered?

"Oh, and some nice chambers would be pleasant," he said. "Some proper clothes, as well. I'm tired of dresses and all this female frippery."

But those are my things! Andín yelled inside the sudden prison of her mind. She had the notion of taking back her body and voice. How dare you? I won't wear men's clothes!

«Shut up,» he snapped, exerting a very unpleasant iron control. She struggled but found she could do nothing.

"Y-yes, Your Imperial Majesty," the steward said. "Right away. Shall... shall I call for a ladies' maid, or a manservant?"

"Neither, just leave the clothes and leave me be!" Andín's voice roared at the man. He quickly bowed his way out of the room.

Soon after, another servant came to show Andín to their room. She was suddenly back in control, the emperor's presence reduced to a lurking, exhausted anger in the back of her mind.

This would be over soon. It had to be. She didn't know how much more she could take.

◆ ◆ ◆

Once they were alone again, she sat on the bed, feeling worn out. "You didn't have to be so cruel to him. And I will not wear men's clothes!"

«*You won't*—I *will. They won't take me seriously in a courtly gown! I won't stand for it.*»

"And why should you get to say? It's my body that's being covered! You act like I'm not here at all!"

«*I don't care what you think,*» he growled. «*You are nothing but an inconvenience I must endure in order to regain what is mine. You should be glad I don't have you imprisoned for speaking to your emperor in such a fashion!*»

"You aren't emperor now," she said, voice low and fierce. "The steward was right. You're dead. Your son's the emperor."

«*It's all one,*» he said lazily, «*or it will be soon enough.*»

A knock came on the door, a servant with a pile of men's clothes. "Forgive me," he stammered. "I, um, had to estimate the size."

"Thank you," Andín said sourly, snatching the pile away and shutting the door. She sat on the bed and sorted through them. "Well. They're nice. But this is too long, and I don't see how these pants will fit at all."

«*Put them on.*»

Andín skeptically examined the unfamiliar clasps and buttons.

«*I'll guide you if you need it, if you'll only put them on!*»

"Fine!" She began the long process of undressing. She glanced in the mirror once she was entirely naked. A very harried-looking seventeen year-old girl stared back.

She felt *him* watching and quickly turned away.

"Don't do that," she snapped.

«*Close your eyes, then,*» he said, clearly amused.

She balled her fists, trying to control her anger. "You are horrible," she said. "Horrible!"

He said nothing, but she thought she could hear him chuckling in her mind somewhere. Her skin crawled.

"I am not here for your amusement," she said, furious, pulling on the clothes as fast as she could. "Or any man's."

She did up the ties and fastened the buttons as best she could, not daring to ask for his help.

The men's clothes strained in some places and were far too loose in others. Still, she didn't look half bad, she had to admit. If she gathered her hair up like so, she might have passed for a boy. She tried it and realized with a shock that she did look very much like a young noble boy—if one ignored the curves betraying her here and there.

So this is how girls run away to sea, she thought, letting her hair fall again.

«*The sea is great fun!*» he said, flipping through images of massive pleasure boats.

"I don't think they run away to that kind of sea," she said.

"Merchant ships, that kind of thing."

«*I rarely saw the inside of those,*» he said, «*but I toured them at the port.*»

"Hm," she said, pacing around the room, feeling her legs in the trousers. Very different. Unsettling, even.

She looked around the room and spied a piano.

"Ah!" she said, glad for the distraction. She sat on the intricately carved bench and experimentally plunked a few keys. The sound was nice, if a bit muffled. She played a scale.

"It's out of tune," she complained. "Has anyone ever played it?"

«*I don't know. It was a gift, I believe.*»

Well. She paused over the keys for a moment, then launched into a few bars of "Mader's Complaint."

«*Not that song!*» he protested. «*I despise that song. There was an entire season where the girls did nothing but play it!*»

"Any requests?" she asked, frost in her voice. "I'd hate to offend you."

«*Something nice.*»

She sighed, annoyed. "Fine." She thought for a few moments, then started playing the simple if lovely old folk song "Vasi's Run," about a girl running from an attacker, and all the tricks she played on him to get away. She sang the tune as she played, always coming back to the refrain:

I'll run to the hills and the faraway sea;
For as long as I live you'll never catch me.

She knew this one back and forth and added her own complex flourishes when Vasi turned the man into a fish at the end.

When she finished, she could feel the demon's grudging appreciation.

«*Not bad,*» he allowed. «*I like that old song. I haven't heard it in many years. I'm surprised it's still around.*»

"He never does catch her," Andín sighed, wishing she could say the same for herself. She examined the piano critically. "I could do better if this were a properly tuned piano."

«*I haven't had much interest in playing music for many lifetimes. Perhaps I should take it up again. It was once a very sweet part of my existence,*» he mused.

"I play when I can," she said. "My brother is the one with the real musical talent, though. You heard him on his fiddle, he's very good. We had a piano at home, but we had to sell it."

«*Too bad.*»

"It is. I miss the old thing."`

She paused.

"And here we are, talking like real people instead of fighting," she said.

«*How strange,*» he agreed.

They were interrupted by another knock on the door. The steward hesitantly popped his head in; the court wizard had arrived, and would see them now.

Chapter 6
The Emperor of Antriman

Syr fan Porlab was the exact opposite of the steward; tall and thin to the point of gauntness, he exuded a menacing confidence and authority. He wore the formal scarlet robes of a wizard, augmented by a sedate three-cornered hat. His deep-set eyes were severe and searching.

His mere presence was enough to terrify Andín. Even the demon went silent; she could feel his sudden guardedness.

She was ushered into his presence by several guards, who then took up positions along the wall. The wizard acknowledged her presence with a slight tilt of his head.

"Wizard fan Porlab," she said—or, rather, she reluctantly allowed the demon to say through her, "you've been informed, I presume? What can you tell me—why did this take place? And what can be done?"

The wizard arched an eyebrow, looking over her clothing.

"Well," he said at last to the trembling, jowly steward, "that most certainly sounds like the way Askar talked."

"How dare you say my private name in my presence?" the demon roared.

"A moment," said the wizard, holding up a hand. "Ah, yes. Hold perfectly still."

He cast a fine powder into the air; it settled around Andín.

A golden halo shimmered around Andín's body for a moment, then flashed blood-red before turning golden again.

Magic, she thought, trying not to panic.

"Yes, he's in there," said the wizard. "Very interesting. I wouldn't have thought a peasant girl, but why not, I suppose? And where are you from, girl? Are you still in there?"

She pushed her way past the furious demon. "Yes, I am. My name is Andín dal Rovi. I'm from Viko Station in Lofkandi province."

"Ah," said the wizard, "a Lofkand. Even more interesting. I imagine he bored you with details of the Battle of Viko?" She smiled slightly, amused despite herself. "I thought so. Well, Your Imperial Majesty and Miss dal Rovi, you've both come all this way and so quickly. I'm impressed by your resourcefulness. Too bad it's for nothing, really."

"Why are you acting in this way?" the demon demanded, pitching Andín's voice lower and biting off the ends of the words. "What can be done about this? I must not stay in this body!"

"Nothing will be done about it," said the wizard smoothly. The steward, now behind him, shifted nervously. "Nothing at all."

Both the demon and Andín shouted at once. "What?"

"It will be explained," said the wizard, looking behind them at the hall. "Yes. Here he is now."

Andín turned around and gasped as the Emperor of Antriman strode into the room.

♦♦♦

Emperor Hular Molasca started laughing at once.

"A girl! And a *peasant,* too! Oh, Syr. Well done. He must be furious, chained up in there." He peered closely at Andín. She wilted, wanting to run and hide from his penetrating stare, but the demon held his ground. "Dressed like a man, too, eh?"

The wizard bowed. "It was not my intent. The essence of the demon flew where it would do no harm to the succession, and for reasons beyond my knowledge ended up there." He waved a finger in Andín's direction. "Random chance."

"And yet, it's nicely done," said the new emperor. "So, he's there, and secure? He can't jump to me?"

"What is going on?" Andín asked. It was a shock to see this

man she'd only ever seen in grainy black-and-white photographs standing in front of her. He was so short! "Aren't you going to remove him from me?"

«*It was a trick,*» the demon snarled. She could feel his cold, furious outrage. «*They did this. They knew!*»

"What?" she said aloud. "You *knew?*"

"Yes, girl. Or am I talking to my father? Hm. Sit down, won't you? Syr, old man, please remain." The emperor turned to the guards and the steward. "The rest of you may wait outside."

They hesitated.

"Oh, don't worry, I'm perfectly safe. Syr is with me and this one can't hurt a fly. Go."

For a moment Andín felt a frightening and oddly familiar gathering of dark power within her. In just that instant, she felt like she might not be so helpless after all.

But then, just as abruptly as it had come, the sensation of power vanished again.

The guards bowed and withdrew, shutting the double doors behind them.

The emperor sat and beckoned to a chair. Andín reached automatically for skirts and grabbed air. Right. She sat down, the trousers feeling doubly strange as they clung to her legs.

"Father," he addressed her, voice low and serious. "Or... ancestors, perhaps? Forebears?"

"I demand to know the meaning of this," the demon said. But some of his bluster had gone. Andín could feel his uncertainty and what might have been the beginnings of panic.

"You should know that we did this only after a great deal of consideration," said the emperor.

"I don't know what *consideration* you mean," said the demon through Andín. She had never heard her own voice growl like that. "This is treason. A coup!"

"Is that what you think it is?" said Emperor Hular intently. He seemed more curious than angry. "Isn't the coup instead what *you* do? What does the law say? The son shall follow the father. It says nothing of a demon possessing each of the line in turn."

The demon, furious still, said nothing.

"And yes," continued the emperor, "I learned of your plans from Syr many years ago. He was wise enough to inform me. He sought to enlist me in this project of his, and of course I quickly agreed. I was young then, and I was afraid my own personality would simply be lost in yours. Some men envy their fathers, but few want to entirely become them."

"It's... it's not like that, boy," the demon said. "You don't get lost. It's more a merging. We become something new."

"No, I know that now. Syr showed me the journals previous wizards had kept. It seems less a subsuming of personality than an augmentation or a combination." Emperor Hular looked thoughtful. "I would have grown a bit more like you, but you would have grown *much* more like me. Or so they say."

Andín listened with growing fascination. Was that what was happening to her?

"So why do this?" the demon demanded.

"Very simple," the Emperor Hular said. "I decided that I still didn't want a thousand-year-old demon in my head. The very thought repelled me." His expressive eyes suddenly turned hard. "And it is my head, my body. You have no claim on it, Father. Syr and I worked for years to devise a way to channel the demon spirit away from the crown and break the curse."

"It's no curse! Boy, look around—"

He held up a finger. "No. Don't call me 'boy.' I am the emperor now."

"You are no such thing! You alone?" the demon scoffed. "You have no right to the throne; you have no training or experience! *Boy.* Why do you think this land has known peace, prosperity, and expansion for so long! How is it that we have become the most powerful nation on the continent? It was I. My experience is a wonderful gift! When Askar Molasca ascended the throne and found the demon in his, in *my* mind, it was terrible for a while. Oh yes! I raged and ranted against it! I would have agreed to foolish plots if treasonous wizards had proposed them!" He glared at Syr, who smirked back. "But gradually I came to be glad of the experience; we would not have won the war against Yarun if I had not had it. So too will you be. Take me back, boy, and find out."

Andín could sense his desperation. So could Emperor Hular, who merely fixed a placid smile on his face.

"Maybe so. But have you seen the city lately? Have you been out and seen the marvels that exist in the streets here? Father, our world is changing so fast."

"Of course it is! Too fast. It's dangerous. You need my experience and wisdom to guide you," the demon insisted.

Andín thought of the anti-monarchist, Fevín dan Halda, and the immigrant slums. She remembered how dismissive the demon had been of them.

"Do I?" asked Emperor Hular. "Or would you simply try to stop progress in its tracks? Come, Father, you have always been conservative. You paid no attention to the people clamoring for more of a voice in parliament, and for the parliament to have a greater say in the affairs of the empire."

Was that true? Andín wondered as the demon raged.

"They are ridiculous," the demon spat. "Fools!"

"Perhaps, perhaps not. You were always so worried about change. You see it even now as something to be weathered instead of embraced. It doesn't matter, though; your time, at long last, has passed. It's time for something new. This is the way the world should have worked. The son follows the father. We've put things back onto their natural course."

"You'll be doomed without me! If you dare to give the rabble an inch, you'll find you won't be emperor for very long at all! They'll sweep you off the throne."

"It could be," said the emperor, looking thoughtful. "And would that be so bad? Maybe the time of emperors and empires has passed, as well."

The demon and Andín both gasped. "You're mad!" the demon exclaimed. Andín couldn't believe he'd said such a thing. Even Syr fan Porlab looked mildly shocked.

"No," said Hular Molasca. "Not mad. I'm a man of my time. A thing you have not been in, what, a thousand years?" He went to the window and stared out at the city below. "In any event, you will not be restored. We could find no way to banish you back to whatever demonic world you came from, but the link between you and the crown of Antriman is broken forever. A very neat little revolution, if I do say so myself."

He turned back to them. "I think you'll find we have been thorough," he said. "Even if you kill the girl you won't find yourself inhabiting me. You might find yourself inside her little brother or sister, for instance, or somewhere else entirely."

"Palyar?" said Andín, speaking again at last. "No!"

«*Shut up!*»

"No, *you* shut up!" said Andín. "I don't want you in my body, and I certainly don't want you to happen to Palyar!"

Emperor Hular held up a hand. "Enough. It is a moot point. Father, you are deposed."

The demon charged to the front again. "I won't let you! I'll find a way to take the crown back!"

"Ah, I'm afraid not. I don't think a peasant girl poses much of a threat, but We have decided in Our Imperial wisdom to not take any chances." He cleared his throat. "Andín dal Rovi and the demon carried within you, you are both hereby exiled from the Antrimanian Empire permanently, without hope of recourse or reduction. Syr fan Porlab, Imperial Court Wizard, will magically seal the borders against you once you leave the empire. Sentence is to be carried out at once."

Andín's heart dropped into her feet. The demon, for once, was stunned into silence.

The wizard handed him a piece of paper, which the emperor examined briefly and then signed.

"There. Done. You'll be taken from here and into custody, then brought on a special train to a port of exit of your choice. Do you have a border crossing in mind?"

She could find nothing to say.

"No? Well, then, the nearest is—"

"Shuyu!" Andín exclaimed. "That's where I want to go."

Emperor Hular seemed a little startled. "So far? And why is that?"

"I always wanted to travel there. And the line would run past my town again," Andín said, starting to cry. "I want to see it again! Your Imperial Majesty, please, I'm innocent in all of this, must you banish me as well? Can't you do anything to help me?"

The emperor briefly looked stricken. "I'm so sorry. Poor girl. Please do understand, we never intended for anyone but the demon to suffer."

«*I'll make him suffer!*» the demon roared.

"Shut up!" she yelled at him. "Shut up, shut up! He won't ever be quiet! I hate having him in my head!"

"I am sorry," said the emperor again. "Please, try to understand. If it wasn't you, it would be someone else. I wish the game had not played out for you this way. But," he said, straightening, the hard look back in his eye, "this is the only way to be sure. This had to be done, for the good of the empire, and I must keep this nation safe. So you will be exiled. Don't think we're entirely cruel. You're doing the empire a great service and making a great sacrifice. A goodly sum of money will be given to you, and a line of credit extended by my embassy for your use. Wherever you decide to settle, you will be cared for." He stood. "And that is that. Syr, anything else here?"

"No, Your Imperial Majesty," said the wizard. He gave Andín a gloating look. She wasn't certain which of them it was meant for—her or the demon. "Nothing at all."

"Good. If you'll excuse me…"

At that, the Emperor of Antriman swept out of the room. Syr fan Porlab followed, scarlet robes swirling behind him. Neither gave Andín a backward glance.

♦♦♦

She slumped in her chair. This was not happening. She was going to wake up in her bed at home and find it had all been a terrible dream.

The steward re-entered, but now he didn't seem afraid of her at all. "Miss dal Rovi? Please, this way. The guards are waiting to take you to the train station, and then you will be taken to Shuyu."

"Pero!" the demon cried through Andín. "You must help me. Surely you're not in on this plot as well?"

"I'm sorry. His Imperial Majesty is the emperor now, and I can only do as he commands," the steward said smoothly.

"Well then, help me now! Please, old friend. Don't let them send me into exile! Find a way; hide me here in the city. He'll never know!"

The steward looked at Andín, expression unreadable. "No," he said at last, his voice clear and calm for once. "No, you were always so cruel to me. Emperor Hular is a good man. I think he'll be a good emperor, and I don't want to disobey him." He snapped his fingers, and the guards appeared. "Please take this young woman to the private railway station. By order of His Imperial Majesty."

Chapter 7

Into Exile

Soldiers hustled her into one of the two train cars, then withdrew. She had it entirely to herself; guards sometimes peered in through the door to the next car, but they never entered. Her compartment had an almost military sparseness to it. A desk, a bed, a cabinet. They had neglected to include any of her things.

«*My private car*,» the demon whispered and then went silent. A brief memory of riding in it to some state function or other only a few years before surfaced and then dissipated.

Of course. They were sending the old emperor off in ironic style.

Andín dashed around the car, looking for a way out. She pushed and pulled, but the exits were firmly sealed.

This wasn't how this was supposed to go! She pounded on the door, yelling for the guards to let her out, panic consuming her.

"What do we do? Emperor? Demon? Askar? What do we do?" But he would not answer; he lay sullenly at the back of her mind, a black pit of depression.

The train's whistle sounded. She put a hand on the heavily reinforced window. The steward was watching impassively. Next to him the guard she had talked with just yesterday stood quietly. A sudden hope seized her, and she banged on the window, trying to catch his attention.

His eyes flicked up, then away again. The train jerked and slowly began rolling forward.

"No!" she called. "No! Please!"

The train pulled out of the station. She abruptly realized she was still wearing men's clothes. She thought about tearing them off but she decided against it. She had nothing else to wear.

She sank into a seat, not wanting to look at the cityscape passing this time. She couldn't bear to think she'd never see it again.

Next stop: Shuyu.

◆◆◆

They picked up speed; this train was much faster than the passenger train she'd taken from Viko Station. Was that only yesterday? It was impossible to believe, but now she stared out the window despite herself, the view hers alone as the same scenery unrolled in reverse.

The train sped through the grimy vastness of the great city and out into the newer suburbs. Then she saw the fields, farms and villages of the plains. Stations whipped past, often too fast for her to read their names.

They ascended into the rolling hills of Lofkandi Province, and she kept her eyes peeled for signs of home. What would her family and friends be doing there? Would Palyar be playing his fiddle? Would he be making excuses for her? What had Valsin told her parents, if anything? Surely they knew where she'd gone. Surely they'd discovered her ruse.

Well, she thought disconsolately, there's something. They're probably so mad at me that they don't care if I'm gone!

She knew that wasn't true.

Finally she spotted the familiar tower in the station square. Her family was in that town, her entire life!

"Stop!" she called, pounding against the window, hoping against hope. "Stop! Stop the train! Mama!"

But Viko Station flew by, vanishing all too quickly behind them.

◆◆◆

Shuyu. She was going to Shuyu. She'd looked up at that station board and dreamed of it countless times, but to go like this, and to never be able to return? Exhilaration warred with terror until at last the rush of travel faded, and all she was left with was a restless ache.

She paced the cabin. There was no way out of the fine, beautifully appointed room. The door to the next car was firmly bolted from the other side. It was a gilded cage.

She picked up a lamp and threw it as hard as she could. It shattered into a million pieces against the door. She waited, chest heaving with fury, another lamp in hand. They didn't come.

Clearly they didn't care.

She dropped the lamp, and it cracked apart.

Inside her mind, she could feel the demon actually wince.

"Don't like that, do you?" she snarled. "I'm breaking your wonderful imperial things? Too bad!" She picked up a plate from the cabinet with the Molasca house arms on it and let it drop to the floor. She felt his anger spike. She picked up another one, and he tried to take control. She batted him away with shockingly little effort and let the plate fall.

"Oh, how sad!" she mocked him. "All this precious dinnerware! But what do you care? You had so much more! While the country is poor and depressed, you have nothing but the best! We starve while you eat off of plates that are worth more than my father's house. That's the imperial life!"

«*You have no idea what my life was like,*» the demon said furiously.

"Don't I? I know you! Arrogant ass! You don't care about any of us! That was my home that we just passed back there!" Tears started running down her face. "I'll never see it again because of you, and all you care about is battles and glory and *dishes*." She kicked the remains of the plate.

«*Stupid girl! You know nothing about what this really cost! You have no idea what it means to be Emperor of Antriman!*»

"Then why don't you show me?" she screamed.

He did.

◆◆◆

Hours later, as the sun rose high overhead, she lay shivering on the compartment's narrow bed, the floor covered in plate shards and lamp bits.

"You killed them," she whispered.

«*Yes.*» The demon's voice had lost much of its arrogance.

She shut her eyes, and she saw the terrible scenes again. An executioners' scaffold. Bloody swords and axes. A dozen and more men, women, and children lay bleeding in the dust, and in the baskets... no! It was too horrible to think about.

She had seen it all. Every stroke of the pen, then every stroke of the axe or the sword.

"They were your family," she said.

«*I know. They plotted against the realm. They were traitors. They would have let foreign armies into Palascena to support their cause. It would have been civil war, a nightmare for everyone.*»

"But... but I know this story. They didn't do anything. They were innocent."

He paused. Then: « *I know that now. But I didn't then. I acted on the best evidence I had. And I would do it again, given the opportunity. That is what it means to be emperor. The empire is the only thing that matters. Everything else is nothing to me.*»

"You're a monster!"

«*I am. And so are you, now. Congratulations, girl.*»

"No!" she said, horrified. "I'm nothing like you!"

The demon laughed, its voice echoing around in her head. She clamped her fists over her eyes, trying in vain to make it stop.

But a vision appeared, unbidden. The cruel, wizened face of Askar Molasca hovered in front of her.

«*You're more like me than you want to admit,*» he said. «*There's a wonderful streak of righteous fury and ruthlessness in you. You'll do anything to get what you want. Won't you? You'd make a fine emperor.*»

Visions of plots, murders, poisonings, assassinations, executions, and horrific scenes of torture sprang into her mind. All for the safety of the realm. All of the good of something she couldn't even begin to wrap her mind around. The darkest ghouls of Antriman's long, bloody history lurched before her.

«*All me. And you are me now.*»

"No!" she cried. "No, I'm not like you!"

«*You are,*» said Askar Molasca, taunting her. «*Far more so than my fool of a son Hular! Proud and headstrong and arrogant. And in time, you'll become more so, won't you?*»

The demon's image turned and twisted, and she gasped. She was looking at her own cruel reflection now.

"N-no," she stammered.

«*Oh, yes,*» her doppelgänger said, his voice dripping with cruelty. «*In some ways, you already are the emperor. That was the deal. The crown and the demon go together, and now you* hold *the demon. So, Your Imperial Majesty, behold your empire as it passes by.*»

The visions vanished with the demon's oppressive presence, and she was left alone on the bed.

Shaking uncontrollably, Andín looked out at the passing landscape. Trees and flowers and farms.

The empire... every corner was bathed in blood and misery. She shut her eyes again. No. Cruelty and violence were wrong. It wasn't an excuse.

She was not like him.

No, no. Please, Goddess, no.

She slept and dreamed of terrible things.

♦♦♦

The journey took four long days. The train crossed again over the Antroi River, narrower here than in Palascena, then climbed up a steep grade into the green, wooded Purka Mountains. Then they descended into deep, shaded pine forests, through river-watered greenery and down to another vast plain. They passed through small cities and logging towns, through highlands and lowlands. The empire went on and on.

All of this, won with so much blood and tragedy. Every inch. Antriman's history was one of ruthless, bloody expansion, followed by repression, suppression and eventually the long but tense internal peace they'd enjoyed for more than a century and a half.

Even her own people, the Lofkands, had been brutally conquered and then suppressed by the Antroi tribes long, long ago. Now that ancient war was nothing but the dimmest of memories and a lingering resentment directed at Palascena. For other peoples, though, the hurt and shame was much closer to the surface.

The empire was at peace, but over much of the land it was the peace of the sword.

The demon had done it. She was starting to remember him doing it. And sometimes it felt like she had done it, too.

Long marches… towns on fire. People captured and brought in chains back to Palascena. Cultures eradicated, whole peoples removed from their lands, languages forced to extinction. The real history of Antriman was nothing like the safe, heroic fantasy they taught in her books.

Over it all, throughout the centuries, the demon had presided. The goal was always a larger, more powerful, safer empire. He had pursued it, with some stops and starts, relentlessly and ruthlessly for nearly a thousand years.

And yet… the empire was so beautiful, despite everything. A small part of her saw new horizons in every direction and was glad.

She lay on the bed or stared out the window and turned it all over and over in her mind. Am I like him? Am I going to become like him? Who am I now?

She tried to ask, but the demon had fallen entirely silent again. She could feel him back there, raging helplessly at this exile, but he didn't speak again.

◆◆◆

The train stopped but rarely. On one occasion, though, the door to her compartment opened and the guards threw a pack in at her. She opened it; inside were a heavy leather and cloth dress and cloak. Meant for travel, she assumed. The pack would come in handy, too.

She changed into them. She thought of throwing the men's clothes away but carefully packed them instead.

That night she dreamed of bloody days and the scratching of a pen across paper. She signed, and the axe fell. Villages burned, women shrieked, armies marched. Somewhere, someone sang a mournful song, waiting in vain for her husband and son to come home again.

Scratch, scratch, scratch again, and her shoulders grew heavy with consequences and guilt.

♦♦♦

The demon continued his now-sullen silence. Good. She wanted nothing from him.

Still, she knew without having to ask when they passed through the former domain of the Forest King, midway through the second day. She looked out the window and had almost an instinctive sense of where in the empire they were.

She couldn't bear the thought of exile now. The empire felt like a part of her in ways she couldn't even begin to express. This was the work of the demon, she knew, but she felt the attachment regardless. It was impossible not to.

On the third day the loneliness began to eat away at her.

"Talk to me," she demanded as she watched the empire roll by. "You're in there. Talk to me. I know you're listening."

He said nothing.

♦♦♦

Andín sank into depression and, after a day of glumly staring at the ceiling, edged back into fury at the unfairness of it all. She banged on the doors and yelled at the phantom guards who pushed food through a slot in the door. After a while she gave up, exhausted, and started to sing a few old songs she knew.

Then she fell silent again.

She watched the scenery go by and let herself be lulled by the rumble of the powerful engine several cars in front of them. She watched, entranced, as the landscape rose into sharply angled mountains and back down again.

At some point she accepted that the demon wasn't going to speak to her, and she banged around trying to find things to do besides look out the window. She occupied herself by reading some of the deadly dull books of economic statistics and trade figures the emperor had left in the train, or by composing and discarding and composing a long letter to her parents. She wondered if they'd find out somehow. Surely the new emperor would tell them what had happened to her. Surely Hular Molasca wouldn't be cruel enough to let them wonder forever.

Just in case, though, she wrote to them.

It was a short note, in the end. It didn't say much beyond the fact that she was safe and not to worry. How could she explain anything beyond that?

Andín sealed the letter up and put it in her pack. She hoped they'd let her send it when she finally got off the train.

◆◆◆

On the fourth day they rose into a high desert. The vegetation faded from green to brown, and the grass became dust and then sand. The towns went from widely spaced to nonexistent, and the rivers went from shallow and muddy to dry, snaking beds. In the bright morning light she caught a glimpse of jagged, high mountains off in the distance. They grew larger as the train rolled over the flat, sandy wastes and up into rocky foothills. She could make out snow on some of the higher peaks.

She knew them. How could she not know them?

The Yahzu Mountains, at last. Beyond them lay the mountain kingdom of Shuyu.

◆◆◆

The imperial train chugged into a weathered wooden station in the shadow of the mountains, and whined slowly to a halt, brakes hissing and squealing.

A soldier unlocked the door to her cabin and stuck his head in.

"Come on," he said gruffly. It was the first words any of them had spoken to her for the entire trip. Andín silently gathered her few belongings together under his impatient watch, put them in the pack they'd given her, and followed him out into the dry, cool mountain afternoon.

The wind hit her face as soon as she left the train. She stood on a rocky, windswept plain surrounded by endless miles of nothing. A few scraggly trees poked through the rock and dust, but little else besides brown grass seemed to grow here. The railway station was minuscule in comparison to the vastness of the wilderness.

They led her down a dirt road to a small garrison fort surrounded by a crude wooden palisade. Inside, soldiers sat sullenly on carts or next to buildings, watching her go by. This place seemed to have no town or life beyond the military base.

It struck her as she struggled to keep her hair from blowing in her face just how far she was from the heart of the empire.

The soldiers brought her to a low building at the center of the camp. She was unceremoniously ordered into what passed for a cell and left alone with her thoughts.

"Well?" she asked the air. The demon stirred again in the back of her mind but said nothing. "Here we are. The edge of the world. I hope you're happy."

He didn't respond, but she could feel his despair and grief radiate through her for a moment.

"Serves you right," she said in a low, biting voice, "for all the evil you've done."

He still said nothing, to her immense irritation.

◆◆◆

She waited for what seemed like hours, until a soldier with a long mustache and an unkempt officer's uniform finally came to see her. Some demon impulse wanted to bark at him about the order of his gear, but she restrained herself.

"I'm the lieutenant here," he said. He looked her over with a searching, appraising eye. She wanted to shrink into the ground. "So, they were right, you're just a girl. What did you do, pretty girl, to be exiled from the empire like this? And all the way out here, too?"

She shook her head. It was impossible to know where to begin. He smiled knowingly.

"Can't say, eh? I understand." He cleared his throat and spat on the ground. She winced. "Well, we've done this before, so we have a way of doing it. The usual protocol is to toss you over the border as soon as the paperwork with the Shuyans is done, but it's getting late for that sort of thing today. You'll stay here, safe, for a night. Then we'll take you to the border tomorrow, bright and early."

"Thank you," she said, meaning it. She wondered at the idea of a "usual protocol" for this situation. Did people get exiled here often?

Of course they did, she chided herself, thinking of the scratch of a pen across paper. She remembered: the empire was not a forgiving place.

"Well, it's all I can do for you. I'll see you in the morning. Give a yell if you need anything. Oh, if any of the men come in the night, scream as loud as you can," he said in a disturbingly matter-of-fact way.

He left. She didn't feel reassured.

◆◆◆

The wind howled all night long. She lay awake on the hard bed, trying not to think about what she would do now.

Every creak and moan of the roof timbers was a soldier coming for her. Every rustle of dust was the garrison lining up outside. She pulled the covers over her head, terrified.

"Where are you?" she asked the demon. She found herself searching for him, desperate for his now-familiar presence in an alien world.

There he was. There. He responded slightly, and she was pathetically glad of it.

◆◆◆

Andín slept fitfully, her dreams confused and chaotic. Then everything snapped into sharp focus, and she knew she was dreaming something true again.

She was on horseback, far from home, in the middle of dry, rocky hills.

"There," said someone dressed in an ornate army uniform from centuries ago, and she followed his finger to the high mountains. She knew them. The Yahzu Mountains, the border of her land. "That's Shuyu."

She turned to one of her generals. "Do we press on or turn for home?" she asked, her voice that of an unfamiliar man.

The general shook his head. "Even with the number of men we

have, it would be suicide to attempt to fight in those mountains."

"We can force the Tsimu to parley with us. Trade concessions."

The general seemed weary. She bristled at his weakness.

"You coward! Ahead is the great *unknown*! Only trade caravans have ever come this far, yes?"

"If we go there, we'll be at their mercy," said the general wearily, the insults sliding off his back. "We've seen it. They fight like demons in their own country."

"Demons," she giggled. "Ha." In this incarnation, she was less stable than she had been before.

"But, Your Imperial Majesty, don't you think it's time to go home?" the general pressed. "What of events in Palascena? Your cousin—"

She shook her head. "Oh, no! I don't worry about *him*. Foolish brat. I want those mountains. Forward. That is my command."

And then she awoke into predawn gray, certain in the knowledge that the expedition had been a failure.

The demon would wake from the fall he took during a fatally cold forced retreat from the Shuyans to find himself in his cousin's bed in Palascena. He would curse fate and his own foolishness and then set about consolidating the empire as it was. Antriman wouldn't commit forces so far west until the war with Larunsliat a century later.

"You failed," she said, looking out at the morning sun peek over the eastern horizon, "and now we're going back there."

He said nothing. She could feel his presence and almost taste his fear.

"Say something," she pleaded.

He remained silent, though, as the soldiers came to get her.

◆◆◆

They handed her a new travel pack and several letters of commission. She would be able to draw on a line of credit backed by the imperial government at any Antrimanian embassy; assuming she was ever able to find one.

They also included a supply of money, military rations, and travel clothing. That was it.

"You're a strange one," the lieutenant said, eyeing her. "Sent here on the emperor's train like you were, with a golden letter of commission. I do wonder what—or who—you might be carrying with you."

She turned to him, confused, before she realized that he meant he wondered if she were carrying some inconvenient child.

"Nothing of that sort," she retorted.

He shrugged. "As you say, miss. We'll take you to the border now. Get in the wagon."

She was about to comply when sudden shouts of alarm echoed from one of the fort's walls. The lieutenant's head whipped around, and he was off like a shot.

Curious, she followed. No one stopped her. It struck her that she could run while they were distracted, but where would she run to? She was surrounded by miles and miles of arid nowhere.

Instead, she clambered up the ladder behind the lieutenant, kicking her thick travel skirt out of her way and swaying dangerously as she pulled herself from rung to rung.

The men were pointing and exchanging worried glances at something she couldn't quite see yet. She heaved herself up onto the planks of the walk, grabbed the lip of the wall, and peered out to the southwest.

She stifled a scream. The plains were as they always were except for one little spot next to a lone, leafless tree, which was simply... *not there*.

It wasn't colorless. It wasn't shadow, it wasn't light. It had no color at all. It had no defined shape. It was *nothing*.

She felt sick just looking at it. It slid away from her perception. Her mind couldn't fathom it. She'd seen emptiness before, but not like this. This wasn't the kind of empty you'd find in a barren field or the inside of an abandoned home. This space was empty of everything; it was a place where things were not.

It was as if something had made a hole in the world itself.

She wrenched her gaze away and looked up at the lieutenant, taking relief in his solid there-ness. He glanced back down at her, and she flinched to see the haunted look in his eyes.

"I... I haven't seen one so close to the post," he said.

He'd seen this before?

The demon stirred in the back of her mind but neither spoke nor remembered. She could feel him watching with interest through her eyes, though.

"What is it?" she asked.

He gave her a hard look, as if deciding how much to tell her. "We don't know," he said at last. "They happen from time to time. We've been seeing them for a few months. It's no threat as long as we don't go near it."

A battle mage with red piping on his uniform appeared next to them, grimacing. "It feels just as awful as the last one," he told the lieutenant. "Like the world has a piece missing."

The lieutenant glanced around at the others and cleared his throat. "Send another report to headquarters. Keep an eye on it, and tell me if it gets noticeably larger. Don't look at it directly for more than a few seconds at a time. Clear?"

They stammered an affirmative reply, Antrimanian military discipline finally kicking in.

"As for you," he said to Andín, all business and bluster again, "it's time to go. To the cart."

She took one last stomach-lurching look at the *nothing* out among the rocks of the plain and turned to climb back down the ladder. She wanted to be gone from this haunted place.

♦♦♦

A tired-looking mule hauled the cart up a narrow, winding road until they reached a small guard post flying the blue, white and green Antrimanian tricolor with the imperial badge, a crown and two swords, in the center. Two soldiers exchanged places with the men in the cart and then nodded to Andín.

She lowered herself to the ground, shouldered her pack, and turned to the soldiers. She withdrew the letter she'd been keeping.

"Will... will someone send this to my parents? In Viko Station, Lofkandi. Tell them where I've gone... and that I'm sorry."

The soldiers looked at one another.

"Sure," said one, taking it. He looked abashed. Good, she

thought spitefully. "Now... get going. Here are your papers."

She took a wallet full of official documents. They casually unslung their rifles; one gestured at the road up the hill. A low gate was in the middle of it, beyond which an ornately busy yellow and brown flag flew in the mountain breeze. So this was the border between one country and another.

The soldiers started talking to one another. She caught snatches of their conversation. A new one, nearer the post, they were saying. The blank space, she thought, feeling a sudden chill.

One glared at her and pointed with his rifle. She got the message. Time to go.

Andín gathered her courage and tried to calm her breathing. She took one step, then another, and soon the guardhouse was behind her, the gate in front. She showed her wallet of papers to the Shuyan men at the gate, both of whom were dressed in loose-fitting yellow uniforms. They nodded and raised the gate, handing her wallet back to her.

She stepped through, and they closed the gate behind her. She sagged as she left Antriman's soil, feeling suddenly empty.

There was a shimmering sound, and the hairs on her arms rose. She felt a need to be gone from the border area. They'd sealed the border against her, as they said they would. She could picture the wizard Syr fan Porlab smirking, back in Palascena. They'd finished what they started. She would never be a threat to the throne again.

Andín dal Rovi had left Antriman and its bloody, painful history behind.

She took one last look at the imperial soldiers chatting and the familiar green, white, and blue Antrimanian flag snapping in the stiff breeze behind her, then she squared her shoulders and marched up the hill into Shuyu.

Chapter 8

The Mountains of Shuyu

Andín walked through the Shuyan foothills for miles but saw no one and nothing on the rocky, hilly road leading up into the mountains. There was a stark beauty to this place, she thought. It struck her that she was in a completely different land. She had always wanted to travel. Now she was doing it.

If only the circumstances had been better.

At last she stopped to rest, exhausted. There were no people anywhere nearby. The landscape had been utterly barren since the border station, so she sat by the road on an outcrop of cold, gray stone.

"I would have thought," she said, her voice sounding odd to her ears in the middle of all that silence, "that we'd have seen traders at the very least."

«*There is very little trade with Shuyu,*» a familiar voice said in her head.

"Got you," Andín said smugly.

She was met with surly silence.

"I know you're still in there, you awful parasite. I can feel you."

«*It matters little,*» he said, but his haughtiness seemed dulled. The demon's mental 'voice' was softer, less angry and sharp.

"I felt you watching this morning," she pressed, "when that... *thing* appeared out past the walls of the fort. Since you're listening and apparently willing to talk again, what was it?"

He stirred. «*I... I don't know.*»

"No? Not even you, oh great, evil, and powerful emperor-demon who lives in my head and has ruined my life? How surprising," she said, failing to keep the bitterness out of her voice. "There's a lot you don't know, it seems."

«*You know nothing of me,*» he said, his familiar ire returning in a brief flash.

"You said that before, and it's still not true," she said. "I know plenty. I've seen that thing before."

«*You have?*»

The thing she'd seen back there had been horrible but also familiar. She thought the demon might know what it was.

Then she remembered: her dreams. The crack in the sky. Somehow, this was the same.

Those dreams had been real. It didn't surprise her, not after everything.

"That Alavesh woman. She showed it to me in my dreams somehow," said Andín. "I have no idea what it is, but I've seen it before. So that's one thing I know that you don't."

The demon grumbled in the back of her mind. Andín continued hammering at him. It made her feel a little better.

"Another thing I know is that you decided the best thing to do since we left Palascena was to hide and whine like a coward instead of trying to help me figure out what we should do next. I also know you had no clue that your own son and the court wizard would conspire to keep you from the throne again. What a clever emperor you were!"

He didn't rise to the bait. She threw her hands up, frustrated. "Ugh! You make me sick. You're not only horrible and ruthless and a murderer, you steal people away! What you do to survive is awful. Inhabiting poor innocents without even telling them first! That's the way it always works, isn't it?" she asked, knowing for certain that it was true. "You just leap into people without their consent. Without even letting them know what was waiting for them! I don't blame Emperor Hular for getting rid of you one bit; it serves you right. The country will be better off."

«*How dare you?*» He actually sounded hurt. «*How dare you say that to me! It was the only way to keep the country stable! It—»*

"Oh, please," said Andín, letting her words be coated in the bitterness she felt. The wind had started up again. She was cold, and it was sinking in just how far from home and alone she was out here. She had come to the end of the world. She'd never see her mother, her father, her brother or her friends ever again. That warm room where she'd slept since she was a girl was gone now. She lashed out at the demon, trying to keep from collapsing into a sobbing wreck. "That's not how it started, is it? You just wanted power. You wanted to be king of the Antroi Men. And then you wanted to be emperor."

«*Antriman prospered under my rule! How dare you—*»

"Stop saying that! How dare I what? How dare you? What gives you the right to do anything you've done? How dare you believe you deserve any of it?"

She waited, though he said nothing more. He stormed around in her mind, an active and malevolent presence.

"I'm exiled from my home because of you," she seethed. "I'll never see any of them again. My mother, my father. Valsin. Palyar! I did nothing. I was just sitting there! It's only because I'm carrying you around in my head that this happened!"

«*I was betrayed,*» he protested weakly.

"I won't have it," she said, standing and scanning the rocks above. A sudden memory flashed into her mind, and she seized it. "Ah. There. Let's get this done."

«*What are you doing?*» He seemed panicky, uncertain. Good. She climbed up the steep rock face, muscles screaming in pain with each foot gained.

"Do you remember Kanzki dav Yoshen?" she huffed once she was at the top.

«*What? No! Stop!*» He made a mighty, desperation-fueled effort to control her, but she clamped down. His days of inaction came in handy; he was rusty and weak.

Or maybe she was stronger now.

She strode to the cliff's edge. "I knew he died this way, but I didn't know why until now. The Emperor Kanzki simply couldn't accept it," she said to the stiff breeze blowing in from the plains. "He didn't want his consciousness mingled with that of a foul demon. He hated the things that he remembered! He was afraid of what he'd become. He wanted to stay pure, he wanted to stay himself. I remember him. I remember being him."

«*Your memories and mine are mingling,*» he said, and for once he seemed worried. «*It's disorienting, I know. This is a delicate time. Andín, please, think about what you're doing!*»

"No," she said. "No! I won't be in exile. I don't want to live in some horrible mountain land where no one knows me! And I don't want a demon in my head."

«*I'll just go to someone else,*» he said with relentless logic. «*You can't kill me. Who knows who might be next? Your brother, maybe!*»

That gave her a moment's pause. "You don't know where you'll go. That's the worst part for you, isn't it? It was hard to appear in me, with no foreknowledge. It will happen again." She grinned, feeling sinister. "Maybe you'll just disappear! Maybe you'll die with me."

She spread her hands.

"Mama, forgive me," she said despairingly. "Please understand." She stepped forward, her heart pounding.

«*Wait!*»

She felt invisible hands grab her and hold her back. She struggled, wrenching against the force, feeling a secret, shameful relief.

"Let me go!" she cried.

«*It isn't me,*» said the demon, just as baffled.

Then Andín saw the young Alavesh woman, the one from the hillside and from her dreams, hovering in midair in front of her.

"Oh no," the Alavesh woman said. "You don't get out that easy."

"Whatever you're doing, let me go!" said Andín.

The Alavesh woman crossed her arms over her slight chest and smirked. "Heh. So I still have some power in the world, do I? Good. Now, you don't really want me to let you go, do you?"

For a split second, the hand loosened. Andín shrieked in terror as she pitched forward, arms pinwheeling. Then the invisible hand returned, holding Andín firmly in place.

"There," said the Alavesh woman as Andín's heart pounded in her chest. "Thought so."

«*You have to listen to me,*» the demon said. Could he even see the Alavesh woman? He hadn't been able to sense her before, in her dreams. «*We can make this right again. There must be a way. I don't want to be inside of you any more than you want me here. I have a plan. Step back!*»

"If—if you really had a plan you would have tried it already."

«*I promise you, I do have a plan. Step away!*»

"Why?" she asked, sensing she had the upper hand. She looked out over the vast, rocky loneliness of the Shuyan mountains. She struggled again but was held fast. "If I die you'll go back to Antriman. You can go home; I can't."

«*Will you listen? This is what we should do. The Shuyans worship different gods, they're one of the only peoples on the whole continent who don't worship the Holy Pair.*»

"So what?"

«*Their priests are mystics. They know many, many things lost to us, including wisdom about demons! We should go to the chief temple at Azu and see what they know. Maybe they can find a way to undo this. Do you know why I wanted to attack Shuyu so badly? It was for the demon lore those priests possess!*»

"I—I don't believe you," she said, glancing down and gulping. It was a long fall. She stopped struggling and rested, braced against the drop.

«*It's not a lie. Many places in the world have demon lore. Alavia, Yarun... but those are too far. We can actually get to Azu. We're so close.*»

"Why didn't you say this before?"

«*I didn't want to think about it. Please, step back.*»

"Why?" she asked.

«*I don't wish you to die,*» he said.

She gritted her teeth and leaned back toward the ledge. She felt the invisible hand pushing her back.

The Alavesh woman was still there.

"Good," she said. "When you're ready, come to Alavia. I need your help. It'll become clear why pretty soon. In fact, you've already seen it."

"The hole in the world? Who... who are you?" she whispered.

But the Alavesh woman only smiled mysteriously and vanished into thin air.

«*What? Who were you talking to?*»

"I... I can't live like this forever," she said into the air. "It's too much."

«*This was the curse of being emperor. But you're just a girl, in the end. We will find a way to let you live your life again.*»

She bristled. "No one deserves this. But I don't care. I want you out of my head. If... if they can do that for me in Azu, we'll go there. I'll go there. You can come along."

«*Agreed!*»

Choice made, Andín stepped back onto the safety of the ridge. She felt the invisible hand release her, and as she fell to her knees she let go a breath she hadn't even realized she was holding.

◆◆◆

They were walking into the sunset when the demon finally asked, «*Back there. Were you serious?*»

She laughed without humor and didn't answer.

◆◆◆

Soon they set up a camp, and she managed to get a fire going to warm herself. The demon fed her bits of knowledge about the tinderbox, and her freezing hands finally got it to catch.

She worried about brigands and worse, but nothing and no one came. She wondered how the men at the border post lived this far from anything.

The tent was thin and the wind strong, but Andín still managed to stay warm by wrapping herself in the coarse blankets and covering her head with her coat. She could feel the demon in her mind, still, and she could tell he wanted to talk. There was nothing Andín wanted to say, though, and she wrapped her blankets more tightly around herself. Soon she fell into a deep, blessedly dreamless sleep.

When she woke, she remembered more people she'd never known and places she'd never seen. His memories were bleeding into hers more and more. She hiked deeper into the mountains, bound for Azu.

She'd get there, she promised herself through the disorienting haze of memory and emotion. One foot in front of the other.

In the morning they found a village, and a man and his son there were willing to take them in their cart to the distant city of Azu. Antriman began to recede into the hazy past; only Shuyu lay ahead.

◆◆◆

It was afternoon, and the sun was high in the sky. Andín still shivered in the cold mountain air as they jostled and bounced along in the cart next to pumpkins and crates of mysterious, scented woods. Andín watched the scenery crawl past, listening to the incomprehensible speech of the driver and his son.

Bet you wish you'd learned Shuyan, she thought at the demon.

«*I never needed it until now.*»

She stretched, yawning. The boy, who was about her age, grinned back at her. He had an infectious smile and bright, expressive eyes. Like most Shuyans, he was paler than Andín, with dark, shaggy hair worn long and delicate features.

«*Cute,*» the demon observed, then grumbled, «*I haven't said that about boys in centuries. I blame you.*»

She hadn't thought of the boy as cute but enjoyed the demon's disorientation anyway.

Her mind suddenly filled with memories of very attractive young women, and she flushed, her heart rate increasing.

«*For that, you can blame me.*»

"How are you?" the boy asked, snapping her out of it. He had a smattering of rudimentary Antrimanian. "Okay?"

"Sure," she said. "Thank you."

He smiled again. He was passably cute, she had to admit, in a girlish kind of way.

His father thwacked him on the shoulder, and he quickly faced front. The father then touched one of the religious medals on his chest.

«*If I had to guess, he doesn't like you,*» said the demon.

You're brilliant, Andín thought tiredly. She knew she was a strange sight—a foreign woman, alone in the vast rocky wilderness, begging for a ride to Azu. She was grateful they'd picked her up at all; she could endure the father's disapproval.

The boy in the front started to hum a tune, elbowing his father to join in.

Soon, reluctantly, the father did. They hummed and then sang their travel song together, harmony and melody, voices rising and falling in tandem as afternoon slipped down into evening.

Andín closed her eyes, letting the music and the rhythm of the road roll through her.

♦♦♦

As night fell they camped in a rocky outcrop, barely sheltered from the howling mountain winds. The boy and his father quickly set up their own sturdy-looking tent and started a fire. They ate a thin stew, then retired. It was clear that Andín would not be welcome in their tent.

Well. She still had her own flimsy Antrimanian tent and sleeping roll in with her supplies. She took out her tent and started setting it up. The boy and his father pointed at it and said what she was certain were some disparaging things.

What did they know? She'd survived last night, right?

♦♦♦

In the small hours of the morning she shivered in her flimsy tent, numb and weak as the winds tore through her. She had never been so cold. The winds here were worse than she'd ever imagined.

"I could have gone to the university," she whispered, her small voice drowned out by the roar of the wind. "Maybe I could have. Or… even if I hadn't, I would have found some other way to leave home, to travel… to study. To be a scholar, a traveler… I'd have found a way. I could have. I could. Or… or I could have stayed in Viko Station. Maybe it wouldn't have been so bad."

She discovered she was crying. She couldn't feel her feet anymore. Dimly, she realized that was bad.

"I wonder what everyone is doing back home? Is Valsin wondering if I got to Palascena okay? I wonder if she told Mama and Papa... The shop! Who will mind the shop? Who will take care of Papa?"

Her head swam and darkness beckoned. How ironic, that she should be so close to throwing herself off a cliff one day and find herself here the next.

«*Andín, Andín,*» said the demon's faint voice in her mind. She could feel dark energies, like the ones she'd felt for the first time long ago in Viko Station, pooling around her, waiting. «*Speak these words:* Moak Zyerala Havyanti Aszh! *Speak them! Be warm and speak.*»

"Don't want to speak," she said, her words slurring together. "Want to sleep."

«*No sleep. Not yet. Speak the words. Moak...*»

"M-moak..." she said, her voice barely audible even to herself.

«*Zyerala...*»

"Zyerala..."

«*Havyanti Aszh!*»

"H..."

«*Havyanti Aszh! Now, Deeny!*»

"Havyanti Aszh," she murmured, her voice barely a whisper. "And... don't call me Deeny."

When she spoke the last unfamiliar word, she felt a little jolt of something in her chest. She felt dark power swimming around her, focused by the words. Then the fog lifted from her mind, and she breathed in warm air.

"W... what..."

«*Magic,*» the demon said, satisfied.

"I can't do magic," she mumbled. "I was tested. I can't do it."

«*Ancient words, used to channel energy. I have so little access to magic now, but what I have we can use to stay alive. You... you are the first in many generations to be able to actually wield it. I wasn't sure that would work. But I'm glad it did.*»

He seemed so sincere, so much less the haughty emperor than before. She lay in her bedroll, feeling wonderfully warm despite the howl of the same merciless wind.

"I didn't know you could do that," she murmured. Magic. She'd made magic. Very few humans could work magic, and most of those were snapped up by the military.

«*We can do many things. For now, sleep.*»

"Okay," she said. "I..."

And then it was morning. Sunlight streamed through the tent flaps, and the boy and his father were moving around outside. She was cold again, but not terribly freezing. She crawled out of the tent bleary-eyed.

The boy smiled cockily at her. "Good sleep?" he asked.

"It was a nice warm night," she said, returning his cocky grin. He laughed.

♦♦♦

As they bounced along in the wagon again, she had a thought.

If you can make magic, she wondered, why didn't you do anything to the guards? Or the wizard? We could have escaped or fought back!

«*Well...*» he said, reluctant to explain, «*there are many reasons. For one thing, you and I need to be together for a while for the magic to start working. But the main one is that my magic is... not what it was. It was once incredibly powerful, and I could do great things. But after so many human hosts it's become dull and weak. Many hosts couldn't use it at all.*»

She snorted. "Some demon," she said out loud.

A head whipped around in the front seat. "Dee-mon?" asked the father, suspicious. "*Vinyon? Vinyon Antrimayak?*" She had to communicate through pantomime and a few spoken words that, no, she had said something that wasn't remotely related to 'demon.'

For some reason, he knew that word. That worried her.

♦♦♦

Days passed as they crawled through the rocky landscape. The sharp Yahzu Mountains eroded into rolling, rock-strewn hills.

Herds of goats and thin cattle grazed on the sparse grasses; farmers eked out minuscule crops from rocky and rainless lands. Villages clustered together in stony defiance, poverty and desperation clear on everyone's faces.

Andín knew a little about Shuyan geography. The mountains and hills would eventually flatten into a broad, grassy steppe in the west. Nomads and herders lived there, where villages were few. Where the hills and the steppe met stood the ancient capital of Azu. Soon they'd be there, Andín told herself. It had to be soon.

But they kept traveling on and on.

In some villages they stopped to sell, and the curious came over to peer at Andín's brown, clearly foreign features. A few seemed to be laughing at her or making fun of her. She said little but sat in silence while this happened. She sensed it might be dangerous to react.

The boy and his father were in high spirits, however, since they were drawing customers and making money. It was worth it to her if they were happy with her, so she endured.

At last they started following a tiny stream bordered by some of the few trees they'd seen; it grew to a babbling brook and then became a rushing, wild river. The river led them down through villages of increasing size into a basin-like valley, at the heart of which lay what looked to Andín like a town maybe twice the size of Viko Station. The boy pointed and said proudly, "Azu." So this was the Shuyan capital. From here it was nothing but distant walls and hints of blue.

«*It's in a wide valley. It looks so easy to take,*» the demon sighed inside her mind. For a moment he was the emperor again. «*If only we could have passed through the mountains.*»

"But you couldn't," she said out loud. "The mountains are the city walls." She was surprised at the insight; maybe he was rubbing off on her.

The boy turned to look at her and nodded slowly in understanding.

"Azu safe forever," he said seriously. "Always. No one take."

«*Bastards,*» said the demon ruefully. «*It's a wonder just to see this place. I would have loved to have it. We could have taken all of the Astanav Valley from here.*»

She ignored his gauzy, rheumy visions of conquest, instead watching and listening as they descended toward Azu.

At last, weary and lulled by the road, she slept.

Chapter 9
Visions of Home and Water

Andín walked down the cobblestoned main road of Viko Station, dodging the rattletrap streetcar as the factories belched their smoke high into the midmorning sky.

Home! How good it was to be home. It had all been a terrible mistake, just a simple misunderstanding. She'd never leave again.

She ran up the path to her house and called for her mother, her father, her brother. But no one answered. She raced up the stairs to her room—and found the Alavesh woman smiling at her from her bed.

"You," said Andín. Her shoulders slumped in defeat. "This… this is a dream, isn't it?"

"It is," said the Alavesh woman.

Andín collapsed into her chair. It felt so real—it even squeaked when she leaned back. "I hate you," she said, but without any real feeling.

"I know." The hint of a smile played about her face.

Andín leaned forward. "You saved me, on the cliff. Why?"

"You know why."

"No, I don't," insisted Andín.

"You do. Things are moving, out there, and I need you. I don't have time to start over."

"You won't use me," said Andín, temper spiking. She rose, hands balled into fists. "I won't let you!"

"I beg to differ," said the Alavesh woman. She snapped her

fingers, and Andín's room, the house, Viko Station, and she herself vanished.

◆◆◆

A heavy, cold rain fell as she trudged through the muck. Beside her, a grim-faced woman in some kind of stylized robe with Goddess symbols all over it rode a donkey.

Once again, she saw through someone else's eyes. It didn't seem so strange to her this time, maybe because she'd seen so much of the demon's lives. She could grow used to anything, maybe.

"There," said the robed woman. She pointed to a gloomy-looking walled town perched on the end of a promontory sticking out into the middle of the gray, heaving sea. "Kingstown. You can see Shapylar Castle and the Temple—those are the big spires on the far end."

"Great," Andín heard a grunt from whoever's eyes she was looking through.

"Lynde, you should be more excited!" the other woman said. *Lynde?* thought Andín. Was that this person's name? "You've received a great honor!"

"Oh, an honor? My husband divorced me when he found out I stole his sword," she, or rather Lynde, said moodily. "No one in my whole town will have anything to do with me now. They think I'm a thief, or a witch, or both. Now I have a magic sword that sings so loudly I can't sleep at night, and you've dragged me a hundred miles though the rain to this awful place. I don't feel honored."

The woman with the sword from her earlier dream, Andín realized. She was seeing separate pieces of someone else's story. Why?

"You're serving the Goddess," said the woman airily. "It's the highest calling of all. Come. We're expected at the Temple."

Lynde muttered something Andín couldn't quite make out, and the scene changed again.

◆◆◆

She stood at attention inside a creaking, ancient great hall. Two women sat at a table. Andín recognized them both from her previous visions: the crazy-eyed woman who looked sort of like the Alavesh woman from her dream, and the old woman from the valley in the circle of mountains.

They were together? They knew one another? All the dreams… were they part of a greater whole, somehow?

"If she has the sword… I could be famous. They'd have to listen to me then!" The crazy-eyed woman banged her fist on the table. "I knew you'd know what to do!"

"When she comes here, hold her," said the older woman. "Don't let her leave. Trust me."

Were they talking about Lynde? This wasn't Kingstown. It was somewhere far away, in the mountains of a continental country. Alavia, maybe.

Andín was going to try and find out more, but the scene abruptly changed again.

◆◆◆

A young woman, maybe Alavesh, worked a ribbon into her hair. She was so beautiful she took Andín's breath away.

She swept the young woman up in her arms and kissed her.

"Hello, my love," said the woman, and the scene fell apart.

◆◆◆

She polished a large brass railing until it shone. She peered at her own face reflected in the brass—graying hair, dark complexion, furrowed, wild eyebrows. She glanced upward; a massive bag filled with air rose high above her.

"I think it's about ready," she said, and her voice was that of a man.

"You're sure, Rikan?" a man in an ornate uniform asked. "It will fly?"

"Of course," she, or rather the man named Rikan, scoffed as the scene changed.

◆◆◆

Her family's home again. Andín's heart leapt. She was at the table, she was with them! The Alavesh woman was nowhere to be seen this time.

Mama sat down next to Papa, and she glanced down at her own hands. They were light and delicate, but not her own. She realized with a start that she was looking through Palyar's eyes.

"No word from the capital," sighed Papa. "The police captain said they're doing all they can. Valsin's been of no further help."

Mama looked close to tears. "That girl should have known better!"

"I'm sure it's all right," Andín heard her brother's voice say. "I'm sure she's alive! And wherever she is, I bet she misses us."

Oh, I do! I do! Andín's heart broke as the scene shifted. *But why didn't you get my letter?*

◆ ◆ ◆

…Somewhere deep underground, a woman slept on a bier, a thick layer of dust covering her like a blanket.

Was it Andín's imagination, or did she stir ever so slightly?

◆ ◆ ◆

The world was water, hints of light and shadow, the taste of brine and life. Was she a fish? She swam and breathed underwater without any effort.

She turned and saw a massive hole in the sea, just like the one she'd seen at the fort, just like the one she'd seen in the sky.

No, no!

The hole expanded, and the fish was caught.

◆ ◆ ◆

She hovered in the middle of nothing, suspended, without a place to put her feet.

The Alavesh dream woman hovered in front of her, a wry smile on her face. "See? Things are moving out there," she said. Her expression grew more serious. "This is why I need you to come to Alavia, Andín."

The fury returned as Andín flailed, trying to orient herself. "How dare you tell me what to do?" she seethed. "Just because you saved me on the cliffside doesn't give you control over my life!"

The Alavesh dream woman shook her head. "You aren't paying

attention. This isn't about control. It's about what's happening out there. The world's in a lot of trouble, Andín, and I need your help to fix it."

"Me? Why me?"

"I'm sure you can work that out," said that Alavesh woman.

Of course. The demon. Always the demon.

"We're going to Azu," said Andín. "And I'm going to get this damned demon out of my head. Then I'm going home. I am *not* going to Alavia, or anywhere else!"

"There's nothing but trouble waiting for you in Azu," said the dream woman. The wry smile returned. "But if that's the way you want to play it, fine. I'm patient. But don't take too long. I don't have a lot of power or time left." She gave Andín a measured look, then said,

"Alavia. Be there."

She snapped her fingers again, and the nothingness swallowed Andín whole.

◆◆◆

Andín woke as the cart bounced and jostled down the rutted road.

«*What is it?*» The demon asked. «*What happened? Are you all right?*»

So he hadn't seen that, either.

"I'm fine," she lied, voice low. "It's all right. Just more dreams."

That seemed to satisfy him, at least. So they rode on towards Azu, Andín more unsettled than ever.

Chapter 10

Azu

The walled, cramped Shuyan capital felt more like a rural temple complex than a real city, especially after the grandeur and crowded intensity of Palascena. This felt like something out of the distant past, the way cities might have been before rifles and railways and streetcars. The demon seemed to agree; memories of a smaller, older Palascena floated to the surface.

They passed through the crumbling walls and onto the narrow cobbled roads of the town, where the smell of cooking meat mingled with incense and spices she couldn't place. Almost every building was made of stone painted light robin's-egg blue, and the streets were lined with colorful banners. Many people wore bright, vibrantly colored robes and complex, square hats. The result was a calliope of colors combined with unfamiliar sounds and smells.

The sight of the city, so foreign and strange, made Andín ache for home.

"Here, get off here," the boy said as they pulled into a narrow alley.

"Thanks," said Andín.

He shrugged. She felt the impulse to reward them more for their kindness and trouble and pulled out some more coins. "Here," she said, holding them out to the driver.

He grimaced. "No, no," he said angrily. "No! *Vinyon.* Go away from us. Bargain done."

And with that, he turned and marched away. The boy shrugged

gamely and followed after. Andín stood by the cart, listening to the large, sturdy horses breathe.

What was that about?

She sighed and put the money back in the pouch.

"Let's look for a place to stay," she said.

♦♦♦

There were several inns in the city; she chose one relatively close to the main temple complex at the heart of the city. Heads turned to watch them pass as Andín entered, then turned back again.

"Um, do you have room?" she hazarded in Antrimanian.

"Ah, yes!" he said in the same language, spoken with the flat accent of the Shuyans. "We get eastern guests here often! Come!" He named a price. She agreed, to his apparent surprise, and then he led her upstairs.

He put her things down in the narrow room next to the mostly-clean bed, and, after an awkward moment where she wondered why he was remaining, handed the innkeeper a handful of coins. He bowed and left.

She sat on the bed. It made a squishing noise. She thought she heard something scuttling underneath it. She sighed and thought of how much money it had cost.

"This is horrible," she said softly.

«*I quite agree.*»

"Shut up," she said, irritated at the demon again. "If it weren't for you, we wouldn't be here."

She immediately felt a wave of remorse, but for the first time she couldn't quite tell which one of them was feeling it.

"You're a monster," she whispered, "and now I'm becoming one, too."

«*We'll fix it,*» he assured her. «*Tomorrow we'll go to the temples. There must be someone there who can help us.*»

"You'd better be right," she said, voice perilously close to cracking. His interior voice stilled, but she could feel the cacophony of emotions shouting inside him. Worry, sadness, confusion, panic...

He seemed even more blunted and muted, though. More of the

arrogance of an old, powerful man had bled away during the long, bumpy journey to Azu.

She, on the other hand, felt like screaming.

How had it all gone so wrong, so quickly?

◆◆◆

Wonder of wonders, the inn had a functioning bath with real plumbing. Maybe, she admitted to herself, Azu wasn't as backward as it had seemed. She took a few minutes for a soak, washing off the grime of the road, and put her hair up in braids. By then the sun had slipped behind the mountains, and she was exhausted and starving.

«*In the old days we could go weeks without eating if we needed to,*» the demon mused. «*That magic doesn't work anymore. Not like it did. Pity. Food is inconvenient.*»

She ignored him and dragged herself down to the common room for dinner. She had no desire for any sort of human company, so she seated herself in a corner with no one else nearby. The woman who took her order spoke little Antrimanian and ended up just bringing her a soup with bits of what Andín assumed were meat in it. She sipped it and made a face, the spices disagreeing with her, but still she worked her way through it. She was too hungry to be fussy.

"It's bad, isn't it?" said a young woman, sliding herself into the seat across from Andín. She had the deep brown complexion and tightly curled dark hair of people from the west. She was strikingly beautiful—and strangely familiar. Andín's heart beat faster. "I think it's mutton and some sort of strained grass, but I can't be sure. There may be vegetables."

"You speak Antrimanian," Andín said, composing herself.

"I speak a couple of languages," the woman said brightly. "My husband's a diplomat in the Alavesh civil service. We think we'll be sent to Antriman eventually, so we prepare." *Alavesh*, thought Andín. She was plagued with the Alavesh.

"I actually thought we'd see more Antrimanians here," the Alavesh woman continued, "since we're so close to the border, but we met more of your people in Larunsliat. They tell me not many

Antrimanians bother making the trip to Azu. So what brings you all the way out here?"

"It's a long story," Andín said hesitantly. "We... I'm... here for the temples."

"Right! Those temples, how strange and mysterious they are! My Jandy has been talking about them nonstop. He's so fascinated by anything that's not the Durovan Church. He wanted to go to Kadana, but you know, that would have been a bad idea."

Andín had no idea why. «*The Kadaan used to be enemies of the Alavesh,*» her demon supplied helpfully. A torrent of facts poured through the cheesecloth barrier between their minds. She winced at the sudden flood of information, desperately wishing she knew how to turn him off for a while.

The serving woman came up to the Alavesh woman, who rattled off an order in staccato Shuyan. The server grunted a response and shuffled off.

"Oh," she said. "How rude of me! I'm Yshe Shadalyan of Kalanae in Martox, though I live in Telesan more often. And you are?"

"Um. Andín dal Rovi, of Viko Station."

"Viko? I don't know it. Is it far from Palascena?"

Andín tried not to think about the familiar spires and streets of her hometown. "Not... not too far. Lofkandi province. A few hours by train."

"Trains!" Yshe said, brightening again. "I can't wait until I can take one again. We have so few in Alavia now, and the ones we do have aren't really reliable. But I've heard Antriman's railway system is the best in the world! Is that true?"

"That's what I've been told," said Andín.

"I can't wait to find out for myself! Do you plan on returning soon?"

Andín stared down into her soup. How she envied this woman! How glamorous and exciting it must be for her to travel the world with her diplomat husband. They probably didn't have to ride in the backs of slow carts or suffer through cold nights in thin tents.

And, best of all, when it was all over, they could go home again.

A single tear rolled off her cheek and landed in her soup with a little *plip*.

"Oh, I'm sorry!" said Yshe. "What is it? Andín, what's wrong?"

"It's... I'm sorry," said Andín, hurriedly wiping her face. "It's a long story."

Part of her desperately wanted to confess the whole story to this wide-eyed, beautiful woman. But another part of her, a part she wasn't entirely sure *was* her, wanted to close her mouth and leave the room.

"I... I can't tell you right now," Andín heard herself say. She stood, trying to wrestle back some control of the situation. "Not here. But... maybe later. Come find me tomorrow. I'll be here. Upstairs."

"I'll find you!" Yshe called as Andín swept from the room.

◆◆◆

She lay on the bed, listening to the wind outside. Did the wind never stop in Shuyu? Was this country anything besides rocks and wind?

Sleep eluded her, and she was glad. She didn't want to dream again. Old memories, old battles, and the confusing chaos of the demon's past kept intruding, making sleep less restful than waking.

She kicked herself for putting Yshe off. She could have used someone to talk to.

Then it struck her where she knew Yshe from and why she seemed so familiar. She'd seen her in one of her dreams.

In that dream, she'd kissed her. She realized belatedly that she must have been seeing through the eyes of Yshe's husband, Jandy. Of course.

He was probably with her now, she thought enviously, then shoved the thought out of her mind. What did she care what Yshe did? She didn't know her. She had no idea why she'd see a random Alavesh woman in her dreams, either.

All of this was the fault of the demon, from exile to the awful dreams to whatever it was she felt about Yshe.

She got out of bed to pace restlessly around the room. There was a piece of cracked glass stuck to the wall, a makeshift mirror.

She glanced in it, and started back, repelled. She saw not only her own reflection but also the ghostly figure of an old man, surrounded by the even less distinct faces of dozens and dozens of others.

She knew them all, of course. The demon had worn each face.

"I don't want you," she said softly. "You are not me. I am not becoming you."

«*Tomorrow*,» they answered in a hundred hushed voices. «*We'll make this right.*»

"I hope so," she said and looked away. She lay back on the creaky bed and let worry and fear chase themselves around her brain until at last she dropped into an unsettled sleep.

◆◆◆

Her dreams tormented her again, of course. Memories flickered past, bits and pieces from the demon's lives flashed by in a chaotic jumble.

Things had gone so wrong so quickly. How had this happened?

Impossible. He—they—could not be cast out of their—her— own land. There must be a way to return. She reached for magic but found pitifully little there.

You are too human. Too human now, the old wizard Esklader said, a smug smile on her face. And that had been a century ago...

What demon am I? She looked in a mirror and saw a familiar yet horrifyingly alien face. She touched her reflection. *Hello, old self*, she thought. *Hello again.*

To end up this way... Well, it had been a thousand years on the same throne, running the same empire. Maybe it was time...

No! She couldn't allow herself to think this way.

There were still worlds to conquer, still things to organize, still enemies to crush!

Except... what enemies were those? The Emperor of Yarun had been toppled from his throne. The rebels in the west were scattered and gone. The southern nations were quiet and obedient. Antriman was the largest and most powerful nation in all the world, and there was peace.

What was left to do?

She felt the usual frustration and anger boiling within her. She had been so cruel, so powerful! Losing her army and her servants was like losing a limb. She kept reaching for her power, only to close her fist on air.

This couldn't be how it ended. She had no plan, no real goals, and only a vague idea of what to do next. The girl, infuriating and difficult as she could be, was her only goal now. She had to find a way to either use her to get back to her throne... or find a way to leave her in peace.

Or...?

No. Time was running short. Soon it would be too late. Then what? She had no idea.

Andín realized with a shock that she was seeing the demon's dreams. He slept? He *dreamed?* She'd had no idea.

She stood and walked away from the dream, down a long, familiar corridor. She felt the presence of the demon, curious, watching her. Then he was beside her—an old man in a dirty leather travel dress, wearing a heavy pack. His arms and face were covered in angry-looking, glowing red symbols.

She opened the door at the end, and emerged into the bright sunlight of the hill above the old Vintoi property. She sat down next to the iron pot. The Alavesh woman from her dreams was waiting for her there.

"So you're both here at last," she said.

"I know you," growled the demon, his voice a strange combination of his own and Andín's.

"Yes. I was there when you died," she said. "Remember? Andín and I have been talking. So. You're coming to Alavia, right?"

"Alavia?" said the demon, confused.

"You showed me Yshe," said Andín. "Why?" The Alavesh dream woman smiled slightly. "I showed you a lot of things. Funny that you remember that one."

"Alavia is full of demon lore," said the demon thoughtfully, "and the sorceress was Alavesh…"

"Tomorrow we're going to the temple," said Andín. "We'll be

separated from one another."

"If you say so," said the dream woman, "but I'm not here to argue with you, am I? I'm here to help. And... oh—"

Suddenly everything seemed to wink out of existence, and Andín woke.

Chapter 11

Yshe

The great temple complexes of Azu, the center of worship for Shuyu's dozens of major gods and lesser spirits, stood on a little hill in the center of the city. They were surrounded by a low wall, around which penitents had spread mats and unusually-shaped bronze objects. Shrines, maybe? Andín knew comparatively little about Shuyan religion.

Most other lands on the continent had gladly adopted the idea of the Holy Pair when they'd met evangelizing Durovan priests in the train of that ancient city's armies. Their own male deities became aspects of the God, female ones aspects of the Goddess. The Shuyans, or so the story went, had gods that shifted back and forth between genders, or lived somewhere in between, or had no gender whatsoever. So they'd told the Durovans and their religion to get lost, trusting in their remote mountains to protect them from Durovan armies. It had worked, and the Shuyans had taken a very different religious road from everyone else.

Andín sneaked glances at some of the statues of the gods, goddesses, and other deities. Some of them were naked, and very… interesting. Others were magnificently clothed or dressed as beggars. Some were animals or fantastical beasts. Penitents sat in front of them, burning incense and saying quiet prayers.

The ornate gate to the inner part of the complex where the looming blue-painted temples rose was guarded by three huge, pale Shuyans in ancient but brightly shined armor. They glowered at her as she approached.

"Antrimayak girl," one said in broken Antrimanian. "What you want here?"

"I..." she faltered. What was she supposed to say? "I want to talk to a priest. Someone. I need to know about demons and how to get rid of them. Please?"

Unfortunately, she seemed to have reached the end of their useful Antrimanian. They glanced at one another, clearly puzzled.

She thought back to the road, and the words the cart driver had used. "Um. *V-vinyon. Vinyon Antrimayak.*" She pointed to herself. "Me. Need help."

Their eyes widened. One drew his short dagger and stepped back a pace. Another made a sign in the air.

That was a bad idea.

"Wait, no—" she said. Clearly that had been the wrong thing to say.

Before she could speak again, one turned to the others and issued a command. One of the guards took off at a jangling run, armor glinting in the sun, toward the inner complex.

"Stay!" commanded the one who knew a little Antrimanian. He, too, had drawn his dagger. "Not go!"

She nodded. "Yes. Not go. Stay." She put her arms at her side and tried to look as inoffensive as possible.

Minutes passed. She and the two remaining guards eyed one another nervously.

Finally, long after her muscles had begun to ache from standing so still, the runner guard came back, escorted by what had to be a priest. He was dressed in robes the same light blue as the buildings, and he had a long white beard. He wore a colorful skullcap, and a complex bronze pendant swung from his neck.

He marched up to her and folded his arms. "Explain," he said in Antrimanian. "You say you are a demon?"

"No! I... I have a demon inside of me," she said. "I can't—I want to know how to make him—it—go away. Is there someone here who can help us? Me? Is there someone who knows about demons? We've traveled a long way."

He frowned and rummaged around in his robe, finally withdrawing a small vial of powder. She caught her breath, remembering the powder Syr fan Porlab had used to determine that she carried the demon.

"We shall see," he said, and poured some of it into his hand. "Be very still."

Without warning, he cast the powder at her face.

Fire spread everywhere the powder touched. It felt like being stung by dozens of bees at once. This was nothing like the harmless powder the emperor's wizard had used!

The demon screamed. Andín doubled over in shared pain, howling his unearthly scream. The air around them seemed to burn.

"Go! *A sha!* Leave, demon! Demon! *Vinyon!* Go away!" The priest held the vial threateningly. "No *vinyon* shall pass through these holy walls!"

She scurried back, pain still shooting through every part of her body. She fell to her knees.

"Please!" she called. "Can't you help?"

He shouted something in his own language and grabbed a guard's dagger.

"Never trust a demon! GO! Go now! Leave the holy city! *Vinyon!*" He threatened her with the powder and the dagger. She quickly scrambled to her feet and ran as fast as she could from the center of the city, followed by the horrified stares of every Shuyan there.

◆◆◆

Andín curled on the bed, shivering, her tears spent. There was no chance of ever getting inside the temples now. If there was anyone in there who could help her, she'd never know. She'd been lucky to get away from the temple complex without being captured or killed.

«*We'll find a way,*» the demon's voice said softly in her mind. She could tell he was trying to be reassuring. «*We can do this.*»

"I wish you'd go back to the hell you came from!" she wailed. "I despise you. I hate you more than I've ever hated anything!"

She felt his remorse and guilt, mixed with a certain amount of annoyance. That just made her angrier.

«*We can still fix this! I promise we can. There are other places we can go. Yarun, Alavia—*»

"You and your promises! I don't believe you."

She glanced at the mirror and immediately wished she hadn't. Dozens of ghostly eyes stared back her. She squeezed her eyes shut and threw herself at the bed.

"There is no way," she said into the pillow. "I can feel you lying. You have no plan."

He said nothing. She lay back on the bed, trying to think of what to do next.

◆◆◆

Sometime later, there was a knock at the door. Andín crawled out of the bed.

«*Wait! It could be the authorities from the temple!*»

Andín kicked herself for not fleeing the city when she'd had a chance. She had no idea how she'd escape from the authorities here. The sum total of the otherworldly demon powers she had was remembering things she didn't want to think about and making a room a little warmer.

"Hello? Are you in there?" called a woman's voice.

Yshe! Andín quickly opened the door, relieved.

The lovely Alavesh woman stood there, blinking at Andín with her big, pretty eyes. "Oh! You are in there," she said. "I didn't know if you'd still be here. Remember me? From downstairs? Jandy, that's my husband, said there was a commotion at the Holy Hill today. He says a young Antrimanian woman was chased away for being a demon. Was that you? Forgive me if that's an intrusive question, but I don't know of any other Antrimanians in the city, and well, I was worried."

She looked Andín over. Andín was acutely aware that she must look horrible. "I can see that it was, wasn't it?" she asked, grabbing Andín's hand. "Are you all right? Did they hurt you?"

«*Tell her to leave.*»

Andín ignored him. "Oh, uh. No! Well, maybe they did a little.

But I'm all right."

"Do you want some company?" Yshe asked, still holding Andín's hand. "I'm having some tea in my room. Would you like to join me?"

«*No. Tell her no,*» the demon said sulkily. Andín was suddenly aware that the demon couldn't take her over and do it himself; he was relying on her, now. Something had shifted.

Andín grinned. "I'd love to," she said. "Give me a moment, will you?" The manners her mother had drilled into her kicked in. "I'm afraid I'm in a bit of... a state."

Yshe favored her with a gracious smile in return. "Oh, but of course! My room is at the end of the hall." She pointed. "I'll be getting things ready."

Andín thanked her again and retreated into the room. She stared defiantly into the mirror.

«*I still don't like this,*» the demon repeated. «*I don't care how pretty she is. She's Alavesh.*»

"That's idiotic," Andín said. "She's not a pickpocket in Palascena, and she's not that... that dream woman. She's nice."

«*She's dangerous. You don't know what she could do.*»

"You're worried I'll tell her everything. Well, why shouldn't I? What's the worst that could happen, that she could throw demon powder at me and run me off with a dagger? Oh, wait, that happened already. And it was *your* plan! So. Shut up and let me have someone to talk to!"

Abashed, he said nothing. She tried not to think too much about the fact that a week ago, he'd have told her what a miserable, awful girl she was and stopped her from going. She didn't like dwelling on the demon becoming more pliable.

She fixed her hair in the mirror as best she could, ignoring the ghostly images staring back at her with fixed expressions, and, after trying to smooth down the rumpled travel dress, she changed into the fancy men's clothes she'd worn in Palascena. At least they were clean, and she sort of liked the idea of showing up at a pretty young woman's door wearing them.

She wiped the tear-streaks from her face. What she would have given for a bit of Valsin's eye makeup or powder now! She'd never liked the stuff so much before, but she desperately wanted to look presentable for Yshe.

Most of all, she wanted to look and feel human again.

She glanced in the mirror again and ran a hand through her hair, picking out some of the tangles and smoothing it down where she could. It would do.

♦♦♦

When she'd made herself look as nice as she could on such short notice, Andín gathered her courage and strode down the hall to knock on Yshe's door.

"Come in, come in!" Yshe called in her lilting, accented voice. Yshe sat on a pile of cushions on the floor of her comfortable, well-appointed room. Soft cushions and draperies were everywhere, and a fire crackled merrily in the fireplace. A red-and-white Alavesh flag was pinned to the wall. "Oh, are those men's clothes? How daring and wonderful!" Yshe giggled, and Andín swelled with pride.

"Your rooms are lovely," Andín said.

"Well," Yshe said, beaming, "I try to keep them up. We've been living here while the embassy is built, since it doesn't have rooms for the diplomatic staff yet. In a few months, they say. In the meantime, I'm happy to live here. The government pays for it, after all."

"The embassy is still being built?" Andín asked, settling onto the cushions. Yshe poured her some tea that smelled strongly of exotic western spices.

"Oh, yes. Shuyu was one of the first countries to recognize the Republic of Alavia when we became independent, but it's taken a long time to really do anything but rent some space in the Selessian embassy here in Azu. The new building is over on the far side of the city, in the new quarter beyond the walls."

"Is it going to be painted blue?" Andín asked slyly.

Yshe giggled. "Yes, yes! Everything here is! I like the color, but I'd love to see something red or green. At home in Telesan the houses are all colors."

Andín smiled and sipped her tea. It tasted rich, with a sweet hint of oranges. She made a happy noise.

"Do you like that? I brought it from home. It's from Debanae, which is a big city on the coast. They have the very best markets there; I think there's spice from Througe-Sandair in the tea."

"It's delicious," said Andín.

"Have you ever been to Alavia?"

Andín shook her head. "No. I... I speak a little Alavesh, though."

Yshe clapped her hands together, delighted. "You do?" she said in Alavesh. "Really? Can you speak a little of it to me?"

Andín reached deep, and then replied in her demon-gotten language, "Yes, of course. We can speak it instead of Antrimanian if you like."

The demon grumbled but didn't really resist.

Hard to resist a pretty girl, isn't it? she thought at him.

«*You would know,*» he replied.

Yshe was clapping her hands again in delight. "Oh, you speak so well! You sound like my cousins who lived in Antriman! They speak differently there, but I love hearing it!"

"A lot of Alavesh live in Antriman," said Andín, letting the language expand in her mind again. "I met a few in Palascena."

"Did you? I'm not surprised. So many people left after the Prytt took over the country, and even more left during the war." A shadow passed over her fine features. "The war was terrible. Your country is lucky it didn't come to you. I know you sent troops, but..."

"There was war in the southwest," Andín said, "but that's far away from my home. We sent men away, and some of them died, but it never came near us, thank the Goddess. Antriman is huge. I never... never knew how much until I traveled across it."

Yshe nodded soberly. "During the worst of it we had to leave our village and hide in the woods. The armies came and went three times. The princess' armies came, then the Prytt came back, then the Selessians, and the princess again. Oh, it was so awful. So much was destroyed. We're still rebuilding. We may be rebuilding for a long time." Her face twisted. "I hate war."

"I don't blame you," said Andín, her heart going out to the

other young woman. Yshe had reminded her of Valsin at first, but she was so much more worldly and interesting.

"I'm so glad Jandy is a diplomat. Talking is so much better than fighting. But enough about me!" Yshe chirped, shedding her sadness as quickly as she might shrug off a coat. "Were you really at the Holy Hill today? What happened? Do you mind talking about it?"

"I was," said Andín, closing her eyes. "It was me. And I don't mind at all, but it's a long story."

Yshe waited expectantly.

Andín took a deep breath. The demon made a weak attempt to restrain her, but she ignored his hold. She launched into a very abbreviated version of her story: She was possessed by a demon through no fault of her own. She'd been exiled from her country. She was looking for a way to get the demon removed. She left out the part about the demon being the former emperor. She wasn't sure why—either it didn't seem relevant, or the demon had influenced her again. It bothered her that she couldn't tell which.

When she'd finished, Yshe looked poleaxed.

"And that's all true? You swear it?"

"I do. I swear on the altar of the Goddess herself. It's what happened to me."

Yshe threw her arms around Andín, who stiffened in surprise. "And that means you can't go home again! Oh my poor Andín!"

Startled, Andín began to cry and let herself sink into Yshe's embrace. She smelled like her tea. Her soft warmth was reassuring—and something more. *Stop that!* she thought at the demon.

«*Wasn't me. I don't even like her.*»

"How dare those arrogant priests treat you that way?" said Yshe, breaking the hug. "You'd think they'd want to help, wouldn't you?"

Andín shrugged. "I have no idea. Honestly, we were hoping they would, but who can know? They must have their reasons."

"You're right about that," said Yshe. "Well. I'm going to ask Jandy when he gets home. You'll like him. He's smart and knows a lot about the world. He might know something that can help you!"

"That would be lovely of you," said Andín, feeling a little pang of jealousy at the mention of Yshe's husband. She remembered the dream where she'd seen through Jandy's eyes, that kiss they'd shared... She quickly shook the memory off, trying not to stare at Yshe's lips.

"All right, then!" Yshe was saying, blessedly oblivious to Andín's emotional turmoil. "I'll ask him. In the meantime, would you like to play a game? I have some cards. Do you like cards? Oh, I hope I'm not being too forward! It's just that I've been so alone here."

Andín saw a familiar loneliness in Yshe's eyes. She'd seen that same expression reflected back at her in her horrible, haunted mirror.

"I don't know many card games," she admitted, "but I'm willing to learn."

◆◆◆

They chatted about trivial things as they played. At length, after Andín had lost too many card games to count, Yshe rose and stretched. "I have to excuse myself," she said. "I have a party to go to with Jandy at the Lyndani embassy tonight, and I must start preparing! Oh, I wish I had a maid or someone." She eyed Andín speculatively. "I don't suppose you have an experience with dressing a lady for a formal event?"

"Sorry," Andín said. Dressing Yshe seemed... dangerous, somehow. "My friend Valsin always told me I could never get it right, that I made her look worse than if she'd done it herself. I mean, look at what I'm wearing." She gestured at the men's clothes from Palascena. "All I know is books and running a shop." And being an emperor, though that didn't seem worth mentioning.

"Oh, too bad," pouted Yshe. Then she brightened again almost immediately. "Oh, books! I have many books if you want to borrow one. Do you read Alavesh as well?"

Andín's eyes lit up. She hadn't had anything to read since the train from Palascena. "I don't know," she admitted. "Can you show me?"

Yshe led her to a small case packed full of dog-eared volumes.

"Take whatever you like," she said.

Andín picked one out and hesitantly opened it. The alphabet was fluid and made of curlicues and loops instead of blocky Antrimanian type, but after a second of unpacking it made sense to her. She read a few pages with near-perfect fluency.

"I can read it!" she exclaimed. *Thank you*, she thought with a certain reluctance to the demon.

«*See? Good for something after all.*»

"Good. Take what you like! And I'll talk to Jandy tonight. Oh, that book's a good one; it's full of battles and danger and history. I'd start with that if I were you." She smiled and vanished into another room. Andín was clearly dismissed. She read the cover as she walked back to her own room. *Shashalnikya's Song*. She'd never heard of it before.

«*The Shashalnikyas were the royal family of Alavia before the Prytt invasion*,» the demon filled in.

"I know that," Andín said testily, "but I don't know this book."

«*Neither do I.*»

She'd give it a try. What else did she have to do?

◆◆◆

She paged through the book, curled happily on her creaky bed. The story was written in verse, about a young Alavesh woman named Judy Shashalnikya who had led a rebellion against invaders hundreds of years ago. A woman—imagine that! She'd even worn men's clothes, as Andín was wearing now. Andín read on, devouring the slim volume. There were words she (meaning the demon) didn't know, but they were few.

"I wonder what that means," she mused after reading the same word several times on a page. "*Shadarant*. It keeps comparing her to *shadarant*."

«*I never heard the term. Sorry.*» The demon seemed bored.

"Doesn't your magic help you fill in those gaps?" she prodded him.

«*I didn't learn Alavesh by magic.*»

"How, then?"

«*The old-fashioned way*,» he replied grimly. «*One of us had an*

innate gift for languages. We remember. My memory is excellent.»
"Oh," she said. "Well, too bad he didn't learn this word." She sighed. "This is a good story. I like it."

«*It's true, at least in part.*»

"Really?"

«*Oh, yes,*» he said, relishing the chance to give her a history lesson. «*Judy Shashalnikya is a legend to the Alavesh. She was a contemporary of my original host.*»

So about a thousand years ago. Interesting.

«*She did lead armies against the Selessians, who back then were fierce warriors instead of dull clock-makers and merchants. All of Alavia's monarchs are descended from her, or they were until the Prytt conquered them. Some of them still live in Antriman.*»

"And her sword? There's a magic sword in here."

«*That I know nothing about.*»

Too bad. She could have used a magic sword. "Was she queen?"

«*I don't believe so. Her descendants ruled, though. Why don't you read the book and find out?*»

She propped herself up on her pillows. "You don't like Yshe."

«*I don't dislike her. But I don't trust her.*»

"Why? She's going to help us!"

«*All the Alavesh I've ever known have been thieves or madmen. The Shashalnikya royal family was the worst of the lot. I allowed them to settle in Antriman to spite the Prytt, but they made my life miserable. So many requests for maddening things.*»

"Your old prejudices have nothing to do with Yshe," said Andín, noticing that the demon sounded less like a haughty lord now, and far more like a complaining housewife. "Serves you right in any case."

«*Hardly. They were guests at my court! They could have behaved better. I made my youngest son deal with them.*» Andín caught a flash of three haughty, well-dressed Alavesh women surrounding a skinny Antrimanian prince, berating him with demand after demand. Andín giggled.

«*Poor boy. I was very hard on him. He grew up to marry a cruel woman, too.*»

"I bet he was nice," said Andín.

«*He was. One of the few who were. He died too young. So.*»

"So?"

«*It was good to hear you laugh.*»

She sighed. "I haven't forgiven you, and I still hate you."

«*Fair enough.*» Andín could tell he was pleased; she didn't know whether to be happy or throw something.

◆◆◆

Late that evening, as Andín read by the light of the oil lamp in her room, a knock came at her door. "Oh, Andín! It's me, Yshe!"

Andín set *Shashalnikya's Song* aside and jumped to open the door.

Yshe threw her arms around Andín. She smelled of tea and the outdoors. "Hello, dear! I've brought Jandy with me. We've just come from the party!"

Andín stepped back, taking her friend in. Yshe was dressed in a heart-stopping green dress with an intricately patterned wrap over it. Behind her stood a tall, solemn-looking young man with bright, nervous eyes, dressed in an ill-fitting black suit.

"Oh, please come in," she said, remembering her manners. The man ducked his head under the low door frame and folded himself into the one chair in the room. Yshe settled onto the bed while Andín leaned against the wall and waited.

"Andín dal Rovi, this is my husband, Jandy Shadalyan. He's an officer in the Alavesh Diplomatic Corps."

Jandy inclined his head slightly. "How do you do," he mumbled.

"I told him everything! Well, not everything. But I told him enough, and he had some ideas!"

"Thank you," said Andín, ignoring the grumbling demon in her head.

"Ah," he said. "First, you made a stir this morning. The Shuyans talked about it at the party." He shifted his long legs, trying to get comfortable. "They think it's, well, a bad omen. That's what they said."

"Oh," said Andín.

"They don't know it was you, but they're going to start looking around, so you might want to leave Azu," he said, fixing her with a very serious look.

Andín shot Yshe a questioning look. Yshe shrugged, looking sad. "I'd hate to see you go," she said, "but the Shuyans are very firm about protecting their city from what they see as threats."

"Right," said Andín. "I understand."

"The, er, second thing. You do have a demon in your head?" Jandy asked. "Truly?"

"Truly," confirmed Andín.

"Can I... can I speak to it?"

"I suppose, if you want," Andín said. "He's never not here, so speak away. He can respond, too."

"Ah. Well, demon," said Jandy, "what will become of you after you leave Andín's body?"

Andín surrendered control as the demon bubbled up to the surface. It took much longer than it had before.

"I will go to another host," said the demon. Strange. It felt more like they both spoke at the same time instead of the demon taking full control. The thoughts popped into her head, she presumed from him, and she said them. She'd expected him to fully take over. Maybe he couldn't anymore.

"Ah, and what happens to them? The other host? Isn't that just as bad?"

"Perhaps. But there is a host I was meant for, who is not blameless. Andín is not that host."

"I... see," said Jandy. "And you do require a host?"

"Yes. I can't exist in this world without one."

"I see. Well, demon... Um, we in Alavia have some experience of demons, or at least minor ones."

"I know. I've heard stories."

"Mm." Jandy continued. "There were many types of demons that lived in our lands long ago, before the Alavesh crossed the mountains from Larunsliat into what is now Alavia. There are old folk tales about Alavesh wizards drawing up treaties with them in the ancient times. If anyone has knowledge of how to work any sort of demon-related magic, they would be in Alavia. Perhaps in

Corgal. The Blue Temple there has a long history; the Patriarch's library may have some answers. The Shuyans, on the other hand, are mostly worried about demons invading their lands. Their stories are all about evil spirits from Antriman."

Andín flinched.

"Just stories!" Yshe tried to reassure her. "But you do understand why they treated you that way? They've been worrying for years about demons coming from the east. They're a bit obsessed with it, I think."

"So it would seem," Andín said dryly, remembering the pain caused by the powder. The demon settled back down into wherever in her mind he was living, tired out by the experience.

"I'll need to ponder this," said Jandy. "There's more to consider. But Corgal in Alavia, that's a start for you. Have you considered going to Durov, as well?"

Durov, the ancient holy city far to the southwest, was the cradle of religion for most of the continent's people and a center of ancient knowledge. Durov had been a mighty empire long ago, and the Durovans had collected knowledge from all over the continent. "No," admitted Andín, abashed that she hadn't thought of that, "but perhaps we should."

"I'd recommend it. For now, the Blue Temple in Corgal may be able to give you clearer moral guidance. I think there certainly is a question of morality to be considered here."

"Jandy," Yshe said warningly.

"It's true, though," insisted Jandy. "By removing the demon you either kill the demon or it will go to another innocent."

"No, it's all right," said Andín, swallowing hard. "That's fair. Thank you for all your help."

Jandy rose and bowed awkwardly. "A pleasure. And now, if you'll excuse me, I'm exhausted and must retire."

"I'll catch up," Yshe said to him. Jandy bowed again and let himself out of the room, trailed by Yshe's bright eyes.

Yshe deflated a little once the sound of his boots on the wooden floors had receded. "I'm sorry for him. He comes off a bit... abrupt? He's had a long night," she said, "and I told him not to go into all that moral nonsense."

"He has a good point, I'm afraid," admitted Andín. It had been weighing on her mind lately, too. If she were rid of the demon, he'd just go somewhere else. Right? Did the new emperor really deserve that? Did anyone? What if he did go into Palyar? She'd never forgive herself. "I've tried to work that all out myself."

The demon stirred uneasily.

"I told him that for us here and now it's about saving one person, and not so much about what happens next," Yshe said, "but he worries about that sort of thing. Always thinking of consequences and problems and the moral nature of things. It's why he's good at his job... But still." She sighed again. "It's not a lot of fun."

Andín gave Yshe what she hoped was her brightest, most fun-loving smile. "Thank you for asking him anyway. It's more than anyone's done for me in weeks."

Yshe grinned back. "Make it up to me. I know—we'll have breakfast together tomorrow! How does that sound?"

"Lovely," said Andín, meaning it.

Chapter 12
The Fall of Azu

The next morning, Andín was up and dressed long before Yshe knocked on her door.

"You're ready!" Yshe exclaimed in her lilting Alavesh. "I know a place down the street; they make this sort of fascinating fried... well, I don't really know what! Some kind of meat and peppers and other things. It's delicious, and they serve it with tea. Come on!" Yshe grabbed Andín's hand and pulled her down the stairs and out into the cold mountain morning.

The streets were bustling for so early in the day. The city smelled like wood smoke and a tangy scent Andín had noticed since the first day but couldn't place. Spices, maybe, or incense.

She adjusted her pack on her back. "Oof."

"You should have left that behind," said Yshe.

"I'm thinking of buying a few things," said Andín. "I need more clothes and supplies."

"Oh, shopping!" said Yshe, delighted. "I rarely get to go. It'll be fun!"

"I know it will be," said Andín sincerely. She didn't have much in the pack right now beyond her dwindling pile of Antrimanian money and a few odds and ends. She'd left her letter of commission back at the hotel; she didn't want to chance losing it to a thief. Still, she hoped to make it to the Antrimanian embassy before she left Azu; maybe she could renew her funds. Might as well cash in on the imperial largesse.

Yshe's little place down the street was a shack with a counter, a wood stove, and some rickety-looking tables, but a surly-looking man produced a platter of fried objects and two jars of lukewarm, spicy tea without much fanfare. Andín hesitantly bit into one of the fried things. It was surprisingly moist and flavorful, and the tea was spicy and warming. There was even a little jar of honey they could dip their food in.

"Jandy and I talked more about it last night," said Yshe, sipping her own tea. "He still thinks it might be for the best if you left town soon."

"I know," said Andín. "I'm planning on it."

"There's a rail line that runs west down the river. You can get to the navigable part of the Astanav that way. From there you can sail to Roshden, and there's a train to Alavia from there. Do you have money? We can help you if you need it."

"No, no," said Andín, touched. "I can get more money. I'll be fine. But thank you, sincerely."

"Jandy said the Shuyans are the way they are because they believe in so many gods that they're always looking for false ones. It didn't make a lot of sense to me, but Jandy has a lot of ideas like that." Yshe sighed. "I don't know, I just think they aren't used to outsiders in this city. The people in the western part of the country were much friendlier. It's sad. In all the time I've been here none of them have opened up to me. It's very lonely!"

"I can imagine," said Andín, thinking it might also be because Yshe was not as dirt-poor as a lot of the people around here and didn't seem all that aware of the fact.

"I told Jandy it might just be because they're in the mountains," Yshe continued. "My grandmother lives in the mountains up in Eusalee, which is in the north part of Alavia, and all the people in her village are so suspicious! Any time someone from 'the lowlands' comes they all start gossiping and frowning. Jandy says it has more to do with history, but I don't think so. I think people are by and large the same."

"Do you two talk a lot?" Andín asked.

"Oh, yes! Jandy tells me all about what's going on at the

embassy, and I have all kinds of opinions. It's lovely. The other wives envy me, I can tell. But they don't talk with me much." She looked crestfallen.

Andín grabbed her hand. "I'm sure it's not your fault," she said, though she had her doubts about that. Yshe could be a little... overwhelming. Andín found her charming, but she could see how someone else might not.

"They're all so much older anyway. I wish you didn't have to go!" Yshe said, shoulders drooping. "You're the first real friend I've made since I came here! Oh, do you mind if I call you that? I know it's only been a day! I'm sorry, I don't mean to offend."

"Not at all," said Andín. She squeezed Yshe's hand. "Not in the least. You're my friend, too."

"I wish those horrid priests could have helped you more," Yshe said. "It's not your fault, after all."

Andín shrugged. "It is what it is," she said, feeling fatalistic. The demon inside seemed to sigh restlessly.

"But Jandy's right about the Blue Temple in Corgal. There are lots of mystics there these days, some may know demon lore. Who knows? Maybe they can find a way to trap it so it doesn't move on to another host! Or even kill it."

"Well, I don't know if that's what we want," said Andín slowly. The demon, dead? That thought unsettled her. "But... I suppose you never know. Maybe there's a solution we—I—haven't thought of."

Before Yshe could respond, they heard sharp shouts off in the distance. "What's that, I wonder?" Yshe asked. "We never hear shouting here."

The shouts got louder. A woman screamed.

Yshe and Andín looked at one another. "Let's go see what it is!" Yshe exclaimed, springing to her feet.

"Are you sure?" Andín asked. Yshe seemed awfully quick to rush off into danger.

"Of course! It'll be fun. Come with me!" Yshe grabbed Andín by the wrist again and hauled her out of the shop.

◆◆◆

Several streets away dozens of Shuyans were gathered in a tight, excitable knot, pointing up at the Holy Hill. Andín's stomach did somersaults. There, right in the middle of the temple complex, was a patch of *nothing*.

"Oh, Goddess," breathed Andín, "not again."

It was the same sort of hole in the world that they'd seen at the outpost back on the border, except now it was right here in the middle of the city. It had sliced off a patch near the wall, by the gate where Andín had tried to enter the previous day. The streets, the wall, the little shrines—they were all just *gone*.

People were shouting and pointing; a few screamed. One man turned and fainted. The nothing was maddening to look at.

"What... what is it?" Yshe asked, shaking visibly. She clutched Andín's arm. "It looks like someone ripped a piece of the city away! Andín? Do you know what it is?"

"No," said Andín, "but I've seen it before."

The priests stood at the front of the crowd, waving their arms or silently praying. One of them spotted Andín and pointed, shouting.

"*Vinyon!*" he cried. The people turned as one, fear and fury in their eyes.

«*Run!*» the demon cried.

Andín turned and sprinted as fast as her legs would carry her out of the square, Yshe running close behind.

◆◆◆

Far outside the city walls, but still close enough that she could still see the columns of thick black smoke rising from the fires raging all over Azu, there was a cluster of gray rocks in the middle of a field by the road. Andín huddled against them, cloak wrapped around herself, shivering in the cold.

She had run away from the square until her lungs felt like they would burst, hiding in alleyways and behind boxes. The tide of people had forced her and Yshe apart, and she hadn't seen her since. Somehow fires had started, sweeping through the old quarter of the city with terrifying rapidity. She tried to go back to the inn to find Yshe, but the inn was in flames. Then people had recognized her again, and she'd been forced to flee for her life.

Andín ran and ran, then joined the crushing throng of people getting out of the city. The gate guards had abandoned their posts. She covered herself with her travel cloak so no one could see she wasn't Shuyan and so left the city with only the pack on her back. She sat back against the cool stone, watching the smoke curling up from now-distant Azu.

"This… this is your fault," she whispered, her heart growing cold. "All of it. The travel documents. The letter of credit. They're back at the inn. I never got to go to the embassy to take money… We have nothing left except what I'm carrying. No food, no change of clothes, only a little cash…"

«*We can make our own way.*»

"How?" She gazed out at the windswept plain. "With what? Where will we go?"

«*We must—*»

"Don't you tell me about *must* and *should*, demon!" she spat. "We got run out of that town! We're lucky the mob didn't grab us and rip us to shreds. I can't even blame them—you saw that thing." She shivered at the memory. "You must know what it is. The Alavesh dream woman showed it to me. I've seen it in my dreams."

«*I don't know what it is,*» said the demon, and his voice was soft, as indistinct from her own thoughts as it had ever been.

"Then what good are you?" Andín said bitterly. She rummaged through her pack. Not much left. Some extra clothes. A small amount of Antrimanian money. Stale travel bread from the imperial border post.

Her hand brushed something hard. She withdrew it—the book Yshe had given her, *Shashalnikya's Song*.

She pressed it to her chest for a long moment and flipped through it.

Her finger landed on one page. An etching of a face, done in a very old style, stared up at her.

It was the Alavesh dream woman's face. Underneath was the caption, "JUDY SHASHALNIKYA."

"What?" she said. "No. No… what does this mean?" Her head spun. "Demon? Is this true?"

But there was no answer. She glanced back at the smoke rising from Azu and suddenly felt the need to move.

"Let's go," she said. "They'll come for us sooner or later. I wish I could feed you to them when they do."

♦♦♦

She found a little valley where she pitched her tent and set up a camp. As night fell, the wind tore through her.

«*Say the words, Andín. We're too cold,*» the demon begged.

"No. Go back to whatever hell you came from," said Andín through her chattering teeth.

«*Say them. We need sleep!*»

"I need sleep. You need to be gone from me," said Andín. "And if you want the warmth so badly, go ahead and make me say it."

«*I can't. I couldn't before, even to save us. I'm not strong or separate enough. Please… please.*»

"Fine," said Andín angrily, dredging the words from her reluctant memory. "*Moak Zyerala Havyanti Aszh.*"

The tent was filled with warmth again.

"Happy?" she asked the demon. But he didn't respond.

She lay listening to the howling wind, wondering if they'd be discovered by the mob from Azu at any moment, until at last she fell into a fitful sleep.

♦♦♦

She walked down the same long corridor in her dream, but this time it led only to a pitiful old man sitting on a rickety wooden chair. He was dressed in Andín's traveling dress and cloak, and his body was covered with glowing red symbols.

She was filled with fury. "You!" she cried.

He looked back up at her, resentment smoldering in his eyes. "*And you,*" he said, rising unsteadily. "*So glad you agreed to use my magic and skill to keep us alive another day.*"

"How dare you?" she said, balling her hands into fists. "You stole everything from me, you get us run out of Azu, and now you insult me?"

"*Azu was not my fault,*" protested the demon, "*and I never asked to be put into such a whiny, ungrateful, and incompetent brat such as you!*" The symbols glowed redder for a brief instant. "*You've done nothing but complain. But my own son turned against me, and I lost my realm. Antriman was the place I lived and breathed and built for a thousand years! And now it's lost to me.*"

"You were nothing but a tyrant," she cried.

"*And you are nothing but an ignorant peasant girl.*"

Andín howled with frustration and anger and launched herself at him. She battered him with her fists, and he struck back but soon fell to the ground. He was frail and weak, and her anger made her strong. She kicked him and dove atop him.

"*No!*" he cried, shielding his face.

She shook him again, tears running down her cheeks. "I want to go home," she cried.

"*We can't go home,*" said the demon, and suddenly his form was far, far less distinct. He seemed to blur before her eyes. "*I'm sorry. We were both betrayed. And now—and now I'm becoming less like I was—*"

There was the sound of something tearing, and the demon's form resolved in front of her.

"*And more like you.*"

Andín stared at her own face, covered in angry red symbols. She gasped and sprang to her feet, backing quickly away.

"*I'm sorry,*" the demon whispered in Andín's voice. She—for the demon seemed in no way masculine now—gathered her leather travel dress around her, and looked imploringly up at Andín. "*Now I've lost all that I was, to become someone new. It's like dying. It happens... every time.*"

Andín wavered between horror and sympathy. "I don't want you to be me," she said.

"*It's inevitable. It's my nature. To live, I must change.*"

The demon looked miserable, sitting there on the floor like that.

Andín's anger finally burned itself out, and she knelt to give the demon her hand. "I'm sorry, too," said Andín. "Of course. We've both been betrayed. We've both lost so much."

The sound of someone clapping her hands echoed behind them. The Alavesh dream woman had appeared.

"Well," she said. "I wondered when you two would finally start getting together for real."

"*You again,*" said the demon, but there was no anger in her voice now.

"You're Judy Shashalnikya," said Andín. "I saw it in my book."

The Alavesh dream woman spread her hands. "Fair enough."

"But you died. A thousand years ago. I don't understand."

Judy Shashalnikya folded her arms in front of her, looking peeved. "Here I am in your dreams alongside the demon you're carrying around in your head, and that's what bothers you? We don't have time for this. Look. You need to come to Alavia."

Andín and the demon glanced at one another. "Why?" Andín finally asked. "You never told us why."

"The world needs help. Just… come. Get across the border, and I'll guide you from there. And make it fast, I don't have a lot of time left."

Andín started to say something else, but Judy Shashalnikya cut her off.

"No arguing. Come to Alavia."

Everything suddenly became much dimmer again, and Judy Shashalnikya seemed to fade out of existence.

Andín woke into darkness.

◆◆◆

She'd risen well before dawn, and decided to be on her way. There was light enough to see by.

She was glad for her tough travel boots and thick cloak. The Antrimanian troops had given her sturdy gear, and she was grateful to them. She couldn't hate them; they'd only done their duty. Yshe had probably thought her strange for wearing the heavy dress and cloak, but it had come in handy.

Andín let herself think about Yshe. The panicked people of

Azu had been targeting foreigners as they rioted. She worried Yshe might have been caught.

«*People like her are charmed,*» the demon said. The demon's voice was much like her own now, and she found she thought of the demon as a young woman, not a man. Strange. «*She'll be fine, I imagine. Fortune favors the foolish.*»

Andín shook her head, smiling. "Yshe's not that foolish. You're still being insulting. You don't change."

«*Of course I do.*»

"Yes... I suppose you do. Every time you change hosts, you change." It was a strange thought, even now. "How... how are you?"

The demon seemed taken aback by the question.

«*I... I am doing quite well, I believe,*» the demon said.« *I've certainly had better years. But I am durable. How are you, Andín dal Rovi?*»

"I've had better years," she said grimly.

«*But you, too, are durable,*» the demon replied.

"Am I?"

«*Yes. You've come this far, and you're still on your feet. What you've gone through would break a man of twice your years, and yet here we are,*» said the demon. «*You're doing well, Andín. I'm proud of you.*»

"Thank you," she said, touched. The demon had never been so kind to her before. Was it because he—she—had changed?

«*It is. But I've never been all bad. Here... see for yourself.*»

Some of the demon's memories filtered to the surface.

In one, he was a young man sitting at home with a plump woman dressed in beautiful clothes, bouncing a laughing baby boy on his knee. A merry fire crackled and popped in the hearth. Here, he kissed his daughter as she presented a frayed piece of woven cloth. For me? You are wonderful. He swept the little girl into his arms.

Five children played in an ancient room, a thousand years ago. This is why, said the cruel king who had imprisoned a demon in his mind. For them. I want them to have everything. A man is his family.

He kissed a young woman on the top of her head. He played

cards with three shrewd old ladies. He bantered with his friends, a young man again for a little while. And then, as always, he went home to his family. They were all his family.

«*You see? It's not all so terrible.*» The demon's voice was only a whisper; she was having a great deal of trouble distinguishing it from her own thoughts. «*You're making me remember kindness again.*»

"You're surprising," she murmured into the cold night wind. Her breath warmed the air.

«*I am many, many things. My last host was cold and cruel, and so I was, too. But I was loving and bright and friendly and hopeful before. And now perhaps I shall be stubborn, sharp-tongued, adventurous, kind, and inquisitive, like you.*»

She laughed. "Didn't you call me ruthless and a spoiled brat before?"

«*Yes. You're that, too.*» How strange, she thought, to hear light teasing from the demon instead of mocking sarcasm.

"I'm not really most of those things," she said quietly. "I'm more like you than I want to admit. I'm not that kind or friendly or loving."

«*You are all of those and more. I've felt myself change to become like you every day.*»

And I to be like you, she thought. She did have a ruthless streak. She also wanted very badly to continue and to have her way in the end.

"So," she said. "Alavia, and Judy Shashalnikya. Are we going?"

«*If we must. But I don't like it.*»

"Neither do I," agreed Andín. I don't like feeling that I'm being called like a dog by its master, used like a pawn in someone else's game. How is this Shashalnikya any better than Syr fan Porlab?" She shook her head. "But... it's a direction. We have nowhere else to go. And maybe... maybe if I go there I'll see Yshe again someday."

«*So we go to Alavia?*»

"For now. Yes. But only because we choose to go."

◆◆◆

Somewhere on the moonlit plains of Shuyu, Andín dal Rovi marched west. She slowly chased the moon across the sky, watching as it outran her to the horizon.

"You know things," she said, addressing the demon. "You've been in a palace for a long time, but I bet you remember how to survive in the countryside."

«*Yes.*»

"And you know how to ride. And fight."

The demon seemed surprised. «*I do.*»

"I want you to teach me."

The demon said nothing for a moment.

«*The knowledge is available to you. All you need to do is remember.*»

Andín laughed again, trying to banish the lingering sadness. "Fine. I'll learn. I'm good at learning. I would have been great at the university in Palascena, no matter what you think!" She could feel a trickle of regret from the demon. "But you're better than any university, aren't you? I can learn and travel at the same time. Maybe that's what I wanted all along. And I bet you know more magic, too, than you're letting on. We'll see. I'll have it all from you eventually."

«*Yes.*»

"Yes! Yes I will. That's fine."

She stopped and looked up at the tapestry of stars overhead. It was so beautiful. She let the night surround her, her breath a pale, brief ghost before her eyes.

♦♦♦

The next day broke clear and cold.

Andín thought of home as she walked tiredly towards the wide western plains. She thought of her friends, her parents, and her brother. She thought of Kalu dav Rasa, the boy in school who had chased her around the playground. She thought of clever, strong, curvy Plavis, Valsin's older sister, who had been her obsession as a child. She thought of how the light hit the square in just that peculiar way in the morning if there weren't clouds. She thought of the station tower and the whistle of trains.

She knew in her heart that she would never see any of it again.

She would never find a way to get the demon out of her head, and even if she did, she'd still be exiled from Antriman forever.

«*Now, that's not a way to think—*» the demon began, nervous.

Andín laughed, a strange sort of joy bubbling up through her. "Oh, oh, poor demon. No, it's fine." She sighed. "It's fine. It's all right. I've made my choice."

She started to sing as she walked. The tune came to her in scraps; it was old, far older than even the demon. They had sung this song around Antroi tribal fires a thousand years ago, and she sang it in the ancient language.

Come home, sing home
Men come over the hill
Swing pail, sweep floors
Men come through the dale

Wander far, travel near
Men march, march home
Sing home, come home
Come home, sing home.

It went on like this, for many more verses. She sang loudly, the simple, guttural Old Antroi words springing easily to her lips. These words hadn't been spoken, much less sung, in hundreds of years.

She remembered a daughter singing the song as she worked at her sewing, a wife humming the tune as she bustled around a fire, and the women of a village belting it out at a fair. The song was the history of her land, buried for centuries beneath the surface.

She could never go home herself, but maybe she could carry a piece of Antriman with her on her travels.

Come home, sing home.

She could feel the approval of the demon, and she sang the song over again as she looked ahead to the winding road running down into the wide plains. Behind, she could almost hear the snip of the scissors slicing through the slender silvery thread running between her and Viko Station.

Let them come find me if they will.

She was on her own from here on in.

The sun rose behind her; the road down into the valley stretched out before her.

PART TWO ☉

Chapter 13

Endless Grasslands

Andín walked for days away from Azu, keeping herself warm with the rudimentary heat spell she'd learned, but the one thing she couldn't do was stave off hunger. She ate what she had in her pack, but it was hardly enough to keep her going. When she couldn't stand it anymore, she stopped in a small hamlet and bought some bread with some of her few remaining Antrimanian coins.

She avoided any more villages and stayed off the main road after that, for fear of riders from Azu recognizing her. So she walked down dusty trails through tall grass, utterly lost, legs and feet aching. She followed the setting sun, hoping that if she went far enough to the west, she'd make it to the river Yshe had described.

Her dreams were quiet, as was the demon. In fact, Andín was having more and more trouble telling her own thoughts from those of the demon and eventually gave up on it.

What did it matter? They were becoming the same.

On the morning of the third day out from Azu she spotted a trail of smoke to her right as she walked. She wanted to stay away, but hunger gnawed at her so she headed towards it. Maybe there was a village there, or a house. She could buy a little food, maybe, or trade.

Her stomach growled as she hiked through the tall, waving grass. Copses of scraggly-looking trees rose here and there, and high above birds flew through the windy sky. There were four carts in a circle in a trampled-flat clearing, surrounded by striking-

looking horses munching on grass. Three men dressed in warm
clothes sat at a cooking fire. Something smelled delicious.

They eyed her warily as she approached, their eyes registering
mild surprise. They probably hadn't expected an Antrimanian
woman to come out of the grass. Soup was bubbling in a pot over
the fire, and they had set their steaming bowls down to wait for
her to approach.

"Hello," she said in Antrimanian. They simply looked blankly
at her. She experimented with Lyndani, Old Durovan and Alavesh.
Nothing. Curse the demon for not bothering to learn Shuyan.

She spread her arms to show she didn't have a weapon. Her (or
the demon's) subconscious suggested that this was a good idea.
"I, uh… hungry." She gestured at the food. "Pay. Money. *Gerlin.*"
She hesitantly pronounced the Shuyan word for their currency.
They waited expectantly. "*Gerlin.* I have. Well, not *gerlin gerlin*,
but Antrimanian money. Here." She slowly opened her pouch and
took a coin out. She mimed eating, and gestured with the coin.
"Well?"

One of the men said a few words to the others. Then he smiled
and passed her his bowl, brimming with soup. She tried to hand
him a coin, but he looked at her like she had lost her mind and
refused it.

She shrugged and dove in.

The soup tasted wonderful. She finished her bowl, and they
immediately refilled it. The man whose bowl she'd borrowed was
patiently waiting for her to finish. She swallowed the last of it and
handed it to him. He gestured at the pot; she shook her head no
and smiled. They smiled back, nodding, and said a few words to
her.

Then the man with the bowl sprang to his feet, gesturing at her
to follow. He led her to a rickety covered wagon. She hesitated,
but his smile was open and friendly. Warily, she walked forward
and peered inside.

It turned out to be full of random goods. The man was clearly
the proprietor of some kind of traveling shop. She sighed. So that's
why he wouldn't take money for the food.

He held up various things. Here, a strip of some kind of leather. There what looked like a ball of rough wool. Er, a wooden slat? What would she do with that?

He held up a finger and then withdrew a deep blue shawl with a few typically blocky Shuyan patterns on them.

"Oh!" she said. "It's lovely!"

She shouldn't. She had only a small number of coins left, and she didn't have her letter from Palascena to get more now. But it was so, so beautiful...

"How much?" she asked, pointing at it.

His smile grew wider, and he held up three fingers. Three of the coins she had given him earlier?

"Oh, no. I'd have next to no money left! One." She held up a single finger.

He scowled, but brightened a moment later and held up two.

She made a show of thinking about it, then gave him his two with much frowning. She took the shawl and wrapped it around her; it was wonderfully warm and soft. He held up another finger and brought out a set of sky-blue clothes. Her eyes widened.

"Oooo," she said. She petted them experimentally. "Oh, these are wonderful!"

Clearly he could tell she was in love from the sound of her voice. He held up five fingers.

She could afford it. But... she needed food more. Didn't she? She could starve if she had pretty clothes again, right?

She sighed and pointed at some dried meats. He nodded and scooped some into a bag, holding up a single finger, making a very serious face. She didn't barter this time. She needed the food too badly.

She paid up, made a show of looking over the rest of the seller's wares, then nodded. She thought about how to ask where the roads to down to the Astanav River might be might be, but decided against it. She had no idea how to even start.

◆◆◆

As she was walking in what she hoped was a westerly direction along a narrow path through the high grass, she heard a commotion behind her. Someone screamed.

Andín didn't hesitate; she turned and ran back toward the encampment, having no idea what she'd do once she got there. She burst into the clearing and saw six men on horses, each with a rifle, menacing the trader and the others from the camp. They had drawn short daggers and were trying to surround the horsemen, but the horsemen's rifles were quick to seek them out. Everyone was shouting. They didn't notice her.

Bandits, thought Andín. Ten centuries of hatred for bandits causing trouble on the empire's roads built up in her, and she felt a bubble of dark, hot energy build up inside her.

«*There is a word you can say, to release it at them,*» whispered the demon.« *It will hurt, not kill.*»

Andín held out a hand as the dark energies built to a crescendo, and the word formed in her mind.

"*Shih!*" she said, and a wave of energy flew from her hand at the horsemen.

Three of them were caught by the blast and fell from their rearing horses. Spooked, the still-mounted horsemen rounded on her.

She held her other hand up. "*Shih!*" she said again, and a weaker wave buffeted them, knocking one's rifle from his hand.

The other two might have gotten a bead on her, but the trader and the members of his camp had swarmed over them, daggers flashing. The men on the ground were quickly overwhelmed. The still-mounted bandits turned and rode off as fast as they could.

The trader grinned at her, holding up his bloody knife, and said a word in Shuyan that probably meant something like thank-you. Andín bobbed her head in acknowledgement, trying not to think about the three bandits who had just been stabbed because of her.

Was she even sure they were bandits? What if they'd come looking for stolen property? What if they'd been the authorities here, and the trader the bandit?

She sat on the ground, feeling sick and numb, while the trader and other members of the camp picked through the bodies and rescued the horses. In time the trader came up to her, bearing a bundle.

He said something in Shuyan, gesturing at her.

"For me?" she asked, taking it hesitantly. It was the sky-blue Shuyan outfit. Her eyes widened.

He grinned and summoned a small boy. He led one of the bandits' horses and carried a rifle. These he also presented to Andín.

Andín shook her head. "I can't pay."

"Your share," said the boy in something like Lyndani. He grinned, and his grin was the same as the trader's. They were father and son, she guessed.

Part of her didn't want any of it. They'd belonged to a man who would be alive if not for her. But... that man more likely than not had been coming to steal from these people.

"Thank you," she replied in the same language. "They were... bandits?"

The boy nodded his head fast. "Very bad men, Father says."

She took the clothes, the horse, and the rifle. The trader held up boxes of ammunition, and then held up two fingers. So much for gratitude. But with the rifle, she thought, she could hunt. She could eat.

Maybe she could even get through this. She paid for the ammunition, thanked everyone again, and left before she completely fell apart.

◆◆◆

So now she had a horse. She knew nothing about horses, but memories of how to ride flooded her mind as she walked the mare through the grassy paths. The demon had known plenty about horses. She decided to wait to ride until she was a little more certain of the memories.

At last she changed into her new clothes, which thankfully had trousers instead of skirts. The blue riding outfit with the shawl was even better suited to travel than the men's clothes she'd taken from Palascena, and it was wonderfully soft and warm.

Finally she steeled herself and mounted the horse. The well-worn, stained saddle had a neat little mounting step built into both sides; perhaps that was where her feet were supposed to go.

The Shuyan tack was different from Antrimanian, but the demon's memories were close enough. Thank goodness the mare wasn't a tall horse!

The first few minutes were disorienting and terrifying, but soon she discovered the demon's memories and felt at ease. Within the hour she was riding like the old hand that, in many ways, she was.

She knew she should be afraid of that kind of power from the demon, but in truth she wasn't. What was left to be afraid of? The worst had happened so many times.

Andín found that thought even more bracing than the wild grassland winds.

◆◆◆

The western Shuyan plains stretched on and on. Andín rode west and north for weeks.

She quickly came to love her startling sky-blue outfit, embroidered at the edges with the complex squares-within-squares motif that Shuyans seemed to put on everything, and she tossed her heavy travel dress away.

She slung her rifle over the back of the saddle with her pack, where it was within easy reach. She had practiced with the rifle and was getting better.

Here in the wilds between Azu and the Lyndani border there were few villages. It was better this way, if lonely. She sometimes went five full days without seeing any signs of other humans.

Andín rode, and she sang as she went.

Wander far, travel near
Men march, march home
Sing home, come home
Come home, sing home.

◆◆◆

Andín dal Rovi rode for many weeks across the high, grassy plains of Shuyu. She rode west, ever west, towards the river. Alavia called to her, so far away.

She soon found herself much better able to access precisely the memories she wanted. Once she'd gotten onto her horse, she'd wanted to know how to ride better. The information had appeared in her mind, and soon, with some practice, she was spending most of her time in the saddle. There wasn't much she or the demon could do about saddle soreness and an aching back, but she managed.

She fashioned a better, thicker tent from materials she bought or found, and she traded for a box of tinder so she could light a fire at night instead of relying on the limited magic she could call. She spent the last of her coins buying more ammunition.

The demon knew how to shoot (of course), and once she accessed and internalized those memories, she took a certain delight in holding something in her sights, then felling it with a pull of the trigger. The first time she'd tried to shoot something, she'd almost fallen over from the recoil, but soon she learned, or remembered, how to plant her feet and anchor the rifle butt with her shoulder. She had to train her muscles to react the way her mind remembered, but with every day that passed she improved.

She could almost hear the demon laughing at her. It didn't matter. She was laughing at herself, too. Soon she was bringing down the game of the plains. She knew next to nothing about how to prepare the birds and small animals she shot and botched it very badly the first few times. She was left with very little usable to eat and ended up looking like she'd butchered a mammoth. The demon's knowledge was scarce, sadly. As a noble man in Antrimanian society, she'd rarely cleaned and prepared her own meals.

Soon, though, hunger and concentration forced her to improve, and as she traveled she ate—if not well, then adequately.

At night in her makeshift tent she dreamed of times long past. She led her men down a corridor in a ruined fortress, she dispensed rudimentary laws to the people of the Antroi, she reviewed official documents in a drafty palace, she held her son, she kissed her wife, she played with her grandchildren.

Sometimes she dreamed of her own home in Viko Station and her parents. It took an effort to remember that these were hers, and no one else's. They seemed so far away.

She battled hunger and cold and fatigue. She spent days searching fruitlessly for food. Her time of month stopped coming, though whether from the demon or lack of nutrition she wasn't sure.

The wide western steppes had few villages, and she only rarely encountered nomads and their carts. If she found them, she discovered she could exchange the hides of the beasts she'd caught for a cup of stew and the safety of the campsite. Sometimes they even welcomed her when she didn't have those things. They turned out to be a warm and friendly people, especially compared to the paranoid city-dwellers in Azu.

They thought her strange, but they didn't try to impede her. At some point she realized that they thought she was a foreign boy. Well, why not? She rode and shot, she was thin enough now that her figure wasn't apparent, and her riding outfit was that of a man. She'd used someone else's knife to cut her hair shorter, wanting to keep it from tangling. She found that it didn't bother her. She remembered being a man, and it didn't seem so foreign anymore.

This life suited her, and she was sometimes happier than she'd ever been.

And yet she sometimes felt achingly lonely in the middle of the plain, thinking of Valsin's laughter, Palyar's shy kindness, or Yshe's easy company. When she stopped to rest, she took *Shashalnikya's Song* from her pack and read the story of a woman who had risked everything in battle a thousand years ago.

She read until the light was gone, or her eyes were too tired from squinting against the firelight, and she thought of the Alavesh dream woman. Were they truly one and the same? She hadn't seen her in her dreams for months.

She also thought of Yshe, and of all the other people she'd left behind. She missed them, but she'd always been solitary by nature. She might be lonely at times, but things could be so much worse. She was still alive, still moving.

Dark thoughts and images from someone else's past still troubled her. She rarely, if ever, looked into the glassy surface of the ponds she came across, fearing what she might see.

◆◆◆

One day, as she was riding over a hill, she came face to face with a huge brown bear.

He roared and reared back on his legs, surprised. The horse backed off nervously. For a moment, Andín was terrified he might charge them. She reached back to unhook her rifle, but her horse's panic made her knock it to the ground instead.

The bear snarled.

She held a hand out and spoke.

"*Shih!*"

A wave of power burst out from her, buffeting, if not harming, the bear. It stopped in its tracks, cowering.

"Go," she said, voice full of menace. Dark power shimmered all around her. "Go!"

The bear turned and ambled off to the east. Andín waited a while, then dropped to the ground to fish her rifle out of the tall grass.

I am the meanest, most dangerous thing out here, she thought with satisfaction.

Chapter 14
The Astanav River

Slowly Andín wound her way across the trackless western Shuyan plains. She told herself that she was in no hurry, and her dreams were still quiet, so she took her time.

Gradually the plains gave way to more rocky hillsides, and then one day she found herself staring out over a majestic valley spreading out as far as she could see.

A shining white-blue ribbon of river ran through the valley, far off in the distance. The Astanav, larger now than it had been in Azu. Here, then, was the great riparian highway that linked a small slice of Shuyu to the nations of Raza, Lyndania, Larunsliat, and Narlland. Somewhere beyond this valley were the Vandan Mountains, and across those lay Alavia and the nations of the western coast.

Here, she thought. At last, I've come to the edge of Shuyu.

She thought of the girl who had left for Palascena. How long ago? Three, four months, perhaps? Her sense of time was unmoored by slow travel and days that seemed much like the ones before and after. That girl had been someone utterly different. If they'd met on the streets, they likely would not have recognized one another.

That girl had been lost, swallowed by whoever this new person was.

She thought sometimes that she missed her old self. But there was nothing to be done, except to ride forward.

She urged the chestnut mare on and descended into the valley below.

♦ ♦ ♦

The riverside Shuyans had built a small trading outpost where the navigable portion of the river began, and it was to here that Andín rode. It was basically a small cluster of weathered-looking blue wooden buildings surrounded on three sides by a rickety palisade fence. The river wound slowly past; a few ships were tied up at the docks. The Shuyans here, apparently transplanted nomads, were clearly not all that interested in the river trade. Still, maybe there were people here Andín could talk to.

She rode her horse up to the gates, trying to think of what to say to gain access, only to find them wide open and unguarded. A few people, some Shuyans and a few others who were clearly foreign, hung around eying people who came and went. Their eyes lingered on Andín. She knew she must be an odd sight; an Antrimanian carrying a war surplus rifle on a nomad's horse fresh from the steppe. She probably smelled terrible, and she couldn't tell whether they saw a boy or a girl when they looked at her. She tried to tell herself that didn't matter, but maybe she'd get fewer questions if they thought she was a boy.

She saw plenty of nomads here, strangely enough. They were filthy and had hollow looks in their eyes as they wandered through the streets or sat, drinking something strong from bottles. Pulled in by the town, she thought, only to find themselves trapped here. They didn't even raise their heads as she rode by.

She poked around some more. Maybe there was a place she could trade what little she had for passage on the river. She hadn't seen so many people in one place since she'd left Azu months before, and the sudden press of humanity unnerved her. She was jumpy and paranoid, starting at every strange sound, constantly on guard. A part of her wanted to run back to the calmness of the open steppe.

She rode down the muddy street, the only one in the post, when she heard a startlingly familiar voice cutting through the chatter.

"No!" it said in lightly accented Alavesh. "This isn't the one. I ordered some of the green, and this isn't it! Do you have the one I ordered?"

It couldn't be, thought Andín, heart leaping with sudden hope. Impossible.

But it was: there Yshe Shadalyan stood arguing with a fabric seller, who didn't seem all that enthusiastic about talking with her.

Andín's mouth moved. Her lips formed the words. But her voice would not come.

Yshe turned to storm out of the seller's stall when she caught sight of Andín. "And what are you looking at, boy?" she said. Andín tried to say something, but Yshe's gaze slipped away again.

No! Wait! She tried again, opening her mouth to call after her, when Yshe spun round again.

"By all the spirits in the woods," she breathed, eyes wide.

"Y-Yshe," stammered Andín. The sound of her voice was strange in her ears.

"Andín! It is you! But—but how did you get that horse? And your clothes, your hair! What *happened* to you? I thought you were some strange Shuyan nomad boy! Is—is that a gun?"

At Yshe's horrified, indignant summation of her current state, Andín began to laugh with something approaching desperate relief.

◆◆◆

She sipped hot spiced tea, savoring the flavor and the warmth, while Yshe delicately cut into some kind of meat pastry. The town had a single mediocre restaurant, and they were stuck in it. Still, Andín was grateful for the food, which Yshe had graciously paid for.

Andín told her friend as much as she could think of about where she'd been and what she'd been doing since she left Azu. Yshe's eyes grew wider and wider as Andín talked about the nomadic Shuyans of the steppes.

But she left out the part where she'd blown the men off their horses with her powers and had then seen them butchered before her eyes. Instead, she concocted a barely-believable tall tale about finding a mystical cure for a young nomad boy and being gifted with a horse, the clothes, and a rifle for her trouble.

"Amazing! So you healed that little boy?" Yshe asked. "I never knew such a potion existed! You'll have to write it down; we can sell it!"

Andín shook her head. "I, um, don't remember the exact proportions. Still, demon knowledge isn't always a bad thing."

She could feel a little glimmer of amusement somewhere deep inside her; or maybe it was just her own sense of humor growing back.

"I suppose so!" Yshe's normally open and bright face was shadowed by worry and care. "And then you just... rode here? I'm astonished, I really am. Even by the quickest route, that's a long way! Shuyu is a huge country. Jandy and I took the train here from Azu, and it took four entire days! To be fair, it was a slow train, but still! It's much larger than Alavia."

Andín laughed. It had taken four days to cross all of Antriman on the Emperor's fastest express train. Shuyu was still small compared to the vastness of the empire. "Is Jandy here?"

"Oh," said Yshe with a sad frown. "No. He had to go back to Azu to try and reopen the embassy."

"How are things there?"

"Oh, Andín, Azu is a mess," said Yshe, shaking her head. "We stayed on as long as we could, but we had to relocate here after they started making threats against anyone foreign. The city was in an uproar for days. You'll be glad to know you're infamous now. Foreign witches and all that."

That didn't make Andín feel any better. "And... the hole?"

"Oh, that thing," Yshe shivered. "I don't know. Likely still there. They'd built a tall fence around it when we left so no one could see it, which was fine with me! I haven't heard from Jandy since he went back there, sad to say, and I doubt I will. Mail service here is awful."

"I'm sorry to hear it," said Andín sincerely.

"It can't be helped," Yshe sighed. "I'm actually here waiting for a ship to Roshden, up in Lyndania; I've been waiting for weeks while they get it all settled. We're finally leaving tomorrow—it was lucky I saw you when I did. Otherwise I might have left and missed you completely."

"Tomorrow?" So little time...

"Yes, first thing. They decided to send the embassy wives home; that's why I'm here. This means I won't see Jandy again for a long, long time. He'll be here, doing the work he needs to do, and I'll be sitting at home in Telesan."

Yshe looked like she was about to cry. Andín impulsively grabbed and held her hand for a moment. Yshe smiled in return. "Thank you, my dear. Oh, I don't mind going home. I just wish Jandy were coming! I do miss him. It's always so hard to live without him. But... that's the risk, so he says."

"I'm sure he'll send for you again as soon as he can," said Andín.

"No doubt," said Yshe, her eyes heavy and sad. "And you never know. We may be off to your Antriman or somewhere else next. Shuyu is a lonely post in any case. Well, that's my story. And what about you? Now that you've ridden across the grassy steppe like a wild nomad, what will you do next?"

"Actually," Andín said carefully, "I'm heading for Alavia, as well. I... thought I might see what they know of demon lore at Corgal, like you suggested."

Yshe clapped her hands together in sudden delight, her expression blooming into a grin. "Really? You are? You must travel with us! Andín, do! I can pay for your passage on the ship, and we can be together!"

Together. Andín could only stammer, "Yshe, I... Are you sure?"

"Of course I am! Oh, please do say yes! I can't stand the other two women. They treat me like I'm nothing! I have no one to talk to; I've been so lonely here. And you've had such adventures—I want to hear all about them while we sail!" Her tone dropped into seriousness. "Please. *Please.* I need a friend."

"Then I'll come," said Andín firmly.

◆◆◆

Andín stayed in Yshe's rented rooms that night at Yshe's insistence. She'd actually planned on camping outside the post, but Yshe would hear none of it. Instead she found herself in a heated, comfortable room for the first time in many weeks.

Andín worried that it might be awkward or strange, that she might not adjust well after being outside for so long, but once Yshe flopped on the bed like Valsin used to do back in Viko Station and started talking nonstop in rapid Alavesh, everything began to make a beautiful kind of sense again.

Andín sank onto the bed beside her, feeling herself unwind. Yshe told her all about everything that had happened in Azu and the boredom of the long train ride with the other embassy ladies. "It wouldn't have been so bad if I could have talked to them about anything, but they wanted to go on about their children and their clothes! I like clothes, but this is a bit much!" Yshe said. "Jandy and I would always talk about everything. He loved telling me about the world, and I always liked asking, but these women wouldn't ever say anything about all the places they'd been except to say how horrid they were. 'All those filthy foreigners!'" She imitated one of the ladies, using a high, piping voice. "'I don't think I could ever staaaaand them. I stayed inside with my fuuuurniture!'"

Andín giggled. "Well, believe me, I don't care much about furniture."

"No, I suppose you don't," Yshe said, her eyes merry. "Though you have, ah, unique taste in clothes, to be sure."

Andín smiled, plucking at her blue Shuyan travel outfit. "I suppose I do."

Yshe hesitated before asking, delicately, "Do you have any other clothes?"

Andín thought. "Oh," she said, rummaging around in her pack. "I had the travel gown I was in when you saw me last, but I threw it away. This is all I own now."

"And when was the last time you washed it?" Yshe's nose wrinkled. "Here. We're going to wash your things before we leave. And you are going to take a bath before you get in this bed tonight!"

◆◆◆

Andín let Yshe lead her to the bath, which was even less

modern than the one in the inn in Azu. She ducked behind a screen, stripped her clothes off, and dropped them outside. Yshe bundled them off and promised she'd pay the laundress extra to get it done by morning.

Andín slipped into the lukewarm water, suddenly very conscious of her naked body, and sank up to her chin. After a few moments she stretched out and scrubbed at her hair with the chunk of strong-smelling soap and the dirty cloth they'd provided. At last she began to unwind, and she floated in the tub, letting the water cool around her, feeling her muscles un-knot.

She looked down at her body and winced. She hadn't really seen herself naked and clean since Azu; she hadn't expected to be so... scrawny. She could see bruises all over. Where had those come from?

She ran a hand over the deep bronze skin on her belly and sighed. Her body didn't seem quite her own.

The door opened, and someone left something on a chair. Then it closed again; feet padded away.

Curious, Andín got out of the tub, dried off, and peered around the screen. Yshe had left one of her own gowns for her to wear.

Andín quickly put it on—it was a little too short, but it covered her well enough.

She put her nose to the soft fabric and breathed deeply. It smelled like Yshe.

There was a mirror, and she hesitantly looked into it.

The gown hung loosely, but it looked decent. Yshe's figure was fuller than her own, especially now, but their waists and hips were basically in the same places, and Yshe was only a little shorter. Andín stretched her arms out and turned back and forth experimentally.

A single face stared back—her own.

For a moment she wondered if maybe the demon had gone, but she knew better. Still, no other faces at all? She hesitantly probed for the demon, and as she did so ghostly faces appeared behind her reflection.

"Ah," she said, "there you are."

The Emperor Askar smiled his grim smile but said nothing. The others were too indistinct to read expressions. They faded away again as fast as they had come.

In the meantime she looked utterly strange to herself with short, unkempt hair, a too-thin face, and eyes that seemed so much more distant than the ones she'd been used to. She picked up the scissors the inn had left and clipped experimentally at her hair, trying to even it out. After a while she gave up. Any farther and she'd have next to no hair at all!

Maybe she could buy a hat.

◆◆◆

Andín sat on the bed again with Yshe, feeling brand new. The gown felt luxurious and strange against her clean skin.

"We'll sail downriver for almost two weeks," said Yshe. "It's a slow ride, but it should be a peaceful voyage. I loved the river on the way up. This should be quicker and more fun!"

"I don't think I've ever sailed on a riverboat," said Andín. It would be odd to be carried along instead of riding.

"You'll like it! And we'll pass through the loveliest countryside. There are towns and cities, too, which I'm looking forward to seeing again. Civilization! After everything that's happened in Shuyu, a little civilization is just what I need."

"It should be nice," said Andín distantly.

"Andín? What is it?"

"Just thinking," said Andín, "about Azu."

"Ah," said Yshe, her good cheer melting away.

"I didn't get a chance to tell you," said Andín softly. "I saw a... hole... like that in Antriman, when I was being exiled. It was at the border fort there; we saw one off in the distance. I went up to the ramparts to see it, and... it was just like the one in Azu. I don't know what it was, but I can't help but wonder..."

"Well everyone started talking about them after," said Yshe, picking up on her train of thought. "And I've heard that this isn't isolated at all. I don't think anyone knew about the one in Antriman, but there are many more."

"More?" Andín's heart skipped a beat.

"Jandy told me about it that night, when we were in the new hotel. The Alavesh government says there have been dozens reported all around the world. No one knows what they are! They haven't appeared in the middle of a city like this before, but they have been appearing."

"Everywhere?" Andín asked.

"Oh, yes," Yshe assured her.

"God and Goddess," breathed Andín. Antriman, Shuyu, the ones she'd seen in her dreams, and now other places, as well. What was happening to the world? Was this what *Judy Shashalnikya* wanted them to stop?

Suddenly getting to Alavia seemed a lot more important.

"The people back in Azu think it's, well, demon magic," said Yshe. "Not surprising. The ladies from the embassy say it's some punishment of the God and Goddess on the world for being wicked. Jandy says it might be something to do with plate tectonics." She made a face. "I think that one's silly."

"Yeah," said Andín, worried.

"It might not be so bad," said Yshe, putting her hand on Andín's arm. She had small, warm fingers. "The world is always in one crisis or another, Jandy says, and I believe him."

"Maybe," said Andín, though she couldn't shake the foreboding she felt.

"Well, we should be sleeping soon," Yshe said after a moment. "We have to make ready to leave tomorrow, after all. Oh, it'll be so good to be on the move again!"

Andín thought so, too. After all this time on the road, she had little inclination to stay in one place.

♦♦♦

She curled up in the bed with Yshe, trying not to be too aware of the other woman. Thankfully she'd mastered falling asleep quickly, so she dropped off without too much fuss.

That night, Andín dreamed of Lynde, the sword-carrying woman, for the first time in months.

Lynde was hiking through the woods, carrying the rusty sword in a scabbard. It sang quietly to itself; even Andín could hear the music now as she looked out through Lynde's eyes.

This mountain range was endless! Andín could feel Lynde's awe. She'd never seen such a forest, but she found she loved the tall wooded shade and piney scent of the place. Everything here seemed muffled and still.

She rounded a bend and pulled up short. An Alavesh woman with tight braids and a hard look in her eye stood there, glaring at Lynde.

Andín recognized her. Judy Shashalnikya. She tried to shout, she tried to warn Lynde off, but Lynde couldn't sense her.

The Alavesh woman seemed to flicker in and out of existence. One moment she was there, the next Lynde was alone in the pine forest. Then the woman appeared again.

"Lynde Shevariat, this way," she said, pointing to a side trail. "Hide the sword. You won't get to keep it long otherwise, and you need to have it."

"What?" Lynde asked. "Why?"

"I don't have time to explain it!" the other woman said. "Just do as I say!"

The sword by her side suddenly began to sing louder than it ever had. She touched the hilt and felt a shock of electricity.

The sword seemed to be agreeing with the Alavesh woman on the path.

"Okay," Lynde sighed. She sounded so weary. "Lead away."

The woman—Judy Shashalnikya—pointed again, giving Lynde a very significant look. Clearly she wasn't going to be doing any walking herself. Lynde shrugged and followed where she pointed, into a clearing with a huge rock. She hid the sword carefully in a craggy space there.

She walked back to the main trail, missing the constant music of the sword, and looked around. "It's done," she called.

But Judy Shashalnikya was gone. Lynde wasn't surprised. Magic was a funny thing.

Lynde looked all around, trying to memorize everything about the place. Yes. That tree, there. The rocks, just so. The bend of the trail. Fine. She marched on into whatever danger she was heading into.

Andín separated from Lynde with a burst of static and found herself alone in the clearing.

No. Not alone.

Judy Shashalnikya stood there, arms folded. But she was indistinct and wavered in the breeze.

"What is she walking into?" Andín asked. "She's in danger, isn't she? What are you doing?"

"I didn't think you'd care," retorted Judy Shashalnikya. "You seem to have lost interest. Where have you been for the past three months?"

"I don't care about your games and your visions!" snapped Andín, "and I don't care for being used by you."

"And yet, you're still coming," observed Judy Shashalnikya. "Interesting."

Andín smoldered. "You know what's going on. It has to do with those holes in the world. What's happening? Why won't you tell me?"

"Isn't it obvious?" said Judy Shashalnikya. "Things are coming apart. I need your help to fix it."

"What will happen if I don't help you?"

"Then the world is done," said Judy Shashalnikya.

She looked around as the scene dimmed again.

"I'm running out of power and time," she said, and there was, for the first time, a note of panic in her eyes. "Please. Hurry. Come quickly."

The dream fell apart completely, and Andín woke, the smell of the pine woods fresh in her nostrils. She didn't sleep again, but lay awake listening to the reassuring sound of Yshe's soft snores.

◆◆◆

The day dawned clear and brisk, and they got up early to take care of business before meeting the boat. Yshe had slept like a log; watching her blearily get ready was actually kind of charming.

Their boat was a long, narrow river craft with a single mast, atop which the scarlet flag of Lyndania fluttered and flapped in the breeze. They'd be traveling downriver, which meant north, to a port in Lyndania. Then they'd take a train across Lyndania, cross the Vandan Mountains, and arrive at the divided city of Gantritt on the Pryttland-Alavia border.

Andín had been forced to sell the horse. She hadn't wanted to part with the mare. They'd grown close during the long walk across the steppe, but as Yshe said, she needed money, and she couldn't take a horse on the river voyage. She felt a lump in her throat when she handed the beautiful animal over to the buyer, but she did it anyway.

She got her money in Selessian silver, which was one of the coins that just about everybody on the river and points west accepted. The Selessians were, among other things, a nation of bankers and merchants.

Once that was done, they loaded their possessions, which for Yshe was several trunks of clothes and other things and for Andín her beat-up pack and her gun, onto the boat. The two other embassy wives, both of whom were much older than Yshe and Andín, gave them both severe looks. Andín, who wore a dress she'd borrowed from Yshe and her patterned Shuyan shawl, steadily returned their gazes. They looked away.

Andín stood at the rail and watched as the crew scurried around, making ready. Then, with a groan, the ship pulled away from the dock and maneuvered to the middle of the river. Andín asked one of the crew a question in hesitant Lyndani, guessing their nationality from the flag. The crew told her that it would be several weeks before they made port in the Lyndani capital of Roshden. The boat was slow, and they planned to make many stops to trade and take on passengers.

For the first time, Andín had the sense of time running out. She hoped the boat would be faster than they said.

"I didn't know you could speak Lyndani," Yshe said when the crew had gone. "I have only a few words of it myself!"

"I speak a lot of languages," Andín said, tapping her head. "Useful."

"But not Shuyan?" asked Yshe, puzzled. "That seems like a

strange omission."

"I don't know why," said Andín. "When the time came for picking up languages, the demon just never learned that one. It's all random."

Yshe shook her head. "How wonderfully strange! I'll never understand it, I don't think. Well, I'm going to go below and get situated in our cabin. We're sharing, I'm afraid. I do hope that's all right. Short notice and all."

She sounded so apologetic that Andín had to keep from laughing. "I've been sleeping outside for weeks! Yes, it's all right," she assured her. "It sounds lovely. You go ahead. I want to stay out on deck for a while."

"I'll be below, then!" Yshe chirped, setting off.

♦ ♦ ♦

Andín sat on the deck and stared out past the iron railing into the river. The Astanav River was wide, even here, less than two hundred miles from its mountain source, and slow. If she looked behind her, she could see the low hills rising into the high Shuyan steppe.

She thought of endless tall grass, wide open sky, and the smell of the horse beneath her. The wilderness called to her, and all the rough nights in the open, all of the cold and hunger, vanished into the past. She could only remember that sense of being absolutely free.

And yet she was moving on.

Well, she thought. Here I am. Halfway across the continent and looking to go farther still. The trees here looked different, somehow. Everything was unfamiliar; the people looked unusual and spoke foreign tongues, and yet she felt perfectly at home. She'd wanted to travel, and she found it suited her at last. She chuckled to herself.

Perhaps exile wasn't so bad.

Chapter 15
River Women

In time she joined Yshe below. She was still arranging their cramped cabin, working with what little light filtered in from the single porthole, as Andín entered.

"I'm so sad to leave this country behind," Yshe said. She hung a tapestry on the wall; Andín recognized the Shuyan designs on it. "There's much I won't miss, but there's something about it here. So different and unique."

"I know what you mean," said Andín.

Yshe sighed. "Jandy seems so far away."

Andín did what she'd always done when Valsin had been in a sour mood; she sat next to the other woman on the bed and put an arm around her. "It's all right," she said.

Yshe rested her head on Andín's shoulder. "That thing... the hole, in Azu. I see it when I close my eyes sometimes. It's in my dreams."

"I know how you feel. The holes are horrible." Andín squeezed Yshe's shoulder and, half-remembering wives and girlfriends from someone else's past, absently kissed the top of her head.

Yshe jumped back, eyes wide. Andín immediately realized her mistake.

"I'm sorry!" Andín exclaimed. "It's—in Antriman we, um, kiss more easily than in other countries! I forgot! It—it doesn't—"

Yshe laughed nervously. "Oh! Oh, of course! I should have known. Just... don't do that again." She shook her finger at Andín.

"Showing up looking like a beautiful boy is bad enough!"

Andín flushed, feeling horribly embarrassed. She wanted badly to explain, but how could she?

Yshe thought she was beautiful?

She decided to change the subject. "Oh, I meant to tell you, I have your book." She opened her back and withdrew *Shashalnikya's Song*.

"My book!" Yshe jumped at the chance to change the subject. "Oh, Andín! This is wonderful. I'd thought all my books were lost in the fire!" She took the book and turned it over, scratching furiously at a bit of... something... stuck on the back cover. "I forgot you had it, to be honest."

"I did, too," Andín admitted, "but I read it. Most of it. It was good company when I was all alone out there." Again she left out the most important piece, the fact that Judy Shashalnikya was haunting her own dreams. How would she ever explain that?

Yshe's face fell again. "And here I am talking about my problems! You've been through so much worse." She put a friendly arm around Andín and hugged her chastely. "I won't kiss the top of your head, though," she teased.

"Heh," Andín said, her cheeks burning.

"Did you like the story?"

"I did," said Andín. "It's true, isn't it?"

"Partly, I think," Yshe said. "Jandy knows more. But Judy Shashalnikya was a real person, and she led armies against the Selessians a long time ago. I don't know about handing herself into the arms of the enemy to save Queen Alyshaane, or going off pregnant with Dal an-Gantritt into the north, or anything like that, but she did exist. We Alavesh women all have copies of this book." She smiled secretly. "Our Princess Diya is her descendant."

"Diya? She led the revolt against the Prytt, didn't she?" Andín asked, trying to sort through her memories. "During the war?"

"Yes, that's the one," said Yshe. "She's a bit of an embarrassment now, but she was quite famous for a while in Alavia. She likes saying she takes after the original Shashalnikya. You should keep the book, though. Keep it as long as you want, finish reading it."

"Thank you," said Andín. "It meant a lot to me to have it when I was out there. It reminded me of you."

They shared a long look. Yshe looked away and picked up a blanket. "Ah, here, help me lay this blanket out on the bed?"

Andín did so, noting with something bordering on anticipation that they'd be together in a single large bed again. And why was Yshe so nervous all of the sudden?

These feelings were getting complicated.

◆◆◆

The river slipped by as they sailed north with the current. The crew announced that they'd crossed into Raza, a nation Andín knew next to nothing about. Just like that, Shuyu was behind her. She glanced back but saw only flat valley farmlands and river. What had she expected to see? Tall grass? The blue buildings of Azu? Temples? Nomads and bandits hiding in the bushes?

She sighed and faced forward again. Another border, the second of her life. She knew there were many left to go.

Raza was a mystery, but soon she felt that unsettling *unpacking* in her mind, and then she knew as much as she ever cared to: history, politics, exports, and trade. The demon as emperor had known plenty of dull, dry trivia about this land. Andín, who once drank in such facts like water, wearily tried to push it all back out of her mind. But instead she remembered diplomatic missions, dreary meetings with ministers, stacks of official reports, and idle, boozy conversations about the country. The upshot was that the court in Palascena had a low opinion of this place, which helped Andín not at all.

Days passed slowly on the river while they sailed through farmlands, forests, and even occasional industrial areas. Yshe and Andín spent hours in conversation about everything from the war times to their families to Yshe's moping over being apart from Jandy. At night they slept in the same bed. Andín wore a nightdress Yshe had loaned her, and she often woke to find the two of them back-to-back, huddled near one another for warmth. She got quickly out of bed so Yshe wouldn't know.

Andín pushed whatever feelings she had for Yshe aside. She had no energy for them, or so she told herself.

Damn this demon, she thought when she was sitting alone on the deck, watching the land roll by. He had changed her. He had to have. She'd never liked girls like this before.

Right?

Sure, her relentless memory agreed, if you didn't count the year she'd spent following Valsin's voluptuous older sister Plavis around, hoping to get a glimpse of her changing out of her clothes...

That was only childish, innocent curiosity, she told herself firmly.

Of course it was, a demonic voice that sounded just like her own whispered in her ear.

You be quiet, she told it as she daydreamed of beautiful Yshe.

♦♦♦

After several idle days on the boat, they finally passed through hilly Raza and were approaching the border with Lyndania.

One of the crew came up to her. "If you look to the right," he said in Lyndani, "you'll see a little piece of your homeland." He didn't look all that happy about it. "We are not stopping, but I thought you would want to see."

He was right. They passed over the border, and on one side of the river was Lyndania, and on the other side, the eastern side, was a fortress town with the heartbreakingly familiar green, white, and blue flag of Antriman fluttering in the breeze overhead.

"Oh!" she said, clutching the railing.

Home! Home! Her heart seized.

Yshe ran over to her. "Deeny? What is it?"

"Look," Andín whispered.

"The Kyrgan Corridor," said Yshe. "Your empire took it from Lyndania decades ago. Isn't that right?"

Andín nodded tightly; she knew the history. The Kyrgan Corridor was a narrow hundred-mile-long strip connecting farthest northwest Antriman with the river. She knew what the town was. She remembered the battles, the reports coming in from the field, the decrees she'd signed long before she was born. They'd wanted a port on the river, and they'd taken one.

Tears ran freely down her face as they sailed by. She wanted nothing so much as to leap overboard and swim for shore. Yshe put an arm around her; Andín allowed herself to lean against her for comfort.

"Home," she said in Antrimanian. "I want to go home, Yshe. I want to go home." The boat steered a little to the east, towards the town. Suddenly Andín felt an intense pressure on her lungs and a terrible burning sensation all over her skin.

She screamed in pain and surprise. Yshe jumped back.

"Andín! What's wrong?"

"The town! Steer away from it!" Andín gasped in Antrimanian and then forced herself to repeat the command in Lyndani for the crew. Magic! The smell of it filled her nostrils. She remembered now—the damned old wizard had put a spell on the borders to keep her out. "Please!"

Yshe and the crew member called out the instructions to the person manning the wheel, and the boat veered away again. Andín felt the pressure ease as the town slipped away behind them.

Yshe held onto her as she started to cry in pain and grief.

They passed the town by, and then both sides of the river were Lyndania. The small slice of Antriman vanished, swallowed up by the ceaseless river currents.

◆◆◆

Andín flipped through *Shashalnikya's Song* from time to time as they floated north towards the Lyndani capital of Roshden. She had trouble keeping the Alavesh characters straight: everybody had names that started with "Sha" or "Sho." She'd been training herself to look past the first three letters, but it wasn't easy.

She kept going back to one part, the climax of the story when the Selessians and the rebel Alavesh armies were locked in a standoff. The Selessian general, Sarda Shorvaine, made an odd request for peace: General Shashalnikya must surrender herself into their captivity in return for a five-year truce.

*"And though her queen and her men and her friends
Cried 'No! No! Go not with the enemy!'*

Judy Shashalnikya set her mind to the future
The great General and Shadarant of the Alavesh
Set her mind to the fruits of peace;
She said to Shorvaine, 'I will come with you.'

And so on the day of the raven she crossed the field alone
Into the waiting arms of the Selessian host.
The Queen, Alyshaane ShaGalana an-Telesan,
Fortress of her people, last of the line of Galana,
Wept bitter tears."

Somehow that stuck with Andín. She read it again and again; General Shorvaine's request, Judy Shashalnikya's brave agreement, Queen Alyshaane's grief. There were, she noticed, little hints here and there that Alyshaane acted like she'd lost more than a friend and companion; she'd lost a lover.

Judy Shashalnikya had eventually escaped with the help of another lover, Dal an-Gantritt, and they had fled north. Their son had lived to become king of Alavia, but of Judy Shashalnikya and Dal an-Gantritt, nothing more was known.

North. Andín didn't know what was north of Alavia and Selessia. Was there anything? The story fancifully described a circle of mountains by the sea, with a little valley in the middle.

She asked Yshe about it once, and Yshe said she knew of no such place.

"It's just a story," she said. "The writers made up a lot of it, I think! That's the way the world is; it's half rumor, half made-up. The book was written four hundred years after it all happened, you know."

"No, I didn't know that," said Andín. It struck her that even with her demon knowledge she knew next to nothing about the Alavesh. The many emperors of Antriman had paid little attention to Alavia. And why would they? It had been a tiny, remote kingdom until its conquest by the Prytt, and then it had been only a tiny piece of another, somewhat larger, remote kingdom. They had demon knowledge, to be sure, but so did many other places.

Palascena was the center of the Antrimanian world, and Alavia was a very long way from it.

◆◆◆

One day, as they sailed north through Lyndania, she happened to overhear one of the crew mention the date. She stopped him and asked if it was true. He said it was.

Andín started to laugh, shaking her head, as he left.

"Why does it matter?" Yshe asked, curious. "You've never seemed to worry about the date before."

"It's my birthday," Andín said with a rueful grin. "I'm eighteen today."

Yshe's eyes bugged. "God and Goddess, Andín! You're *so young*. I had no idea!"

Andín shrugged. "It doesn't really matter so much. I feel like I've lived a hundred lifetimes and more with all I remember now."

"Never mind the demon, today we should celebrate you!" Yshe said. "We should celebrate Andín!"

She ran and told the cook, who, delighted, baked Andín a tray of sugary treats.

Andín ate them and effusively thanked Yshe and the cook, all the while wondering who, exactly, it was they were celebrating.

◆◆◆

She spoke of it to Yshe later, as they watched the sun set over the distant western hills.

"It seems so strange," she said. "A year ago I would have been so happy to be eighteen. Now it feels like nothing at all."

"This is why we need to get you to Corgal," Yshe insisted, "to get that demon out of your head."

Andín said nothing for a long moment.

"You do still want to remove it, yes?" Yshe said uncertainly.

"I..." Andín said, her mouth suddenly dry. "I don't know who I'd be without it anymore."

Yshe hesitated, then put an arm around Andín. She sank onto Yshe's shoulder and put her own arm around Yshe's narrow waist.

"I don't hear the demon's voice anymore," Andín whispered. "It sounds just like my own thoughts. And when I was on the plains, it felt like we were becoming the same person. Not Andín dal Rovi, not Askar Molasca or any of the others who came before, but someone new."

"I like Andín dal Rovi, though," said Yshe. "I like her very much. She's my friend. And she's a good, strong young woman who's been through a lot."

Andín shook her head. "You never knew her. She was gone long before I ever came to Azu, I think. You only know me."

"But you *are* Andín," insisted Yshe. "Or you are to me. You're very special. To me."

Andín looked at Yshe, beautiful Yshe.

"I'm sorry," was all she could think of to say.

Yshe bent her head toward Andín's and kissed the top of her head.

The river passed by below.

♦ ♦ ♦

The days went by quickly after that. Andín and Yshe grew ever closer. They talked and laughed and played games during the day, much to the annoyance of the other women.

And if, late at night, Andín's mouth found Yshe's at last, and their eager, trembling hands found one another's bodies, who was to know?

♦ ♦ ♦

Andín opened up to Yshe more than she had for anyone. She told her stories of her adventures, and Yshe told her about being a diplomat's wife.

"The world is such an exciting place," said Yshe, her lovely eyes bright with the memories of the places she'd seen. "Jandy's first posting was in Narlland. It's so cold there in the wintertime, but we only spent a single year, thank the Holy Pair. The country is ruled by a woman, and always a woman. The Narldefang, that's their parliament, elects a new queen every ten years. Can you imagine?" She leaned in to Andín. "Just think what the world would be like if all the kings and princes and presidents were women."

"When I was in Palascena I saw all kinds of new things," said Andín, nodding. "There was a woman giving a speech there. Fevín dan Halda."

"You saw dan Halda speak!" Yshe grabbed Andín's arm. "She's a legend to those of us who believe in the equal rights of women."

Andín laughed. "Is she? I can see why. I had no idea who she was." She gave Yshe a look. "You're one of those?"

"In my own small way," said Yshe, looking down modestly. "Jandy and I both believe in it. You're so lucky, having seen her. Last I heard, she was in prison."

"She likely is. I saw them take her away," said Andín.

"What did she say?"

"She said 'Man is equal to woman, as the Goddess is equal in every way to the God,' I believe," said Andín. "She spoke about how men destroy women's confidence."

"Yes," said Yshe. "Even Jandy does this. He never means to, but he does. Men are all taught how." She sighed. "He's a good man. But he has his flaws."

"Everyone has flaws," said Andín.

Yshe took Andín's hand. "You don't."

Andín flushed. "I have more than you think," she said.

"And you have fewer than you accuse yourself of," said Yshe, kissing her lightly on her cheek.

Andín brought her mouth up to meet Yshe's, and soon they forgot everything else.

◆◆◆

Andín was pressed against Yshe's back, arms curled around the other woman, breathing in her scent. They were spending a day below decks; there was a steady patter of rain above.

Yshe made a happy murmuring sigh.

"You are a good friend," she said.

"So are you," said Andín. "The very best."

"But…" Yshe began hesitantly.

Andín sat up, worried. That had the sound of something bad.

"What?" she asked.

Yshe shook her head. "This… this is the river. And we're like this, here on the river. But when we come to port… maybe we should leave this here. On the river. Does that make any sense?"

Andín felt cold. She got out of bed, pulled her dress back on and sat on the edge of the bed. Yshe looked crestfallen.

"Yshe…"

"I'm sorry," said Yshe softly, "but you know we can't continue like this."

"Why?" Andín said, suddenly angry. "Why can't we?"

"I have a husband," said Yshe. "I'm a good wife. All the other men say so. And I love him. He's wonderful. Though he isn't you… and his hands aren't as skilled as yours."

Andín flushed again. "Yshe!"

"It's true! You… you are incredible. But when this ends, I must go to Telesan and be in that house." She plucked at the bedclothes, a serious, almost studious expression on her face. "I have to be who I was—who I am. I don't want this to end. But it must."

Tears ran down Andín's face. "Maybe I should sleep on deck," she said roughly. "Maybe—"

She couldn't finish the sentence. She kicked the copy of *Shashalnikya's Song* into the wall and ran from the room.

♦♦♦

Yshe found her later, sitting on the deck, drenched by the rain. "Come below," she said. "You'll catch a cold!"

But Andín wanted to be miserable. "Go away," she said. "I've suffered worse. You… you have no idea what I've had to go through."

Yshe sat next to her. "I'm sorry," she said. "Please come back down below. I—I didn't want to spend our last days on the river fighting."

"That didn't work out, now, did it?" Andín said, still stinging.

"What did you think could happen?" Yshe said softly. "That we could continue being… like this?"

Andín said nothing. But she remembered so many women, from so many past lifetimes. She remembered how some had stayed, and some had turned, and some had turned though they wanted to stay.

She knew which this was.

"I don't want to lose you," Yshe was saying. "You fill me with the most... confusing and wonderful feelings. But when this boat comes to shore we must face reality."

Andín nodded through her tears. "I know," she said. "You have to be a diplomat's wife. And I have to be... whatever I am. And do what I have to do."

"Yes," said Yshe. "I'm so sorry."

Andín slumped, feeling miserable and heartbroken. "I'll take a separate train. I have some money. We can part ways at the dock."

"No!" said Yshe. "I said we'd travel together and I meant it. I won't be separated from you. I—I don't ever want to be. We just have to be... friends. Nothing more."

Andín looked up at her, hurt and love warring with one another. "I... I kicked your book."

Yshe put an arm around her, and Andín was shocked to see that she was crying, too. "It's all right. Please come back below."

Andín reluctantly let herself be led, and so their last few days on the river passed by.

Chapter 16
The Divided City

At last, the boat pulled into port in the vast industrial city of Roshden, the Lyndani capital. It covered the west bank of the wide Astanav River for as far as she could see. Andín was briefly reminded of Palascena, though Roshden seemed smaller, poorer, and dirtier in general. Their stay would be a brief one; the train to Alavia left the following day.

Andín stepped off the boat onto the shore and felt the weight of everything that had happened to her, and everything that she had yet to do, crushing her. She had to go to Alavia and find out what the centuries-old ghost of Judy Shashalnikya wanted, at the very least.

She also had to figure out what to do about Yshe.

♦♦♦

She and Yshe didn't talk about it. They shared a hotel room, but Yshe had made it clear back on the boat that she would sleep in one of the chairs while Andín had the bed. Andín hadn't tried to argue with her.

The closer they had come to the port of Roshden, the more closed-off Yshe had become. The river… maybe it had just been a holiday from their real lives.

Andín felt broken, hurt, and confused. She knew why Yshe was acting this way, and she knew why it was necessary. It would be a scandal at best; at worst, Yshe could lose her husband, her position in the world, and even be thrown in jail. Fevín dan Halda's words came back to her now: "We may be crushed at the whim of a man, simply for being ourselves."

The hotel wasn't as private as the boat had been. Keeping some distance between them was the right thing to do.

But it still felt like Yshe had turned her back on her, and Andín ached.

Yshe went out to see some of the sights while Andín stayed in their very posh shared hotel room, moping. She didn't feel much like seeing the city.

She glanced at herself in the mirror and summoned the face of Askar Molasca. It floated there in front of her, indistinct and faint.

"What would you do, now?" she asked.

«*What you're doing*,» the demon seemed to say in reply. Once again, the face spoke with Andín's voice. «*I can't imagine doing anything else.*»

She banished the image again. When had she learned how to do that, she wondered and shook her head. Yshe was right about one thing: she'd already changed so much that it didn't matter if there was any real distinction between Andín and the demon.

The sounds and smells of Roshden wafted in through the open window. Another city, another country. She'd traveled so far. It was wondrous, in its way, but she looked east and missed Antriman. She looked west and thought about Alavia, beyond the distant mountains.

She wondered what her parents and Palyar were doing right now. Probably asleep, she thought. It would be dawn in Viko Station. She hoped their dreams were happy ones, free of worry.

♦ ♦ ♦

Yshe came back to the room that night with a bottle of something labeled in blocky Lyndani script. Some sort of liquor.

"We're going to drink all of this," she said quietly. "You and I."

Andín didn't object. She'd never drunk any sort of alcohol herself, but the demon had, and she relished the chance to experience it again.

Yshe poured out glasses and they drank.

♦ ♦ ♦

A few hours later they were wound around one another in bed, clothes everywhere, the sheets tangled up and cast aside.

"Do… do you still want me to sleep on the chair?" Andín asked, her tongue feeling heavy in her mouth.

Yshe broke into giggles. "No. No! There's no point now, silly."

Andín rolled over. "Thank you. For this. You didn't have to. I… I understood."

Yshe looked up at her, eyes brimming with tears. "I wish you were a man. I could have married you instead of Jandy."

Andín gritted her teeth. "But… you still love him."

"I do," said Yshe. She began to cry again. "Oh. Oh… it's too much. Can't we just have our happy night? Just one last night?"

"I thought that was last night," teased Andín, trying to make her feel better.

"Oh, Deeny, don't," said Yshe. "I don't know what I want. I wish… I wish I did. Just hold me, would you? Just for tonight."

Andín gathered up the sheets, covering both of them, and curled up around Yshe.

She didn't sleep much and was up well before the morning.

♦♦♦

The next morning they were on their way again.

They made their way through the city from their hotel. As they stepped out onto one of the narrow, crooked avenues leading out of the old city towards the train station, they passed by an old, bearded man ranting on a street corner. Andín was prepared to ignore him, but as she passed he jumped in front of her and grabbed her shoulders.

"It's all nothing but someone's hallucination!" he shouted, his fermented breath assaulting her nostrils. "It's coming apart, and the gods can't stop it!"

"Let her go!" snapped Yshe, stepping between them. "Keep your hands off her!"

As Yshe dragged a shaken Andín away, the man bellowed, "There are holes! Holes in the world itself!"

Andín stopped.

"Deeny," whispered Yshe. "Come on. Ignore him."

"But…" said Andín.

"We have to catch the train. He probably just heard about it from someone. Come on!"

Reluctantly, Andín let herself be led away.

◆◆◆

They boarded a creaky-looking train at Roshden's ostentatious main railway station and found themselves a compartment. The other embassy wives had disappeared; perhaps they weren't even on this train.

The conductor walked down the aisles, making his same announcement in Lyndani, Prytt, and Alavesh: this was the Trans-Vandan Express from Roshden, Lyndania to East Gantritt, Pryttland. They would arrive in 48 hours. Yshe and Andín were crammed into a six-person compartment as the train got underway.

Yshe immediately struck up a conversation with the other people in the compartment. They were all Alavesh and chatted about places they knew. Andín felt far less sociable and plastered her nose to the window to watch the scenery roll by.

So much of the world is like this now, she thought as she looked out at the factories, smokestacks, and filth of Roshden. So much has changed in all these centuries. And yet, there was a part of her, maybe the part that was most Andín, that thought it looked modern and exciting.

She thought she might understand her parents a little better now. Papa and Mama had been suspicious of novelty and innovation. At the time she thought they were foolish, but maybe they'd just seen too much change in their lives.

The city passed out of view. Soon she'd be in Alavia.

◆◆◆

The wide, flat green river valley turned to hills and charming villages, and then to dark, rocky, forest-covered mountains unlike any Andín had seen before. Darkness fell as they chugged ever upwards on the precarious track that ran between the high peaks and deep crags. Sure-footed goats perched on the rocks, impassively watching the train as it passed.

They converted the car to sleeper bunks, and Andín slept on the opposite side of the cabin from Yshe. She dreamed that they were together, but woke in the night to find her out of reach.

When the light was bright enough to see by and they converted the car back to seating, she found that they had come down from the mountains into a dry scrubland.

Then, abruptly, the train stopped. They were in the middle of nowhere as far as Andín could see, except for a small outpost with the red flag of Lyndania and another she hadn't seen before. A border, then. They were crossing into Pryttland.

Officials paced through the car, asking for documents. Yshe showed her travel papers, had them stamped, and said very clearly that Andín was with her.

The officials rifled through Andín's pack, and found her stash of Shuyan coins. They gave her a speculative look, then took half the coins and moved on.

That could have been worse, her demon knowledge told her. Somehow that didn't make her feel much better.

◆◆◆

They rolled on through the dry Prytt countryside. The rocky scrubland hills turned to wide treeless plains carpeted with gently blowing grasses, and for a moment Andín was reminded of Shuyu. Villages became more common, and they passed through vast flatlands with huge herds of cattle grazing on acre after acre. They pulled through two larger towns, and then, abruptly, they were on the outskirts of another city. The train slowed, and Andín watched, fascinated, as they wound through neighborhoods filled with barbed wire, fences, and half-erased red graffiti. The most common was nine letters arranged in a box:

S H A
D A R
A N T

"What does that mean?" Andín asked Yshe.

"This is Gantritt. It's an Alavesh city," Yshe whispered, looking around in case the Prytt guards who had stayed with the train overheard. "Half of it's still occupied by the Prytt. The border with Alavia is the river between the two halves of the city. The Shad— the people that sign says—are Alavesh who are still fighting the Prytt. Same organization as was in the war and before, mostly. It's complicated."

"Ah," said Andín.

"I'll explain more when we get over the bridge," Yshe promised. She frowned. "I don't like this city. It feels like everyone here is on edge, all the time. Even the Alavesh half is bad. It's wrong to divide a city like this."

The train slowed and then finally ground to a halt in a tumbledown station with a massive canopy over the tracks. Andín shouldered her pack, grabbed Yshe's bags, and followed Yshe out into East Gantritt.

The air here smelled like dust and gunpowder. The station itself was full of uniformed men with rifles who glowered at everyone who passed. They glowered especially at Yshe, who was by her dark complexion far more clearly Alavesh than the fairer-skinned Prytt who streamed all around her. They didn't know what to make of Antrimanian Andín and stared openly at her.

"Come on," said Yshe, glancing this way and that. Andín had never seen her so nervous. Was it her? This place? Both? "We need to get across the river."

She thought she heard Judy Shashalnikya whispering *hurry, hurry* as they headed west through the cramped, crowded streets of East Gantritt. Yes, yes, she thought testily. I'm coming. Almost there.

The people largely looked like Yshe, with dark skin and deep brown eyes, but Andín could pick out many Prytt faces in the crowd. Strange smells and sounds assaulted her senses.

Heavily-armed Prytt soldiers were everywhere. They walked in groups or rode on horseback or stood stoically on street corners. Were things in this city so bad, Andín wondered, that they needed armed guards everywhere? In answer to her question, they rounded a corner and saw a burned-out building. Someone near them muttered something about a bombing.

Red graffiti was everywhere. The Prytt had clearly been painting over it, but there was always more.

At last, they emerged into a bright square by the side of a shallow, narrow river.

"The Debanae River," Yshe sighed. "I grew up next to it. Farther downstream, of course! But it's so, so good to see it again. Such a beautiful river!"

It looked like a muddy brown trickle to Andín, but she didn't say a word.

"This is the border. We'll see what we can do about your papers," Yshe said. "The Alavesh guards ought to let you through on my say-so or refer us to the local authorities. We should get in if the Prytt let us through." She strode confidently to the bridge. Andín followed close behind.

Two Prytt soldiers stopped them before they stepped onto it.

One growled something in his native language. Andín knew little of it, so she couldn't follow along.

"Since when do I need papers to cross back into my own land?" Yshe demanded in Alavesh.

"Papers!" he barked in halting Alavesh. "Or go back!"

Yshe shrugged and took her papers out. The guards unhappily examined them for a while, then grudgingly handed them back with a stamp on them. "You, pass." He looked at Andín. "Your papers!"

"Oh, she's with me—" Yshe began.

"No exceptions! All must have papers!" said the Prytt guard.

"I—I don't have any," Andín said. "I'm from Antriman, and I lost them, and—"

"Antriman! Devils in that country," said the guard. "I should have known, you look like a demon girl! If you have no papers, then get off the bridge."

"No!" Andín cried. She was so close. They were going to separate her from Yshe! "You can't. You have to let me pass! I have some money in my pack—"

"How dare you?" the guard roared. He gestured with his

weapon. "Try and bribe me. I should haul you into jail! Get away! Go!"

Andín gave Yshe a pleading look. Ahead, red and white Alavesh flags fluttered from the far end of the bridge. So, so close.

She fought the dark, demonic powers rising in her. She couldn't. Not here in the middle of a crowded square, and definitely not in front of Yshe. She had no idea what would happen if, say, she blew a hole in the bridge and ran for it. Probably nothing good.

"I'm sorry," said Yshe. She looked terrified by the Prytt soldiers. Andín remembered that when Yshe had been little, the Prytt had occupied all of Alavia. "Go to the Alavesh consulate in Great Maklav Square," Yshe instructed. "I can try and help you from this side. Please do it! I promise. I'll get you across!"

"I will!" promised Andín.

"Good," said Yshe. A deep shadow crossed her fine features. "I'll make it right. I promise."

And with that, she turned and walked across the bridge into Alavia, leaving Andín behind in Pryttland. Andín watched her go, her heart breaking.

"I love you!" she shouted at Yshe's receding back.

Yshe stopped then, without turning around, strode forward quickly beyond the gates.

"Get off the bridge," growled the guard, giving her a hard look. Andín looked one last time at Alavia, so near, and turned back into Pryttland.

◆◆◆

The fortress-like Alavesh consulate turned out to be no help at all. After a three-hour wait behind dozens of Alavesh, she finally got to the head of the line. She explained her situation, but the consular agent said simply, "Are you a citizen of Alavia? No? Then I can't help you. Ask at the Antrimanian consulate."

"Where is that?" Andín asked.

He smiled thinly. "In Roh. The Prytt capital. Two hundred miles away."

"What? Please, my friend is going to send—"

"I'm sorry," he said, irritated. "Next!"

She tried to argue with him to no avail. The guards escorted her out through the security barriers and back onto the narrow streets of East Gantritt.

Now what would she do? She walked through the streets, trying to ignore the gathering twilight. *There are always ways across borders*, the demon's knowledge said. But this was a heavily guarded crossing. How could she get across the river? Should she try and swim for it? That seemed like a very bad idea.

Should she try to go to the Antrimanian consulate in Roh? She'd have to get back on a train, and that meant money—which she didn't have much of. And what if Yshe found a way to get her across in the meantime, or the Antrimanian consulate turned her away? She had no proof that she was who she said. She looked like an Antrimanian, and she spoke the language well enough, but that was no guarantee. She could very well end up just as trapped.

She could try and wait for Yshe. But what if she never found a way to get her across? Yshe had her own life in Alavia. Why would she expend so much energy on Andín?

Why wouldn't she just continue and leave Andín here? It was the solution to the problem they'd been dancing around. Yshe could go back to her life and forget Andín ever existed. It was probably better that way.

As for Andín, she needed to get to Alavia. Judy Shashalnikya called her.

There are always ways across borders.

Andín made up her mind to seek them out.

◆ ◆ ◆

The cheap rooming house she eventually found was dirty and noisy, but Andín at least was able to use her remaining Shuyan coins to buy her own room. This hotel didn't mind where the coins were coming from, as long as they existed. She eventually changed some more of her money into the local Prytt currency and bought a meal. Her bag of coins was getting too light. She couldn't afford much more of this.

Not for the first time, she cursed the Prytt soldiers who had stolen her money on the train and bemoaned the fact that the ones at the Alavesh border had done the same.

She lay in the narrow, musty-scented bed, listening to the sounds of the city below. People yelled in Prytt or Alavesh, train whistles sounded, horses neighed, carts clattered past.

She had magic. She wracked her brains trying to think of something useful to do with it. Didn't this demon know any invisibility spells? No spells to move from one place to another? No confusion spells that would let her walk past the guards?

There had to be something she could do. With all this knowledge and magic, she had to be able to use it in some way. Tomorrow she'd walk along the border and see.

She tried to plan, but all she could think of was Yshe. She saw her face everywhere; she remembered the sight and the smell and the taste of her.

That night she dreamed only of sitting in some dark, dank place, smelling the scent of rotten food and watching daylight creep across the floor, hour by hour. Her body didn't feel like her own, but she knew the waiting would be worth it.

When she woke, she resolved to escape East Gantritt somehow, no matter what.

♦♦♦

The next day she went again to the consulate to see if Yshe had sent word. Nothing. They turned her out again, this time with a warning not to waste their time.

Andín began to doubt that Yshe would ever send word. She was probably halfway to Telesan by now, gratefully leaving the strange burden of their relationship behind. Andín went back to her hotel room and wept into a pillow.

She roused herself, empty of tears, and looked in the mirror. She concentrated, and called forth the face of Askar Molasca. It was the only way she could think of to get the demon to talk to her directly; otherwise, the demon's voice just sounded like her own thoughts.

"Demon," she said, her voice sounding hollow in her ears. "Talk to me."

Askar Molasca's face once again twisted and morphed into an

eerie parallel of her own, covered in red symbols. *«I'm sorry,»* her reflection said. *«First love is always hard.»*

First love? Was that what this was?

"I miss her," said Andín.

«I know. You may see her again. But it will hurt for a long time. I remember many first loves. It rarely ends well, and it's always painful to lose them.»

Andín smiled ruefully. "Aren't you supposed to tell me it will be okay?"

«I am a demon, remember,» her reflection said, fading away.

Andín sat on the bed and called up the memories of first loves. Beautiful young women and a few men flickered through her mind, and she felt the shock and despair of losing each.

Somewhere deep inside, she knew this was what it was always like, to fall in love for the first time. She knew it was silly and sharp and awful and wonderful, and she knew that even if she never saw Yshe again, the pain of losing her would fade into something cherished and half-remembered.

She also knew, deep within the merged and demon-haunted core of her being, that she'd never had Yshe. Not really. Yshe herself had tried to explain it to her; there was their life on the river and then everything else.

Andín thought of Yshe's smile, her laughter, and the way it had been when they were together, and her heart ached.

◆◆◆

Moping wasn't getting her anywhere, so she took herself for a walk along the river to see what the border looked like. Some borders were just imagined lines across sand and rock, but this one was more like an armed camp. The Prytt side was lined with high fences and barbed wire, dotted with guardhouses and towers. She could only see the Alavesh side through gaps in the fence.

Andín had impulsively dressed in her Shuyan clothes, and she attracted plenty of stares and whispers. She began to wish Yshe hadn't convinced her to leave her gun behind in Shuyu. She eventually came to the edge of the city, which was protected by even more guards and barriers. Papers of anyone who didn't look

Prytt were being checked.

Apparently the Prytt weren't interested in letting the Alavesh or anyone else who wasn't like them leave through any route. It was infuriating. East Gantritt felt more like a prison than a city. Andín turned back.

She turned off the avenue running alongside the river barrier and into a crumbling Alavesh neighborhood. It didn't take long before she found herself surrounded by skinny boys with knives.

One of the boys sneered at her. "You a boy or a girl? And what's those clothes?" he asked.

"Let me pass," she said, keeping her voice neutral.

"We'll take your coins first," he said. They fanned out around her with practiced ease.

She reached for the dark energies she felt swirling just out of sight, and gathered them to her. She could feel power building up. "You should let me pass," she warned. "I'm in a really bad mood today."

The boy passed his knife from one hand to the other, casual in his easy menace. "Don't like waiting," he said. "Let's have it now." He took a step forward, and Andín's dark energies built to a crescendo.

She wanted to hurt this sneering boy, to make him fear her. She scowled and raised her hand.

He brought the knife to bear.

"*Shih!*" she shouted, throwing all her anger, frustration and hurt at him. Waves of demonic energy slammed into the boy, knocking him back onto the dusty street. Everybody else sprang back, shocked.

Andín was smart enough to turn and run as fast as she could back towards the river. She could hear them shouting behind her, but they didn't follow.

She slowed to a walk, hating herself a little for what she'd done. But what choice did she have? And… to her shock, she discovered that she'd enjoyed it.

I am becoming ruthless, she thought. Askar Molasca had rubbed off on her after all.

Good.

So lost was Andín in thought that she didn't notice the three men watching from the shadows, taking careful notes.

♦♦♦

She stayed two more nights in the Prytt half of Gantritt. Each day she went to the Alavesh consulate, and each day she came away empty-handed. No word came from Yshe. Andín began to despair.

She thought about going to the Antrimanian consulate in far-off Roh but found she couldn't even get back into the train station without papers. There'd been a bombing in the south of the city a week ago, so security was tight, and everyone was on even more on edge than usual.

If she couldn't get into Alavia, and she couldn't leave the city, what was she going to do? All of her demon knowledge hadn't prepared her for this.

Restless, she went out walking again, this time down one of the major avenues in her more pedestrian dress and a hat, and saw even more red graffiti. *Shadarant. Shadarant.*

The rebel organization. Maybe, she thought with wild, reckless hope, they could help her.

Something didn't feel right about that. The demon memories which kept constantly trickling into her consciousness had made her wary of anti-government groups, especially armed insurgents.

Still, growing desperate, she resolved to find them.

She began to keep an eye out, seeking out the sorts of places where the kind of people she needed might lurk. She stopped in shops in dodgy neighborhoods and made a few clumsy inquires, relying on the demon's surprisingly scarce knowledge of skulking around dealing with shadowy groups. Emperors were bad at some things, apparently.

She worried about dealing with the Shadarant, but it was the only thing she could think of to do that had any chance of success.

♦♦♦

They found her sooner than she imagined. She decided to go look in another neighborhood on the north side of the city and fought her way through the narrow, heavily guarded streets. She picked up a newspaper and flipped through it. There had been another bombing somewhere near the river. The paper said ten, including two children, had died. The Shadarant took responsibility.

«*Civil war is brutal*,» the demon's quiet, memory-like voice whispered. «*This is what it's like. Everyone's a target. No one is safe. These people you're looking for aren't safe.*»

"You're sure?" she whispered. "You're sure they're not safe? I'm not Prytt. I can pay them."

The demon lapsed back into silence.

She knew the demon was right, of course. But what choice did Andín have? Every day she remained behind the Alavesh border was frustration and torment. She glanced back toward the river. What was over there, in Alavia? *Come to Alavia*, Judy Shashalnikya had commanded. But where? And why? What was she looking for? What was the point?

She told herself she was looking for demon lore, but deep down she had the feeling that she was actually searching for something much more.

She longed for the freedom of the open, grassy steppe. This tense, dusty city felt like being stuck in a bottle.

Hungry, she picked a café in a run-down neighborhood, ordered some sort of fried noodle dish with goopy vegetables and a thick, tangy white sauce she couldn't identify, and sat down to wait for inspiration to strike.

After a few minutes, an Alavesh man in shabby businessman's robes sat across from her. She was almost surprised. "So," he said, helping himself to some of the food on her plate. She glared at him. He laughed. "Some hospitality. Antrimanians, eh? You're the one who's looking for us."

Her eyebrows rose. "You're one of …those."

"I am," he said, cutting her off before she could say the name 'Shadarant.' He looked casually around. "This is friendly territory.

But we should go for a walk." He jerked his chin out towards the street. "After you."

"Oh, but I don't—" Andín stammered, trying to stall for time. This man radiated menace.

"It's not really a request," he said, not unkindly, gesturing again towards the street. She thought she glimpsed a pistol beneath his robe. She stood, annoyed and afraid, and went out into the street. If she needed to, she could take care of him. He was close behind her. Once she was out of the shop, she was immediately flanked by two others.

"The alley," said the man. She turned right.

"So you were looking for the Shadarant," the man said, falling into step beside her. The buildings of the alley loomed up on either side. No one was around. "You've found us. This makes it easy. We were told to watch for you."

"Oh!" said Andín, flooded with relief. Yshe must have told them, who else could it be? Yshe hadn't forgotten her after all. "I'm so glad, I thought—"

Someone clamped something with a strong chemical smell over her mouth and nose. As she sank to the ground, darkness rushing in all around her, she dimly realized that Yshe hadn't sent these men after all, and she was in a world of trouble.

Chapter 17
The Princess of Alavia

The rhythm of the road jostled her awake. She started up and tried to look around, but someone had tied a heavy, musky-smelling blindfold around her head. She was also bound hand and foot.

"You're up," a man's voice said in thickly accented Antrimanian. "Good. Good."

"We're... are we still in Pryttland?" Andín asked groggily in Alavesh.

"You speak our language! Even better," he said, switching over. "Yes. For now, but we'll be out soon. A few more miles to the northern border. It isn't far from the city. The province of Eusalee in Alavia is beyond."

"Oh," she said, trying to fight nausea. Her head throbbed, and the bouncing of whatever she was traveling in was making her sick. Motorcar, she realized belatedly, recognizing some of the noises and fumes. She'd never been in one before. "Why... why did you...? I would have come with you. I want to get to Alavia."

"We're taking you to someone special," the man replied. "In Eusalee. She's the one who told us to watch for an Antrimanian girl who did magic, and here you are. You even came to us. What luck! We didn't even have to work for it."

"Please take the blindfold off at least," said Andín. The nausea was getting worse. "It's making me sick. I won't fight you or run away. I promise. I have nowhere to go."

"Huh," said the man, whoever he was. "I can't believe that. But we'll have to untie you before the border crossing anyway, so we might as well do it now. The guards are our friends, but even they get jumpy when there's a tied-up girl in the back of the wagon. So."

Hands fastened around the blindfold and tugged, then the world was bright again. She squinted in the sharp sunlight as her wrists and ankles were untied. She found she was riding with three armed men in the back of an open-top motorcar. The land here was full of pastures and cows, and they bumped along a badly-paved road between tall fences.

"It'll be quicker when we get out of Maklav," said the man who had spoken. Their faces were covered, so she couldn't see anything distinctive about them.

"What's... Maklav?" she asked, too nauseated and aching to search her memories.

"This is," said the man, sweeping his arm out to encompass the dry, hilly land they were riding through. "All of this is part of the province of Maklav. It was part of the old Kingdom of Alavia. It was always Alavesh; most of the people here are Alavesh even now. It fell with the rest of the kingdom to the Prytt." He spat, both for punctuation and expression. "It's still part of Pryttland now, thanks to the cowards in Telesan who signed the treaty. We lost this land to them, and parts of Northalv and Kish to the Selessians."

"I see," said Andín. The demon part of her remembered that treaty. Information unspooled in her mind. She remembered reading the treaty and thinking it was a brilliant win for the Alavesh. "You... you got a country for yourselves. And most of the mines and the trade routes," she said. "All in return for a little of the worst land. You did really well. It was a smart treaty. Get the rest back... maybe in a hundred years. If you can. But... don't poke the bear just after you took his dinner away."

They all laughed. "You know nothing of us, Antrimanian girl," said the man.

She lapsed into silence at that but thought, I know you better than you think.

♦♦♦

After another hour they finally came to the border. "Smile," her captors instructed. "We have papers for everything. Just smile."

She did. The guards at the post were clearly on good terms with the Shadarant. Money changed hands, papers were stamped, and they were waved on their way out of Pryttland. The Alavesh guards on the other side gave them a casual salute, waving them through, and they passed through the red-and-white striped gate into Alavia.

Andín waited for something, some kind of sign or message, once they crossed the border. She waited for Judy Shashalnikya to appear and tell her what to do next.

But nothing happened.

♦♦♦

They rode in the motorcar to a ramshackle village where they bundled Andín onto an ancient-looking coal train. From there, the train groaned northeast into the steep hills rising beyond the village.

Another train, thought Andín tiredly. Would this travel never end?

Worse, here she was in Alavia, but so far Judy Shashalnikya hadn't reappeared. There was no message from on high, nothing but this headache and a slow train that smelled like dusty men. She had no idea what to do next, except be borne along to wherever they were taking her.

She wished she could do something, take some kind of action, but the demon part of her knew there was value in waiting to see how the game played out.

They chugged slowly through deep pine forests and into a greener, wilder, and craggier land than she'd seen since leaving Antriman. It reminded her a little of the trip up the mountains from Roshden, except with thicker forests.

This, she thought approvingly, was a glorious redoubt. Even the Forest King himself hadn't had such magnificent cover.

The train finally ground to a halt at a station in what seemed like the middle of nowhere. A few houses were clustered around the station; no one else seemed to be around. The Shadarant ordered Andín out and took her to a group of waiting horses.

"You can ride?" the man asked her. She nodded. "Good. Get on."

She threw herself on the horse. The men laughed uproariously, and she realized she should be riding sidesaddle. Her skirts bunched under her; she obviously looked ridiculous. She missed her Shuyan riding outfit, and wondered what had become of it. She resolved never to leave another hotel room without taking all of her things with her.

She rearranged herself, cheeks burning. However, she found holding on to be almost impossible and shifted back, embarrassment be damned. She needed to get another pair of breeches, she decided as they set off again into the dark pine wood.

◆◆◆

At last, as the sun was setting, they arrived at an old stone manor house in a wide clearing. The rambling house stood atop a hill with a commanding view of the valleys below; a small contingent of armed men drilled in formation on its lawn.

A military stronghold, her demon memories helpfully filled in for her.

"Welcome to Shadarant headquarters," the man said. "You're expected."

She was brought into a drafty hall that smelled strongly of mold and burnt meat and told to wait. The man she had been talking with loitered with her while the others took up positions nearby. "The princess has been looking forward to meeting you," the man said. "Princess Diya Shashalnikya. You know about her, yes? Even in Antriman?"

"I-I know a little," said Andín. "She led the independence fight here."

"Of course! And more. She's a national hero. But the new government exiled her here, where no one can see her, because they think she's a threat. Idiots!" The man's expression twisted. "If she were in Telesan, the people would want her to be queen. And they can't take that. So here we are. But she does us all a service by heading the Shadarant, even as we fight for Maklav, Kish, and Namnar."

"What does that mean, 'Shadarant'?" asked Andín. If she had to wait here, she'd at least have her curiosity satisfied.

"It's an old word," explained the man. "There were women who used to fight in the old days, and that's what they were called. Scary bitches. They'd take some kind of drug, then strip naked and run into battle shrieking at the top of their lungs."

"Ah," said Andín. She shivered, suddenly was aware of how filthy and disheveled she must look. "You should... I should wash up. If I'm going to meet a princess."

"Oh, don't worry about it," said a sharp female voice. A gaunt, middle-aged woman strode in, dressed in a severe black and red jacket, shirt, and pants, her hair pulled back into a bun. The only sign of her rank was a small golden pin on her collar. The men immediately stood to acknowledge her. "I don't care about that now. You're the girl, the one I was warned about."

Andín gulped. "I'm sorry, P-Princess, I don't know what you mean."

Diya Shashalnikya sat across from Andín and stared piercingly into her eyes.

"You're an Antrimanian girl," she said slowly in Andín's native language. To Andín surprise, she spoke with a Palascena accent. "Come a long way. And you're carrying the demon-emperor of Antriman around in that head of yours. Isn't that right?"

The world seemed to slow to a crawl around them. Andín could feel every beat of her heart. Her first impulse was to deny everything. "I—I don't know what you're talking about!" she said, trying to sound indignant.

"Yes, you do," said Princess Diya, still in Antrimanian. "Askar Molasca. Or you were, until you died a few months back. Yes. Here you are."

Andín held her ground, stubbornly saying nothing.

Diya abruptly changed the subject. "You're the host, girl. Where are you from?"

"Viko Station," said Andín. "It's in—"

"Lofkandi province, yes, I know," said the princess curtly. "I've been through there on the train. Many, *many* times. It's near enough to where some of my family lived." She glanced at Andín, reading her expression. "Oh? You didn't know I was Antrimanian by birth? It's true. When the Prytt conquered my country, the Shashalnikyas fled to Antriman, where the damned demon of an emperor proceeded to ignore us for a hundred years."

Andín laughed at the memories she saw expanding into her consciousness. "You were a nuisance," she said.

"There," said the princess, eyes disturbingly intense. "You see? You are what I said. The emperor."

Andín felt like someone had made her swallow a cold stone. "I am myself."

"Are you, now?" the princess said, her voice ice. "Your family isn't the only one with secrets, after all. Oh, no. We Shashalnikyas figured you out a long time ago. Demon lore is one of the things we Alavesh are good at." She stood and snapped her fingers rapidly at Andín, clearly trying to unsettle her. "Ha! And how do you like that? Demon-emperor, the thousand year-old monarch, couldn't be bothered to help us or even see us. It would have cost you next to nothing, to give us what we wanted! A few thousand men, some money, that was all. But it never happened, and now here we are. You're in my home, in my country. The tables turn! Wonderful. I had thought they were working on a plan to get rid of you, and oh! Here you are. In a peasant girl."

She laughed, and the laughter was a little too loud and lasted a little too long. "A peasant girl! Why a peasant girl? What a strange retirement! Was it a mistake? A plot? It hardly matters, it's brilliant. What a treasure has landed in my lap, wouldn't you say?"

"I... I don't have anything of value," Andín said, trying to keep her nerve.

"No? But of course you do," said the princess. "You are, as you said, yourself! You have the demon inside you. I'll send to the current emperor at once. I'll wager anything he'll pay quite a nice sum to get you freed."

"You don't understand," said Andín, fighting hurt and anger.

"He doesn't care about us. He exiled us from Antriman."

"He'll pay," said the princess, ignoring her. "Oh yes. He'll pay to get you back. The accumulated wisdom of a thousand years— he'd be a fool not to!"

"You'd think so," murmured either Andín or the demon or both.

Princess Diya continued her ranting. "Antriman won't ignore us any longer. And then when he does pay I can fund my troops in Gantritt at last. We'll make the streets run red with Prytt blood!" She turned to her men and repeated the phrase in Alavesh. They clapped politely.

Diya fixed her intense attention back on Andín. "So. You're *here*, you're here, as my sorceress said you would be. Excellent. My men do good work. I'm pleased. Pleased! Oh yes. The men in Telesan won't be able to ignore me if I hand them Gantritt, or if I have Gantritt and keep it... wouldn't you say? Imperial Majesty?" She smirked at Andín.

"You're insane," Andín spat, anger finally breaking. "I'm in exile; the government of Antriman won't pay anything at all for me, and you've brought me here against my will. You've done nothing but make me angry!" She could feel the dark energies building up all around her. "If—if you want nothing else of me, let me go! There are places I need to be."

The princess smirked at her. Andín waited, seething, dark energies swirling around her.

"Go ahead," said the princess softly, "and those of us you don't affect with your magic will shoot you dead in the next instant."

Andín looked around at the men set up all around the room. A few had ever-so-casually brought their weapons to bear.

There was no point to this. She gave up, defeated. The dark energies ebbed away.

Diya turned to the men and said in Alavesh, "Take her below! Lock her in. Make sure she's cared for, but keep her here."

◆◆◆

They dragged her down a flight of dark stairs into an equally dark and dank basement. Inside, she could see the daylight filtering in from the barred windows. Iron bars separated a row of a dozen cells; most were empty. One held a filthy, miserable young Alavesh-looking woman. They shoved Andín into the cell next to her, turned the key, and left.

Andín sat, utterly defeated. She should never have gone looking for the Shadarant; she should have trusted Yshe to come up with a solution.

Yshe! Andín thought with alarm. Sweet, lovely Yshe would never know what had happened to her. Now here she sat in the home of a madwoman, waiting for a ransom that would never come. What would this princess do with her? There was no way to know.

She buried her head in her hands. All of the misery of the past year came back, and she started to cry.

"Hey," said a voice in accented Alavesh from nearby. "Stop crying. Please? It's all right."

"I—who are you?" Andín asked, wiping her nose. That voice sounded familiar.

"Over here," said the voice. Andín looked over, and saw the young woman in the next cell looking at her through the bars. Andín couldn't see her too well, but she had a kind, open face, wide brown eyes, and the dark skin of the Alavesh. For a split second Andín was reminded of Yshe. "It's not so bad down here," the other woman said. "They feed us, and the guards aren't cruel."

"Are you here for a ransom, too?" Andín asked.

"Ha. No," said the young woman. She was maybe a few years older than Andín, though it was hard to tell. "I had something Princess Scary up there thinks is hers. It's not. But I hid it, and I won't tell her where it is."

"Really?"

"Yeah. She'll never get it, either. It's powerful. Magic. There's no way she should have it."

"Magic," said Andín. Dark powers rose and fell inside her. Now that no one was pointing guns at her head, she might have a chance to actually use it.

"That's right," the other woman said. "What's your name?"

"Andín dal Rovi," said Andín.

"It's nice to meet you, Andín," the young woman said sadly. "My name's Lynde Shevariat."

Chapter 18

Secrets

"Lynde," said Andín, scrambling to her feet. Maybe this was the message! "Lynde! I know you!"

"You do?" asked Lynde, confused. "I'm pretty sure I've never met anyone from the east."

"I dreamed of you!" exclaimed Andín.

Lynde rolled her eyes. "Oh."

"No, it's true," insisted Andín. "You're from somewhere really cold and rainy, by the sea. And you had that singing sword!"

"Shh!" Lynde said, eyes wide. "Don't talk about it!"

"Why?" asked Andín. "I'm sure they know."

"Yeah, but they might think you know something more," Lynde said, giving her a look. "You do know something, don't you? How do you know about that damn sword?"

"I thought you didn't want to talk about it," said Andín, keeping her voice low.

"Yes, but now I have to know," whispered Lynde. "Come on. That sword is the bane of my existence, and I still don't know the first thing about it."

"I don't know any more than that," admitted Andín. "I saw you with it, that's all. But… maybe you're tied in with all this. Did anyone tell you to come here?"

Lynde shrugged. "The sword did, sort of. *Find my mistress,* it said. *Take me to her.* All day and all night it said that. Worse, it *sang* it. Ugh. The divines at the temple in Kingstown said I should come to Alavia and try to return the sword to its rightful resting place. Apparently they think it'll fix the world. I don't know."

"Are you not from Alavia?" Andín asked. Lynde was speaking Alavesh, though with an accent that was somewhat hard to follow.

"Nah," said Lynde. "I'm from Rath. It's a little island kingdom in the sea, mostly Alavesh people there."

"So Judy Shashalnikya didn't appear to you in a dream telling you to come here, huh?" said Andín. There went that possibility.

"Judy Shashalnikya?" asked Lynde, eyes wide. "You sure the princess didn't tell you about the sword?"

"No," said Andín. "Why?"

"That's whose sword it is," said Lynde. "I was sent from Rath to bring it to her grave."

♦♦♦

Andín paced her cell, filled with restless energy.

"You're making me tired just looking at you," complained Lynde.

"Sorry," said Andín. She turned to face Lynde. "You have to be the sign. It has to be you. You're why I'm here. *She* orchestrated this whole thing, I'm positive."

"Ah," said Lynde.

"Look, we need to get out of here," said Andín, ignoring Lynde's obvious sarcasm. "We have things to do." She looked around; no guards. Good.

She held her hands out in front of her and called the dark energies. The air around her shimmered with power.

Lynde's eyes widened. "Oh, hell."

"Stand back," she said to Lynde, who cursed but she did as she was told.

"*Shih!*" she shouted. A wave of energy slammed into the cell door—and bounced off harmlessly, ricocheting back at her at full force. She screamed as the wave picked her up and hurled her against the wall, knocking the wind out of her.

She staggered to her feet. Lynde was sprawled on the floor on the far side of her cell; the diffused wave had gotten her, too.

"Lynde!" she gasped, lungs burning. "Are you—?"

Lynde picked her head up. "Ow."

"I'm so sorry!" Andín said, wincing at the pain in her side. She hoped she hadn't cracked a rib. "I had no idea it would do that."

"You do magic," observed Lynde. "Great."

"Not that it does a lot of good," sighed Andín.

"Princess has a wizard or two running around here," said Lynde. "Probably had one of them do something to the door."

Andín nodded. It made sense. There were probably charms and wards everywhere. "You know much about magic?"

"Not really," said Lynde, sitting up. She rubbed her head. "Most of my experience with it was that sword. People said there was a witch at the edge of the village, but I think she was just an old woman that nobody liked."

"Great," said Andín, feeling a certain renewed dislike of wizards.

She sat gingerly back on the floor, genuinely at a loss for what to do next. She was certain that Judy Shashalnikya had guided her here; she was certain that she'd seen Lynde hiding that sword in the woods. But she had no idea how they were going to get out of this dungeon and do whatever it was Judy Shashalnikya wanted.

Her mother would have told her to have faith. Andín wasn't good at having faith in anything but herself, and she was stuck in a dungeon.

Her memories expanded again, and she saw the insides of several nasty, ancient dungeons from the bad old days. At least one of them had led to her death and a change in dynasty. That was how the Molascas, who were originally from the far north and had kept their foreign names since, had come to power.

Something to keep in mind, she thought morbidly. *We don't always win.*

"So why does our friend upstairs want you?" Lynde asked after a while.

"Long story," said Andín.

"Sum it up for me," said Lynde.

"Well… That idiot princess thinks I'm worth money. I'm not."

"Ah," said Lynde. "That seems rather typical."

"She's not exactly sane, is she?" Andín asked quietly. "The princess."

"Sure she is," said Lynde. "She's the sanest person here; she just has a funny way of showing it. People all have their demons."

Ouch, thought Andín.

"So," Andín asked, trying to feel this other girl out. She felt like she knew her already, at least a little, but there were lots of gaps to fill in. "How long have you been here?"

"No idea. Probably a few weeks. Maybe more."

"And all for the sword."

"Right," said Lynde. "She's a Shashalnikya; she's Judy Shashalnikya's descendant, so she thinks the sword belongs to her. She thinks if she goes down to Telesan and waves it around, the old men who run this country will make her queen."

"But they won't," said Andín. People rarely gave up power willingly.

"No. Alavia's a republic," said Lynde. "No kings, no queens, no emperors. Pretty good deal. Who would ever want to go back?"

"Right," said Andín. She thought about what Hular Molasca had said about the time of emperors ending. Diya Shashalnikya didn't seem to want to let it go.

They sat in silence for a while longer.

"They do bring food, you said?" Andín said at length.

"Sure," said Lynde, "but it's not very good. Even I think it's bad food, and my ma said I'll eat anything."

"Just like my brother," said Andín, feeling a little pang of homesickness.

"Yeah, but brothers can get away with it. Ma always said I'd just get fat."

"Same," sighed Andín. Mama had always been after her about her figure.

"So you're from Antriman? The empire? You have the look."

"I am," said Andín.

"We used to get Antrimanian traders in to buy whale oil," said Lynde. "Long way from home."

"Rath," said Andín, her demon memories kicking in at last.

Facts tumbled out of her. "Mostly whaling. Poor. Was an Alavesh colony before the Prytt conquered the rest of the country. Useful trading stop on the northern route."

"That's us," agreed Lynde. "My husband was on a whaling ship. My pa and brother, too."

"You're married?"

"Well," said Lynde. "Not anymore."

"Oh," said Andín. Had she known that? It sounded like something half-familiar. "I'm sorry to hear it. What happened?"

"You're blunt. I like that." Lynde smiled, but it didn't reach her eyes. "He divorced me after I stole his sword. It wasn't his, of course, it's Judy Shashalnikya's, but he's the one who found it. He and everybody else was sure I'd become a thief, though, and when the local temple started getting involved and saying I had to go on this quest, he threw his hands up and got rid of me. Just like that."

"That's awful," said Andín. "He could do that?"

"Yeah," said Lynde. "I didn't even have to be there for him to do it. They just sent me a notice in the temple. Real nice."

"I once heard a woman named Fevín dan Halda speak, back in Palascena," Andín said. "She said that men can crush women just for being themselves."

"I bet I'd like this Fevín dan Halda," said Lynde. "So you came all the way from Palascena? That's farther away than Rath, I think."

"It is," said Andín. "I've been traveling for about… six months?"

"That's a long trip," said Lynde, impressed. "You get homesick?"

"I do," said Andín. "I really do. Do you?"

"Yes," Lynde sighed. "I miss home. I don't miss my ex-husband, I don't miss the people, but I miss the place."

"Tell me about it," Andín encouraged her, "your home."

"Ten Fish was its name," said Lynde. "It was a nasty little village out in the middle of nowhere, but we had the big whaling ships come in every year. They docked there in the winter, and we all helped keep them from rotting away. We went hungry, and it was cold, but it was great to look at the high mountains and rocky cliffs coming down to the sea and big trees everywhere. When the sun came out, it was amazing. I've never seen a place that's as beautiful, and I've seen a few. Maybe you have, I don't know. You've seen more of the world than I have."

Andín thought of the windswept grassy plains of Shuyu. "Maybe."

"Anyway, I thought you said you'd dreamed about me or something," said Lynde. "So don't you know?"

"I only saw bits and pieces," said Andín. "I saw you get the sword, I saw you on the way to Kingstown, and I saw you in the woods. You met a young woman there, and you..." Andín glanced around to make sure no one else was nearby.

"You saw me hide it," said Lynde, her voice soft.

"I did."

"Huh," said Lynde. "You dream about people often?"

"Only lately," said Andín. "My life's been... strange over the past couple of months."

"Mine, too," said Lynde. She groaned and leaned back against the iron bars of her cell. "So here's to having strange lives."

♦♦♦

The day turned to evening and night. Someone came to drop off food and light a torch on one of the walls, and that was all the light they had to see by. The food was terrible, as Lynde had said: cold gray paste spread over undercooked rice and bread. She ate it anyway.

Andín thought the princess might send for her, but she didn't. She chatted some more with Lynde, and they swapped stories about living in little villages halfway around the world from one another.

The only thing she didn't bring up was her demon. There wasn't much of a reason to, and while she found she liked Lynde, she had no idea if she could trust her.

At last Lynde rolled onto her little cot and began snoring loudly. Andín sat up, watching the torches gutter.

There would be no ransom. She would be left to rot here, captive of an unhinged princess with a grudge against Antriman and the Molascas, while whatever Judy Shashalnikya had wanted her to do went undone.

She slept and dreamed of the freedom of the grassy Shuyan steppe.

◆◆◆

The morning broke, and with it came Princess Diya in a terrible shrieking wrath. She first went to Lynde and hollered at her, over and over. "Tell me where it is! Where did you hide it? I'll come in there and pry your fingernails off; I'll make you tell me!"

Lynde sat still, enduring in her stoic way. The princess picked up a little bit of stone and hurled it at Lynde. It glanced harmlessly off her shoulder.

"Hey!" Andín protested, "Leave her alone!" The princess ignored her and threw another chunk at Lynde's leg. This one left an angry-looking red gash.

Lynde grimaced but said nothing. She didn't even cry out.

Princess Diya whirled on Andín at last. "And you! Demon girl! Did you tell your friend here that you're really a thousand year-old demon-emperor? Did you? Because I think she'll want to know. Askar Molasca, you old goat, I have you in my power at last!" she taunted. "You wouldn't give my father the time of day, but here you sit in my dungeon, in my house, in my kingdom! How does it feel, to be so powerless? How does it feel? Answer me!"

Andín, angry, opened her mouth to respond but caught Lynde shaking her head slightly, no. Let her rant herself out. Andín shut her mouth.

Diya caught the motion and went back to berating and throwing things at Lynde. After a while she left, trailed by two long-suffering Shadarant.

There was silence for a while. Then Lynde got up and started to wash off her wounds with the little bucket of water she had in her neat and tidy cell.

"Are you all right?" Andín asked, impressed by the other girl's stoicism.

"I am," said Lynde, a strange look in her eye. "Thank you for sticking up for me. ...What was that about being a demon? I haven't heard that one from her before."

Andín sighed, resigned. There was no hiding it now. "It's true, actually. I am."

Lynde cocked her head. "Huh. Okay."

Andín laughed. "I usually get more of a reaction than that!"

"Eh," said Lynde, shrugging. "A year ago I would have thought you were nuts. Then I got an obnoxious singing sword that belonged to a woman who's been dead for a thousand years. So. Tell me about it."

Where to begin? Andín took a deep breath and started at the beginning.

♦♦♦

She told Lynde an abbreviated version of the demon's story, leaving out a thing or two, but she told enough. She didn't say much about Yshe, but did tell her about the dreams, and the young Alavesh woman, and all of her travels and hardships.

Lynde listened intently through the whole thing. When Andín finished, Lynde shifted in her cell and tapped her fingers on the ground, thinking. Andín waited nervously.

"You swear that's all true?" Lynde asked at last. "Swear by the Goddess?"

"I swear it," said Andín, "by the Goddess."

"All right. Good," said Lynde. "Great. Demon girls. Why not? Wish it could get us out of here, but I had a singing sword and couldn't do much, either."

"There's one thing I didn't say," said Andín. "The woman from my dreams? I'm pretty sure she's Judy Shashalnikya herself."

Lynde blinked. "Really. Interesting. A ghost?"

"I don't know. She never explained. But… this is all connected. I'm sure of it. You, me, those holes in the world I told you about, everything. It all has to link up somehow."

"I'd agree, but how?" asked Lynde.

Andín shook her head. "I wish I knew."

♦♦♦

The evening came, and Princess Diya came down to the basement cells again. Her eyes slid past Lynde and fixed on Andín.

"You," she said. "Molasca girl. Why are you still here? Be ready for dinner in an hour."

And with that, she turned and left.

A Shadarant followed after her and put a key in Andín's cell door. "No magic," he said, "or it will go badly for you. Understand?"

Andín nodded slowly.

"Good. You're to be taken upstairs to have dinner with the princess. We have a room where you can change. Your things from Gantritt are there, but the princess strongly hopes you'll wear one of the gowns she's provided. Follow."

The Shadarant unlocked her cage and marched off up the stairs.

Andín exchanged a quizzical glance with Lynde and followed after him.

"Have a nice dinner," Lynde called after her. "Save some for me."

Chapter 19
The Sorceress Vi

The Shadarant brought her up two flights of stairs to a narrow, sparsely furnished room. There were a few crumbly pieces of wooden furniture, including a bed and bookcase, some old books, and a threadbare tapestry on the wall. The door shut behind her with a click. She tried the handle after a few moments—locked. The window was too narrow to squeeze through, and she was at least two stories up. There was no escape.

She could try blowing a hole in the wall. Her memories suggested that the demon's magic might be able to do that, and she'd seen its power herself on the grassy plains. But she might find herself thrown back again, and she didn't want to risk worse injury than she'd suffered downstairs.

Only one way to find out. She let a little of the dark energy that always lurked just beneath the surface lately pool around her, then pointed at the wall and said, softly, "*Shih.*" A very small wave of power pushed into the wall—and bounced back. She staggered a little as it hit her, and a book or two fell off the shelf, but that was all.

"Lesson learned," she murmured. She thought of something else and murmured a few words. The air immediately became warmer. Then, just as fast as it had come, the heat dissipated again.

The wards here were astonishing, and they were everywhere. Who were the wizards in this place? Andín desperately wanted to meet them.

Maybe they'd know something about demon lore and help her get out of here. Maybe they could even send the demon on its way back to Hular Molasca, and then she could go home. It was a happy fantasy.

She sighed and sorted through the clothes laid out on the bed. There were a few rather nice old-fashioned gowns that were likely too small for her, but she put these aside and found her own things. Here were the dresses Yshe had loaned her, freshly laundered.

Then there was the blue Shuyan riding outfit. That probably wouldn't go over well. Andín wished she still had the black men's clothing she'd worn to meet the emperor back in Palascena.

It occurred to her that she probably shouldn't provoke her unstable hostess. But maybe she ought to remind her that she was more than she seemed.

She shrugged out of her dress, another loaner from Yshe's plentiful wardrobe, and into the Shuyan riding outfit. It felt like putting on a part of herself she thought she'd left behind on the grassy plains. She immediately felt more at peace and centered.

She glanced in the mirror, checking her outfit. I rode across the steppe, she thought. I'm Andín dal Rovi. I can do anything.

Bored, she poked around the room and examined the few tattered, dusty books on the shelves. They were all written in Prytt. That was strange. She forced her way through a few pages, but her command of this language was too shaky. The demon hadn't learned more than the rudiments, apparently, and she couldn't hold it all in her mind. The books seemed to be children's fables, but she couldn't tell much more than that.

She looked around, wondering. The faded tapestry on the wall showed a fanciful scene of two people riding horses through an enchanted wood. Strange and wonderful things grew all around them, and odd but friendly creatures galloped alongside or hid in the trees.

This had been a child's room, she realized. Did the princess have children? She'd seen no sign of them in the house. Why would she allow her children to read Prytt, in any case? She poked around a little bit more and found a faded blue chest in a forgotten corner.

She opened it and withdrew little wooden horses and a doll. They were well-used and worn.

She put the toys back in the chest and dusted off her clothes. If there had been children here, they were long gone now.

Andín sat on the bed and waited, looking out the narrow window at the mountains rising to the east. Another part of the Vandan range, she thought. On the other side of those mountains was the broad Astanav River valley and plains, and then, even farther east, were the Yahzu mountains and then the varied vastness of the Antrimanian Empire. Maybe, a thousand miles and more to the east, the Emperor Hular sat in his rooms in Palascena. She wondered if he ever thought of her—or, more precisely, of the demon within her.

Memories of Palascena and home trickled into her consciousness. Some were her own. She remembered Viko Station and dinners with her parents and brother. The other memories seemed random. Long marches. Cold nights. Lovemaking with a woman or women, or sometimes a man. Youth. Middle age. Battle, exercise, hunting, dining, poring over papers, debating barons over finer points of policy. Death.

Lives upon lives upon lives.

She was lost deep in thought and memory when someone knocked on the door, telling her it was time to come down to dinner.

◆◆◆

Princess Diya arched an eyebrow at Andín's outfit. "There were some very nice gowns there," she said. "Were they not good enough for you?"

"I wore this when I rode across the plains of Shuyu," Andín replied simply.

"I see," said Diya. She herself wore another military-style tunic, this one a deep forest green. It had clearly been cut for a man. "Interesting."

"Thank you for having me for dinner," said Andín, trying to stay polite.

Diya laughed but said nothing further. A few others filed in and sat at the modest table in what might once have been a lavish dining room. A servant whisked in and delivered a plate of gristly sliced meat and runty-looking potatoes.

"I should make introductions, I think," said Diya in a ghoulish parody of a polite voice. "This is Orley, who is the commander of the troops here. He's been with me since the beginning. And this is Lokas; he's our security master and king of spies." Lokas nodded. "And this is Vi, who is my sorceress. I used to have a whole regiment of battle mages, but she's all that's left. Ingrates."

"Ah," said Andín, studying the sorceress. Vi had gray hair and more than a few lines on her face, but she didn't look particularly old. She reminded Andín of someone, but she couldn't quite place her. She returned Andín's gaze, her eyes cool and steady.

"Everyone, this is someone who wandered in off the street," said Diya, gesturing at Andín. "She's the Emperor of Antriman!"

Andín cleared her throat. "My name is Andín dal Rovi," she said. "I'm from Viko Station, Lofkandi Province, Antriman."

"You speak Alavesh very well," said Orley.

"Thank you," said Andín, deciding to keep explanations simple. "There are many Alavesh living in my country."

"I lived there," said the princess, stabbing a piece of meat with her fork. She gesticulated at Andín with it. "You all know that. I grew up in Antriman. I speak Antrimanian better than this country wench. Dressed as a Shuyan boy though she may be, that's what she is. Lofkandi! Ha!"

Lokas humphed a laugh, but the others clinked their forks against their plates in resigned silence.

"All of the better class of refugees from the First Prytt War went there," she continued, looking at Andín. "When the Prytt took the country, the nobles and their servants went, then everyone else followed. My family was there, too. Thousands and thousands of us! And did the Molascas care one bit for any of us? Did the demon-emperor ever bother to lift a finger to help his Alavesh subjects? No."

Andín bit her tongue. It wasn't her place to say anything, not now. She had to try and act nice.

Diya grinned at her. "I bet you'd like to blow me halfway across this room. I bet you found it doesn't work." She turned to the servant who had brought the meal out. "This is delicious, Polnya, thank you."

The servant bowed and hastily withdrew. Andín envied her escape.

The rest of the dinner was just as awkward. Princess Diya alternately talked logistics and strategy for Gantritt with her lieutenants as if she still commanded a massive army and heaped abuse on Antriman, the Molasca family, and Andín specifically.

She did notice that the one person who said nothing at all during the dinner was the sorceress, Vi.

Once the meal was done, Diya glared at Andín. "You may stay in the room you were in. For now."

"Thank you, Princess," said Andín, grinding her teeth as she bobbed her head.

"You do not have the run of the house," said Diya, "but you may move freely on that floor in that section. If we see you anywhere else, you'll be back downstairs with the thief." Her expression softened. "You see? I can be magnanimous."

She stood, banged her plate on the table to signal she was done, and left.

Andín looked around. No one else would meet her gaze except for Vi, who seemed lost in thought. Andín decided she'd had enough and so pushed back from the table and headed upstairs, trailed by a Shadarant.

◆◆◆

Long shadows stretched over the poorly-maintained, much-trampled lawn outside as the sun set. Andín watched darkness creep over the land, transfixed by the light and color after more than a day of captivity. She thought of Lynde in the basement and wished she could bring her upstairs or at least send her some better food.

There had to be connections here, but she still had no idea where to begin.

Frustrated, she focused her energies on the window and again let a little of it fly. It bounced back immediately.

"I can tell when you hit my shielding, you know," a voice said behind her. Andín started and whirled around. Vi herself stood in the door, a smile on her warm, lined face. "But it hardly matters. Not even you can get through them. The magic I use is even older than you are, believe it or not."

"Parts of me are very, very old," said Andín.

"Oh, I know," said Vi. "I know indeed, child. Yasharay, it's good to see you again."

Yasharay, Yasharay, Yasharay! Andín felt in her bones, the name, the Name. A terrible gnashing of teeth, the ripping of flesh, the red world engulfing her. She gasped, and the room returned to normal again.

Vi nodded sagely. "Ah. It hasn't revealed its name to you, yet, then? Perhaps trying to spare you. Yes? Is this why?"

Andín didn't dare answer. She could, for the first time in weeks, feel the demon as a separate entity from her. It lurked, considering, in the back of her mind.

Vi examined her with a practiced eye.

"Interesting," she said. "I had hoped you'd join me for some tea. I know that dinner wasn't terribly appetizing."

"I can't leave this floor," said Andín, hoping the sorceress would just go away. She was feeling frayed and shaky and wanted to be alone.

"That's fine," said Vi, pointing to the left. "I live in the next room over. Come with me, the tea is on." She gestured for Andín to follow and vanished out of sight.

Andín trailed after her, lured in by the bait Vi had deftly dangled in front of her.

♦♦♦

The sorceress' rooms were full of light, forcing back the gathering gloom outside. Balls of bright yellow and gold energy floated in the air, casting a warm honey glow over everything. Andín studied them intently; she'd never seen such a thing, not even from the great wizards in Palascena.

Books were neatly arranged on the shelves along with all manner of what Andín's demon memory identified as wizard tools. Here a round ball with a green vine in it, there a brick that changed colors as she watched, and over there a glove made of what looked like moss. The room was warmer than the rest of the tumbledown manor house, and it smelled like a chaotic mix of spices.

A tea kettle steamed and popped merrily on a raised platform in the middle of the room. Andín could see no fire or any other heat source. More magic?

Of course, magic. The whole room reeked of magic.

Vi sank into an overstuffed armchair with a happy sigh and waved Andín over to another chair opposite. She tapped the kettle, which leaped and burbled and glowed with the same honey light as the floating baubles.

"There, it's done. I have a lovely lemongrass green tea. Would you like some? I know Antrimanians love their tea."

"Please!" said Andín, eyes lighting up. Tea!

"We don't have much here to put in it, I'm afraid," said Vi.

"That's all right," said Andín. "I like it as is."

"Wonderful, so do I," said Vi. She poured the kettle's steaming contents into a waiting teapot, then after a minute or two poured a golden liquid into two pewter teacups. It smelled delicious. "Careful, it's hot."

Andín took hers and cradled it, relishing in the warmth spreading into her hands. "Thank you, this is lovely," she said, meaning it.

"Did you have much tea at home?" Vi asked lightly.

"Oh, yes," said Andín. "My mother made some every day. We ran the town shop, and Papa always had the best teas." She cocked her head at Vi. "You're speaking Antrimanian. I hadn't even noticed."

"You're a delightful polyglot," said Vi with a smile. "Is that all demon, or some of the girl, as well?"

"The demon," said Andín. "I was awful at languages before."

"Ah," said Vi. "In any case, I thought it might be nice for you to have a taste of home again."

"It *is* nice," admitted Andín wistfully. Tea, Antrimanian, such a warm and cozy room in this strange place...

She thought of her mother sipping her tea in the sunny breakfast room at home, chatting with her father while Palyar made eggs and she read the newspaper. Palyar would make jokes about eggs while her mother laughed.

A treasonous tear slipped down her face. "Oh," she said, wiping it away. "I'm sorry—"

"No need to be," said Vi gently. "You're so far from home, here on the other side of the world, and you've had to face so much already. Parts of you are very old, but the rest of you is so, so young."

Andín nodded, trying to contain her sniffles, and took a sip of the tea. It burned the roof of her mouth and scorched her throat, but it was absolutely delicious. "Thank you," she said when she trusted her voice again.

"You're welcome. I'm afraid you haven't been given much of a reception here so far," she said with a little sigh. "I had to insist that the princess let you out of that dank basement."

"I very much appreciate it!" said Andín. "There's another girl down there, too, did you know?"

"Oh, yes," said Vi. "Lynde, but the princess won't let her out for anything. Not until she gets that sword in her hand. Our princess is a little... well. *Focused* is a word I might use."

Andín snorted.

Vi shook her head sadly. "This has not been an easy decade for her," she said. "I know how she seems now, but she wasn't always like this. She led armies against the Prytt during the war, and the people of Alavia owe her a great deal. It was inspiring to follow her in those days."

"But she's cut off here in the mountains by the government," Andín said. "She's a threat to them."

"It's more than just that," said Vi. "Think about the room you're living in over there."

"I had wondered," said Andín. "Was there a child living here once?"

"Several, when the house was full. One of them was Diya's daughter, Lyshan. She lived in the room you're in now. Her son

Dalya lived on the opposite end of this hall." A shadow fell across Vi's face. "The government keeps them and her husband in Telesan now, under house arrest. She hasn't seen them in years."

"Oh," said Andín. She thought of her own family, far away in a place she could never get back to. "That's horrible."

"It is. You wonder why she acts the way she does. It's more a way to avoid thinking about her troubles than any actual madness, I believe. The government hasn't been kind. They don't want the family to be a rallying point, either," said Vi. "It's such a strange fear. The people of Alavia really and truly love Diya, but they don't want a queen. They prefer the republic; there's no chance they'll sweep the government out in favor of a restored monarchy, but the prime minister is utterly paranoid. So Diya has been cooped up here for nine years with next to nothing to do. You've seen her Shadarant?"

Andín nodded.

"There used to be thousands living at the house and in the village alone, not to mention all around the country. But they all vanished with the peace. Now she has maybe twenty diehards left here and a few dozen more in Gantritt. Most of the other Shadarant in East Gantritt don't report to her any longer; they're separate now. You and poor Lynde have nearly her entire attention, I'm sad to say."

"She doesn't really think Emperor Hular will ransom me, does she?" Andín asked.

"I don't know," replied Vi. "It's entirely possible. Or maybe she just wants to watch you writhe." She sipped her tea. "Ah, it's good today. But tell me a little about yourself."

Andín prepared to launch into yet another explanation of her travels when the sorceress held up her other hand.

"Not where you've been, mind. I've seen the world for myself. I want to know what you and that demon are doing. It seems you may not be entirely integrated yet. Is that so?"

Andín paused and thought about it. "I thought we were, but you showed me just now that I may be wrong. You know a lot about demons," she said.

"I do," said Vi. "More than anyone living, perhaps."

At last, after so long, someone who knew about demons. Andín thought and thought of what to say. "I don't think we're completely integrated yet," she said at last, "though I have access to so many memories, and I can do magic."

"The memories are the most difficult part," said Vi. "You'll experience memories that seem like your own but aren't your own. Are you overwhelmed by them? Is it constant?"

"No," said Andín thoughtfully. "Just a few at a time now. When I look for them."

"So the demon's learned," said Vi. "It... some of them, when they jump to a new host, flood them immediately. Insanity or at least a great deal of mental confusion can result, which is tricky for everyone."

Andín's heart leapt. *Other demons!* "There are others? Do you know anything about them? About demon lore?" She could barely ask the next question; she'd given up hope so long ago. "Can you help me?"

The sorceress Vi paused, teacup halfway to her lips. "There have been a very few others, at least here in this world. I don't know if any remain, but they did exist at one point. And as for help, that depends: what do you want?"

Andín shook her head. She wanted so many things that she couldn't sort it all out anymore. "I... I want to go home," she said at last. "I want my old life back."

"Do you? Really?"

Andín shrugged, thinking of Viko Station. Would she really be happy going back there to live as some provincial man's wife? She couldn't imagine it, not after everything.

Not after the steppe. Not after Yshe and the river. Not after Gantritt and the Shadarant.

"Maybe not," she said at last, "but I would like to see my family again."

"And do you want the demon gone from you?" pressed Vi.

The thought would once have filled her with joy and hope, but now it seemed less like the removal of a tumor and more like cutting off a limb. The prospect was a strangely lonely one. As she'd said to Yshe, she wasn't sure who she'd be without the demon now. "I don't know," she said. "I... I thought I would, but..."

"But now it's hard to tell where you end and it begins. And you've had a taste of its power, and it doesn't frighten you. Hm. I wondered if this would happen." Vi set her teacup down. "You have become highly integrated with it in a relatively short space of time. This is how these kinds of parasite demons work. You've got an old and powerful one, to be sure, but they're all the same at the heart. They jump into a host, and then become an integral part of whomever they're using to survive. Tell me, does it feel like you're losing yourself inside the demon?"

"No, actually," said Andín. She looked up at Vi. "I thought I would, but maybe... maybe it's the opposite? Or, at least, I think I feel like me." She balled her hands into fists, feeling that familiar, painful frustration. "I don't know. I don't know *what* I am!"

"Calm, calm," urged Vi, putting a hand on Andín's arm. "I know it's not an easy thing. You feel out of control for a while. It's so hard, especially when it happens to someone as young as you. You become unsure of who you really are."

Andín nodded miserably.

"It's all right to feel that way," said Vi. "The demon does change you. But everyone changes, and I know for a fact that the demon has changed far more than you have. It's normal to feel the way you do. You can get through it. Let me assure you, the actions you take are your own. The decisions you make are your own. After the first few weeks the demon can't control what you do unless you wish it."

Andín sighed. "It sounds like you've seen this happen a lot."

"I have," said Vi. "There are others like you, or at least there were once, long ago. Though I must admit I've met this demon before. Isn't that right?" she asked, changing the tenor of her voice to address the demon. "Why have you not shown her that yet?"

Shocked, Andín gasped as the demon stirred within her, asking for control. Andín allowed it to speak.

Andín's mouth moved without her for the first time in ages, as the demon spoke for itself. "*She is not ready.*"

"Of course she is; you're just embarrassed," said Vi. "You have become so human, Yasharay. Show her. She has a right to know you in full."

The demon hesitated, and then Andín was borne away in the wild river currents of its memory.

♦♦♦

There was a red world, somewhere below this one or maybe apart and aside from this one, and the demon lay there in wait. It had no gender, nothing familiar for Andín to latch onto. There it spent its time spinning its webs, hatching its alien plans, and feasting on the nectar that dripped up from the lowest of the below places. Nothing made sense, up was down, chaos and order mixed and laughed and laughed and laughed, and Andín felt her mind slip into the dark—*Hold*, the demon said. *Watch*, and his —her—its voice was Andín's own. *Come, come*, said the bright world, and the demon looked up. *Come!* A silvery hand reached down from above and grabbed hold.

It squealed and fought and unleashed its meager power against the hand, but it had no effect. It appeared into a horrible new world of light and freezing cold, and for a terrifying moment it had no body. It could feel itself start to break apart, scattering to the merciless winds.

Somewhere a voice spoke, high and clear. "You're sure?"

"I am. Do it!"

And then the demon was within a man, and the man and the demon warred with one another for many weeks. When at last they awoke, fused like metals heated and stuck together, they saw the face of a woman staring down at them.

"Good," the young sorceress Vi said. She had dark hair and no lines on her face but was otherwise much the same. "It's done, and now you have a demon inside you. You poor, arrogant fool."

♦♦♦

Andín gasped and returned to herself. The demon prowled

restlessly behind her eyes. She felt betrayed and scared. She looked agog at Vi.

"You," she said. "How...?"

"I am older than I look, hard as it is to believe," said Vi with a mischievous little shrug. "And yes, I helped a chief of the Antroi Men take a demon into himself so he could become powerful and unite his people. He did it, too. He had a terrible time controlling the magic, it was so wild and dangerous to him, but he became very powerful indeed. Everyone feared him. He won many victories, and by the time he died he was the undisputed king of all the river people. His life was short, the stress of the demon was too much, but when it passed to his son it was much tamed. Every time it becomes more like us, more human. Despite that, as you must be aware, it is still a demon. It's from a different world, a place created by an intelligence we can't possibly fathom, which would be a terror of heat and insanity for people like us."

Andín shook and trembled, remembering the nauseating, mind-bending red world. "I... I didn't know."

"No reason you should. This happened almost a thousand years ago now. Even the demon barely remembers it, but that is where your magic comes from."

Dark energies flowed around her. This is what's inside of me, Andín thought, feeling cold. This is where my magic comes from. I draw it from the red world.

"This is what it didn't want you to see," said Vi. "If you had, you might have tried to send it back there."

"What? Send it back? Can that be done?" Andín asked.

"It can," said Vi, but she held up a hand before Andín could say anything else. "But you should know: the demon has been so changed by its long life here that going back to the red world would be very difficult and likely fatal for it. It couldn't survive there, not as it is now."

Is that true? Andín wondered.

The demon rustled in her mind. Again she heard that familiar mental voice, very soft but once again distinct. «*Yes. I believe... I could not go there. Not the way I am now. I would have to change*

*in many ways to go home again. I don't believe I can change in those
ways. It would kill me.»*

She could taste its fear. She knew it—he—she—was telling the
truth.

"Can the demon be put back into Hular?" she asked, carefully
stepping around pronouns.

"Maybe," said Vi, "but I know for a fact that the wizard Syr
fan Porlab has guarded against that. There is a very specific barrier
around Antriman now, and it's keeping you—and the demon—
out. Syr knows the flavor of the red world's magic, and he knows
how to guard against it. It's different from the magic of this
world—the energies are very different—but it can be guarded
against. They're very powerful, the wizards of Palascena. So am I,
of course, but there might be... consequences... for both of you,
even if it could be done."

"Like what?"

"Neither of you might survive it with your minds intact," Vi
said grimly.

"Oh," said Andín. "Then... what do I do?"

"That's for you to decide," said Vi. "You can do one of four
things. First, you could try to send the demon back to the red
world and pick up your life where you left off, if possible." Andín's
eyes widened. "All of your demon memories and powers would
vanish," Vi continued, "and if we could convince the emperor
that it was truly gone, and you were no threat you might even
be able to return to Antriman. But that could kill the demon—it
would certainly be very painful for it. The process might damage
you, too: be aware of this. You and the demon are very closely
intertwined. The chance of damage to your mind and body is not
insignificant."

Andín nodded, scarcely daring to breathe.

"Second," Vi said, ticking them off on her fingers, "we could try
to pass the demon on to Hular Molasca. But this has its problems,
too, as I've said. It may not even be possible, and you may both
suffer greatly if it fails."

"I see," said Andín. She could feel the demon's worry building.

"Third, we could put the demon into someone else. This would work well enough, I think, though it wouldn't exactly be easy to accomplish. We'd have to trick the demon into thinking you'd died so it would jump. But we'd have to find someone to, ah, infect." She smiled thinly at Andín. "That would be good for you but bad for them, unless we can find someone who wants a demon." Vi sighed. "I could think of a few who might, but none of them is a person I'd want to have that kind of power." She glanced at the door, clearly thinking of Princess Diya. "Even then, the demon might just jump to your closest living relative, trying to follow the pattern I set down a thousand years ago."

"And the fourth thing?" Andín asked, thinking of Palyar.

"You do nothing. You choose to accept who and what you are, and you live this way."

Andín scrunched her hands against her eyes. "There... there must be something else. Some other option."

"I'm afraid there isn't," said Vi. "Those are your choices. Which do you prefer?"

Andín shook her head. "I don't know," she said, miserable. "I don't know what I want."

"That's not a surprise. It's a difficult decision, which is why I've done my best to be as honest as I can with you." She gave Andín a penetrating look. "I know it isn't easy to sort your feelings out on this, but it is of great importance that you do so. When you're ready to decide, come and see me."

"Why? Why is it so important?" Andín wondered.

"Because you matter, Andín," said Vi. "Trust me. You do."

"Just because I hold the demon," Andín sighed. Judy Shashalnikya had said much the same thing.

Vi shook her head and smiled. "And for so many other reasons, as well."

◆◆◆

That night Andín lay in the narrow, creaking bed that had once belonged to Diya's daughter, running the options through her mind.

What to do?

She found that despite everything, she didn't want the demon to die. It—she wasn't sure how else to think of it now—had been part of her too long. She had remembered the demon as the emperor doing terrible things, but she had seen great kindness, too, and it had helped her when she needed it. The demon seemed much more like an actual piece of her now than a horrible infection.

That was likely just what it wanted her to think, but it felt true.

Sending the demon back to Emperor Hular seemed out of the question. The Emperor's wizards were too strong. There was no way to tell what would happen if they failed, either. She worried about that—what if after all this, she ended up as broken as Old Mama Yava from the children's stories anyway? What kind of life would that be? It wasn't worth the risk.

She didn't want to force the demon on to another unsuspecting person, either. That wasn't fair, and she knew she wouldn't be able to live with herself. Maybe she could find someone to take him, though... But how? She thought briefly of Princess Diya, but that thought was unsettling in the extreme. What might an already demented and bitter woman do with demon powers? And, as Vi had said, the demon might just jump to a family member like Palyar anyway.

She sighed. The last choice... she didn't want to stay like this forever.

Did she?

Judy Shashalnikya had said she was important. So had Vi. But was she important only because she carried a demon within her?

Or was there another reason? She just wasn't sure anymore.

When sleep came at last, she was no closer to a decision.

That night she dreamed of her brother playing his fiddle. She and the demon, who looked just like Andín but with red tattoos on its arms and face, danced together while Palyar fiddled and stomped his foot, and they all laughed and sang along.

◆◆◆

The next morning Diya came up the stairs, flanked by guards. She had an unusually sober look in her eyes.

"You," she said, pointing at Andín, "come with us."

"Where are we going?" Andín wanted to know.

"*Come*," Diya commanded. "The sorceress says you should see it, too, though God and Goddess know why."

Andín shrugged and followed.

♦♦♦

To Andín's surprise, Lynde Shevariat squinted in the bright sunlight of the lawn in front of the house.

"They let you out!" Andín exclaimed.

"She... she said I should see it, I might know something," murmured Lynde. She was bound hand and foot. "It's so *bright* out here."

"No more talking!" snapped Princess Diya. The sorceress Vi appeared next to her, her face lined with worry. "Follow!"

The princess strode ahead. She had dressed in yet another sharp-looking military uniform. She marched with purpose; Andín could almost see why men had followed her for so long.

She led them to the edge of the woods and down a path to a spot overlooking a ravine. She stopped and pointed downwards.

"There," she said, turning to Andín, eyes full of something approaching nervousness. "Demon, explain that to me."

Andín looked, and her heart skipped a beat. There, in the chasm below, was another blank space, another hole in the world.

Chapter 20
Judy's Sword

The nothing space was suspended in midair, but it seemed to extend both above and below where it was fixed. One of the Shadarant guards had to look away; another started to shiver violently. To her credit, Diya Shashalnikya stared directly at it, her gaze unflinching.

"Well, Molasca girl?" she demanded, still looking at the hole. "Tell me what that is. You're a thousand years old. You must know."

"I..." said Andín, her mouth dry. "I've seen something like that before. But... it's only been recently. In the past six months."

"And what is it?" Diya demanded.

Andín caught the eye of the sorceress. Her expression was perfectly neutral.

"I don't know," said Andín after a moment. "I wish I did. I saw one on the border between Antriman and Shuyu, and another in Azu. They seem to appear at random."

"Or they're following you!" Diya said, her eyes wild again.

"No, that can't be right," said Lynde, stirring at last. "The matriarch of the temple in Kingstown said something about holes in the world. She must have meant this."

"Did she?" said Diya dryly.

"Yes," insisted Lynde. "They thought it had something to do with the sword. That's why you need to let me go. I need to return the sword to Judy Shashalnikya's grave. That will fix it!"

"Superstitious nonsense! That sword belongs to me!" Princess

Diya snapped. "I—"

But her gaze was drawn downward again.

"You say there are more," she said after a moment. "Do they disappear again?"

"I don't think so," said Andín. "I haven't heard of that. I think they stay."

"If there are more and more and more of these, and they keep appearing," said the princess, "then eventually they will overwhelm the world. Will they not?"

"They might," said Lynde.

Andín blanched. The thought was sickening.

Diya glared at her. "Is this some trick of yours, demon?"

"No," said Andín, shaking her head. "I swear by the Goddess."

"I can fix it," said Lynde evenly. "Just let me go."

Princess Diya seemed at war with herself. Then, without another word, she turned on her heel and marched back to the house. The Shadarant herded them along behind.

♦♦♦

They waited under guard in the foyer of the crumbling manor house while Princess Diya met with her advisors. They'd tied them both to chairs for good measure.

"Do you think the sword will really fix this?" asked Andín. "How?"

Lynde shrugged. "No idea. But everybody at the temple seemed to think returning it to Judy Shashalnikya's grave would make a difference somehow. Even the sword's convinced."

"So you weren't making that up," said Andín.

"No," said Lynde. "If I had, I would have thought up a better story."

At that moment the sorceress stepped out of the room where she'd been meeting with the princess.

"Well?" asked Andín.

"The princess wants you to fix that hole," said Vi. "Both of you."

"How?" asked Andín.

Vi merely looked at them.

"So you'll let me go," said Lynde. "I can go to Salaz with the sword."

"Ah, no," said Vi. "She wants you to fix this specific hole. Right now."

"That isn't what I'm supposed to do," insisted Lynde. "The sword's supposed to go to Judy Shashalnikya."

"You may find," Vi said gently, "that the sword has many uses, and when combined with demon magic it may provide a temporary... calming effect on what's happening to the world."

"How do you know?" Andín asked. "Do you know what those things are?"

"Go and find the sword," said Vi, ignoring Andín's questions. "Those are the orders of the princess. She promises not to take it from you, especially if it proves to be useful."

Lynde folded her arms over her chest, her face like granite.

Vi sighed. "It's the only chance you're going to get to complete your mission, Lynde. Now go get the sword. The Shadarant will ride with you."

♦♦♦

They rode down the narrow road towards the village below. Lynde clung to Andín, who was glad she'd worn her Shuyan riding outfit again.

"I hate horses," said Lynde through clenched teeth.

"You do? Why?"

"I just do. Too alive. Why couldn't we walk?"

"Right," said Andín, trying to think of a way to distract her. "Um, so you've considered that this is just a way for her to get her hands on the sword and capture us again?"

"I know," said Lynde. "But we do need it, so we're stuck. Tell you what, if she tries anything, we can run for it. I'm good at that."

"Where are we headed?" asked Andín.

"Tell you when we get near it."

They rode on in silence for a while longer. Their Shadarant guard trailed behind.

"Here," said Lynde. "Stop here."

She slipped off the back of the horse and disappeared into the woods with her pack. She returned a few minutes later, and Andín helped her back up.

"Did you get it?" Andín asked.

"Ride," said Lynde. Andín shrugged and urged the horse forward.

They rode in complete silence for a few minutes. Then Lynde said, "No. I didn't get it," in a low voice so the Shadarant guard couldn't hear. "It wasn't there. But if they were going to attack us and take it, they would have just now. We'd know, and the sword would be safe."

"Good plan," said Andín in admiration. "You really thought this through."

"I had a lot of time to think down there," said Lynde. "We're going to have to circle back into the woods. We can take that path over there; I remember it. I did a lot of running and hiding when they were after me the first time." She pointed to a dirt trail running into the pine forest. Andín nudged the horse onto the side trail.

♦♦♦

They rode through the thick forest, the bored Shadarant trailing behind until at last they turned off the path again. They eventually came into a small clearing with a great gray rock in the center. Lynde slipped off the horse and ran up to the rock. Her hand darted into a little crevice, and her face lit up as she withdrew something long, wrapped in rags.

"Here it is," she said, unwrapping it. She held the rusty, thin piece of metal up to the sky. "Judy Shashalnikya's sword. Nice, huh?"

"Looks its age," said Andín.

"It was on the bottom of the ocean," Lynde said. "My ex-husband found it in a net. Figures. He should have brought up some fish instead." She closed her eyes. "I can hear its song again," she said. "It's been so long."

"I don't hear it," said Andín, disappointed.

"Not everyone does," said Lynde, "but it's doing it, don't worry." She carefully re-wrapped the sword. "I thought it was annoying when it would just sing and sing and sing all day and night, but I guess I missed it. Huh." Her eyes widened as she looked beyond Andín. "You."

Andín whirled around to where Lynde was looking. A ghostly vision of Judy Shashalnikya stood in the clearing with them. The two Shadarant guards stood stock-still.

"Hurry," she whispered, and then vanished again.

"I saw her," said Lynde. "Right here. I saw her."

"That's Judy Shashalnikya," said Andín. Lynde raised an eyebrow, nonplussed. "We need to get back to the house. Right now."

Chapter 21
The Hole in the World

Princess Diya stared hungrily at the sword in Lynde's hand. They were back at the overlook with several Shadarant and the sorceress.

"When this is done..." Diya said.

"I can't make promises," Lynde said. "We'll have a lot to do first." She turned to Vi and Andín. "Now what?"

"Do what you think you must," said Vi.

Andín felt that dark energy swirling around her. It tasted the sword and reached out for the hole in the world.

She had the sudden sense that a piece could be put back here. She only had to get close enough.

If only she could get inside.

But that seemed like the worst kind of stupidity. It seemed like suicide.

And yet she was utterly certain that they could fix it.

She closed her eyes and thought of home. Then she steeled herself and made her choice.

"Come on," she said, grabbing Lynde's hand.

To her credit, Lynde didn't protest, even when Andín led her up onto the ledge.

"We—we need to jump into it," explained Andín.

Lynde nodded soberly. "I thought so. The sword's song is louder than it's ever been." She pulled the rusty sword from the scabbard and grabbed Andín's hand. "When you're ready, demon girl."

"Now," commanded Andín, squeezing Lynde's hand. They jumped out into space.

Lynde and Andín hit the event horizon of the hole and were immediately engulfed by nothingness.

◆◆◆

The world is a dream, something whispered in her ear. *And now we wake. Now we wake.*

Andín opened her eyes, but there was nothing there for them to focus on. She tried to call on her dark energy, but it failed to respond to her. She felt naked and alone, stripped of herself, hollowed out. She seemed to float in the middle of the nothingness. She glanced up and saw the tear in the world overhead. She knew she was alive only because of the protective magic of the demon and whatever powers Lynde's sword contained.

But where was Lynde? She felt woozy, unsteady, and imbalanced.

There. Lynde floated near her, holding the sword in her hand. It glowed steadily, but she could tell it was lacking something.

"Lynde!" she called. "Over here!"

Lynde looked at her, frowning. "Andín!" she said "Asoya a kshalve na yo? Pelayara damrashna?"

"What? What language is that? Lynde, what...."

"Ya shera ya ve," Lynde said. She reached out her hand for Andín.

Andín shook her head, uncomprehending. Lynde had spoken Alavesh, she knew that. But she couldn't understand a single word of it.

Something was dreadfully wrong. She felt weak, lighter, alone.

She looked beneath her and saw a thin line stretching down into a great, blood-red crack.

The red world.

She grabbed hold of the line. "Wait there!" she shouted to Lynde, though she knew she was speaking only Antrimanian, and Lynde wouldn't be able to understand. "I'll come back!" She began to pull herself along the line, down towards the pulsing red crack.

◆◆◆

She pulled for what seemed like hours or even days. Her arms ached, though the pulling was no effort at all.

She sang as she pulled:

"Come home, sing home
Men come over the hill
Swing pail, sweep floors
Men come through the dale

Wander far, travel near
Men march home, march home
Sing home, come home
Come home, sing home."

She sang in modern Antrimanian. She couldn't remember the words in the old language, and she guessed at the tune. Why couldn't she remember? The words, though, she knew by heart. So she sang.

She looked ahead and saw the great pulsing gash of the red world there, starting to fill her vision. Andín pulled onwards.

♦♦♦

She saw a small figure crouched on a small plane by the line to the red world, and she slowed as she drew up to it. She couldn't quite see the edges of its jagged, scaly form.

She knew it at once, of course.

"So there you are," she said, and knew at last why she felt so strange. She was alone in her head, only herself and nothing and no one else, for the first time since Viko Station.

She reached out and put a hand on the demon's soft, cold shell.

"Yes," the demon croaked, and its froglike voice was like nothing she'd ever heard. It looked sad, small, and alone. She pulled up to where it crouched and sat on the small plane next to it. "The... the hole. We became separate. Between, where we have come, it's like this. All travel alone."

"I haven't felt like this in so long," she said in wonder. "It feels... lonely."

"Yes, to me as well," said the demon. It seemed even more indistinct to her now, almost as if it couldn't hold its form. It seemed to shift under her hand.

It glanced down into the sea of redness.

"That's home for you, isn't it?" she asked.

"My world. Red world. Another place. Your world is so *bright*. I forgot how it hurt at the start."

Andín looked at the dark threads of the line she held in her other hand, and followed with her eyes as they spiraled down and down towards the red world. "You could go home."

It stirred. "It is not home now. So long in your world... I can never go back. I am changed. As you are changed."

"Yes," she admitted, sitting on the little plane with the demon. "I thought... I thought I would be happy if you left me for good. But I'm so used to you, now. And... I need you, don't I? If I want to help fix that up there." She raised her head. Far above was a bright rip, through which she could see the blue of the sky.

She looked around. There were other rips and tears up above her, so far away.

But farther away there was a cacophony of bright whorls, pulsing green discs, blue balls, and bright shining suns.

How many worlds were there? It had to be thousands.

She ran her hand over the demon's shell. This seemed to calm it.

She opened her mouth and sang again. "Come home, sing home," she sang quietly, and she remembered the tune.

The demon seemed to ripple with contentment or perhaps grief and then joined her song. It sang in the ancient Antrimanian language, gone a thousand years.

They sang together, voices intermingling, becoming whole again.

When at last they fell silent, she sat and thought for a long time.

"I used to wonder," she said at last with a wistful sigh. "I used to think that I didn't have any idea who I was, and what I wanted. Back in Viko Station... I thought I was the kind of person who would run away to the city and be famous."

"I remember," said the demon softly.

"You would, wouldn't you? That seems so long ago. I wanted to run away so badly. I thought I'd be happy if I could get to the city and go to the university. I thought I'd be happy if I could travel and see the world. That seemed like everything to me. And then I thought I would be happy if I could just be free of you. Now here we are. And... I don't know who I am without you."

"Humans are always becoming something new," said the demon. "You never stop changing. You'll change with or without me."

"You're probably right," she said, voice tinged with bitterness. "Maybe I'll never figure out who I am, no matter what happens."

"Maybe," said the demon. "Or maybe you know yourself better than you think."

"Do I? I wonder," said Andín. She glanced up at the gash overhead again.

The demon said nothing, but she could feel its slow consideration.

"The sorceress said I'd have to choose," Andín said. "Tell me. Do you wish you could go back to your red world?"

"No," said the demon. "I doubt I would survive there. I would miss this world. What I like best... I like to be in your world. I like to be out under the sky, in the sunshine. I like the rain and the wind and the smell of flowers. I wouldn't know what to do in the red world now. Nothing changes there. In your world... everything changes all the time."

She patted its hard shell again and stood, lost in thought.

"What do you want to do then?" she asked after a long pause.

"I want to go back," said the demon. "I miss the sun and the sky. It's a little painful, even now. But it's beautiful, too. And I want to be with you."

Andín dal Rovi sighed. "Damn it all. I thought I wanted to be rid of you. But I don't think that's what I really wanted. I think I just wanted to choose for myself. So... all right. I've chosen. Come on." She held out a hand. "We can work together for a little while longer, can't we?"

She felt its hope and its joy, and she smiled.

"Let's go find Lynde," she said. "Then we can start fixing the world."

The demon reached out a spindly limb and touched her hand. At once, they fused together again. Andín felt her—the demon's—*their*—power return, and the demon whispered *thank you* into her mind's ear before sinking back into her subconscious, that old arrogance wholly gone.

Did I make you this way? she wondered. But no, there had long been kindness, humility, and grace in the demon.

As there had been in her.

♦♦♦

Andín looked with newly powerful vision and immediately spotted Lynde Shevariat still hovering far, far above her. Andín gathered her power, spooling it up out of the red world and into her hands, and flew quickly up through the darkness toward her.

"Andín, you came back!" Lynde called, astonished. Andín almost wept in relief, she could understand her again. "I thought you'd gone for good! Where are we?"

"Between," said Andín. "Here. Grab onto me."

"You said that before we jumped," Lynde reminded her.

"We can do this," said Andín. "What does the sword tell you?" It was still glowing dully in Lynde's hand.

"Nothing—it went quiet as soon as we hit the hole," Lynde said. She flapped her arms uselessly, her usual equilibrium shattered.

"Here," said Andín, taking her hand.

Lynde's stopped spinning. "Oh! It's singing again," she said. "Huh. Okay. Good! Let's go up." She pointed the sword up at the hole and, little by little, they ascended.

Help us, Andín prayed to the God and Goddess, thought she wasn't sure they could hear her here. She put a hand on Lynde's sword, which flared as bright as the sun.

Andín fell at once into a deep sleep.

♦♦♦

Trees, rocks. Trees, rocks, water. Water, water, fish, rocks, trees, grass. A thousand years, a million years, ancient rocks and falling water, here. Here. Here. Here. This place.

Place, come. Come home. Be healed.

She saw the place in her mind's eye, though she had never seen it before. She saw it, she felt it, she could touch it. The sword's bright magic and her dark, red world energy combined, the elemental forces of two worlds, and remade what had been lost.

She could feel the presence of Lynde, her bright and industrious soul working furiously to build and repair and heal.

Lynde is magic, Andín thought, far more than I ever realized.

They made and made, and then Andín lost herself in the burbling, bubbling water...

◆◆◆

She awoke to something jabbing her in the side.

"Hey," said Princess Diya. She was poking Andín with her cane. "Hey, you. Demon girl."

"Ugh," Andín said groggily.

"You did it."

Diya pointed up at the cliff face with the cane. There, high above, water fell freely from the rocks. Trees and grass grew on the banks. Fish swam in the clear mountain water, and birds sang overhead.

Lynde stirred next to her, sword still in hand.

"We did it," said Andín.

"Yeah?" said Lynde, rubbing the back of her neck. "Great." And with that, Lynde collapsed back onto the grass. Diya regarded them for a moment more and started making her way laboriously back up the steep hillside toward the house.

The sorceress crouched next to Lynde. "She'll be fine," Vi said to Andín as she laid a hand on Lynde's forehead. "She's just exhausted."

Andín felt like passing out herself, but she managed to focus on Vi.

"We healed the hole. Didn't we?"

"Yes and no. It's only temporary," said Vi. "It helps. For now. But it doesn't solve the larger problem."

"What's happening?" Andín asked. "Out there in the world. You know, don't you? I saw the way you looked at the hole, like you'd been expecting it."

Vi fixed her with a look of pure, aching grief. "The world is dying. And now that you've fixed one hole, everything has been set into motion at last. The end will come very rapidly. You must finish your mission quickly. Now, perhaps, you see why you're important."

As Andín tried to digest that, two Shadarant came to help them back up the side of the hill. Two more carried the still unconscious Lynde and her sword.

Andín could only laugh as they were brought back to the manor house, where they were installed in two sumptuous bedrooms under heavy guard. She fell asleep reliving memories of the demon's first days with the sorceress, a thousand years ago.

◆◆◆

Princess Diya came to see her the next morning, once she'd bathed, dressed, and eaten. Andín and Lynde had gathered in the room Andín was staying in.

"Vi said there are many other holes in the world," Diya said to them. "She also says you can fix it."

"Yes," Lynde said, her voice even and calm.

"You have a lot of faith in yourself," said Princess Diya tartly. She seemed to wrestle with herself for a moment, and then she sighed angrily and fixed them both with a glare. "So. My family said my great ancestor lies in Salaz, in the north of Selessia. Now you know."

"Salaz," said Lynde. "That's what the sword said, too."

"Did it, now?" muttered Diya.

"So… that's in Selessia?" Andín asked. She'd never heard of a place called Salaz.

"Yes," Diya said. "In the north, beyond Salasee. Where the mountains and the sea come together, or so my grandfather used to say."

"It's a start," said Lynde.

"Thank you," said Andín.

Diya's glare deepened. "The sword belongs to me by rights. You are impudent for keeping it, Lynde Shevariat. But in this case I'll allow you to keep it to complete your mission—on the condition that you bring it back to me when you're done! Understand? I want it back."

Lynde nodded. "Of course. Deal."

They shook hands. Andín wanted to laugh at the absurdity of all of it.

"I've spent nine long years confined here," Diya Shashalnikya said, and for a moment her voice and eyes were clear. "But I have not lost all perspective. These things are a threat to my Alavia. I've dealt with threats before, but nothing like this. I can't defeat this with armies, or so Vi tells me. So."

She looked over at Andín. "I suspect there's a reason you're both here, and I suspect that my infuriating sorceress is at the bottom of it all. I hate coincidence. But... I know in my heart that Hular Molasca is like as not glad to be rid of you. So you're free to go and fix things. Both of you. Go before I change my mind."

They both sprang to their feet and ran off to pack.

♦♦♦

A horse was waiting for them at the entrance to the manor house. Princess Diya herself waited, flanked by her guards.

"I have only one horse to spare, but you may borrow it if you can ride," said the princess. "One of my men will return it after you leave for Telesan on the train."

"Thank you," said Andín and Lynde together.

"You may also have these packs we put together. Clothes, food, a bit of money, other things you may need. You're to take them and use them."

"We appreciate it," said Andín.

"Hm," said Diya. "Take a gun or two, as well. I have many." She gestured to a pile of war-surplus pistols on the ground. Andín took one and tucked it into her pack. Lynde demurred.

"Is the sorceress here?" Lynde asked.

"No," said Diya, some of the old anger returning to her voice.

"She left yesterday. Her rooms are empty. No one has seen her. That's why I only have one horse; she took the other one."

Andín started to laugh.

Diya scowled. "Hear this, demon Molasca: I charge you both with the elimination of these... these holes. Don't you dare return to my domain until you've done as I command. In the name of the Princess Royal of Alavia, I, Judiya Aruka Alyshaane Shashalnikya an-Palascena, you are so charged." She handed each of them a small, round token with her seal on it. "Now get out of here and come back with my sword soon."

They rode out of the yard and onto the dusty road that led to the village.

♦♦♦

Lynde and Andín rode through the tall woods. Lynde, a little calmer on the horse this time, fiddled with the sword.

"I swear, it seems less rusty," she said.

Andín nodded absently, lost in thought. It felt good to be on the road again.

Her past flowed around her, bright faces surfacing in whirling dark energy. Her parents, Palyar, Valsin, the boy on the road to Azu, Yshe, the nomads, Lynde. Vi. Princess Diya.

She had a purpose and a direction at last. She bent all her will towards it. She would find a way to save them all. The demon stirred.

Yes, it said. *We will.*

PART THREE

Chapter 22
Telesan

Andín dreamed.

She walked with Palyar over the hill and sat herself on the wash pot.

"I'm the Queen of Wash Pot Land," she informed him, "and you're my knight!"

He sighed. "It's time for that to end, Deeny. Nothing lasts forever. It's time to wake up."

The old, beaded ranter from Roshden was there, and he shook his head sadly. "It's all someone else's dream," he said, "and what happens to us when she wakes?"

The pot cracked and vanished into itself, leaving only a deep hole in the ground where it had been. Andín stared down into it, and then suddenly she was falling, falling...

She jolted to a halt, her skin prickling and hair standing on edge. Something was wrong. She looked around. There was a curtain. Curious, she pushed it aside and walked into brightness.

Andín found herself in an unfamiliar room. She wandered through, certain that she was both there and not-there. She caught glimpses of people chatting and talking, and then she caught a breathtakingly familiar voice.

Yshe!

Sure enough, there she was. She stood in a parlor somewhere, drink in hand. She was talking with someone in Alavesh. They talked of nothing. The weather. Friends. Things seen in the city.

Telesan, Andín knew. They were somewhere in the Alavesh capital.

"Yshe!" Andín cried. "Yshe! I'm here!" But Yshe couldn't see or hear her.

Yshe separated from her companion and went to the window. It faced to the east, though it was dark out. Andín knew this for certain.

Her mouth moved, two syllables formed. *Jandy.* Or maybe it was *Andín.*

"Yshe!" Andín screamed. "See me!"

Yshe sat on the window bench and sipped her drink.

"Yshe, I'm sorry! I'm sorry I didn't come," Andín said. "I waited, I did! I meant to come. I thought you—I'm so sorry. I wish I'd stayed. I know you would have found a way to get me out of Gantritt. You're so clever and resourceful. You would have."

She put her hand on the woman's shoulder; it seemed to pass right through her. "Oh, Yshe," whispered Andín, her heart breaking.

Yshe looked up, as if she had heard. Her mouth formed the syllables.

Andín.

Andín reached for her, but the scene broke apart. She saw a ring of mountains surrounding a little valley near the sea, and there the sorceress Vi walked up and over a hill and down to a little house. At last Andín remembered where she'd seen her before—a dream, much like this one. Vi was standing in the doorway. The two women, each exactly like the other, touched hands.

"They're together, they've fixed one break already, and they're on their way," said the Vi who had arrived.

"At last," the other Vi murmured. "And in time, too. Well done."

"It may not be in time," said Vi. "The situation outside is getting much worse."

"Yes," said the old woman. "It is. But that isn't your concern. Come to me."

There was a surge of light, and where two identical women had stood now was only one.

Hurry, whispered Judy Shashalnikya as Andín woke.

She was aboard the train again. She glanced out the window; she could see trees whipping past in the dark gray predawn light. Lynde snored beside her.

She lay awake as they rolled into the mountain city of Markorae, worry and fear chasing one another around her head.

◆◆◆

They changed trains in Markorae, a tumbledown city that Lynde said was the capital of whatever Alavesh province this was. The steep mountains and pine forests gave way to rocky hillsides and then to a green-gray, gently rolling plain.

This countryside looked so like home, thought Andín, except that the sun shone less brightly here. She could almost believe that they'd pass by Viko Station.

Lynde stared out the window, a thoughtful expression on her face. Andín didn't want to bother her, so she took out *Shashalnikya's Song* and read passages of it to kill time as they chugged through the flat, featureless plains of northwest Alavia.

The forsaken General delivered her child
Boy of destiny, great king in waiting
And went with Dal an Gantritt to the far north.
Kind men and women bore the babe to Alyshaane
Princess, now Queen, who waited in Stonehold still
A birth, and the loss of her General
A joy and a loss, for Shashalnikya never returned.

She'd given herself for this land, thought Andín. She'd sacrificed everything, including her life, so that Alavia could go on. The train crossed a wide river, then passed through a series of industrial towns, each of which was more depressing than the last.

At last, as the sun set again, they pulled through the filthy industrial suburbs and slums of Telesan. Factories belched smoke into the air in the midst of dense, desperate-looking neighborhoods. The Alavesh capital seemed even more dark and dreary than

Roshden, which Andín had traveled through what felt like a lifetime ago. A smoky haze hung over the entire place.

"Wow," said Lynde, watching the city go by. "Nice."

"'Nice'? Really?" asked Andín, agog. Lynde seemed to use that word to describe everything.

"Better than Kingstown," said Lynde with a shrug. "I like big places like this. Debanae, where I got off the boat, was the same way. Smaller, but a lot like this. There's a lot of movement and action here."

At last they arrived at the station nestled between the river and the great hilltop complex of government buildings and palaces. They gathered their things and went out into the station to wait. Andín checked the tickets to Salasee they'd bought in Markorae; the time listed was three hours ago. Had their connecting train left? She asked a man in a ticket booth.

"Oh," he said gruffly. "That again, happens all the time. Here." He took their tickets to Salasee and ground them up. New tickets were issued. "This one leaves tomorrow at noon. The lines from Markorae are always running late, see." He didn't seem very apologetic about it.

Andín was about to say something about the lines in Antriman always being on time, but swallowed her tongue. That probably wouldn't help her any.

"It looks like we'll have to stay the night here," she said. "The train doesn't leave until tomorrow. We can try to find a place here in the city..." She looked around. People were sleeping on the rows and rows of benches.

"We don't have much money," said Lynde. "Maybe we should stay here."

Andín looked around and sighed. She'd stayed in worse places, but this would rate near the bottom of the barrel. The station looked like it had once been very grand, but there were barely patched holes in the roof and entire sections roped off where it looked like the structure had begun to cave in.

"I can buy us a room," she said. "We shouldn't pass up a warm bed if we can get one."

Lynde shrugged. "You're the boss."

They gathered their belongings and headed out into the busy station square.

◆◆◆

Telesan was somewhat reminiscent of Palascena from fifty years ago, though it was far more modern than backwater Gantritt or Azu. There were gas lamps set up everywhere, and horses drawing coaches clopped over cobblestone streets. A few puffing motorcars fought their way through the throngs of horses and people. Everyone here wore suits of somber black and gray.

They walked down a well-lit lane, Andín drawing open stares and hushed conversations because of her blue Shuyan outfit and foreign complexion. They probably think I'm a Shuyan myself, she thought. If they know what a Shuyan is.

They walked through narrow streets up a steep, overbuilt hill and then entered a huge square at its summit. There in front of them was a massive, blocky stone building with the white and red Alavesh flag flying from a pole attached to the front.

"The old palace," said Lynde, standing still, expression unreadable. "I've seen pictures of it. The kings and queens of Alavia used to sit here."

"Right," said Andín, remembering with a mix of fondness and anxiety a dozen imperial residences back in Palascena. The last one, which looked as ancient and crude as this, had been abandoned a century ago. "Sure. Not bad."

Lynde opened and then closed her mouth again. "During the war a lot of Alavesh nationalists came to Rath for supplies, and Rath soldiers went back with them to fight the Prytt. Our ancestors were Alavesh. We never forgot that." She touched the wrought iron of the railing. "It's just funny, being here."

Andín let her have whatever moment she wanted to have. At last Lynde straightened and turned her back on the palace.

"Okay," she said, nodding her head briskly. "Let's find a place to stay."

◆◆◆

They headed back down the hill and found a street full of cheap hotels. They got themselves a cramped room with a stuck-open window overlooking a busy street.

Lynde, surprisingly, turned in at once. She cheerily stripped down to an underdress of some kind and burrowed in under the odd-smelling covers. Andín reluctantly followed suit. Soon Lynde was snoring, leaving Andín wide awake.

Thoughts of Yshe came unbidden to her. The last time she'd shared a bed with another woman, they'd tied the sheets in knots.

She didn't even remotely feel that way about Lynde. Still, she found herself replaying every scene on the riverboat, every moment with Yshe in the hotel in Roshden.

"Wherever you are," she whispered. "I miss you."

At last she fell asleep, and dreams carried her away.

♦♦♦

She found herself walking through knee-high, waving grass. The sky was piercing blue overhead, and the high, cool steppe stretched broad and flat all around.

Shuyu. She walked and walked through the grass, not so much pushing it aside as passing through it, without so much as disturbing a single blade.

In time she came to a wagon, and then another. There were men and women around a fire, and they spoke among themselves. A boy sat there.

She knew these people—the traders she'd saved, long ago. She raised a hand, but none of them seemed to see her. So she was invisible again.

They talked about trade and weather and the daughter of someone else in another camp. They gossiped and laughed. They spoke their own language, which Andín hadn't known, but now was somehow able to understand.

A young boy turned and looked at the space where she hovered, and he smiled, almost as if he could see her. She waved, but he turned back to his family.

She stood and walked through their camp and then back into the grassy plains. She walked and walked, smelling the familiar scents and feeling the wind blowing through her hair until finally she awoke, feeling more at peace than she had in many days.

I choose to be myself, she thought as dawn broke over Telesan. Whatever I've become, I choose to be who I am.

◆◆◆

Andín rolled out of the bed, trying to be careful not to wake Lynde. She stumbled, but Lynde continued to snore. Well, that wasn't really a surprise.

She used the communal washroom at the end of the hall, then paced restlessly around the room. They had a good half day left until their train to the Selessian capital of Salasee.

"Lynde," she said, shaking her awake.

Lynde stared at her through bleary eyes. "Huh?"

"I'm going out to see more of the city. Do you want to come?"

"Nuh," Lynde said, rolling over.

"Are you sure? You liked the palace."

But Lynde was already snoring again. Andín shrugged and let herself out of the room.

◆◆◆

She walked up the hill again through the early morning calm and past the rambling medieval stone palace.

People were beginning their days as she ventured into a neighborhood of solid-looking homes on the other side of the hill, and the streets were filling up. The people in their somber clothes stared at her sometimes, but they left her alone. Just another strange foreigner, perhaps, in a city that was becoming more cosmopolitan all the time. She thought she glimpsed two other Antrimanians but didn't pursue them.

She bought some pastries from a street vendor who scowled at her while muttering something about foreigners under his breath, and then she strolled back down towards the river.

The neighborhood here was pleasant enough. Well-kept row houses, all painted in bright, clashing colors, lined clean streets. This, though Andín, was the kind of place Yshe might live.

It hit her that Yshe *did* live in Telesan, at least part of the time.

Of course. How had she managed to forget that?

Maybe she'd wanted to forget.

On impulse she waylaid a man walking by. "Excuse me," she said in Alavesh. "I'm supposed to deliver something for Yshe Shadalyan. I was told she lives in this street, but I don't remember the number. Can you point the way?"

She held her breath. The man looked her over with the sort of frown she'd seen people leveling at her all over the city. Then, obviously deciding she was harmless enough, pointed down the road.

"The Shadalyans don't live here, they live down on the Washaliat Row," he grumbled, pointing to a nearby street. "The third on the left." And with that he hurried away.

Andín's heart pounded as she walked slowly towards Yshe's house. Then, as she rounded the corner and looked at the third house on the left, she felt herself root in place.

"This is stupid," she muttered to herself. "Just go up and say hello. Just tell her you're okay."

How would it play out? Yshe would squeal with delight, they'd fall into each other's arms, their lips would lock—

Or Yshe would look at her the way she had the day she'd set boundaries, the day she'd drawn a line between the river and the land.

"I can't face her," she said to herself.

She withdrew the little book, *Shashalnikya's Song*, from her bag. She held it in her hand for a moment, then strode quickly up to Yshe's house. Before she could think twice, she pushed the book through the mail slot and left. She rounded a corner a block away and waited.

A beautiful young woman emerged, the book in her hand. The way she moved was stamped on Andín heart. She looked right and then left.

Her mouth moved, and Andín heard her voice, high and clear. *Andín! Andín!*

She almost rushed to her. But instead she turned away, tears in her eyes. She dashed around the corner, out of sight of the house, and headed back towards the hotel.

They had a train to catch and a mission to complete.

◆◆◆

Andín came back to an empty room. Frantic, she rushed out into the street, looking all over for Lynde.

There was a small, rather shabby temple right across the street. Maybe... Andín dashed inside. She blundered her way into the women's section, her eyes adjusting to the dark.

Lynde sat on one of the cushions, quietly chanting a prayer to herself. She grimaced when she saw Andín but waved her over.

Andín knelt next to her but didn't interrupt.

She could remember endless days in temples, of long ceremonies on the men's side. But her own memories were of the stuffy little temple in Viko Station, holding her mother's hand as they walked through the welcoming crowd of women to offer prayers and coins to the service of the Goddess.

She exhaled and tried to trust in gods. Goddess, keep us safe. Goddess, help us do what needs to be done.

"The Goddess will be good to us," Lynde murmured to Andín. "She gives us just what we need, and no more than that. It's up to us to use it. Or so they say."

She lay the sword at the feet of the statue of the Goddess in her fearsome warrior aspect and said a soft prayer over and over.

Andín looked up at the face of the warrior Goddess, cold and angry. She'd always favored other, softer aspects, but the warrior seemed appropriate now.

They sat together, Lynde lost in prayer, until it was time to go.

Chapter 23

Shashalnikya's Trail

Andín was glad to leave Telesan behind as the train, filled to capacity with passengers, finally chugged out of the station.

"You seem moody," said Lynde.

"Oh, it's just…" Andín sighed. "It's nothing."

Lynde raised an eyebrow. "Hm. Boy trouble?"

"No," said Andín flatly.

"A man, then?" Lynde said, a hint of teasing in her voice.

"Neither boy nor man," said Andín firmly, her heart beating faster. She was getting close to dangerous territory here.

"So," said Lynde matter-of-factly. "What's her name?"

Andín's mouth fell open. Lynde merely looked curious. "Y-Yshe," said Andín at last.

"Ah," said Lynde, "a pretty name."

"I—I didn't think—" stammered Andín.

"I know," said Lynde. She sat back in her seat, looking thoughtful. "There was a hillside where people used to live back before the big storm," she said. "Two women lived in a cabin up there. One of them grew vegetables in a garden, the other made cloth. Not great cloth, but good enough to sell at the market and keep them going." She fixed Andín with a significant stare. "Everyone knew they weren't sisters, and they weren't just friends. They lived as husband and wife. Some people hated them for it. Most said, let them do what they want, the Goddess will deal with them in the next life if it's wrong. And I thought they were nice people who deserved better than they got."

"Why are you telling me this?" whispered Andín.

"Because you look like I'm about to start cursing at you," said Lynde. "Your Yshe, is she Alavesh?"

"Yes," said Andín, her voice shaking. "She's… an ambassador's wife. But…"

"She's pretty?"

"Oh yes." Andín laughed. "I'm sorry. I'm sorry! I've… I've just never said that to anyone. Not out loud."

"Mm." Lynde nodded. "You think it was the demon, made you that way?"

Andín shook her head. "I thought so, once. But when I think about it, when I really let myself, I think it was me all along. Just Andín. I was always this way."

"Everyone wants something different," said Lynde. "And why not? As for me, I want a man. A *real* man. Not a foolish boy like my husband." She made a face. "He'd come in every night, drunk, and slobber all over me while he did his thing, and then he'd roll over and sleep. Awful. I want someone to treat me right, to make me feel like a lady."

"You deserve that," said Andín, relief coursing through her.

"I do," said Lynde, "but I'll never have it. All the real men are gone." She smirked. "Maybe the cracks in the ground swallowed them all up!"

Andín couldn't help herself, she started to laugh. "That—that shouldn't be funny," she gasped, "but it is!"

Lynde grinned wickedly. "Damned right it is."

"Thank you," said Andín.

"For what?" said Lynde, turning back to the scenery rolling by outside.

◆◆◆

Andín was lost in thought when the train screamed to a sickening, lurching stop. They were slammed back in their seats, while the other two in the compartment pitched forward, screaming as they fell.

Lynde was helping them up when someone shrieked in terror.

Andín looked out into the crowded corridor. "What is it?" she called.

But all she saw was confusion and panic. What could be wrong? A conductor shakily forced his way by.

"Sir?" Andín asked. "What stopped the train?"

"N-nothing," he stammered, his face ashy and eyes hollow. *Oh, no.* Andín felt sick. She'd seen that sort of look before. "It's nothing!" She threaded her way to a door and leaned out.

Sure enough. A huge swath of *nothing* had swallowed up the railway ahead.

"Oh, Goddess," she breathed. The holes in the world they'd seen so far had been relatively small and self-contained. This one, though, was miles across. It stretched north and south; she could barely see the other side of it.

And now that you've fixed one hole, the sorceress had said, *everything has been set into motion at last. The end will come very rapidly.*

Whatever was happening to the world was getting worse. This train would never go forward. She ducked back into the train.

"Come on," she said to Lynde, starting to gather their things together. "We're going."

"What is it?" Lynde asked.

"A hole," said Andín simply. "Huge. Across the tracks."

"Ah," said Lynde. "Should we try to fix it?"

Andín shook her head. "I don't know. It's huge. Come on, we need to get out. The train won't be able to get across."

Lynde picked up her pack and the sword. "I'm ready."

◆◆◆

They knew immediately upon looking at this hole, however, that they wouldn't be able to do anything about it. The hole stretched as far as the eye could see.

"Too big," Lynde pronounced after a long moment of taking it all in. "Fixing just a little one knocked us out. This would be worse."

"Agreed," Andín said, trying not to let her fear show. The world really was coming apart.

"Now what?" Lynde asked.

"We're going to have to see if we can get around it," said Andín, trying to project calm. "Maybe… maybe we can catch another train to Salasee on the other side."

Lynde gave her an uncharacteristically worried look but agreed. They set off over the empty fields.

◆◆◆

They hiked north around the maddening hole, trying very hard not to look at it too much. Just being near it was making Andín anxious.

Whole towns had been half-swallowed by the hole this time. Fields were cut off, rivers and streams poured into it and disappeared. Roads ended, houses vanished in the middle.

It was a horrible, unsettling sight.

People sat with their backs to it, or with their heads covered. Some wept and wailed, and Andín wondered what happened to the people who were caught sitting, walking or just existing where the hole appeared.

They must have vanished along with everything else.

Several times Lynde turned to look at the hole and grabbed the hilt of the sword, but turned away again. After the third time Andín said, "You know we can't fix it. We don't have time."

"I know," said Lynde.

"If we fixed it we might not make it out," said Andín. "We might be trapped in there. Or we might even be sucked dry."

"I know that, too," said Lynde, annoyed.

"Well… all right then," said Andín, chastened.

They continued to walk north. The road they found leading north from the tracks was eaten by the hole after a while, so they crossed through severed fields and dismembered meadows until they found another.

"When I was little girl my uncle's boat was caught in a storm," Lynde said after a while. "The morning after the storm we went down to the beach and looked out at the ocean. We could see this little black lump bobbing in the water. It was the underside of his boat. It had capsized within sight of the land. We sent out boats but it was too late. They were all gone."

"I'm sorry," said Andín.

"Don't be," said Lynde. "It was a long time ago. But this… feels like that. The sea is awful and cruel and doesn't care who or what you are. It kills for fun, and there's nothing anybody can do. When the men come home on the big whaling ships there's always happiness, but we always count the people who are missing. The captains give the widows the dead man's possessions as soon as they come off the ship. I remember when it happened to my mother. I was six."

"Lynde," said Andín softly. "I had no idea."

"That's life in Ten Fish," said Lynde, shrugging. "We all knew it. That was part of the price of making a living from the ocean. Sometimes bad things happen, and people die. The waves carry them away, and nobody can fix it."

She turned to the ghastly rip in the world, where towns, fields and roads once had been, her eyes hard and determined. She opened her mouth as if to say something, then closed it and glared out at the nothingness.

"We'll fix this," said Andín. "I promise."

Lynde nodded sharply, and set off again. Andín jogged behind her to catch up.

◆◆◆

At last, after more than three hours of grim, silent marching, they reached the northern end of the hole and turned west.

"What do you think?" asked Andín, her mouth dry, as they walked along a dusty westbound road. "What do you want to do now?"

To the southeast, the horrible blankness of the hole loomed.

"We can turn south again," said Lynde. "We can follow the hole back to the tracks. We might be able to find another train to Selessia if we keep going."

"I'd rather not," said Andín, shuddering. Constant exposure to the hole had made her extremely jumpy and unnerved.

"I don't blame you," said Lynde. Andín wondered how she could remain so calm.

"So what, then?" Andín asked.

"Let's take a look at the map," said Lynde, relentlessly practical. "Maybe we can find a way to Salasee from here." Lynde pulled the map the princess had given her from her pack and spread it on the ground.

"We're here," she said after a few minutes, stabbing the paper with her finger. "Holvae. I saw that name on a village back there. This must be the road we're on. Ah. We're near the border. The railway goes south and then back northwest, but we can just cross right over in a few miles. Then there's a border town, maybe we can find transportation to Salasee from there."

"And maybe somewhere to sleep, too... that sounds like a good idea to me," said Andín. She was weary; skirting the hole had taken a lot out of her. She missed her Shuyan horse.

Lynde, on the other hand, seemed like she could walk a hundred miles more.

They set off again.

♦♦♦

They hiked north and west, away from the rip in the world. The plains here were even flatter and more dismal than before, but compared to the hole, Andín thought they looked like the most beautiful thing ever.

It had recently rained, and they struggled over the muddy ground. Lynde had a pair of sturdy leather boots, but she couldn't keep the mud off her dress. Andín's blue Shuyan riding outfit was warm and comfortable, but soon it was more a muddy brown than blue.

They passed by old, moss-covered stone markers every once in a while. Lynde leaned down to examine one and nodded soberly.

"This is Shashalnikya's Trail," she said. "See?"

There were a few faded symbols carved into the rock, including a distinctive grouping of three swords. "What does that mean?" Andín asked.

"Judy Shashalnikya was brought this way by the Selessians after they'd captured her," said Lynde. "There are stories about this trail; they marked it a long time ago. People would walk it for luck. It's an omen. We're on the right track."

Andín looked at the marker, then up at the cloudy sky. She'd had her share of signs and portents, but somehow this didn't seem like one of them. "I don't know," she said dubiously.

In response Lynde stood and ripped the sword from its scabbard. Andín stepped back, worried.

Lynde closed her eyes and turned slowly all the way around. She eventually ended pointing in the direction they were headed.

"This way," she said, opening her eyes. "The singing is stronger if I point it this way."

"You can sense directions?"

"I can now," said Lynde. "The sword..." She stared at it, her eyes thoughtful. "It's getting stronger than it was. It seems a lot less rusty to me, too. Doesn't it?"

For a wonder, it actually did. The sword fairly gleamed.

It seemed that they were being led to where they needed to be by a magic beyond Andín's knowledge or control. The thought was unnerving. Who was leading them? Judy Shashalnikya? And what was her real purpose?

Lynde, oblivious to Andín's thoughts, broke into a hopeful grin. "Come on! We're on the right path, we'll succeed for certain!" She strode off determinedly through the mud; Andín had to run to catch up with her.

◆◆◆

"Do you think she was scared?" Lynde asked Andín as they walked through the gathering gloom. The border was closer now. Andín thought she could see a cluster of buildings on the horizon; that had to be it.

"Who?" Andín asked.

"Judy Shashalnikya, who else? Do you think she was scared when the Selessians took her?"

"I know I would be," said Andín. Why was Lynde asking her that? "They were taking her to prison, weren't they? She's lucky they didn't just kill her." She shook her head, remembering. "We were tough and mean, in those old days. Not a lot of mercy."

"And you'd know, wouldn't you?" said Lynde. "I forget,

sometimes, what you are. I think you're just a girl like me."

"But I am," protested Andín, not knowing how to explain. "I really am."

They trudged on in silence down Shashalnikya's Trail toward Selessia.

Chapter 24
Selessia

The border turned out to be a nightmare. Dozens of Alavesh were waiting there, possessions strapped to their backs, fleeing from the rip in the land that had swallowed whole villages back in Alavia. The Selessian border guards held firm, insisting that not even people with proper documentation be allowed to cross. The border, they said, was closed.

"There must be another way across," said Andín. She knew she and Lynde didn't have enough identification to get across this border, not now. So what to do?

The border here was a bridge over a wide stream, much as it had been in Gantritt. They had nowhere to go and nowhere to sleep for the night. All of the lodging was in the town on the other side of the bridge.

To make matters worse, the clouds had finally opened, and the long-threatened first drops of rain spattered Andín's hair and face.

She was tired. She was terrified and traumatized. She was in the middle of a field in some horrible Goddess-forsaken country halfway around the world. She was being led towards some northern place to do who-knew-what. The world was coming to an end.

And now she was wet.

"That's it," she said in a low voice. "Move aside!"

She marched up to the annoyed-looking Selessian border guard and addressed him in what she hoped was the command form of his native language: "Get out of the way! Now! These people need shelter!"

He blinked at her. "I'm afraid not, miss," he said haughtily. "Not in this crisis, border's been ordered closed! Now move along, and—"

She didn't let him finish. "*Shih!*" With a surge of dark energy, she blew him and his comrade off the bridge and into the river.

"Go!" she cried, urging the crowd of Alavesh forward while the guards splashed and cursed below. "Go! Run!"

The Alavesh, along with Lynde and Andín, stampeded across the bridge and into Selessia.

♦♦♦

They hid under the eaves of a barn on the outskirts of the village, trying not to make a sound. Somewhere out there, the police were still searching for them. They'd already found a few of the other Alavesh and unceremoniously kicked them back across the bridge into Alavia.

The trudging of heavy-booted feet passed, and the only sound they could hear was the rain falling softly on the eaves above.

"Maybe I should have thought that through," Andín said miserably. Lynde put a hand on her shoulder.

"It was brave," said Lynde.

"I guess. But it was stupid, too. I didn't think."

"You know," said Lynde, "sometimes, that's the best way to get things done. Don't think. Just act. If you think about everything, you'll spend the whole day worrying about the 'what ifs.' That's what my grandmother used to say."

Andín put her head in her hands. "You're right. Ugh! I think the hole... whatever it is... I think it got to me."

"It got to me, too," said Lynde. She smiled ruefully, and for a moment Andín noticed that Lynde had a subdued sort of beauty, worn down by the sea and the wind and the rain but all the more marvelous because of it.

"You got us across," said Lynde, snapping her out of it. "We'll get out of here soon and head for the north."

"I hope so," said Andín.

"Hey," a voice called in accented Selessian. "Hey, who's out there?"

They froze in place.

A man with a steady-burning electric lantern rounded the corner. He lifted the lantern and looked at them.

Andín gathered her energy, preparing to strike. Lynde took hold of the sword's hilt. Then Andín stood, the energies dissipating. He seemed eerily familiar, as did his voice.

"You two look wet," he said after a moment, speaking in strongly-accented Alavesh. "Got nowhere else to go, have you? Come from across the border, yes?"

Andín and Lynde nodded.

"Well then, come on inside and warm up. Then maybe you can tell me why you were sitting in the back of my barn." He fixed them with a stern look and ushered them into the nearby farmhouse.

◆◆◆

Andín shivered over a bowl of hot tea while the man studied them with a watchful eye. Lynde had gone to use the man's washroom with assurances that she wouldn't go anywhere.

"Thank you," said Andín softly in Selessian, sipping the tea. "This is very good."

"You speak Alavesh, yes? Then do that," he said in Alavesh. Lynde, who didn't know any Selessian, relaxed. "Though by the look of you, you're not from anywhere near here. Am I right?"

"I'm from Antriman," said Andín.

"Thought you might be," said the man. He had a lined face and graying hair above well-wrinkled eyes. She struggled to remember where she'd seen him before. "You have the look. Long way from home?"

"I am," said Andín.

"So the border patrols said a crazy foreigner and an Alavesh girl blew the guards off the bridge with wicked magic and let the refugees through. Would you know anything about that?"

Andín and Lynde exchanged a quick glance but said nothing. This man could be capable of anything. Andín kept the reserve of dark energy near, just in case.

"Well," he said, "good for you if you did. Serves the Selessian bastards right."

"You're... not Selessian?" asked Andín carefully.

"No, girl!" he said, surprised she was even asking. "I'm Alavesh! This is Kish, and here in the west of Kish we're all Alavesh people living under the Selessian crown."

Lynde nodded in understanding.

"Oh," said Andín. Like Gantritt, then, a place where the Alavesh were outside of their own country. This part of the world seemed needlessly complicated.

"And we don't mind it when someone shows the Selessian police a thing or two," he continued. "My name's Rikan Shollaire; this is my home."

Rikan. *Rikan.* The name finally tied together all the nagging sense of familiarity Andín had been feeling. She'd seen him before. She remembered a table cluttered with blueprints, a brass railing attached to... something massive.

Had Judy Shashalnikya wanted them to come here? Did Rikan have a part to play, as well?

Rikan Shollaire was still talking. "I live here with my boys, though they aren't here so much these days. Just me, mostly." He fixed them both with a steady, firm stare. "Now then. The truth. What's happening over there? Everyone says there's a crisis, but no one's saying what it is."

Lynde and Andín exchanged glances again. "There was a sort of... rip in the world," said Andín. There was no reason not to say; it would be common knowledge soon enough. "It's hard to explain. But where there were land and people, now there's just... *nothing.* Less than nothing."

"It's like a blank space," said Lynde, shutting her eyes. "The absence of anything at all."

The man, Rikan, looked evenly back and forth between them. "I've heard some rumors of that," he said at last. "All the same, I wonder how such a thing could be."

Lynde opened her mouth but then glanced over at Andín and

stopped herself.

"If you'd seen it, you'd think differently," Andín insisted. "Maybe you could tell us how to get northwest from here?"

"Train to Salasee," he replied, "but you'd need to leave town. The police are looking for you. Stay here tonight, leave tomorrow."

"I, um, have a little money," said Andín. "We can pay for a night's stay."

"I'd appreciate it," he replied gravely.

And with that he left them alone.

"I thought he might let us stay for free," said Andín, disappointed.

"Nobody's perfect," said Lynde. They shared a grin. Never turn down a warm bed, Andín thought.

How did the rest of the song go?

Never turn down a warm bed,
Never pass by a good meal,
And bring along a friend to share your trials with.

She hummed the old tune, something they'd liked around the fires in camp five hundred years ago, as she finished her tea.

When she was sure he was gone, she whispered to Lynde, "I've seen him before. In a dream."

Lynde rolled her eyes. "Who haven't you seen in a dream?"

"He might be able to help us. I don't know. I just know I saw him."

"Great," said Lynde. "Another mystery. Don't we have enough problems? Let's just try to get through tonight and get out of here tomorrow. Okay?"

"Fine," said Andín, though she wasn't happy about it. She couldn't shake the sense that she was supposed to do something here, but she couldn't imagine what it might be.

◆◆◆

That night Andín's dreams flitted through a dozen places. Princess Diya stalked the halls of her empty home, waiting to hear news of her family in Telesan. People pushed past the fence blocking the hole in Azu, pretending it wasn't there. The carter and his boy rode through the rocky foothills of far eastern Shuyu... then the garrison just over the Antrimanian border, the women in the boarding house in Palascena, even Palyar playing his fiddle in his room back home...

Judy Shashalnikya was nowhere to be seen, but Andín swore she heard her voice saying, *hurry, hurry.*

And then she heard a sound like ice cracking and splintering, coming from absolutely everywhere.

◆◆◆

She awoke to the sounds of wild shouts and screams. She and Lynde bolted out of bed, threw their clothes on, grabbed what they could, and raced out to the front of Rikan's house.

"Oh, no," said Andín, heart pounding. "No, no."

Pools of emptiness scarred the town. A woman nearby wailed at the streak of nothing where her house had been. She called out four names, over and over, willing them to emerge.

Andín looked up and gasped in horror. There was a spidery crack running down the rim of the eastern sky. *It's speeding up,* she thought. *It's getting worse.*

Hurry, hurry.

"We have to go," said Andín. "Now."

"Evil magic," said someone. "Evil foreign magic!" Someone pointed at her.

"Come on," said Andín. They'd worn out their welcome. She remembered enough of mobs that she knew things could turn ugly very, very fast.

But they were already surrounded. Frightened people with wild looks in their eyes shouted and pointed at Andín, screaming terrible things about Antriman's poison and evil witchcraft from beyond the eastern mountains.

Lynde and Andín pressed against the wall of Rikan's house, cut off from the door. Andín grabbed her pistol from her pack and fired it into the air. The crowd stepped back a pace.

"Stay back!" she shouted, calmly reloading. "We didn't cause this!"

"She's the one who blew the soldiers off the bridge!" someone cried. "She's a demon!"

"We can fix this," Lynde's voice, high and clear, rang out, "but you have to let us pass!"

But the crowd wasn't going to allow that. There was another cracking sound from above, and the crowd screamed.

"Throw them in!" someone shouted. "Into the nothing!"

Andín gathered her dark energies to herself. This was at the danger point now. Once, long ago, an emperor had been overwhelmed by a crowd like this one—and he'd fought back. They'd understand force. They'd understand pain.

A part of herself wept as she prepared to blast the crowd back. «Sometimes,» she thought she heard a whispering voice say, «*the emperor must do terrible things for the sake of the empire.*»

But just then there was the roaring sound of an engine and the retort of another pistol firing into the air. A gleaming motorcar appeared from around the side of the house, Rikan Shollaire driving.

"These women are with me," he shouted. "Let them through!"

The crowd hesitated, and Lynde grabbed Andín's hand, leading her through them into the back seat of the motorcar. Rikan hit the gas, and with a groaning of gears and wheels spinning on mud, the motorcar leapt forward, away from the mob.

"Thank you," said Andín, catching her breath.

"Why did you save us?" Lynde asked bluntly.

Rikan drove silently, his jaw clenched tight.

"Judy Shashalnikya," said Andín. "She came to you in a dream. She told you to help us."

Rikan scowled, then pointed to the sky.

"You can fix that?"

"I think so," said Andín. "We're going to try."

"Good," said Rikan. "If the world's coming to an end, I'd like to go out trying to stop it. Where do you need to go?"

"Salaz," said Lynde. "It's where the mountains meet the sea in the north of Selessia."

He nodded sharply. "I know how to get you there."

◆◆◆

They drove through the gray plains beyond the village in shocked silence. The landscape was perforated everywhere with the malevolent blank spaces. In fact, another appeared as Andín watched. The ground seemed to yawn and wrinkle, then it was gone. Above, the crack in the sky leered menacingly at them.

This is a beautiful motorcar, Andín thought ruefully as they rattled and shook over the bumpy roads. She'd likely never be in one again. This could have been the future.

No, it *will* be, she thought. We can't let it end like this.

But as she stared out at the world disintegrating all around her, she wondered how anyone or anything could ever put it right again.

◆◆◆

The motorcar plowed through the muck and grime and turned off onto a side trail with three Selessian flags flying next to it.

"This is a military installation!" hollered Rikan from the front. "If they don't let us through, use what power you might have. Don't be shy about it! There's nothing to lose!"

Right, thought Andín nervously. They could still shoot us, and what would happen then? She glanced at Lynde, who looked like she might throw up.

They rounded a corner and ran into a guard waiting at a very neat little guardhouse. He wore a complex uniform—some sort of Selessian special forces? Andín tensed, ready to act, but the guard took one look at Rikan's motorcar and hurriedly waved him through.

They crested a hill, and Andín's mouth fell open. There, sitting in the middle of a flat field, tethered by four lines, was an airship like the one Andín had seen hovering above Palascena long ago. The great, long tapered cylinder of the airship's envelope loomed above the field, with a partially-enclosed wooden deck attached to the underside. Two huge rotors were embedded in the fins, and the Selessian flag was painted on the hull.

"Of course!" she cried. She remembered commissioning the ones in Antriman, and she remembered seeing this one in her dream. It had to have been that. "Airships! I knew these would come in handy!"

Men in uniform swarmed all around it in a frenzy. *They're getting ready for it to take off!* Andín realized as the motorcar bumped and bounced across the field. She remembered the demonstrations of the Antrimanian ones, only a few years ago now. She had been old and weak, then; they wouldn't let her on the deck. But now...

Rikan pulled up near the airship. "Be ready for my signal to use what you have," he said to Andín. She glanced at Lynde and nodded briskly. He was planning something. She would be on the lookout for it, and so would Lynde.

Another man in a similar complex uniform met them as they walked up to the airship's passenger and control deck. "Dr. Shollaire!" he exclaimed in Selessian. Andín shifted her mind into that language's track while Lynde frowned, trying to understand. "I'm glad you're here! We had just sent to you, but obviously you had the same thought as we all did. And these are...?"

"Assistants," Rikan growled.

"Two *girls*? And... is that one Antrimanian? That's... irregular, Dr. Shollaire, even for you!" said the man. Rikan glared at him, and Andín tensed again. She reached for the dark power of the red world, ready to make a desperate bid for the airship.

"You don't want to start this argument, not now," said Rikan sharply. "You've seen the sky. Are they taking off at once?"

"Y-yes. Fine. Do as you will! Just get aboard and man your station, Doctor. They'll need you." The uniformed man jogged off to another person who was untying one of the lines and started shouting at him.

"So far so good," said Rikan in Alavesh. "I'm a scientist, I'm old, and I'm Alavesh. They expect me to be eccentric. This way. Quickly!"

They ran up a steep temporary stairway and onto the creaky deck of the airship. There were stations set up for steering and navigation. Windscreens were set up along the perimeter, but there was no roof. A ladder provided access to the hull.

"How does it stay up?" Lynde asked. "Is it magic?"

"No, it's hydrogen," said Rikan.

Science, thought Andín. Science will save us. At last.

Two blustery men in uniform accosted Rikan. "Dr. Shollaire! But see here, who are these? You can't bring just anyone aboard!"

"My assistants," he said. "They have special knowledge of this crisis."

Someone below yelled for takeoff. Rikan headed for his station at the back and began to work the levers and dials there. The engines coughed and sputtered to life.

The man followed Rikan, shouting and waving his arms frantically. "They have to leave! You can't have them here. They must disembark at once!"

"Loose the ropes!" commanded someone else.

"Oh, can't I?" Rikan scowled. "Selessians! You can't leave your love of regulations even for a moment. You deserve what you get!"

"What?" gasped the man.

"Now, Andín!" commanded Rikan, a hard look in his eye. "Now! All of them but us!"

Andín had no time to argue. She gathered her dark energy and struck.

"*Shih!*" she shouted. Two men went flying up over the windows and down the side.

"*Shih!*" she cried again, pointing. Energy surged from her. Two more went tumbling down the stairs.

She turned to the last man, who took one look at the magic swirling around Andín and ran for the stairs, panic in his eyes. He threw himself off as the ship rose into the air, its lines cut.

"Done!" she cried, trembling. One of the men on the ground wasn't moving. She felt sick.

Rikan opened the throttle, and with a deafening roar of burning gas the airship began to lift. There was confusion and shouting below, but they left it behind as they rose gently into that terrible morning sky.

Chapter 25
The Shattered Sky

They quickly gained altitude, and soon Andín could see her breath in the cold. Lynde stumbled across the pitching, wobbling deck over to a chest, and opened it. "Coats!" she cried, tossing one to Andín. She gratefully put it on, even though it was a too-large Selessian military greatcoat. It smelled of mustiness and age. She crept forward over the lurching floor to where Rikan stood, piloting the ship.

"They can't follow us!" he shouted over the din of the engine and the wind. "This is the only one we have!" He seemed to be running on adrenaline and pure joy. "Selessian bastards! Ha! I helped build this ship; they used my specifications to make the engine rotors and the frame! They treated me like a fool, but they'll never catch us!" He gazed up ahead, his eyes shining brightly.

"How long?" she shouted.

"I don't know," he shouted back. She strained to hear him over the din. "A while. The north is two hundred miles away, and I don't know how long this ship will hold together—she's still experimental. She may not survive a long trip like this!"

Oh good, thought Andín. They were at the mercy of an untested machine and an unhinged pilot. She felt helpless, more so than she had in months. She suddenly, desperately wished for a good horse, a rifle, and a field of waving grass to ride across.

Rikan whooped and hollered. "That will show the Selessians! Kish and Alavia forever! Ha ha!"

Andín left him to his manic joy and stumbled forward to the front wall of the control deck. Lynde joined her a moment later.

"He seems like he's having a good time," Lynde said. She looked worn out.

"I know," said Andín, shivering in her military greatcoat. "He says it'll be a couple of hours, maybe more. I wonder how fast we're going?"

"Fast," said Lynde. "Did you look down?"

Andín swallowed hard. "No!"

Lynde closed her eyes and rested the back of her head against the wall of the deck. "You should."

Hesitantly, Andín peered through the windows to look at the landscape stretching out below.

"Oh," she whispered.

Patches of blank space had appeared everywhere. The world looked perforated. Cracks of nothing had appeared, connecting some of the holes. More seemed to shift into being all the time.

There had to be hundreds of thousands of people down there. "It can't be like this," she murmured.

She thought of Yshe in her house in Telesan, of Princess Diya in her rambling old manor home, of the Shuyan plains, of her family...

Below, half of a massive city had vanished into nothing.

"God and Goddess!" cried Rikan. "That's Kishran! How in the world can it be stopped?"

Lynde had closed her eyes again. Her lips moved, and Andín realized she was praying.

She thought of all the hopeless battles she'd fought. She had a good idea of when she was beaten. Defeat had a certain feel to it, and she could sense it all around them now. But they couldn't just give up. There was nowhere to go, nothing else to do.

Andín opened her mouth and began to tell a story from the demon's memory.

"Long ago," she said, the memories filling her mind as she talked, "when I was Emperor of Antriman, there was a man who said the world would come to an end. He just marched up to the castle doors, demanded to be let in, and ordered me to surrender my crown to the God Ascendant. That was him. He thought he was the God Himself. He said the world would be destroyed and all of the people killed unless we followed him and did what he said. He was perfectly serious. He had an unkempt beard but sober, piercing eyes. When he spoke, it was with a profound, deep rumble that shook me to the core."

Lynde listened but said nothing.

Andín continued. "Half the court followed him by the end. I thought that I should put him in prison to shut him up, but a wise friend told me that doing so would just make him stronger and his followers more obnoxious. So we did what he wanted, and we waited for the end. He spent the whole day before cursing me for not giving up my throne and preparing his followers for the end. I don't remember what he thought would happen to them. They'd be saved from it all somehow, I think.

"The day came and we all waited. I knew perfectly well nothing would happen. But everyone else worried, even my own close friends and advisers. It was a very long day, but when it ended, I had the man turned out of the city. I didn't imprison him or punish him. He was broken by it. He really, truly believed that the world would end. But I knew it wouldn't, and I was right."

Andín paused. It was a long story and an old memory, and it tasted faintly of former lives and people she didn't like to remember being.

"Why are you telling me this?" Lynde asked.

"Because," said Andín, "I don't believe the world will end today, either."

Lynde sighed. "I wish I could believe that."

"I'm a thousand years old," said Andín, "or parts of me are. So you should listen, right?"

Lynde smiled and gave Andín a friendly punch in the arm. "All right."

Sometimes, she thought bleakly, the emperor looks happy when she feels miserable.

The sky above was clear and blue. If she didn't look too far to the east, it all seemed perfectly normal.

She focused on that and, despite herself, started to doze.

♦♦♦

...*She found herself in a narrow room* somewhere in Princess Diya's ramshackle old house. She was talking in low tones with Orley, her right-hand man.

"No word at all from the city, but our people nearby say the rips in the world are growing bigger and more numerous," Orley said. "One said, and this is just a rumor..."

"Yes?" Diya said, holding her head in her hands. "Out with it."

"One said that half the city has been swallowed by one."

Diya was perfectly still for a moment. "So," she said at last, "this is the end, isn't it?"

Orley said nothing.

"I should go to Telesan," she said. "I should be with my family."

"Your Highness, you can't! The government—"

"They said I can return if I renounce my claim to the throne," Diya said tiredly. "I so renounce it."

His jaw dropped open. "I... Highness, you can't mean..."

"I do mean it," she said, and Andín noted the clear, cold sanity in her eyes. "Sometimes, Orley... sometimes we have to sacrifice in order to do what's necessary. Telesan and my family need me. We should go to them at once."

"Are you sure?" Orley asked.

Diya shook her head. "You've seen it out there. The sky is cracking apart. There's no country left to be queen of and no world to care. All that matters is making a good end of things. Go and get everyone; we'll leave as soon as we can."

Orley bowed and left.

"Andín and Lynde," Diya murmured. "God and Goddess help them. God and Goddess help us all."

Then the scene shifted, and she saw Hular Molasca looking out at the fragmented sky. Chaos reigned in the city below. Already huge pieces of it had been gobbled up by the nothingness.

Syr fan Porlab stood next to him. "I am at a loss," he stammered.

The emperor shook his head. "We are all at a loss," he said.

The scene shifted again, and she was in the front room of her house at Viko Station. The light was the orange red of late afternoon, and the house was warm.

No one was around, but somewhere she thought she heard muffled sobs. She hesitantly climbed the stairs and peered into her room.

It was just as she'd left it, except that her bed was made and all her things meticulously put away. She tried to run a hand over her bed but found she couldn't touch it.

The sobs were louder; they were coming from the next room over. Palyar's. She crept into the room and found her family, her mother, brother and father, huddled on his bed looking fearfully out the window. She joined them and followed their gaze up into the sky.

The crack in the heavens was huge here, and it was everywhere. The whole of the sky seemed to be breaking apart. She glanced out at the town; patches of nothing had appeared there, too. Viko Station was vanishing.

"Oh," said her mother. "Oh, Deeny."

Andín's heart skipped a beat. In all this, her mother was worried about *her*?

She knelt down and put a hand on her mother's shoulder.

It connected for a brief moment, and she could feel the warmth of her mother's skin beneath her knit sweater. The moment passed, and Andín's hand connected with nothing but air again. But her mother tensed and turned, then brushed at her shoulder.

"I'm here, Mama," said Andín, kneeling next to her. She watched the dreadful sky in silence with her family. "I'm here."

◆◆◆

When Andín awoke she found Lynde snoring on her shoulder. Her arm had fallen asleep. She shrugged her off and rubbed her arm, wincing as numbness transitioned to pins and needles.

"Hey," she said. The air was warmer, and the sun shone brightly in the cracked and splintering sky. The effect was both disturbing and hauntingly beautiful.

They were lower to the ground, now. Much lower. They were very nearly grazing the tops of trees, in fact. She stood and wobbled over to Rikan.

"We're losing altitude," he said, his face a mask of concern. "I don't know how much longer we can stay in the air. I had to dive to avoid... there was one of those *things* in the air. I had to go under it, but that jostled something loose. I think there's a rip, too. I turned up the gas to full blast, and we're still sinking."

"How much farther do we have to go?" Andín asked.

He shook his head. "I don't have any idea. Too many landmarks are gone. We've been going all day. You and the other one have been asleep for most of it! Can't blame you. Wish I could have." He looked utterly exhausted. "We're far up the coast, but we've been so at the mercy of these winds that I couldn't say for sure where we might be."

Andín looked out at the patchwork landscape stretching out in front of her. Hills and valleys rose and dipped, mountains loomed off in the distance, and somewhere to her left she thought she caught a glimpse of watery shimmer. The ocean?

Where the sea and mountains meet...

"Lynde," she called. Lynde was just waking up. "Lynde, the sword! Can you tell us if we're close?"

"Right." Lynde scrambled to her feet and picked up the sword. She held it for a moment, concentrating.

"What is she doing?" Rikan asked.

"She says she can tell if we're near," said Andín, "and what direction to go in."

Rikan swore. "That would have been useful two hours ago!"

"I didn't think of it until just now," said Andín distractedly. She was still fighting the memory of millions of people waiting for the end of the world. So many... she had to save so many. It was too much. "I'm sorry. I should have."

Lynde turned back and shouted. "We're close!" She pointed toward the shimmer of the ocean. "That way!"

"Can we take her down?" Andín asked, heart thumping. "Can we land?"

"We need to slow down," said Rikan. He snapped his fingers. "You can help us! Send the same force you used to drive the men off the ship out ahead, and it'll counteract our forward momentum! It'll help us slow down."

She looked at him as if he had grown another head.

"Just try it," he urged. "Now! Sit against the back wall here and send out force ahead!"

She braced herself against the back wall.

"Here goes nothing," she said and put her arm out in front of her.

"*Shih!*" The magic force wave jolted her back against the wood of the control deck. The entire wall of front windows vanished, blown down to the ground. They were buffeted by winds.

"Good!" Rikan cried. "Do it again!"

She did. Slowly but surely, she felt the airship slowing. They sank down near the grass, still going alarmingly fast. She could feel herself wearying with the effort.

"One more big one!" Rikan shouted.

She gathered her fading, erratic energy and sent out one last, huge force wave. The airship pitched wildly, and the supports holding the control deck onto the airship body creaked and cracked.

The front supports snapped with a gut-wrenching sound and sent all three of them tumbling forward. Andín tried to grab on to something—anything—but slid out, down onto the grass.

She hit the ground with a thud and rolled end over end in a cascade of black and red pain.

She kept consciousness somehow and looked up to see the airship career out of control overhead. The control deck hung by a single support, and then the whole thing dipped toward the ground. The deck caught and was wrenched off, and the canvas of the ship tore wide open. They could hear the gas escaping.

"Look out!" Rikan said. "It could explode!"

They threw themselves face down on the ground, covering their heads. The big bang never came, though. When they looked up again, the airship was a mess of twisted wood, canvas and machinery.

"Damn, damn, damn," said Rikan, trying to get to his feet. One of his legs slid out from under him. "Oh," he said, wincing. "I, ah... I think that broke."

Lynde looked up woozily and staggered over to his side. She looked banged up but not broken. "Can you walk?" she asked, putting a hand on his arm.

"I don't think so," he said, shaking his head.

"We'll get that set," Andín said firmly.

"No," he said. "No, you need to go! You have no time. I'll stay with... what's left of the ship. Someone has to. You two go on ahead as fast as you can and do what you need to do."

"Are you sure? We can find a way to take you with us," Andín said. "I don't want to just leave you."

"Go ahead," he said. "I'll be fine. Really. Go. But... hurry back."

"We will," Lynde promised.

"I did what I had to do," he said, grimacing in pain. "What Judy Shashalnikya wanted. In the end… maybe it will be enough."

◆◆◆

They gathered what they could and set off northwest, to where the hills came down to meet the sea. "Not far," Lynde said. "We're so close now."

They weren't too far away from the crash site when they heard a shriek from behind them, cut off in the middle. Both whirled around.

Where Rikan and the airship had been, a vast rip had obliterated the landscape.

Lynde whipped out the sword. "Come on! We can save him!"

Andín grabbed her arm.

"We can't," she said coldly. "We don't have time."

Lynde looked at her in horror, but Andín remembered the ways of crisis and urgency. Nothing mattered as much as the mission.

If Lynde wanted to blame her for it, so be it.

"We can save him," insisted Lynde, eyes hard. "He was kind to us. He saved us from the mob. We owe him, Andín."

"No. We have to go," said Andín, her voice shaking. "If we healed this hole... we'd be out for the rest of the day. We can't risk it. Things are falling apart too fast, Lynde. You know that."

Lynde opened her mouth, then closed it again. She kicked violently at a stone on the ground, sending it sailing off into the nothing. It vanished as it passed into the event horizon.

"Fine," she said. "Damn you."

"I know," Andín said, steering her away. Her heart felt like a lead weight in her chest. Sometimes, she remembered, the emperor left people behind. "I know."

◆◆◆

They hiked northwest through the rough and disintegrating landscape. Lynde held the sword in front of her from time to time, and they followed its lead.

Lynde marched with single-minded determination, saying nothing and wearing a fixed, focused expression on her face.

"Lynde?" asked Andín after a while. "How are you?"

Lynde stopped and lowered the sword. She looked up at the sky, then back at the ground, saying nothing at all. Her face was stone.

"Let's rest a while," suggested Andín. "I'm tired."

Lynde sat next to her as they munched on some dry bread they'd picked up in Telesan.

After a while Lynde said. "All of Rath could be gone by now. The whole island."

"I know," said Andín. "You know... you know about my dreams."

"Right," said Lynde tiredly.

"I had another, when we were in the air. I saw my home," said Andín. "My family. My town was being eaten by those… things. It's only a matter of time." She thought of Palascena and Viko Station. Her empire, her hometown, her family, her friends, all vanishing.

It seemed impossible. It seemed like she might yet wake up and be on a train to Alavia with Yshe.

Lynde's strong hand took hold of hers. Andín, shocked by the unexpected contact, felt tears brimming in her eyes.

"I married a sailor," said Lynde, "and I was supposed to have his babies. It was a hard life, but at least I was away from my mother. Then I found the sword, and I lost everything. My husband divorced me, my town turned its back on me, and I had to leave my island to come here, where I rotted in the princess' dungeon for weeks."

"I know," said Andín. Where was she going with this?

"You lost your home and family, too," said Lynde. "This whole thing… it's bad. Magic swords, immortal, body-stealing demons, and now this." She waved her hands at the disintegrating sky. "When I meet the person who's been manipulating us like this, I'm going to kick them in the face."

Andín laughed. It was actually a relief to laugh. "I'd love to do that."

"But at least we're here," said Lynde.

"Right," said Andín. "We are."

They shared a long look. Andín squeezed Lynde's hand.

"We need to get going," said Lynde.

"I know," said Andín. "Thanks for sitting. I needed it."

They got up and started walking again. Lynde set the pace, with Andín close behind.

"I was going to study at the university at Palascena," said Andín as they walked. "I thought it would be wonderful to be among all those books and teachers."

"That doesn't sound like you at all," Lynde said. "I picture you doing something outside. You're so restless."

Andín smiled. "Well. I thought I wanted it then. I thought I wanted to study history and music, but maybe I just wanted to get away. I don't really know anymore."

"I thought I wanted a sailor's babies once upon a time," said Lynde, "but I don't think I could do it now."

"Yeah, I don't see that somehow," said Andín. Lynde would have been very strange as a mother. "Everyone changes."

"Except when things all come to an end," said Lynde.

Right, thought Andín. She picked up the pace.

"We have to move fast while there's still light," Lynde said, her voice low and grim. "I don't know if the sun will rise again."

Andín followed her gaze off to the west, where the sun was sinking down toward the horizon. Above, the cracks in the sky seemed like they were getting larger. Lynde might be right.

"We're close," continued Lynde. "I can feel it." The sword now seemed to vibrate and twitch on its own.

They were coming out of the woods. Andín blinked, trying to see what was ahead, and she groaned.

Lynde cursed.

Ahead of them lay the biggest and widest pool of *nothing* they'd ever seen.

Chapter 26

The Empty Sea

"What do we do?" Andín asked, trying not to look at the nothingness spread far and wide in front of them.

"I think... I think that's it, over there," said Lynde. "That's where we need to go." She pointed to a rounded peak near the ocean, visible far across the vast expanse of nothing.

"How do we get there?" Andín asked. There seemed to be no way around it. It was too big... and they were out of time.

Andín knew then that Lynde had been right. The sun wouldn't rise again.

Lynde jerked her head up as if she were a dog hearing a high whistle. She looked out at the maddening sea of nothing, and back to Andín. "Wait here," she said. She walked to the edge.

Before Andín could react Lynde muttered something and struck the sword against the nothing... then walked out into it.

For a terrible moment Andín thought Lynde would jump into it without her, but instead a little bubble of not-nothing formed at her feet. She walked into it a little way, then back.

"The sword?" Andín exclaimed. Since when could she do that? "Why didn't you fall in?"

"No idea," said Lynde, her voice quivering a very small amount. "But the sword... it's more powerful now. I... I thought I heard the Goddess saying it would be okay."

"You can walk right across it!"

Lynde nodded, but her eyes were heavy with dread. She

extended a hand to Andín.

"Oh, no," said Andín, backing away. "The circle's too small."

"It's big enough for two. Andín, come on. I need you."

"I can't do it," Andín said softly, shivering at the very idea. She had thought nothing would ever scare her again, not after surviving the plains of Shuyu, but this? This was courting madness. "I'm not as brave as you," she said. "I can't."

Lynde tore a strip off of her shirt. "Here," she said. "It's easy. You just have to hold tight and walk forward with me. You don't have to do anything but walk next to me. Can you do that?"

It was just possible... Andín gulped and nodded. Lynde gently tied the strip of fabric around Andín's head, blocking her sight.

"Now," said Lynde, helping her to her feet. "We both hold the sword. And we just walk. Okay?"

"Okay," said Andín, voice barely a whisper.

They took one step together, and then another.

"Just walk," said Lynde. "Walk forward. No—no! Keep your feet closer to mine. Good. Like that."

They held the sword between them, huddled together with arms wrapped around one another, and they walked forward one step at a time.

Andín tried not to think about the terrible sea of nothing that surrounded them. Even if it swallowed them, they were protected. They could come back out again, even from this.

Right?

They walked for what seemed like forever.

◆◆◆

"Lynde?" Andín asked. "Is it bad?"

Lynde didn't reply.

"Lynde," Andín said again.

"It is," said Lynde gruffly.

"I'll... I'll share it with you," said Andín. They stopped. "Take the blindfold off."

Lynde's fingers deftly undid the knot, and it fell away. Nothingness, the ripped-out heart of the world, spread all around them. Andín fought down her panic, feeling bile in her throat.

She trembled, shut her eyes, got hold of herself, and opened them again.

"Okay," she said, steeling herself and fixing her gaze on the mountains ahead. "Let's walk."

They marched forward.

"Thank you," said Lynde.

Andín hugged her close.

◆◆◆

"I know," said Andín as they walked one excruciating step at a time through the unbearable blankness. "Let's sing a song. It's in old Antrimanian, but I can translate it."

"I—I like songs," said Lynde. Her complexion was ashy gray, and her eyes darted back and forth. Her grip on the sword was tight.

"This is an ancient Antrimanian folk song. It was in my head. People haven't sung it in ages. Listen, then we'll sing it together. Okay?"

"Okay," said Lynde.

Andín raised her voice to the cracked sky, and sang the song in lilting Alavesh:

Come home, sing home
Men come over the hill
Swing pail, sweep floors
Men come through the dale

Wander far, travel near
Men march home, march home
Sing home, come home
Come home, sing home.

"Got it?"

Lynde nodded, tears running down her face.

They sang the song again. Lynde missed most of the words. But it didn't matter. As they sang, Lynde got better and better. When they finished, they started again and again.

They sang and sang the old Antrimanian song of coming home.

Andín sang a harmony to Lynde's melody, and their voices filled the empty space all around them.

Come home, sing home. Wander far, travel near.

And so they crossed the sea of nothingness, and at last reached the circle of mountains at its far end.

♦♦♦

Andín felt it when her feet connected with soft dirt again, and she sank onto the solid ground in relief and utter exhaustion. Lynde put the sword down and collapsed next to her a moment later.

"We did it," Andín said.

"Yes," said Lynde. She put a steadying hand on Andín's shoulder, then lay her head there with a thunk. They sat together, breathing quietly, for a long while.

"This is Salaz," said Andín. "Isn't it?"

She could smell the sea. A low, round mountain rose above them and then ran down to the shore far below.

"It has to be," said Lynde. "The sword says... well, it says we're *here*. We have to go over there."

A path wound its way up the steep hillside. Tall grass swayed by the path, golden in the dying light of the setting sun.

"Let's go," said Andín, feeling her strength returning. "We have to get there."

Overhead, another crack had appeared in the sky. Andín and Lynde struggled up the path, their legs burning and tired.

♦♦♦

The path took them up the side of the hill, weaving back and forth between scraggly trees and rocks. A cold northern wind blew.

"She came this way," said Lynde. Andín didn't even have to ask who she meant. Judy Shashalnikya. "I know she did. A thousand years ago."

"She must have," said Andín. "I'm sure you're right."

"What do you think is up ahead?" asked Lynde.

"A tomb, I guess," said Andín. "I don't know. Something."

I hope. She couldn't bear the idea that this was all for nothing.

At last they crested the hill and looked down, huffing and puffing.

There was a little bowl-shaped valley in between the hills, beyond which the vast ocean glimmered.

"The sea," Andín said, voice full of wonder. "I've never seen it so close."

Lynde pointed towards the sliver of sun still above the horizon. "I come from somewhere out there. That's where Rath is. Or... where it was. In the western sea."

They descended into the valley, hand in hand, as the sun sank below the line of the water at last.

There, in the middle of the valley, was a small house. It was no more than a cottage, really, built from wood and stone and thatch. A little curl of smoke rose from the stone chimney, and a honey-colored light burned in the window. Twilight was fast spreading over the little valley.

They stumbled, tired and worn, down the path to the house. Lynde raised her hand and knocked three times on the heavy wooden door.

For a moment nothing happened. Andín wondered if they'd have to force their way in. But then the door opened and an old woman smiled out at them.

"You!" Andín breathed.

"Hello, girls," said the sorceress Vi, smiling warmly. "Welcome. Come in. I've been expecting you."

◆◆◆

They sat at a small round table in the middle of the cluttered, cheery kitchen while the sorceress made some tea. The house was cramped, packed full of books in every language, plants and jars and assorted strange items. Lynde and Andín exchanged puzzled glances.

"Ah," said Vi, peering outside, "bad weather."

"It's horrible," said Andín. "There's... you saw it. Whole cities and towns. Gone."

"Yes, I know." Her smile flagged, and for an instant everything seemed far less bright and cheerful. "We were supposed to have had much longer. Weeks. Months. Maybe even a year. But what you did, fixing the land, it sped things up. I had no idea that would happen."

"No," said Andín, shocked. They were responsible?

"It isn't your fault," said Vi. "It's no one's fault. Just… bad luck."

"Why are you here?" Lynde demanded.

"I live here," said Vi, "among a great many other places. I've lived a long time; I've had a while to accumulate homes."

"How did you get here? We came as fast as we could!"

"Well, it's complicated. In a sense, I'm never not here," said Vi. "I can send pieces of myself out and then call them back when I need to. That's what you met in Alavia. They can travel very fast when pressed."

"This is where we're supposed to be, right?" asked Lynde. "Is this where Judy Shashalnikya's tomb is? Why didn't you tell us before? You didn't say anything at all! Why?" Lynde was furious and pounded the table for emphasis.

"I thought we had more time," said Vi, a troubled expression crossing her face. "I thought… well. Have your tea first. Rest."

"How can we rest?" exclaimed Andín. "The world is disintegrating out there."

"My dear," said Vi, "you'll soon find that we have nothing *but* time here." The tea kettle started to burble and whistle. "Here, then." She lifted it off the crackling fire. No magic here, apparently, except for the softly bobbling airborne wizard lights. She poured hot water into a set of ancient-looking teacups. "It's Selessian Breakfast Tea, or at least that's what they call it now. In Yarun, where it's from, they call it Afternoon Mist. Neither is really descriptive."

She put the steaming tea in front of them. Lynde held hers for a moment, her hands shaking so hard that it sloshed out.

"My poor little dears," said Vi. "I gather the journey has not been easy."

"No," said Andín shortly. Lynde took a hesitant sip of tea, looking away.

Vi squeezed Andín's hand. "This is the end of the world, I'm afraid. It's not a nice time."

"I don't want the world to end," stated Lynde, determination in her eyes. She set her tea down and pushed it away. "I have to give the sword to Judy Shashalnikya. I have to set things right."

"You don't want tea?" Vi asked wistfully. "One last cup of tea?"

Andín shook her head. "Can you take us to Judy Shashalnikya? She's here, isn't she?"

Vi sighed. She looked incredibly ancient at that moment. "Oh, she's here. The sword brought you right to her. That's what I designed it to do. That's what she wanted, and it worked very well indeed."

"You designed the sword?" Lynde asked.

"Oh, yes, my dear." She stood, and all traces of lightness and levity vanished from her lined face. "She's ready now. Come. See for yourselves why you're here."

◆◆◆

Vi summoned her wizard lights and took them to an unremarkable door that Andín could have sworn was not there before. She opened it, and the musty smell of dust, cobwebs, and incredible age leaked out. Lynde sneezed.

The sorceress laughed sadly, and then, one halting, careful step at a time, led them onto a long, long flight of stairs.

They descended into the darkness for what seemed like forever. Andín started counting steps, but gave up after a hundred. Down and down they went into the heart of the world, their way lit only by Vi's wizard lights floating in front of her. The smell changed from dry and dusty to warm and earthy, like fresh loam. Andín suddenly thought of her childhood and the farm her uncle had run before the war.

Visions floated up out of the darkness.

She saw a short, stocky Alavesh woman in ancient-style clothes trudging across a vast wilderness, all alone. She was on a rolling, windy plain with a few trees scattered here and there. Then she crested a hill and beheld a terrible thing—the great wide lake of nothingness!

The woman had no fear. She stepped into the nothing and was not swallowed. She walked across it into the heart of the breaks in the world. As she went, they healed behind her.

What? Had that been Judy Shashalnikya?

Another vision:

The woman crested the hill and found only a hole in the ground. Was this why she'd come all this way? She crawled in, and then she fell and fell and fell, into the endless dark deep...

A third vision:

The sorceress was there. She took the woman's hand, and then both agreed to something that Andín could not hear. The cracks in the world flared—and healed.

And then a thousand years passed.

Andín's heart pounded.

Hurry, hurry, Judy Shashalnikya's voice whispered from the deep.

They reached the bottom of the stairs. Another door was there, and Vi opened it. "Go ahead," she said. "It's time."

◆◆◆

A woman lay on a raised bier in the center of a perfectly round room. Her clothes, the same as the ones Andín had seen in her vision, were now thin and threadbare. She was in her thirties, and she was more *formed* than she was beautiful. Her hands were gnarled, her muscles hard and well-defined. She had the dark skin of all of the Alavesh.

Andín recognized her at once. "She's older than she was in my dreams," she said, "but I'd know her anywhere."

Judy Shashalnikya.

"Is... is she dead? Or alive? How can this be?" asked Lynde. She reached out as if to touch her, then drew her hand back. "She's cold. But she's breathing!"

"No," said Vi, "she's not dead. She's not quite alive, either. Think of it as a deep sleep but more than that. Deeper, and the dreams are like nothing you could imagine."

Wake me, said the voice of Judy Shashalnikya, but this time everyone heard her. *There is no time. Wake me.*

"The sword," said Lynde. "That's what will wake her!"

"Yes," said Vi heavily. "It will. That was part of the bargain. If that's your choice."

Lynde took the sword from its scabbard and walked it carefully over to the woman asleep on the bier.

"Wait!" said Andín. Suddenly, she was very afraid of what would happen if that sword touched Judy Shashalnikya's hand. "You don't know what will happen!"

Lynde looked over at Vi. "Tell me."

"She'll wake up," said Vi. "After that, I don't know what will happen. Truly."

"Do you know? Judy?" Andín asked the still woman on the bier.

Wake me, whispered Judy Shashalnikya. *Hurry.*

Lynde closed her eyes, whispered a prayer, and put the hilt of the sword in Judy Shashalnikya's hand.

«*No!*» shrieked the demon from deep inside Andín's mind.

The world around them vanished into nothingness.

Chapter 27
The Demon Girl's Song

"Lynde?"

Andín's voice sounded strangely hollow and muted. They stood on a circular plane, distinct from the twilight-dim uncreation all around them.

Somewhere Andín thought she heard someone screaming.

Lynde staggered back from the bier, shocked.

"What happened? Where's everything?" She turned to Andín, grabbing her to steady herself. "Andín, what did I *do?*"

They looked around. There was the sorceress, looking as if she'd been struck. The bier was empty. At the very edge of the plane, a girl who had not been there before crouched.

And that was the entire world. Beyond was *nothing.*

Lynde collapsed onto the ground, her eyes dead. "No," she murmured. "No. I can't have."

"Sorceress!" Andín pleaded. "What is this? What happened?"

"I told you," said Vi. She knelt next to Lynde and put a hand on the young woman's shoulder. "This is the end."

"Wake the sleeper and heal the world," said Lynde, voice monotone. "That's what they told me to do. They told me I would heal the world. But I woke the sleeper and the world *ended*. It wasn't supposed to be like this."

"I'm so sorry," said Vi.

"Why didn't you tell me?" Lynde said, anguish on her face.

Vi shook her head. "You had to make your own choice. We all

do, now. We should have had so much more time."

"You manipulated us," said Andín, her temper spiking. "You made the world end!" She stretched out a hand at Vi, gathering dark energy to herself. The taste of it was far more raw and powerful here, wherever this was. "I should blast you into the nothing!"

"No," said Vi, holding up a hand, fear in her eyes. "Please. I swear to you, that wasn't it. Go. Go ask her why."

Andín looked over at the edge of the circle, where the girl sat, her back to them. "That's... that's her, isn't it? Judy Shashalnikya. That's her become young again."

"Yes," said Vi. "Though that isn't her name, not her original name. And not her name anymore, I don't think."

The girl turned to look at them, her eyes heavy, then turned away again.

"Who is she, really?" Andín asked.

Vi glanced again at the girl sitting at the edge of the circle, who made no movement. She shook her head slightly and turned back to Andín. "She's the creator of this world, I'm afraid."

Andín closed her eyes, listening to the sound of her own heart beating.

"That's impossible," she heard herself say.

"Is it?"

They both looked over at the girl, who glanced back at them. Her eyes were hard and defensive. She looked away again.

"She created this world in her mind. It was a land of heroes and adventure, or at least it was when she made it. It was the kind of place a young girl might dream for herself. And then... she came here. She traveled between her own world and this one. I don't know why or how. Something happened to her back there, I think. She's never said what. But how you see her now... that's what she looked like when she first came here as a girl."

The girl who had been Judy Shashalnikya stared off into the nothingness in stony silence.

"She grew up. She lived her life here. She led armies, fought and bled, and then finally sacrificed herself for the Alavesh. She had a son who became the first of a line of kings. She had great friends and passionate lovers. She found she could no longer create or control the world, but she could be a part of it.

"Unfortunately, she found that it was a half-finished thing and could not survive on its own. Soon it began to fall apart, much like the world has been doing lately."

"Ha," said Andín, "we've been living in Wash Pot Land this whole time!"

Vi frowned. "Wash Pot Land?"

Somewhere, she heard a low laugh. The girl, though she still stared off into the space beyond.

"My brother and I. We made up stories, when we were kids," Andín explained. "I was the queen. I sat on an old pot and gave orders. We imagined it was a whole kingdom, that hill. So you're saying our entire world, everything, is like a big Wash Pot Land for this girl to play in!" She waved over at Judy Shashalnikya. "Like we're nothing! Just fakes!"

"Ah," said Vi, "it's like that in the way a mouse is like a wolf. Both have fur and teeth, don't they? But they're so different at the same time. One is much, much more. And we are real, or we have been as real as anything can be."

"I see," said Andín sharply, though she didn't. "So you found all this out? How?"

A shadow passed over her face. "I was young and foolish, and I wanted knowledge of demons and other worlds. So... I made a bargain with the King of the Red World."

Andín blinked. "The... the king?"

But then she remembered.

Alone among all the demons was a single grand one who moved slowly among them, feeding in a languid manner, giving and receiving many things. More than this she couldn't form in her mind; the memories ran from her. They were too strange, too alien, too much the demon and not enough the human.

Vi shuddered, obviously remembering the same creature. "He told me many things about the way of worlds." She touched what looked like the remains of a scar on her face. "He wasn't kind about it. There was a terrible price, and I was a long time recovering.

But when I did... I knew how to summon creatures from other worlds—and how to anchor a failing world in reality before it shattered entirely."

Andín shook her head. "We knew nothing about this!"

"Only the oldest demons seemed to have this kind of knowledge. You were a very young demon, Yasharay, that's why you were so easy to catch and why you adapted so well. In any case, I took what I'd learned, and I made my offer to Judy Shashalnikya. She accepted. She loved this world so, and she couldn't bear to see it fade away. She wanted so badly for it to live. She gave herself to the world, to act as its anchor to more solid planes. She lay here and dreamed the world; in doing so, she made it whole. That's how it works.

"And in all this time, I've stood guard over her, keeping her safe. I've sacrificed much to stay here as her guardian. My life, my whole long life, has been to serve her and keep her safe."

"Why?" asked Andín at last.

"Because I love this world, too," Vi said simply. "And... because once, a long time ago, I found a gate to the red world. I used it to let a demon loose on this world." She gave Andín a significant look. "I wanted to make up for that mistake, so I stayed here and I guarded her."

"And then you brought us here. Why?" asked Andín. "I don't understand. What could we have done?"

"Ask her," said Vi. "Go and ask her."

◆◆◆

Andín sat next to Judy Shashalnikya. She was perched on the very edge of the round disc of space, her legs dangling off the edge into the twilight space surrounding them. She thought she heard another scream from somewhere out there, but it vanished as quickly as it had come.

"Tell me," Andín said, her anger simmering. "Tell me everything."

Judy Shashalnikya shrugged her shoulders. "When I was young I made this place. Don't ask me why. I don't want to think about it. I don't even know how I did it. But I did. When things went bad back home, I came here." She looked off into the distance. "I woke up in the snow, somewhere near the Debanae River. I knew where I was. A kind woman named Aruka Shashalnikya took me in, and the rest is in that book you were carrying around."

"You made yourself a Wash Pot Land," said Andín bitterly, "and we were your imaginary friends. Is that it? Were we just toys to you?"

Judy shook her head. "Maybe at the start, but after I came here, never. You were real. Flesh and blood, souls in bodies. You're as human as I am, in every sense."

"Except that when you wake up, we all die," said Andín. "I thought a demon stealing someone's body was evil, but you!"

Judy held up a hand. "I didn't make this world on purpose. I was a little girl, imagining a whole world in my mind. What if you woke up and found yourself in your Wash Pot Land, except that it was real? What would you do? Wouldn't you feel responsible?"

Andín couldn't imagine it. Wash Pot Land... all the funny little people she and Palyar had made up, all the stories and games. For an instant, she glimpsed what Judy Shashalnikya must have felt.

"I gave myself to this world for a thousand years," said Judy Shashalnikya. "I slept here so I could be an anchor. It's a way of being more... real. It meant the world didn't just fade back into dreamland. That's what's all around us. Dreams. Nothing. The void. Oblivion.

"But I did it. For all of you. For a thousand years. That's a long time. I'm so, so tired. I couldn't hold it together any longer."

"Damn you," said Andín, still angry. "And now you want to go home, is that it? You want to go home."

Judy nodded. "It's been so long."

Andín put her head in her hands, grief overwhelming her anger. "You're a rotten god. You can't even keep the world from coming apart."

"I'm no god," said Judy.

"Aren't you? You made us. You destroyed us. Sounds like a god to me."

Judy said nothing.

"Why did you call us here? Just to have someone do the final deed, and take the blame? Poor Lynde." Andín glanced over her shoulder. Lynde was resting her head on Vi's lap. They both looked like they were weeping.

"I had an idea that if I brought all the pieces from other worlds here, Vi and I could use them to make some kind of anchor," sighed Judy. "Your demon and that sword were the only pieces not from here, besides me. I suppose the blood in my poor Diya's veins might have qualified, but it's so distant from me now. It's this world's, mostly. But we thought we could combine them all, somehow, and make that anchor. The anchor would have taken my place. We thought it could work... if we'd only had time."

"But you didn't," said Andín.

"No," said Judy. "Everything fell apart too fast. We never realized that would happen. I thought I'd prepared so well. I even asked Rikan to watch for you, I knew his ship could be fast. But it didn't work out that way. If we'd only had more time... we could have done it. I'm sure of it. But now..." She shrugged again. "I knew it wouldn't work. We had no time. So I brought you down here and had Lynde wake me up. That way, we could just end it and be done with it."

Andín shook her head. It couldn't end like this. "I... I wish I'd gone faster."

"You didn't know. And I couldn't bring myself to tell you. I thought... you'd just ignore me."

"Maybe I would have," Andín said, "but maybe not."

"If it helps, I'm sorry," Judy Shashalnikya said. "Look, I can go across to my world from here. You, Lynde, and Vi can come with me. I think you'll be able to survive there just fine. At least you could have lives. You and Lynde were so brave, so smart. You both reminded me of who I used to be, a long time ago. I used you, I know. But, demon girl, you know that the emperor uses people."

The emperor uses people up and throws them away, thought Andín gloomily. They'd been used, but in the end it hadn't changed anything.

A thought stuck her. "Could we make that anchor now? The

sword, the demon..."

Judy shook her head. "We don't have time now that I'm awake. The world needs someone to dream it, otherwise it fades away. Even this little plane will vanish soon. And… I can't do it anymore. What I had to give, I ran out of. Like I said, I'm sorry. You're right. I'm not a very good god."

Andín shut her eyes and heard the scream again. Demons out in the void, she thought. Terrible things.

She thought of brave Lynde, beautiful, clever Yshe, foolhardy, reckless Rikan… and made her choice. "What if I dreamed the world?"

"You?" said Judy. "No. No! It wouldn't work. You didn't make it. It wouldn't… Would it? Vi!" She gestured to the sorceress. "What if Andín took my place as the dreamer?"

Vi thought, and then shook her head. "She didn't make the world… and I think too much of her is of this world to be an anchor. There must be more from the other worlds than just an ancient demon."

"My sword," said Lynde. She'd been listening, and now she came over. "You said it's not from here."

Judy nodded. "I brought it with me from my own place. It was all I had. It can stay. I don't have anything else, though. One sword, one demon… and one young woman. Maybe together… maybe we can make something that will keep the world going a little while longer while we work out a more permanent solution. I don't know."

"Andín, hold the sword," said Vi. Lynde handed it to her. Vi frowned thoughtfully, and shut her eyes. She put a hand on the sword, and then on Andín.

She stayed that way for a long moment. Andín heard the scream again, closer this time. What was out there?

"Lynde, take the sword. Part of it's rubbed off on you. Maybe that'll be enough," said Vi.

Lynde, looking worried, took the sword back and held Andín's hand.

"No," Vi said. "I'm sorry. It's better, but there's not enough. I can't sense that sort of... resonance... that Judy had. With her, it was so easy. But with you, I have to grasp at every single little piece. If I had time... maybe I could come up with someone. Maybe I could go to the red world or Judy's world and find something I could use. But this plane won't last for long."

It was true. Andín could see it beginning to dissipate.

"That's it, then," said Judy heavily. "Come with me. We'll go to my world. It's somewhere."

The scream cut through the silence again, closer and closer.

"Look!" cried Andín. Someone was out there, tumbling through space, heading right for them.

"Impossible," breathed Lynde. "It's the princess."

Judy straightened. "Diya? Diya!"

Somehow, it was. She spun through space nearby, screaming. She would miss the plane by too much. They couldn't reach her.

Hisja, Andín, or something deep within Andín, thought. *Dark energy. Hisja.*

"*Hisja!*" shouted Andín, and for once the dark power didn't leap out of her, but sucked things *in*.

Diya abruptly changed course and sped towards them. She crashed into the ground, rolling end over end. She looked up at them, blinking.

"You have my sword," she croaked at Lynde.

◆◆◆

They quickly explained. Diya took it all in with surprising calm.

"So this world was an imaginary thing," she said. "Dreamed up by my ancestor, who has been sleeping here in order to keep it from fading away. And that ancestor ... is you."

Judy smiled. "Thought you'd catch on quick. Blood tells."

"So it does," said Diya. "You're my great-great-a-dozen-times-great-grandmother, then. And you don't look a day over fifteen."

"In the flesh," said Judy proudly. "It's nice to meet you at last."

"Yes," said Diya, a strange look in her eye. "It is."

"How did you get here? Why aren't you vanished?" asked Andín.

"I have no idea," said Diya. "I was on a broken-down train

to Telesan when everything went blank. I found myself spinning around in this void. I assumed I was dead."

"No," said Vi. "You're quite alive, Princess. Though I admit, that's surprising."

"We need to go soon," said Judy. The plane they were standing on was vanishing from the edges in.

"Wait," said Andín. "Wait! Diya's blood. You said part of it's from your world."

"Yes," said Judy. "I suspect that's why she survived what happened. She's just enough my descendant... you probably didn't know it, Diya, but your mother was also my descendant. Very distantly."

"Of course I knew that," said Diya.

"Inbreeding," Lynde whispered.

"Good pedigree," retorted Diya.

"You have more of my blood than anyone else living," said Judy. "It was enough to spare you. Congratulations, I suppose."

"She might be enough," said Vi, eyes bright. "For the anchor. Diya, grab on to Andín and Lynde."

"Why?" asked Diya suspiciously.

"We might be able anchor the world and bring it back for a little while," said Andín. "It has to be from outside, and it has to be enough."

"Ah, of course," said Diya, as if she understood perfectly. "Proceed."

She took Andín's hand, and Andín took Lynde's. Vi touched them, and gasped.

"God and Goddess," she said. "It's enough. Barely. I think it would last maybe a dozen years, probably less. But enough. We could bring back the world. We could keep it solid while I work on a solution!"

"Then I'll do it," said Diya immediately. "It would be my honor."

"As will I," said Lynde.

"And you can help make an anchor if we do this?" Andín asked.

"It might not work," warned Vi. "There may be no way to make a permanent anchor. I may never be able to get back from Judy's world if I go there, looking for a way to stop this from happening again. But... yes. I think I can."

"Then I'll help dream the world," said Andín.

She reached for the sorceress, but suddenly she was seized by a terrible red pain.

"What?" she gurgled. Then the demon spoke, and it was not her, and did not use her voice.

"You can't decide without me! And I say NO!"

Andín screamed and fell off the circle into the nothingness.

♦♦♦

She was falling, but she could see nothing above and below. She only knew she fell.

There in front of her, another Andín fell. Her eyes were blood red, and angry red markings covered her body.

"You," said Andín.

"Yes!" said the demon, frantic. *"Deeny, please, no! You* won't *make me dream the world! You will not confine me! How can you give up your freedom like this? We—we are to go back to Antriman and be emperor!"*

"But don't you see," said Andín. "There is no Antriman!"

"There are other worlds out there. We can go to those! We don't have to go to the red world, we can't live there. But we can follow Judy to her world. We can live there! We can walk under the sky together and be free! Forget this world."

"How can I?" Andín cried. The wind tore at her breath as she fell faster and faster. "How can I? How can *you?* You lived here a thousand years! This is the world you had a hand in making. All of it would have been for nothing!"

"It doesn't matter. I want to be free! Don't you?"

"Yes," sobbed Andín. She remembered the wide steppes of Shuyu and the feeling of absolute freedom she'd felt. "I do. But... I want to go home, too, and if I can't go home, I want to bring it all back! I want home to be there again."

They grappled as they fell. The other Andín's skin was red-hot.

"*Your home is gone forever!*" snarled the demon. "*Give up this quest! I won't do it! I won't be part of you and Lynde and Diya! I don't want to be chained here!*"

"No!" cried Andín. "You must help me. I can make it again! We can make it again, together! And if I can't go to Viko Station, if I can't hug my mother again or apologize to my father, or tell Yshe... tell Yshe I'm in love with her—" she gulped, tears streaming out of her eyes. "I—I can ensure they have another shot at life!"

"*And what will happen when you want to wake? What if no anchor can be made? What if you have to dream this world forever and never have your own life again?*"

"I don't know. But I want to give this world a chance. You've seen it! Hular was right, you know!"

The demon bared Andín's teeth in anger.

"No, he saw it. Think about it! Motorcars, airships, electric light. This world is becoming something new and terrifying and incredible. All of these people could make an amazing world together! Don't you want to know what happens next?"

The demon fell silent, pushing away from her. The only sound was the rush of air as they fell.

"Help me," pleaded Andín. "I know you love freedom. So do I! But I love the world, too. All those people, all the things we've seen and done together, it must count for something. Please! Make the world whole with me. Sing home with me. I don't believe you don't care, you're too much *me* not to. I don't want to be trapped here forever either, but we must. For what we love. Please, please help me."

The demon wailed, a high, keening sound.

"Please," Andín said, "for love. Because I love you, and I know you love me, too. Because this is who we are now. And because sometimes *the emperor must sacrifice everything for the sake of the people.*"

And then it held out a hand. Andín grasped it tightly.

"*For you, I will,*" said the demon, and Andín hit the ground.

◆◆◆

She opened her eyes. The others stood over her.

"We've decided. We'll help dream the world," she said. "We'll be the anchor. We'll keep it stable until you come back with a solution."

Judy knelt next to her. "Good. You'll see. It's not like sleep at all. It's better. The three—four—of you will understand soon enough."

"Thank you, Judy," said Andín, "for our world."

Judy laughed. "Thank you for saving it."

Andín stood and joined hands with Lynde and Diya. Vi took Diya's hand.

"Here," Judy Shashalnikya stood beside them. She took Vi's hand and then Andín's, completing the circle. "For this, it might take all of us."

Andín closed her eyes, and let the dark energy of the red world build up inside her.

"Now," whispered Judy Shashalnikya.

Andín fell asleep, and she dreamed...

♦♦♦

Andín walked through a sunless land. She could feel the presence of the others, though she could not see them.

It was time.

She opened her mouth, and began to sing a wordless song.

Come, she sang. Return. Be!

Dirt, rocks, earth, the deep fires below. Sky and sea, water and air. Grass and trees, flowers and waving wheat. Rivers, streams, mountains and plains.

Salaz, Selessia, Alavia. Antriman and Shuyu. Pryttland, Rath and all of you, all of Durova, come into being.

Deer and mice, cows and sheep, cats and dogs. Men, women, children, and everyone.

Rikan, Yshe, Palyar, Mother, Father! Come back. Live again.

Live.

Be made!

Power arced through her, bursting through into the void beyond.

Her voice rang through the heavens as the world sprang into being all around her.

Epilogue
Twelve Years Later

Birds called in the sky high above the little seaside village.

Yshe Shadalyan toted her luggage off the pier, sagging in relief to finally be back on Alavesh soil. Jandy had remained behind at his post at the Alavesh embassy in Antriman, perhaps this time for good. Yshe had told him she was tired of being torn away from her life in Telesan when Jandy got lonely and then sent home whenever there was trouble.

Antriman was still recovering from the abdication of the emperor and the declaration of the Republic of Antriman five years before. Various factions were fighting in the streets of Palascena now, as the periphery of the ancient empire broke away at last. The world was changing.

Yshe was changing with it. Jandy had threatened to divorce her after their last fight. She told him she was fine with that. Her lawyer in Telesan would draw up the papers under the newly liberal divorce laws.

At least she'd had a chance to speak with Antriman's leading women's liberation activist, Fevín dan Halda, before she'd gone home this time. Though when she had, she couldn't help but think of poor lost Andín.

No one knew what had happened to Andín dal Rovi. Yshe had even gone to Andín's family in Viko Station, but they hadn't heard from her, either.

By now Yshe told herself that she'd stopped looking for Andín around every corner and behind every bush. Antriman had been difficult; so many people there bore a vague resemblance to Andín.

If only she'd stayed with her in Gantritt. If only she'd done more to get her out of there. If only she hadn't said those things on the boat. So many regrets.

Yshe sighed and trudged over the cobbled streets toward the train station. The ship had been forced to come into port here for some nautical reason Yshe couldn't be bothered to fathom, but at least it was only a few hours to Telesan by train.

She bought a newspaper and sat down on a bench near the station to read it.

The newspapers were full of the shocking reappearance of Princess Diya Shashalnikya after she'd been missing for a dozen years. Apparently the princess had vanished on that awful day when the sky had cracked.

No one could agree on what that day had meant. The world had gone on, shaken and nervous, but they remembered.

But from that day forward, every once in a while Yshe dreamed of Andín, and the dreams seemed more real than nearly everything else she experienced in her day-to-day life.

She scanned the newspaper. The princess had made a splash by renouncing any claim to the throne, and she was now living in the southern city of Rettlia with her family. Apparently she was using her good name to broker an agreement with the Prytt and the Selessians to allow plebiscites in Kish and East Gantritt in exchange for certain other trade and territorial concessions, according to the article Yshe was reading. The people there were expected to vote to join Alavia. Good for her.

Someone came and sat on the bench next to Yshe. She was Antrimanian, which didn't register for a moment as Yshe was very used to being around Antrimanians.

But then the other person's hand touched her own.

"Excuse me," Yshe began to say hotly, turning quickly—only to find herself looking into a heartbreakingly familiar face. The other woman's deep brown eyes danced as she smiled. Beautiful red and blue and green energies seemed to swirl around her.

"Andín?" whispered Yshe, hardly daring to believe. "Is it really you?"

"Hello, love," Andín dal Rovi said, squeezing her hand. The world grew brighter around them. "Hello."

The End

 Susan Jane Bigelow is a fiction writer, political columnist, and librarian. She mainly writes science fiction and fantasy novels, most notably the *Extrahuman Union* series from Book Smugglers Publishing. Her short fiction has appeared in *Strange Horizons*, *Apex Magazine*, *Lightspeed Magazine*'s "Queers Destroy Science Fiction" issue, and the Lamba Award-winning "The Collection: Short Fiction from the Transgender Vanguard," among others. She lives with her wife in northern Connecticut, and is probably currently at the bottom of a pile of cats.

If you enjoyed *The Demon Girl's Song*, please take a moment to review it where you purchased it!

We're always happy for you to come by the site, let us know what you think, and take a look at the rest of our science fiction and fantasy books.

DreamingRobotPress.com

Or email us at books@dreamingrobotpress.com

Continue reading for a sneak preview of *Mirror of Stone* by Corie J. Weaver.

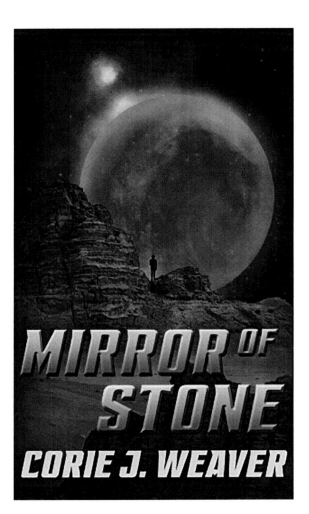

Chapter One

By the middle of the dinner shift, Eleanor Weber wanted to scream or die. She didn't care which.

"Girl!" shouted yet another drunken farmer from the tavern's common room.

Eleanor raised her head from the kitchen table and stared out the window. Ladril hung low in the cloud-filled sky that night. The swirling pastels of the planet above provided a dramatic backdrop for the buildings across the street.

"Girl!" The woman's voice sounded louder, rough with drink and impatient.

Eleanor stood up, straightened her apron and made her way out to the front of the tavern with a loaded tray.

Wiring lay exposed in long runs down the grey ceiling, paired with pipes that despite Eleanor's constant repairs crackled and hissed like old women gossiping, even when the hall stood empty. But ever since the trading ships and their Navy escort arrived at the spaceport outside of Prime, her father's bar had overflowed with customers. A table of Guardsmen argued about recruitment terms, merchants complained about grain that had spoiled in the long delay between ships, farmers speculated on ways to transform more of Travbon's barren rock to good soil and everyone argued about candidates in the next election.

Eleanor could make out the faces of a handful of regulars, but tonight most were strangers in from outlying farms, or prospectors who had rushed into town as soon as the news of the ships' arrival went out. Everyone seemed to be shouting, as all forms of accented

Standard jumbled against Eleanor's ears.

"Here you are, ma'am," Eleanor placed the full wine glass down by the strapping woman.

The farmer didn't bother to look away from her drinking partners as she held her credit chip up for scanning.

At a far table, Mrs. Jameson shook her head at the rowdy crowd. Surrounded by miners and farmers, Mrs. Jameson gave the impression she had stepped out of some fashion vid to model the latest styles from Claro. Eleanor couldn't think of anyone else in town who would bother to stitch designer outfits out of scraps of fabric, but somehow Mrs. Jameson's efforts succeeded. The severe grey and black jumpsuit made the widow look taller, even sitting down.

"Sorry it took me so long to get here, it's a madhouse tonight." Eleanor waved her hand at the crowded room behind her.

"All going well? How's Greg? I only planned to come in for a moment, but can stay and help if you need it."

"No, it's fine. Everyone's wound up, that's all. And I'm sure my father will be down shortly. He's resting for a bit right now." Eleanor wiped down the table and looked away from the older woman's sharp gaze. She knows. Everyone must know.

Eleanor wished her aunt would come out from behind the scuffed bar and help serve tables, even if it meant listening to her complaints later. Susan preferred to reign from behind the bar, only emerging to break up a fight if it came down to that. With luck, this wouldn't end up being that sort of night.

Burly men in plain grey coveralls argued over a section of the map pinned to the wall. Prospectors in from the Newell Mountains to the east, by the pale lines embedded into their faces. Respirator marks. Eleanor had often seen the black molded devices when she cleaned guest rooms. Once she had placed one gingerly over her mouth and nose. It felt uncomfortable, claustrophobic and she had torn it off. Still, the awkward device formed an essential part of the miner's kit.

"Miss? Might there be a room still available?"

Eleanor jumped at the light touch on her arm. At a guess, she'd have placed the old man as another prospector. His travel-stained clothes and the rancid smell indicated it had been a while since his last bath. Not that anyone else in the place smelled much better. His matted grey hair stuck up from his head in tufts around his face.

"I'd have to check, but I think one of the smaller berths is open. Would that be all right?"

"That's fine. I'm not sure if it much matters anymore." The man slurred his words. Perhaps he had brought his own flask.

She shrugged. One fewer table to wait on. She stepped away but he waved her back.

"The Namok flooded. Took me weeks longer to get back than I'd planned. I went to Administration to tell them but they laughed me out of the office." The old man slumped over the table. His gummy eyes gazed past her, focused on something she couldn't see.

"Well, I'm sorry for that. Maybe someone in Administration will listen to you tomorrow." She stepped away. "I'll go set up that berth for you."

As she passed the bar she said to Susan, "I'm setting up a room for that old man. What's open?"

Susan snorted. "Him? Did you get his money first? He doesn't look like he can pay for his wine, much less a berth."

"Watch the front, would you? I'll take a plate to Poppa while I'm up."

Susan shrugged. "On your head, then."

The swinging of the kitchen door cut off the noise of the front room. A few slices of smoked sausage, a piece of hard cheese, a hunk of dense bread fresh from that morning's baking. A glass of fortified water. A set of fresh sheets for the prospector's guest berth. All ready.

Upstairs, Eleanor put the tray of food on the bedside table while she made up the small room. *What an odd man. I wonder if anyone knows he's gone crazy. Maybe nobody cares enough to keep him home, out of trouble.*

She took the tray down to the end of the hall past the sputtering light that she could never get to burn evenly and around the corner to where the family's rooms clustered. She took a deep breath.

"Poppa? It's me. I brought you something to eat."

An empty bed, sheets torn off, faced her. A straight-backed chair lay overturned next to the table littered with empty bottles. The dank sweet smell of rot mixed with the sharp tang of alcohol hung in the air although Eleanor had cleaned the room yesterday. Watery light from the street outside provided the sole illumination.

"Poppa?"

A sob drew her attention to the corner behind the bed.

"There's my girl. My pretty, pretty girl."

"Come on, Poppa."

Eleanor's stomach knotted. Why did he have to be like this? Why couldn't he help, instead of leaving everything to her? He acted as if he alone had been abandoned.

"Come here, honey. Put that tray down. Maybe I'll get to it later."

She cleared space among the bottles on the cluttered table for the tray.

"At least drink the water, please?"

"That sludge? Tastes wrong."

Eleanor sighed. "I've told you. That's because it has vitamins and stuff in it. It'll help you get better."

Pretending to herself that her father stayed in his room due to sickness worked most of the time, but she couldn't lie to herself here among the bottles and the vomit.

"Come here," he repeated. "Wanna tell you a story."

"I don't have time right now. You should come on down, spend some time with everyone. Your friends miss you. They've asked about you all night."

But she cleared a space on the floor and sat next to him.

"I never met a prettier woman than your mother, not in the whole colony." His voice had faded from the baritone she loved to a ragged growl. "Martha. Such a plain name for a beautiful girl. At your age, she had dark hair and sun-gold skin, just like you. Half the boys fell over themselves to get her attention. But she picked me. Me! Never understood it."

Eleanor continued to smile and nod, but didn't listen. She had heard this story too many times. Four years earlier the Kherdan flu had ravaged the colony. Even when the supply ships had flown regularly, there had been shortages, especially of medicines. The fever left her mother frail and easily tired. Weeks would pass without her mother leaving the bedroom, weeks Eleanor remembered of creeping upstairs, peeking through the door to watch her mother sleep, waiting for each breath to come, strands of long hair cascading across the coverlet like embroidery.

She glanced at him. Her father had passed out again while lost in his memories. Over a year since her mother had finally faded away. During her own devastation, Eleanor had hated her father for surviving the final separation so well. It had been an illusion, a charade of functionality. He had been hanging on with his fingernails, waited for her to finish school, even encouraging her to graduate early, before descending into his own collapse.

She jerked the sheets back onto the mattress, then pulled and pushed until she managed to get her father in and covered by the blankets.

Not sure why I bother. He won't stay.

•••

The next morning Eleanor served breakfast to guests as they stumbled down to the common room, bleary from the previous evening's excesses. From their looks, she guessed few had slept well; a storm had advanced up the coastline and the wind rattled the building through the night. Throughout the morning, wind pushed against the building with such force everyone sat huddled, as if they could feel the cold gusts.

She halted inside the door of the kitchen and smiled, not the weak thing she wore for the customers, but really smiled for the first time all morning.

A stocky boy with a mess of sandy brown hair pulled packages of food out of a carry-box and neatly arranged them across the counter.

"Mom said you were due for a reorder. I figured I'd bring up the regular items, save you a bit of a trip." He glanced up and the corners of his green eyes crinkled into the familiar smile.

Doug Reilly reached into the top of a large cupboard to put

away zippacks of grain.

"Not there, I'll never reach them."

"Sure thing, shorty."

"How are your folks?"

"They're fine. The store's been swamped. You know all the things we've been out of? Mom's been placing calls to everyone who backordered. I hope we have enough stock to keep us through until the next ship comes." He shrugged and pushed his hair out of his eyes. "It'd be easier if we could manufacture more things here. We keep asking for machine parts, but somehow they keep getting left off the manifest. Dad thinks it's all some huge conspiracy."

Eleanor flicked her eyes to the door to the main room. "Shhh. You never know."

Doug shrugged and stowed the last of the supplies. "I guess not, but I don't think always worrying about the monitors is going to help. How's it going for you?"

Eleanor flung herself into a chair at the kitchen table and threw her hands up. "Susan's getting bossier and Dad is getting worse. I don't know what I'm going to do, or how long I can live like this. The next person that yells 'girl' or calls me 'dear' is going to get a drink thrown in his face. And I wish Susan would go away. She means well, but we don't need her. Dad and I can do it on our own. I want Dad get back to normal; for things to be like they were before."

She stopped to catch her breath. "I sound like I'm six and want an extra candy, don't I?"

Doug walked behind her chair and put his broad hands on her shoulders. She could feel the muscles begin to relax. "El, why don't you . . ." He hesitated. His hands paused in their pattern.

"Why don't I what? Push Susan down the stairs? Trust me, I've thought about it. Lots."

He chuckled and kept rubbing, found little knots of tension, smoothed them out, one layer at a time.

"I'm worried about you. You know that. You can't stay here forever. It's not healthy for you." He tightened his grip over a stiff muscle and she yelped. "See?"

She sighed. "Even if you're right, what am I going to do about my father? I can't leave him."

Doug sat at the table and put his hand over hers. "I don't know what he needs. He has to want to get better, and I'm not sure he does. Honestly, are you?"

Eleanor pulled her hand away and scrambled to her feet. "Of course he'll get better. How can you say he won't? You sound like Susan."

"Eleanor, wait."

She paused.

Doug rose. Took one step toward her, two. "We need to talk. It doesn't have to be like this."

He raised his hand to her face, cupped her cheek. "We can make it be different this time." And he leaned forward.

Eleanor shoved him back. "What are you doing?"

His wide green eyes roved over her face. "I just thought that we-"

"No! Whatever you thought, you were wrong."

Eleanor grabbed her tray and ran out, but not before she heard him stomp out of the kitchen and slam the back door.

•••

As Eleanor cleared the dishes after breakfast, Susan snapped: "Go roust that old bum you let in. He's either still sleeping or he's already scarpered without paying his bill."

Eleanor focused on her breathing. It's not her place to give orders, not her home, she fumed. In a year I'll be old enough, one more year. But she said nothing.

She rapped on the old man's door. "Sir? Are you ready to come down for breakfast? I need to clean the room."

No answer. She knocked louder to make sure he could hear her over the roar of the wind outside. "Sir? Are you okay?"

She eased the sliding door open and stepped into the room. The stench of feces turned her stomach.

"Sir?"

Chapter Two

Because of the storm it took over an hour for Health and Sanitation to arrive. Eleanor unlocked the room for the pair in orange-trimmed uniforms and looked around the tiny chamber. The frail bundle on the pull-down bed filled the room. The slit window peered out onto the grey cloud-tossed sky. The clothes neatly folded on the shelf by the door, the travel-stained pack tucked beneath. The trace of the man, his habits, made her feel worse for brushing him off the night before.

She stood out of the way of the techs. "I didn't know what killed him, or if there would be contagion or. . ." Her voice trailed off. That poor man. And now there's no telling what upset him so much last night.

"You did the right thing, miss." The female tech scanned the corpse, checked the old man's eyes and tongue. "But he looks fine, no signs of disease. Just old, that's all." She checked her pad. "You should have registered him when he came in, you know." Eleanor started to speak, but the tech cut her off. "No harm, now. But be more careful in the future."

As they loaded the body onto the stretcher, Aunt Susan filled the doorway. She gestured to the small stack of the prospector's possessions.

"Take all of this junk too. We don't want it infecting us."

Eleanor regarded the items. A few clothes, a dusty pack with a bedroll tied to the bottom; somehow, it didn't seem enough.

One of the techs regarded her aunt. "Little to fear there, ma'am. There's no risk of contamination to your family or the guests here."

"I didn't ask for your opinion, did I?" Susan's nostrils flared and Eleanor stepped forward, carefully out of her aunt's reach.

"I'll take care of it, Susan."

Eleanor scrambled to gather the prospector's things, bundled them in her arms and tossed them into her own room.

By the time Eleanor returned to her room that afternoon for a break before the dinner rush, any thoughts about the old man and his death had evaporated. The few pieces of shabby furniture in her small room had been gleaned from the other rooms as items judged too worn for guests. She hadn't bothered to decorate further. But out her window lay another world. She reveled in the clear outlook all the way to the borders of town, provided by living in one of the few two-story buildings on her street. Eleanor took a seat on the wide sill and gazed out.

The battered storefronts marched down the street like weary soldiers, waiting for a relief that would never come, their plastisteel surfaces long since pocked by pebbles kicked up from the street by passing flitters.

Administration had promised to pave the town streets years before, but supplies had been delayed time and time again. Eleanor doubted the project would ever move forward. Dirt roads. Space flight and dirt roads. I'll bet they don't know that back on Claro.

The pale sun glimmered off the beaten metal rooftops and the city transformed to fire before her, contained by the haze of the artificial cloud cover. When she swung away, eyes stinging from the brightness, the sight of the weather-beaten and dusty pack she had tossed in the corner that morning surprised her.

It resembled any other prospector's kit, battered, waterproof and cavernous. The colony on Travbon had been founded to take advantage of deposits of thorium, essential to the process that powered the ship engines and the machinery that kept the air clear. No other colony had been established so far from Claro or on a moon rather than a planet, or had undergone such massive transformation to make it habitable, if still rough around the edges. Prospectors were common enough here, but new tools were hard to come by. She could go down to the general store and sell it and its contents in the morning. She opened the fastenings and spilled the few bits and pieces before her on the bed.

Finely worked tools, a well-worn, oft-mended spare shirt, a respirator. A logbook. A compass and map. A larger something she didn't recognize, like a pale green, heavy brick.

Eleanor turned the object in her hands and tried to make sense of what she held. No matter how she pulled and pried at the edges, she could find no way to open it. A pattern ringed the edge of what might have been the cover, a design of flowers and vines. Similar panels decorated the sides and on the two long sides the vines wrapped around three holes arranged along each centerline.

She rifled through the drawer of her night table, found an old data crystal from class and tried to insert it. It didn't fit. Besides, she'd never heard of anything that would take six crystals. How could it read them all at once?

She pressed along the vines, poked the flowers to see if they held hidden buttons.

Nothing. Bracing for a shock, she poked one finger gingerly into a hole. Still nothing.

I'm going to regret this. This is probably some sort of booby trap. And I'm the booby.

She took a deep breath, braced herself and inserted a finger into one of the holes. Nothing happened. The sides of the hole felt smooth and dry. She slid the three longest fingers of each hand into the holes on either side of the device.

And gasped. Not from pain, but surprise. The front of the device flared into life, became a small vid screen. A city with jeweled spires reaching for pastel-streaked heavens filled the screen, graceful curved domes atop slim towers. Broad opalescent walkways surrounded gardens filled with bright flowers. She could imagine their perfume. Scene after scene rolled by in a parade of silent pictures.

Eleanor sat, entranced. Historical vids she had seen in school, dramas on chips at home, newscasts everywhere, but never something so strange, yet real. It's so close. I could reach through and touch the petals, the walls, be transported there in an instant.

She withdrew one hand to touch the screen.

The picture snapped to black.

She put her fingers back into the empty slots. The screen again glowed with life and displayed the initial views of the city.

She closed her eyes and listened for activity in the hallway. Nothing, she had time. She removed her hands, set the darkened vidplayer aside and examined the rest of her spoils.

She picked up the next item, a small travel-stained notebook. A daily log. On the inside of the cover she found a name and brushed her hand over the spindly script. Joel Zacks. Eleanor bowed her head over the notebook and imagined how awful it would be to die alone and no one even know your name.

She flipped through the thin pages of the logbook, found day-by-day travel notes and sample results at first.

"985.367.465 Another false positive, moving on. Further in than ever before. 984.356.476. Good traces. Planted markers."

Factual daily information changed into seasonal essays mixed with fragments of Joel Zach's personal history, snippets of odd poetry, scrawls.

"I've found them. They've been here all along, watching us."

"Them." Eleanor shuddered. The stories were true. The mountains drove you mad.

In school they'd learned the story of the settlement of Claro, the second planet of the System. The later survey ships, the slow expansion of the colonies, the decisions and reasons to establish each one. Never had a survey found a trace of any other life, not on any of the colony worlds, nowhere in the System. Humans were alone.

She found gaps of weeks followed by small sketches of trees and rock formations. Scribbled in the margins she found a recurring verse.

Mirror of rock
Cold as space
Passage through the dark

The verse appeared for the first time next to a full-page sketch of a rock. Not a particularly interesting rock. Sort of bumpy on the sides and top and smooth on the face. Like a melted picture frame of stone.

But what do I know about rocks or prospecting? She shrugged and put down the notebook. Prospectors might think a certain type of rock promised to be full of thorium. Maybe it marked his claim. No way of knowing. No way of asking.

Worn fold lines threatened to rupture the continent displayed on the tattered map. She rotated it, got her bearings, then smoothed the thin plastic out on the bed in front of her.

She put a finger on the spot near the coast where the town of Prime lay, drew her hand to the northeast, towards the mountains, across wide farmland and forests and paused over a river. The prospector had said the flooded Namok had trapped him, delayed him.

In Eleanor's mind she forded the rushing river as her finger crossed the thin line, then continued east and north. The mountains, she thought. He said he went in further than anyone else, but which way? Where did he go?

Her fingers traced back and forth over the range, as if they could scout the path for her.

Wait.

She stopped and ran her finger over one small area again.

Here.

The section of the map felt textured, as if someone had repeatedly run a stylus over the area.

Downstairs in the bar, prospectors often argued about who had been where, claimed what, mined what. As they made their points, they thrust grimed fingers at the large map pinned to the wall, stabbed it as if the force of the gesture could carry along their heated words. The scored area lay in a section of the mountain range she couldn't remember that anyone had ever argued about.

Eleanor put the notebook down, cleared the other items off her faded blue and green quilt and stowed them back into the old pack. She reached for the strange vidplayer and activated the screen. Lost in the images of the ethereal city as they flickered by, the shout from the end of the hall startled her.

"Tables need washing again before the dinner run gets here."

Eleanor jerked upright and scowled at the door. "I'll do it later," she called. "And the tables are fine," she muttered, "you're never happy with anything."

A deep sigh, audible even down the hall. "Now, Eleanor. You know there's never time later."

Eleanor rolled her eyes but put the device under her pillow and left for the next round of chores.

Hours later she returned to her room too tired to investigate the contents of the pack or the odd video further, but dreamed of towers in a faraway city lit by a strangely colored sky.

•••

In the month after the departure of the trading ship, business returned to its usual steady state. Late one afternoon Susan cleaned glasses at the bar and confided in one of the regulars. "Never seen such a thing. I didn't curl up into a bottle when my Scott died, did I? Sheer weakness on his part. He knows someone will always cover for him. Even as children Greg Weber always left everything to me. He's still at it."

Susan smirked at Eleanor passing by with a tray of dishes. She lowered her voice, but not enough. "And if somebody didn't keep mollycoddling that brother of mine, he'd realize all the sooner he has to get back to work and deal with facts, like everyone else."

Eleanor didn't believe it. Her father had given up all pretense of eating the food she brought him; argued about every sip of fortified water.

She had tried to limit his access to alcohol. When she locked the cellar door, her father tore apart the kitchen and front room looking for the key. It took her a full morning to put everything to rights.

Life settled into a new routine. Every night Eleanor sat in her room and watched scenes of the graceful city in the strange device. The views changed; distant forms passed through the images. Their shapes, how their bodies moved, struck her as unnatural, yet mesmerized her. Fabrics that flowed and shimmered in the light draped over elegant, elongated shapes topped by pale masks shaded with bright colors.

She couldn't hear them. The strange vidplayer showed pictures but no sounds. Instead she imagined stories about the figures, gave them names, made wild guesses as to their hidden faces. Frequently dawn came and found Eleanor unsure if she had slept and dreamt of the city, or stayed awake entranced by the pictures.

Early one morning Susan barged into her room with a round of complaints. "I swear, that man better get himself pulled together. I'm not going to be stuck with this mess."

Susan's voice broke off and she gaped at Eleanor's hands still engaged in the vidplayer.

"Hey now, what's that you've got there?"

"Nothing." Eleanor tried to slide it away under the covers.

"Didn't look like nothing to me. Let me see it."

Susan reached across Eleanor, held her back with one hand while she groped under the quilt. She withdrew the vidplayer with a satisfied grunt.

Susan turned the device in her hands. "So, what is it? How does it work?"

With a surge of anger, Eleanor grabbed the vidplayer with both hands and twisted to free it from Susan's grip.

Susan backhanded her. "Watch it, girl. You've been allowed to get away with far too much in the past, but not anymore."

Stunned, Eleanor lay on the floor as the sting of the blow spread across her face.

"Now, tell me what this is."

The numbness in her cheek made it difficult for Eleanor to answer. "Some junk I found in that prospector's pack. I was only looking at it. It doesn't do anything."

She held her breath as Susan ran her hands over the designs on the sides, paused at the finger holes. Susan tried to stuff one finger inside, but the narrow hole refused her.

Serves you right, you cow, Eleanor thought.

Susan's bulk belied her speed. She swooped upon Eleanor and grabbed her hand, attempted to shove her slimmer fingers into the holes.

Eleanor curled her fingers to her palms.

"Open your hands, girl, or you'll regret it."

Another sharp crack to her cheek and Eleanor let her hands go limp. She put her fingers in the slots and the screen lit.

"It's just a toy. You see them around town sometimes. He must have bought it from the trader ship as a present."

Susan took the device back, squinted at it. "Might be worth something. I'll take it to the store, see what I can get for it."

"But it's mine!"

Susan raised her hand and Eleanor retreated.

"Nothing's yours unless I say it is. About time you learned that."

•••

The view from the window failed to comfort her this time, the shimmer that of a mirage. It's all a trap, she thought. No matter what I do. Eleanor left her hair loose over her bruised cheek. She put down the brush and scrutinized herself in the mirror, then dropped her eyes. I can do it. I don't have another choice.

Eleanor found Susan in the kitchen watching a drama vid. "We're almost out of talik grass and someone always wants it crumbled over their dinner. I'm going to go to the store while it's quiet this morning."

Susan didn't answer for a moment and Eleanor felt her stomach twist. She has to let me go, she thought. I've got to get out of here.

At last Susan shrugged. "I'm glad you've started to think about your responsibilities. Don't be too long, I want you back here before the first guest arrives." And she returned her attention to the vid screen.

Eleanor pulled a heavy jacket on over her jumpsuit and hurried out the back door into the watery light. The wind blew, kicked up dust and chilled her lungs with every breath. The grey buildings hunkered close to the ground, clustered together as if for company. Straggly blooms grew in pots by doors, owners inviting luck to come in, to be attracted by the bright colors. Eleanor tilted her face toward the distant sun, but it did nothing to warm her.

She stood across the street and watched people pass by the store. Old people, children, but far fewer young adults than she had expected. The sun and wind whipped the face of a broad woman. Farmer. White respirator marks on a grizzled man. Prospector. A pair in the dark uniform of the Guards. A merchant or two. No one else bustled down the busy streets of a city of a quarter million people. Of course. The Navy ships that had escorted the traders. The recruiters had been busy.

She dodged two children as they swooped out of the store and shrieked around the candies in their mouths. Supplies and notions of all kinds filled the building, tall shelves stacked to the ceiling. But she noticed gaps, empty spaces on the shelves the slider arms skipped over as they plucked crates down and slid them towards the front of the store.

Around the corner she could hear Mrs. Reilly helping someone with an order. But no Doug. Maybe he's out on a delivery.

"Darling!" Mrs. Reilly stood before her, beaming. "Whatever happened to your face, dear?" She reached towards Eleanor's cheek.

"I ran into an open cabinet in the kitchen." Eleanor forced a laugh. "I'm really clumsy sometimes."

Mrs. Reilly lowered her hand, eyes narrowed. "I see. Well, sometimes there's nothing to be done." She brightened. "But I'm sure you're not here to chat with me. Doug's in the storeroom. Go on back, you'll be a nice break for him."

She came around a corner and found him in the workshop to the side with his head and shoulders buried inside a torn-down engine.

"You don't walk particularly quiet. Hand me that gauge."

"What do-" she spat out, then stopped herself. This had to be done right, this had to work. She lowered her voice. "Doug, come on."

He took the instrument from her but didn't look up. "I'm working."

"And I'm apologizing." she heard her voice rise again and laughed. "But maybe not very well." She sat next to his legs and breathed deep of the familiar scent of machine grease and fuel. "I don't know what to do anymore. I don't know if I can fix this."

The clank of metal on metal stopped, but Doug stayed silent.

"Doesn't he love me anymore?" she whispered. She squinted into the dark corners of the storeroom, focused on distant shapes, tried to tease their purpose from her mind, anything to distract her from the threatening tears.

"Hey. Quit that."

She blinked, glanced over to where he emerged from under the engine.

His lips twisted to the side in a half-smile. "None of that snuffling here, El. You'll make me nervous."

She focused on her hands, rehearsed the next words in her head, over and over. She could only be sure she had finally spoken aloud when his body stiffened.

"Doug, before we argued...before I got angry."

He shifted in place, but didn't answer.

"You know there's no other options. I can't enlist in the Navy, they've already left. Maybe SecDept would have me a year early, but we both know I'd be lousy at it."

"You'd be cute in the uniform, but that's about it," he muttered.

"What else can I do?" She hoped she had read his intentions right. Well, if I'm wrong, nothing's harmed. If I'm right...

And she wasn't wrong.

He put down the wrench he held. He hissed through his teeth as he held her hair back from her bruised cheek. She jerked away from his touch.

"You can't live like that. No one should have to." His eyes searched over her face. "Come here. Live here."

Eleanor leaned back, the wind knocked out of her. She had wanted this, right? Then how could it feel like something crushed her chest, like she couldn't fill her lungs? She forced a smile.

Doug pressed onward. "I know, it would be strange, but we could try. Try with me?"

Eleanor let out the breath she had held. "I think I'd like that." She tilted her face up to his, made her eyes soft, and held her breath.

Hope crossed his face. He leaned over, brushed her lips with his, pressed further.

She forced her mind to be quiet, to be still, and focus on the city, on anything else. He pressed his chest into hers, wrapped his hands over her shoulders and pulled her yet tighter to him. Then, as Eleanor surrendered to the path she had chosen, his lips stiffened against hers. Doug stopped, pulled his face away, searched her eyes.

"You don't want this, do you?" He scrambled away and stood. "I can't believe you'd do this to me, do this to yourself."

She goggled at him, unable to speak.

"You can't stay there anymore. And if this," he flung his hand out at the room, "was your only other choice, what are you going to do now?"

She had no answer.

CPSIA information can be obtained at www.ICGtesting.com
Printed in the USA
BVOW01s0946100916

461638BV00012B/49/P